Saladin!

Andrew Osmond

Hutchinson of London

Hutchinson & Co (Publishers) Ltd
3 Fitzroy Square, London W1

London Melbourne Sydney Auckland
Wellington Johannesburg and agencies
throughout the world

First published 1975
© Andrew Osmond 1975

Set in Monotype Imprint

Printed in Great Britain by The Anchor Press Ltd
and bound by Wm Brendon & Son Ltd
both of Tiptree, Essex

ISBN 0 09 125100 1

Saladin!

For my mother
with thanks

Thanks too to Philippa Harrison, my editor,
whose creative advice was fundamental, and
to Stuart, my wife, who keeps me going.

A.O.

Contents

Contents

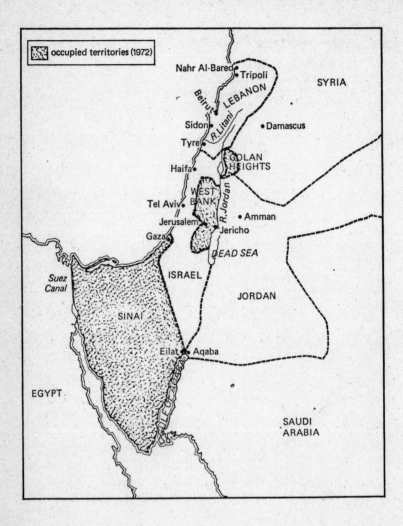

occupied territories (1972)

Nahr Al-Bared
Tripoli
Beirut
LEBANON
SYRIA
R.Litani
Sidon
Damascus
Tyre
GOLAN
HEIGHTS
Haifa
WEST
BANK
R.Jordan
Tel Aviv
Amman
Jerusalem
Jericho
Gaza
DEAD SEA
Suez
Canal
ISRAEL
JORDAN
SINAI
Eilat Aqaba
EGYPT
SAUDI
ARABIA

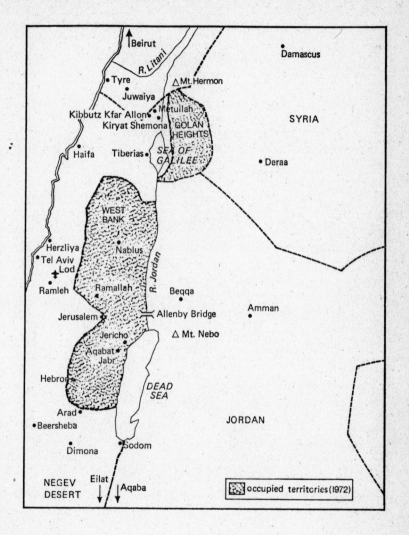

From all that terror teaches,
    From lies of tongue and pen,
From all the easy speeches
    That comfort cruel men,
From sale and profanation
    Of honour and the sword,
From sleep and from damnation,
    Deliver us, good Lord!

G. K. Chesterton

Roscoe and Company

Christmas Eve 1972

1. The House by the Sea

Coming from the west, you approach Roscoe's house across a huge reclaimed marsh. This is the flattest part of England and some say the dullest, an area stripped of all impediments to agriculture. No hunting here, no foxes I suppose, no hedges and almost no people; earth meets sky in a line broken only by occasional trees, but as you move eastwards even the trees disappear and the fields stretch uninterrupted to the coast. The dykes are deep out of sight, so the eye races forward checked only by changes of crop until it comes back to the sky, which here, as in all flat places, is the principal feature of the landscape.

Because of the flatness you expect the roads to be straight, but they are not. They twist and intersect and double back, following the course of ancient tracks across the fens, so that Granby comes into view long before you reach it, a tall red house on the eastern horizon. Around it is a village of sorts – a church, a pub, a few cottages – but Granby is Roscoe's, and what catches the eye is his grandiose residence, appropriately taller than anything around it. Immediately behind the house the horizon lifts slightly and sets into concrete, a long defensive wall which runs along the coast to the limits of vision, holding back the sea.

I approach this place always with a feeling of awe, perhaps explained by the force of the elements – or perhaps it is Roscoe himself, that aloof and unpredictable man whom I idolized at school and whose life seems so dangerous, so large compared to my own. Yes, that I think explains it: largeness of life is what I feel coming up as I leave behind the clutter of the Midlands and drive towards this big bleak house by the sea.

The occasion I have in mind now is Christmas Eve 1972. In those days I always took my family to Granby for Christmas, but now the tradition has lapsed. Because of what happened later that day my wife says she would not feel safe there again.

Although we must have arrived about noon, I remember it was almost dark. An east wind was driving low cloud off the sea and the fields were ploughed bare, white-dusted with frost. From a distance we could see the lights of a Christmas tree shining through a downstairs window, and as we drew closer the details of the house became more distinct: the walls of brightest red brick, the windows picked out in stone, the battlements and four round turrets. Northern baronial, I suppose you would call it.

The gates went for scrap in the war but the posts are still there, topped by stone balls scabby with lichen. The garden has no flowers at all; it is just shaggy lawns with evergreen bushes round the edge, bits of laurel and holly, like a cemetery. The drive curves through it and up to the porch, which echoes the castle motif of the roof.

This is the point at which Roscoe's dogs come baying from somewhere and keep you trapped in your car until he arrives, but that day the place was quiet. No one was about. We rang the bell, walked in with our cases and stood waiting for action.

The hall is, broadly speaking, medieval. To the left is a big marble fireplace containing a portion of tree-trunk, always unlit, and straight ahead are the stairs. Starting downwards in two separate flights, they converge below a stained-glass window and sweep on down between wide-railed banisters, each of which ends in a pewter nymph holding a torch. The general effect is of a stage set for opera, and now, as on cue, it filled with people.

The first to appear was Mrs Parsons, the housekeeper, a strongly built lady from Yorkshire with breasts which reach her waist. Then Roscoe came striding down the stairs, preceded by his dogs and little Georgie, the household's only child. Then from the left appeared two girls, one of whom we knew, the other a stranger, limping on a stick.

To me the situation seemed normal, but my wife, who is sensitive to atmosphere, muttered 'Trouble'.

I remember it all very well. Each detail of that day is imprinted on my mind, because that was the first time I heard about Saladin. It was also the only occasion on which I have witnessed the explosive effects of a parcel bomb.

2. The Sultan's Mantle

After lunch the women went off for a walk while Roscoe and I sat drinking and Georgie ran about in the hall, where the bomb was, underneath the tree in a pile of other parcels.

Roscoe himself was recently back from the Middle East. I had no idea why he had gone there but assumed it had something to do with the army or intelligence. He seemed in good health, lean and still tanned from his travels, though I noticed a change in his manner, as if he had suffered some blow to his confidence – a certain sag in the shoulders, a withdrawal in the eyes – it was so slight I could not be sure, and so made no comment. Roscoe rarely explains himself; but this time he did exactly that. Oblivious of the danger which had followed him into his home, he started to tell me about his long journey and about Saladin, and immediately he had my whole attention.

Saladin, he reminded me, was the sultan who had chased the Crusaders from the Holy Land; the man who had welded a mighty Muslim army to confront the Christian knights on the hills above Galilee and there had encircled them, exhausted them, barred them from water and cut them to pieces before marching on to Jerusalem. In 1187 he had retaken the city for Islam, and his victory lasted well, Roscoe said, in that Palestine had remained an Arab country until the conquests of Israel in 1948 and 1967. Now the wheel had turned full circle: Palestine had fallen to the Jews, and the Arabs seemed unlikely to do much about it, because in modern times they had not produced a leader to match the great Kurdish sultan. Saladin was a phenomenon; not just an outstanding general, but a mystic, humane and incorruptible. He was also a canny negotiator, who united the fractious tribes of Saracens and pursued his aims by slow cautious steps.

Having covered eight centuries in rather less minutes, Roscoe paused and took a pull at his cigar. 'Compromise, that was the trick. Not an Arab talent, I'm afraid.'

Then it turned out that what he had to tell me did not concern the sultan at all but a man who had picked up his mantle; a Palestinian Arab, codename Saladin, who six months before this cold Christmas in Granby had arrived in Beirut with an audacious plan to lead his people to a settlement with Israel.

What follows is the story of this second Saladin.

When I first heard it from Roscoe I confess I could hardly believe it, but my interest, once aroused, became obsessional, and as soon as my other commitments allowed I went back to Granby to interrogate him further. My thanks are also due to his wife, whose recollections were frank and precise. This account is largely based on their memories, to which, as will soon become clear, I have given more detail and colour than a strictly historical approach would allow.

Later I went to the Middle East myself and sought out the others involved. Not all were willing to talk; one is in jail, another has gone mad and several are dead. Nevertheless I am satisfied that the facts as I have them are complete – or rather will not be enlarged upon by further research. Those questions which remain, in particular who did the killing at the end, will I think never be answered. When I come to that I shall set out the evidence and leave judgement open, but now I shall take myself off, since the story is better told straight and seen through the eyes of those who were part of it.

The year then is 1972, and where to begin is no problem. Everyone recalling this period starts with the morning of Tuesday, 5th September, when a group of eight Arabs invaded the Olympic Games in Munich armed with Kalashnikov folding-stock rifles and grenades.

PART ONE

Recruits
and Reprisals

September 5th–September 11th, 1972

1. The Massacre of Munich

They arrived outside the Olympic Village just before dawn, jogging along in tracksuits. One of them climbed the perimeter fence and dropped down the other side. Then another scrambled up and stayed straddling the fence as the weapons, concealed in travel bags, were quickly passed over. Soon all were inside the village. Those who saw them, including a two-man patrol of the German police, assumed that these silent, purposeful, tracksuited figures loping through the early mist were athletes returning from a training session.

In fact they were guerillas and all eight belonged to Black September, the latest and fiercest of the terrorist organizations to be spawned from the two million Arabs made homeless by Israel. Originally formed to take revenge against Arab backsliders, Black September had recently turned its attention to Jewish targets and in three years had picked up a fearsome reputation for sabotage, extortion and murder.

Its strength lay in the quality of its recruits, who were picked from the student population and organized in independent cells. As ready to die as to kill, they also kept their mouths shut, which is not an easy thing for an Arab to do. Black September refused to talk to journalists and at that time its leaders were unknown, though their policy was already clear. No more would young men be sent to die on the Jordan in exchange for three lines in the press; Black September would operate in Europe, where the targets were easier, and its actions would be calculated to shock.

A typical member of the organization in Germany was Ali Ahmad Zeiti, a student of civil engineering at Berlin Free University. Eldest son of a wealthy Palestinian doctor, Zeiti drove a white Porsche and wore the best faded denim. But this frivolous exterior concealed a rabid nationalist. He would take any risk for the movement and had in fact helped to prepare the Munich raid, collecting the rifles from an embassy in Bonn. But on the eve of the attack he flew unexpectedly to London and was sleeping in a cheap hotel in Bayswater Road when his comrades swarmed into the Olympic Village.

Once over the fence they had a short way to go to Block 31, the building which the small group of athletes from Israel shared with the teams from Hong Kong and Uruguay. The whole village had been reconnoitred beforehand and drawn into a groundplan by Zeiti, who was trained as a draughtsman.

The Israelis were asleep, having got to bed at midnight after a visit to the theatre. Two of their number had been trained as security guards but they carried only knives, since the Israeli government had decided that firearms would be against the spirit of the Olympics.

At 5.05 the Arabs mounted their assault. There were shouts, a single shot, then two bursts of automatic fire. No one is quite sure what happened. Within moments both Israeli guards had been shot, but some of their companions had time to jump from the windows and later it was found that two Arabs had knife wounds. After the attack the terrorists were left with nine hostages, mostly wrestlers and weight-lifters. At 5.30 they opened a window and threw down a paper stating their demands. They wanted the release of two hundred prisoners in Israel by nine o'clock that morning and said that unless this demand was met the athletes would be shot.

The Games were suspended for that day. The German authorities arrived to negotiate. Their first aim was to get the deadline extended, and in this they were successful. The terrorists agreed to wait till noon. Throughout the hours that followed the Germans were painfully aware that the lives at stake were Jewish; Munich was the city of the Nazis and Dachau was just down the road. They tried to alter the basis of the deal by offering cash or German hostages, but the terrorists refused. 'Money means nothing to us,' they cried, 'our lives mean nothing to us.'

The Israelis were less squeamish. In Jerusalem Mrs Golda Meir, the Prime Minister, summoned her cabinet and on one point they were instantly agreed: there could be no concessions, even if that meant the death of the athletes. The only deterrent to this kind of blackmail was to yield nothing, ever.

This decision was conveyed to the Germans, who met the terrorists again and persuaded them to wait till five o'clock. That seemed to be the limit. The Arabs were saying they would shoot two hostages unless the talks showed some progress by five, and no one dared to disbelieve them.

The initiative passed to the German police, who had tried to lure the terrorists out with boxes of food and had even considered pumping gas into the ventilators. By 4.30 a large armed force had been assembled, but first a small group went in to reconnoitre – and at this point the situation altered. The terrorists shouted that they wanted to be flown with their prisoners to Cairo.

The choice of Cairo was significant, for although the great Nasser was dead, the Arabs still looked to Egypt for a lead. Nasser's successor there was Anwar Sadat, a dull man by comparison, who seemed to be working towards a deal with Israel. The Palestinians distrusted him, fearing he would overlook their claims, and Black September did not want a settlement of any kind. They hoped by embroiling Sadat in the Munich operation to force him back towards war.

To transport the problem to Cairo seemed an excellent idea to the Germans, but first they had to know if the Egyptians would let a plane land. So Chancellor Brandt, who had flown in from Bonn to take charge, now telephoned Cairo. But Sadat would not take the call, seeing that either way he could not win. If he thwarted Black September, students would burn him in effigy; if he helped them, Israeli bombers would take revenge along the Nile. Better to keep out of it.

There was a last hope of compromise, and this lay with Colonel Gadaffi, the eccentric young ruler of Libya. A fanatical Muslim who preached holy war against Israel, Gadaffi was an outspoken friend of the Palestinians. Black September would listen to him, as would Brandt, since Libya now supplied a third of West Germany's oil. But due to a muddle in the German Foreign Ministry Gadaffi's offer to mediate was not taken up. The situation now acquired the momentum of a showdown.

To get the terrorists out the Germans allowed them to think they were on their way to Cairo and made preparations to shoot them down somewhere between Block 31 and the plane. But the

Arabs were too clever. They refused to leave the building until it was dark. They demanded a bus without a glass roof, and getting out of the bus, they mingled so tightly with the athletes that the snipers could not get a shot. At 10.30 they were transferred with their hostages into two helicopters – each with two pilots – and flown to the military airfield at Fuerstenfeldbruck, where a Lufthansa Boeing 727 had been waiting for an hour.

This too was a trap. The plane had no crew. Three police marksmen were concealed on the roof of the control tower, another two were lying in wait on the runway and the whole scene was floodlit. This was in fact the Germans' best position, but they had not expected to fight the battle here. Five snipers was fatally too few, and again the terrorists did the unexpected. Two of them walked towards the Boeing with a helicopter pilot between them. Then two more stepped out, holding the other three pilots at gunpoint.

Now it was the Germans who were trapped. As soon as the Arabs knew the Boeing had no crew they were likely to do something drastic. The first two were already coming back from the plane and between them the pilot was flashing a pentorch to identify himself.

Seeing they would not get a better opportunity, the police opened fire. The helicopter pilots sprinted to safety. Of the terrorists out in the open, the two in front were killed instantly. But only one of those walking back from the Boeing was hit. The other ran forward and raked the roof of the control tower with automatic fire, killing a policeman and smashing the lights. From the side-door of each of the helicopters came the sputtering flash of a Russian assault rifle. Bullets zipped about in the dark, whined off the tarmac, clanged against the hulls of the machines. Everyone was firing at once – and then there was silence, a sudden inexplicable lull, which lengthened from seconds into minutes and then hours as the world waited breathless for news. Were the athletes now dead? No one knew. The surviving terrorists, if any there were, stayed put inside the helicopters while the cordon slowly tightened around them. Reinforcements were brought up, assault groups made ready. The German police had now been joined by a team of Israelis from Tel Aviv, whose advice was to wait, sit it out until the Arabs lost their resolve, as Arabs usually did. This advice was accepted. A ring of sharpshooters was deployed around both of the helicopters. There were now over four hundred men on the airfield.

For a time nothing happened, then shortly after midnight two terrorists jumped out. One of them loosed off a few rounds before police bullets slapped him to the ground, but the other was able to fling a grenade back into his helicopter. The machine disappeared in a yellow ball of flame. The German assault groups rushed in. Three Arabs were taken alive but all nine Israelis were dead.

When they brought him the news Willy Brandt buried his face in his hands and cried 'Catastrophe, catastrophe!'

2. The Men of Zion

In a London hotel room Ali Ahmad Zeiti wept for his friends, but far to the east, in the refugee camps of Syria and Lebanon and Jordan, the Palestinians cheered when they heard that the athletes were dead.

Watching this exhibition of hate in a camp near Beirut was the man called Saladin, and with him a terse French official of the United Nations. A jubilant crowd was cavorting around them, but both men noticed that the women watched the sky, waiting for the aircraft which would bring retribution.

Saladin turned away and walked towards his car, a big white Mercedes parked among the hovels. Like every other Arab who favoured a settlement, he was appalled by the slaughter of Munich. But at least he had a plan, having decided already that something more drastic was called for from the moderates – an action which would match in its public effect the bloodthirsty tactics of Black September. 'What we need is a professional,' he said to the Frenchman, 'a man we can trust absolutely. And we need him quick.'

Next day the Olympic Games continued. The corpses of the athletes were flown back to Israel, where a crowd of thousands was waiting at Lod airport to escort the coffins, headed by senior rabbis and ministers of the government. Only Yigal Allon, the Deputy Prime Minister, would answer questions. 'They will have to pay the price,' he said.

And now all the numerous vigilante organizations of Jewry prepared to join the fray. The best known of these was the Jewish Defence League of Rabbi Kahane, a former FBI agent; another group called itself Masada. But based in Paris at this time was a tougher and less public organization – the Men of Zion. Financed by a syndicate of wealthy American Jews, the MZ had started to wage a private war on the Arabs and after Munich they came looking for Zeiti in Berlin.

They intended to kill him, and for this they chose Samuel Gessner, the best man they had. A former US Marine, fortyish, bulky, Gessner had served at one time in the New York police. He was a practised assassin but also a man of deep faith, who liked to describe the Men of Zion as 'God's answer to Black September'.

When he got to Berlin he found that Zeiti had vanished from his lodgings, but soon traced the Arab to the Union of Palestine Students in London and discovered that a message had been left for Zeiti there by a man called Dr Bassam Owdeh, telephoning from St Anthony's College in Oxford – this was Thursday, September 7th, two days after Munich. Gessner promptly hired a car and drove down to the university city. Stuck into the top of his trousers was a .38 revolver, a Smith and Wesson of the type widely favoured by the American police. He wore a holster under his armpit but for action preferred the gun in his belt. He liked the feel of it there and could draw slightly quicker if not required to reach across his stomach.

Zeiti was carrying no weapon on his person. His business in Oxford was of a different sort. Bassam Owdeh, the man he had gone there to see, was a young Palestinian academic who had come from Beirut for a conference on Middle Eastern problems.

Zeiti and Owdeh knew each other well. They met with a cordial embrace in St Anthony's common room, then went out to a restaurant to eat. There they had a long and friendly discussion, in the course of which Zeiti announced that he was utterly disgusted by Munich. Black September were dangerous fools, he said, who did nothing but harm to the cause.

Owdeh listened to this with delight; a plump, mild, bespectacled man of pitiable physical clumsiness, who as he grew excited started sweating and shifting about in his seat. He slapped the table to indicate agreement, knocked over a glass but hardly seemed to notice. His speech became oddly disconnected, the sentences trailing unfinished as if they could not keep pace with his thoughts. Such incoherence was familiar in Oxford, indeed it was almost the intellectual patois. But in Bassam Owdeh confusion was real. Now for instance he was filled with affection for his friend but sensed at the same time that he was an enemy, felt a compulsion to trust him yet knew, somewhere else in his mind, that Zeiti was lying.

This duality of thought, when matched with Owdeh's physical traits, could only be explained by a history of mental disorder. Zeiti knew about that, and so did the chief of Black September. Saladin did not.

3. A Visitor to Granby

Throughout these events Stephen Roscoe was working on his farm, a few flat acres surrounding that house on the Lincolnshire coast.

Until March of that year he had served as an officer in the Special Air Service. The SAS, as every schoolboy knows, are paratroop-commandos, a unit first formed to raid behind the German lines in North Africa. Desert forays would have suited Roscoe well, but now the SAS is used for less noble work, and in 1971 he had found himself commanding a secret plainclothes squad in Ulster, making forays in an armour-plated car through the back streets of Derry and Belfast. The job was not to his taste; in fact it was so relentlessly gruesome it poisoned his view of the army and as soon as his contract of service came up for renewal he resigned. A man of some means, he withdrew to Granby and for six months had lived there in broody regret. He missed the fellowship of military life; he missed the excitement and he missed the routine, above all he missed that inflexible structure of rank, in which the British class system still seemed to work and a man of his type could still find a place. In short, he thought he had made a mistake.

Munich caught him in the middle of the harvest. He followed the drama on television and like everyone else was dismayed by the death of the athletes. Two days later, like everyone else, he had almost forgotten it, when out of the blue he was telephoned by Colonel James Marsden, a spokesman for the Arab cause in London.

Marsden sounded strained, as well he might. For two days the press had not had a good word to say for the Arabs.

'Can I come and see you, Stephen?'

'Today?'

'It's important.'

'Very well, come to dinner. Will you stay the night?'

'Thank you no,' Marsden said, 'I shall have to get back. Now, where is this place of yours?'

Roscoe told him how to find the farm, and when Marsden said he would be there by seven allowed another hour. The roads east of Boston defeated all but the highest intelligence.

'Farm' is perhaps too grand a word for Granby. Roscoe has only five fields, for which he keeps refusing fantastic sums of money. His land is too small and his house is too big and he knows it. Granby runs at a loss, but he keeps it because he likes to come back to it; he cannot imagine another place as home.

On the day Marsden called he had borrowed a combine harvester and all that morning drove his small grey Ferguson tractor alongside the big red machine, matching their speeds as the grain cascaded from the chute into his trailer. When the trailer was full he veered away towards the drier, then came back for more, while the crop was cut back to an ever smaller square in the centre and the trapped hares bolted for cover, easily out-stripping his dogs. The noise of the engines, the excitement of the dogs, the sun on his neck and the mounting pile of grain – for Roscoe this was the purest nostalgia, in particular the dry sweet smell of the straw, which reminded him of childhood summers spent on this farm. In those days the place had been bigger, untrimmed by death duty; now the harvest was too quickly over, but some things he tried to keep up. On Sunday there would be warm beer in the pub and hymns in a church full of marrows, then the problems of life would close in again.

Roscoe's problems were not at all serious. One of them was that he was bored and another that current expenditure was cutting into capital. But the main one was Nina Grange Brown, the girl with whom he lived at the time. They could not bring themselves to get married, yet neither was ready to dismiss the idea. In the meantime they quarrelled. So some income was needed, and also some escape; a single solution seemed likely, and while he sat on his tractor Roscoe wondered why Marsden was coming to Granby. Something was about to turn up, he felt.

Marsden was a friend of his father's, a soldier now retired, who had served in Palestine during the last days of British rule; a solitary man, who had that slight upper-class oddness which seems to be a feature of Englishmen attracted to the Arabs.

He had lived for several years in the Persian Gulf then returned to London to run the Atlantic Arab Institute, a body formed by a group of British and American companies with Middle Eastern interests to improve the Arab image in the West.

He arrived when he said he would and stood by his car until Roscoe had stored the last of the grain. Then they walked along the beach with the dogs. The evening was clear, almost windless. With the tide out the sea was half a mile away, a strip of deep blue at the edge of the sand.

From the beach Roscoe pointed to the turrets of his house, projecting above the sea wall, and explained it had been built by his grandfather. 'A frightful old crook. Made his pile in ten years, then quarrelled with the world and came to live here.'

'Still alive?'

'No, long gone. Died of leisure.'

Marsden looked back at the house, shielding his eyes against the sun; a lean, nimble man with neat silver hair and the permanent sallowness which comes from a life in hot climates. 'Very nice,' he said. 'Open air, your own land – what more could you want?'

Roscoe shrugged. 'The place runs itself.'

'Don't you enjoy it?'

'You know what I miss.'

Marsden nodded, and then asked Roscoe what he thought about Munich.

'A mistake.'

'At least it got publicity.'

'Yes, but not sympathy. Everyone feels sorry for the Israelis.'

'Wait till they hit back.'

'Of course, there'll be reprisals, the world expects it. More Arabs will die and no one will be sorry.'

They walked on in silence while the dogs ran ahead, leaping the breakwaters and splashing through the pools. Roscoe's dogs are the terror of the district, a pair of huge mastiffs called Alice and Phoebe, and he himself is to scale, a very tall man with a walk like a giraffe – long slow strides and a slight forward dip of the neck as each foot touches the ground. This comparison comes from Nina Brown, who added at the time: 'About as talkative as a damn giraffe too.' That was unkind, but not altogether unfair. Roscoe sees nothing impolite in not speaking, and sensing that Marsden's questions added up to some kind of test he fell silent, until Marsden said: 'I agree with you of course, and so do many Arabs. Munich was a frightful mistake. But what would you do in their shoes?'

'I think they should operate in Israel, against military targets.'

Marsden nodded again, pleased with the answer. 'Supposing I told you that an organization has been formed to do exactly that?'

'I haven't heard of it.'

'You will, I think.'

'Are you involved?'

'I run the odd errand,' Marsden said carefully, and then added, as if it were an afterthought: 'Actually I came here to tell you they're looking for recruits.'

They walked on in silence, allowing the suggestion to mature. Behind them their footprints were woven with those of the dogs, the only blemish on the beach. Marsden said that what he was about to divulge must be treated as a matter of confidence. 'That in itself may involve you in some risk, so if you don't want to hear more, say so now.'

Roscoe smiled. 'You know I do. I'm curious.'

They had now reached the sea. The waves were curling limply on a bed of black mud; further out a trawler was creeping north to Hull. Roscoe led the way to the left, keeping to the hard rippled sand, which his eyes could distinguish from the soft. As they walked, Marsden talked.

'It's a very small outfit as yet, based in Beirut, but they've got a heap of money. The fellow in charge is an old friend of mine, whose name I'd prefer not to give you. He's using the code-name Saladin – I expect you remember the chivalrous infidel in *Ivanhoe*?'

'No.'

'Ah. Well, take it from me, he's a good man to follow – not a Marxist or a Muslim fanatic. He's going for an independent state between Jordan and Israel.'

Roscoe was surprised to hear that. So far, he knew, no branch of the Palestinian Resistance had dared to promise less than the total destruction of Israel. Yet here, explained Marsden, was a movement which was offering to recognize Israel as first defined in 1948 in return for the West Bank and Gaza – the extra land lost by the Arabs in the war of 1967. Saladin's proposal was that these two areas should be linked and made into a new state of Palestine, to which the refugees could then return as citizens.

'As you'll appreciate,' Marsden said, 'his problem is twofold. First, the Israelis are dead set against such a state, so he has to make them listen. But before he can do that he must get the backing of his people, and he reckons the only way to do it is to upstage the rest of the Resistance, Black September and all, in a fairly spectacular manner.'

Roscoe listened with increasing interest. 'He has to be a hero, you mean, before he can compromise.'

'Exactly. So he plans to mount a major operation in Israel itself.'

'And he wants my help.'

'He wants your help.'

'What's the target?'

'He hasn't told me that. I'm not sure he's even decided.'

'I can't just go killing Jews, you know.'

'Of course not, I explained that.'

'You explained?'

'He wanted to know a bit about you, naturally.'

'I see.' Roscoe stared at his feet. 'Well, let's go and get a drink.'

Returning from the beach, they climbed the sea wall. From the top they could see far inland; the sky had turned pink and lights were coming on across the fens. Nothing appeared to be moving, but in fact the sun was lower, the trawler further north than a few minutes earlier – and for a moment Roscoe felt a spectator of his life. Which course it took did not seem to matter much.

High in the sky a jet was trailing vapour, reminding him of evenings in the war when the air had quivered to the thunder of RAF bomber squadrons. He had stood on this spot with his grandfather, watching the show until his neck was cricked, wondering which plane was his father's. By tradition they had picked the one out in front and Stephen Roscoe, aged six, had gone to bed breathless at the bravery of pilots. Now what amazed him was their certainty: all that jolly lingo, whole German cities smashed without a qualm.

'No trees,' said Marsden suddenly. 'Why no trees?'

'They don't like salt.'

'Salt?'

Roscoe waved a hand at the long concrete wall. 'The sea came through here a few years ago. Hence the Maginot Line.'

'Ah yes, I remember.'

They walked towards the house, across what remained of dunes, and on the way down Roscoe asked why it was that this Arab called Saladin needed the help of an Englishman, at which the dainty silver-haired colonel flashed him a smile and said: 'You used to be handy with explosives, didn't you?'

4. The Man behind the Mask

It transpired that Marsden knew more than he had so far admitted. Sabotage was what Saladin had in mind, he said, a quick in-and-out hit-and-run demolition, of the sort often practised by the SAS. The expertise required was not to be found among the Palestinian guerillas, whose loyalty to Saladin's political aims would anyway be suspect from the start. To lead and organize this raid Saladin wanted a man he could trust, and if that man were not an Arab so much the better, since he would then have the extra advantage of being able to enter Israel openly. Whatever the target selected, casualties would be kept to a minimum, since the object was not to enrage the Israelis but to bring them to the conference table.

Marsden left it at that, and Roscoe said he would give it some thought. But there never was a chance he might refuse. Let me try to make him clearer.

A mutual friend once defined him as 'tough and slightly mad', and he certainly is an odd fellow, taciturn, almost morose, with an air of cold rage buried deep. This coldness has often been remarked on and may derive from the early loss of his parents. Yet he has a dry sense of humour and a taste for practical jokes, which would have inclined him to favour the notion of helping some Arab, however half-baked, to let off a firework display inside Israel.

To look at he is bony and lean, with the physical poise of an athlete, pale blue eyes and straw-coloured hair neatly parted and trimmed. He reminds me of those solemn young men of the football eleven who stare at the camera in public-school photographs and seem, in that click of a shutter, to have posed for their deaths, each face set carefully into the bovine mask which was regulation wear for the Somme. The gentleman at arms – the type is still a favourite with the English, and Roscoe

conforms to it exactly. His manners are nice; he might shoot you
but he will not be rude to you, and needless to say he goes to war
only to protect weaker creatures, a class in which he would in-
clude women, dogs, servants – and now the Palestinians, for
whom he felt an instinctive sympathy.

On the surface then, a good recruit for Saladin. But, it must
also be said, as a fighting animal Roscoe has flaws. He drinks
too much, and in between bouts of anaesthetized violence, he
thinks too much. His basic trouble is that he no longer believes
in the type he conforms to. He goes on conforming for lack of a
better idea, but this weak positive breeds its own negative, a
sullen despair which seems to provoke him into risks, as if he
could only accept his continued existence by increasing the
chances against it. A sad thing to watch. Since his marriage he
has been more settled, but at this time he was plagued by self-
doubt. Marsden's offer was therefore a welcome distraction, a
chance to do the thing he knew best, made the more attractive
by what seemed a respectable purpose.

Coming off the dunes, the two men walked along a track
which passes through the buildings of the farm. Having made
his bid, Marsden was talking now of the first Saladin and his
foe, the Christian Crusaders.

'My God, what a *rabble* they were! Half the riff-raff of
Europe charging down the coast of Asia Minor, eating a Turk
or two when they got hungry – all in the name of the cross,
mind you.'

Roscoe laughed, wondering what god Marsden worshipped
when no one was looking. 'The Pope's idea, wasn't it?'

'That's right, sent them to conquer the Holy Land for Jesus.
The Arabs had run the place quietly for years, and suddenly
this *rabble* descends on Jerusalem. That was the prize of course
– streets of gold, sapphires in the walls – some of them thought
Revelation was a guide-book. But when they got there they
went mad. Slaughtered the whole population, men, women,
children, every living thing. Burned the wretched Jews in their
synagogues . . .' Marsden paused, overwhelmed, as if the
carnage were taking place before him in Granby. 'That is how
Israel appears to the Arabs, you realize. Crusading Franks,
Zionists from Poland – what's the difference? To the Arabs it's
just European aggression, western psychosis inflicted on the east.'

Roscoe doubted the comparison. 'What happened then?' he said.

'To the Franks? They held Palestine for almost a century, and then Saladin caught them at Galilee. Naturally they thought he'd take revenge, but he released half his prisoners and didn't touch the churches – pretty remarkable for the twelfth century, don't you think?'

'But this is the twentieth. We shoot athletes.'

'Come now, be fair. I've told you these people are going to play it by the rules.'

'Ah yes, the rules.'

They turned off the track and walked up the drive to the house, their footsteps crunching on the pebbles.

Roscoe led the way through the porch and the mastiffs trailed behind, spreading sand across the patterned tiles. It was like passing in through an airlock; at each stage the air got colder. As he entered Marsden caught the damp morbid smell of the house, and was glad that he had come. To know a man properly you had to see his home.

As they stood in the hall a door opened, letting out a blast of pop music, and a girl wearing jeans came towards them. Without a glance at Roscoe she walked up to Marsden and held out her hand. 'Hi,' she said, 'I'm Nina Brown.'

Marsden had an impression of beady brown eyes in a discontented face. A small girl, but pugnacious; American, from somewhere in the south. Attached to her other hand was a child. 'This is Elijah,' she said. 'We call him Georgie. Say hello, Georgie.'

The child refused to speak. He had black curly hair and olive skin.

The girl turned to Roscoe. 'What kept you?'

'We went for a walk.'

'You want to eat?'

'Not yet.'

'The old cow will freak. You said eight.'

'Don't worry, we'll sort it out. Good night, Georgie.'

Roscoe mussed the child's hair and the girl led him off up the stairs. Marsden boggled at the two pewter nymphs and their torches. When Roscoe pressed a switch, a light came on inside the smoked-glass flame of each torch. 'This way,' he said, and took his guest into the drawing room, walking straight across to the gramophone to take off the record.

At that point the phone rang. A call from Oxford for Marsden. He took the receiver. 'Ah, Bassam,' he said, 'what's new?'

Roscoe heard an excited voice on the line.

Marsden switched into Arabic, a language in which he was fluent. Then he spoke in English again. 'Very well, I'll be with you tonight. I want to meet this chap. Be careful now . . . Bassam? Hello? Hello? Are you there? Oh, damn.'

Marsden replaced the receiver then stared at it intently, as if wondering whether it would move.

Roscoe passed him a tumbler of whisky. 'Cut off?'

Marsden continued to look at the telephone, then turned abstractedly to take his drink. 'Cut off. Yes, I suppose so. Bloody thing.'

After that they moved to the kitchen and Roscoe introduced his housekeeper. Tending pots on an Aga, perspiring in its heat, Mrs Parsons told Marsden she came from Yorkshire. The Roscoes, she said, were a rum lot. The old man – well, the least said the better; where there was brass there was muck – and the next one, the pilot, he was a sad man, didn't know his knee from his elbow. Stephen, now, had taken up with this woman. 'American. Seen the child, have you?'

'Yes. Nice little chap.'

'Touch of the tar brush there, if you want my opinion.'

Roscoe fed his dogs, filling two large bowls with chunks of pungent meat and biscuit like broken stone. Mrs Parsons asked Marsden what he did for a living and when told, delivered her opinion of the Arabs. 'Mind you, t'other lot's no better. Take your money they will . . .'

Mrs Parsons spoke her mind, and Marsden listened patiently, though his thoughts were with his interrupted phone call. Bassam Owdeh was vital to Saladin's project – the only Arab in the team who spoke Hebrew – but he would need all the ballast that Roscoe could provide. The way he had rung off was odd . . .

5. Vibrations of War

St Anthony's is one of the newest institutions of Oxford, a college devoted exclusively to the study of international affairs and restricted to graduate students. Housed in a complex of ornate Victorian villas, it is, as it should be, far removed from the passions of the world it studies, from the wars and the riots, the skyjacks and terrorists' bombs. At St Anthony's violence there is not; prejudice, rude emotion there is not. However, if you sniff the pipe-smoke with care, you will perhaps catch a faint, titillating whiff of espionage. The college is said to train British spies, a reputation in which its staff takes a certain coy pleasure and which is true to the extent that the Foreign Office send their new boys there to learn about the KGB.

At the time of the Munich atrocity there were a number of Arabs and Israelis in residence, drawn by a two-week conference on Middle Eastern problems. Seated at the long dining tables, they were hard to tell apart – rows of animated olive-skinned faces in the candlelight, all Semites together. Marsden who had dined at the college on Tuesday, had found the sight disturbing, as if he had caught the troops fraternizing with the enemy.

That evening the world had been waiting for news from Fuerstenfeldbruck, but even that brutal event had not disturbed the academic truce. As the port went round followed by squash for the Muslims, Black September had been defended by a Jew – by Michel Yaacov, a rising young major of the Israeli army, who had pointed out graciously that blackmail with hostages was pioneered by Irgun and Stern, the Jewish gangs who had hounded the British out of Palestine. 'Terror breeds terror', he had said, and all the Arabs in earshot had nodded in sober agreement – except Bassam Owdeh, who had trembled with vexation at this equation of Jewish and Palestinian terrorism.

'And justice breeds justice, as you know perfectly well. Those gangs broke up when Israel was created, and so will Black September, when we get our rights.'

Having spoken, Owdeh – or rather Bassam, as he was generally known – had arched back in his seat and stared at the ceiling, eating grapes absentmindedly while his audience exchanged covert smiles. One of the resident dons had perfected a cruel imitation of the gauche young professor from Beirut.

Oddly the man at the table who respected him most was Michel Yaacov, who recognized the quality of this Arab's mind and saw in him also a restraint unusual for his race. Yaacov liked Bassam and tried to befriend him. Bassam liked Yaacov, up to a point, but felt himself obscurely threatened by this smooth-talking Israeli. After each of their encounters he was physically exhausted.

On the evening of Thursday 7th September, that same golden day of late summer that Roscoe had chosen for his harvest, Yaacov and Bassam went walking together in Oxford's park, speaking always of their distant dusty battleground as they strolled across the lawns towards the river. They made an incongruous pair. Bassam's hands fluttered about him, illustrating his argument, but his feet gave him nothing but trouble, colliding, digressing, catching up with an intermittent scurry. Yaacov by contrast was relaxed, hands in pockets, striding easily along as he talked, a man who had fought with brilliance in two wars against the Arabs and could operate almost in his sleep every gadget and weapon in the armoury of Israel's land forces. Yet different as they were, these two men, whom Saladin's initiative was about to pit in deadly combat, understood each other well and even as antagonists communicated on a deeper level than that understood by the British or any other party who had tried to keep the peace between their tribes.

From the park the two men returned to their rooms, which were one above the other in a house on Woodstock Road, and that was where they were about three hours later, just before 9 p.m.

Yaacov had eaten in college, Bassam with Zeiti at a Chinese restaurant in Summertown. Zeiti had gone to find accommodation and Bassam was telephoning Marsden from his room when Gessner came in through the door, not with a cinematic crash, but quickly and quietly, as professionals do. His hand was inside his jacket, but came out empty when he saw that Bassam was alone. Bassam stopped talking and blinked behind his glasses, assuming some mistake. Then Gessner locked the door, turned back with a smile and advanced across the room, holding out his hand for the telephone receiver. Open-mouthed, Bassam passed it over. Gessner put it to his ear, listened for a moment, then disconnected the call. Looking up at Bassam, he broadened the smile to an insolent leer. Then he came up close, face to face, chewing gum with a rapid ceaseless movement of his jaw as he tapped the frightened Arab on the chest. 'So where's Zeiti?'

Bassam backed away, starting to sweat.

Gessner pursued him. 'Ahmad Zeiti, your friend from Berlin. Know who I mean?'

Bassam shook his head.

'You called him in London today, right? Told him to come down here. So okay, where is he?'

Gessner's tactics were stupid, but now he was stuck with them. His information was that Arabs scare easy, and so he went on, pushing Bassam back with short aggressive jabs to the chest, escalating his verbal assault.

'Come on, where is he? You expecting him here, or what?'

No reply from Bassam.

'Look at you, piss-scared already. Man, you'd better tell me or you'll get it too. Where is he? Where's Zeiti, huh? You want it too? Stop fucking around or you'll get it, I'm telling you.'

Furniture was jolted, objects toppled to the floor. Bassam was forced back to the wall, pop-eyed behind his spectacles. He was sweating profusely now and exuding a strange sort of animal odour as Gessner took hold of his collar and shook him.

'Come on, come on, stop shitting me or I'll beat your brains out.'

Still no answer.

Gessner began to lose control. Breathing fast through lips drained of blood he pulled his revolver from his belt and thrust the barrel up hard under Bassam's chin.

'All right now, where is he?'

Bassam stood rigid and quivering, head thrust back against the wall by the gun. Then Gessner stepped back and pistol-whipped him to the floor with one blow.

Bassam did not hear the rattle of the door handle which saved him; did not see Gessner fling the door open then jump back in surprise and after a brief conversation hurry from the room; did not know whose hands had lifted him gently from the floor, until his head cleared and there was Yaacov, sitting beside him on the bed.

Later Zeiti appeared, and Yaacov explained the situation to him. Bassam lay on the bed and listened to them talk. They smiled when they saw he was better but did not press him to speak, and he had no wish to. The room seemed unnaturally still. A plaster had been applied to his cheek.

6. Women and Dogs

Marsden too had been provided with a room at St Anthony's for the conference. He was anxious to get back there but was forced to wait at Granby until he had Roscoe's answer. He had hoped to settle it at dinner, but conversation was impeded by the presence of the girl Nina Brown.

Marsden studied her for clues to his host's state of mind and noted that she had a sort of boyish American charm, robust and direct. Like a pair of boys she and Roscoe called each other by their surnames. Brown was her name and brown her colour; as well as brown eyes she had copper-brown hair, cut short and spiky, and pale brown freckles on her cheeks. All her movements were jerky and quick, like a bird's; her moods came and went with bewildering rapidity.

When Roscoe announced the main dish her laugh echoed all round the house. 'Toad in the hole? I don't *believe* it!' She laughed on, very loud, prodding a sausage with her fork. 'Toad in the hole. Oh my, what a trip you British are.'

Apart from that she hardly spoke. She seemed annoyed by Roscoe's neglect, he by the disruption of his household.

Roscoe drank fast, unworried by the silence, then gave voice to a private train of thought.

'It was rather odd of God to choose the Jews.'

Marsden nibbled at his toad. 'In a way, yes. It is of course a fundamental absurdity of Judaism, the universal god reserved for one race. On the other hand Palestine was just where you'd expect Him to strike – navel of the earth, you see, midway between the Nile and Euphrates – and its still the cockpit today, you know. The Americans commit themselves to one side, the Russians to the other. Mix in religion and oil and ask yourself where the world will end.'

'Jimmy, you're over the top.'

Marsden attempted a smile. 'I don't like the Jews, as you know, but you have to admire them. They gave us religion, psychology, socialism, perhaps even nationalism, which pretty well covers the options. They occupied this central point of the earth and ever since then they have been at the heart of things, the best and the worst. They seem to draw the lightning.'

'Don't know when to stop, you mean.'

'Call it a talent for doom. They invent God and then they annoy him.'

Brown said nothing. Back in the drawing room she put on a record and rolled a marijuana cigarette, then stretched out on a sofa, hissing through her teeth as she inhaled. Roscoe placed himself in front of the fire, his feet deep in mastiff, swilling brandy round a big balloon glass.

Marsden decided he could wait no longer. 'Well, I must be going,' he said, and stood up to leave. At the door he paused, looking back at Brown. 'Mind if I say something?'

She smiled at him, blinking. 'What's that?'

'Go easy with that stuff. I've seen what it can do.'

'Hey, no kidding.'

'Good night then.'

Brown bowed her head in elaborate farewell. 'Nice to have met you, sir.'

Roscoe shut the door on her and the two men walked back together to the farm, where Marsden's car was parked.

'I'll go,' Roscoe said.

'Good for you.'

'Do I get paid?'

'Of course.'

'How much?'

Marsden hesitated. 'Do you need to know now?'

'I do.'

'Well then, let's say two hundred a week, plus expenses of course, and an extra thousand at the end. How's that?'

'Not enough.'

'It's more than you were getting in the army.'

'It is also nothing like enough. Damn it all, I could get myself bumped off.'

Marsden sighed. 'Very well. Three hundred a week, two thousand at the end.'

'Still not enough.'

'What!'

'Come along, Jimmy, you can do better than that.'

Marsden's pique was evident. Like all men without capital he assumed that those with it had no need of income.

But Roscoe stood his ground, pleased to exhibit the talent of his grandfather and well aware, besides, of the going rate for mercenaries. 'If these people have money, as you said, then it's probably oil money. And if it is, there's plenty to spare.'

'All right,' said Marsden curtly, 'so what's your price?'

'Two thousand now, returnable if I turn the job down. Another four thousand if I pull it off. In the interim, as you suggest, three hundred a week plus expenses.'

'Stephen, be serious.'

'I am, and I won't haggle either. All I need is a yes or a no.'

Marsden was silent all the way to his car, then he said: 'The absurd thing is he will probably agree.'

'Of course he will'

'You know, you really are a bit of a bastard.'

'So I'm told,' Roscoe said cheerfully. 'I'll assume it's on then, unless I hear differently from you.'

'Yes, I suppose so.'

'Good.'

Marsden took a deep breath. 'You ought to have a cover, and I think the best is journalism. I'll get a press card made up. Keep it out of sight, though, when you get to Syria.'

'Am I going to Syria?'

'It's best to be prepared.'

Roscoe suspected that Marsden knew more than he was telling. 'I'm not commited yet, that's understood I hope. I'll need to know more before I decide.'

'Of course. Now when can you leave?'

'Any time after the weekend.'

'Tuesday then, the 12th. We'll book you on a flight to Beirut. When you get there behave like a journalist, just nose around the place and wait for Saladin to make contact. Can you be in London on Monday?'

'I expect so.'

'I want you to see a fellow called Hammami.' Marsden explained that Hammami was the representative in London of the

Palestine Liberation Organization, the body which attempted to coordinate the various guerilla groups and acted as their diplomatic arm. 'Hammami will send you round to me for contacts – normal thing for outgoing journalists. But when you get to the Institute, play it straight. If there's anything else to discuss we'll go out to a pub.'

'Any idea how long I'll be away?' Roscoe indicated Granby and all its inhabitants with a single proprietary sweep of his hand. 'It's just that I have to tell them something.'

'You should be back by Christmas.' Marsden got into his car and sat with one hand on the door, his face now visible in the interior light. 'Oh, one other thing. Do you want to take a gun?'

'A gun?'

'I notice you keep a Browning in the house.'

'No, I don't think so.'

'As you wish. If you change your mind I can get it delivered in Beirut.'

'Jimmy, the fact is you're not half as respectable as I thought.'

Marsden had had enough of this. He closed the door, wound down the window and started his car. 'Thanks for dinner. See you Monday,' he said, and drove off briskly into the dark.

Roscoe watched the retreating car's headlamps sweep the fens, then he whistled to his dogs and walked them along the sea wall. They trailed behind miserably, heads hung low, tails between legs. They knew already he was leaving, the way dogs do. And Brown knew, the way women do. 'That Marsden's a fag,' she said, still on the sofa when he came back in.

'Rubbish.'

'Of course he is, an old English faggot.'

'So what?'

'You're going away.'

'Yes.'

'I'm not staying here with that old cow.'

Roscoe refilled his glass and sat down. 'No, you'd better move back to your flat.'

Brown lit a cigarette, the ordinary kind, and paced about the room. Where he was going, or why, was not yet important to her. 'I hope you don't expect me to be around when you get back.'

'You're free to do what you like.'

'So you're going.' She tugged at the cigarette, then buckled it into an ashtray. 'Well, thanks for telling us.'

'Let's go to bed.'

'Okay. Bed.'

Roscoe locked up the house. Latches snapped in the silence, bolts slid, and the unfinished quarrel followed them around like a third party until they were lying in bed, pretending to read.

'Steve, why am I so difficult?'

Roscoe thought about it, wanting to be kind. 'Because you're not dull.'

'I just can't make it, you know. With you, with anyone.'

'I doubt that.'

'You don't understand, the more kind you are, the more I want to kick you. I feel like I'm in a padded cell.'

Roscoe disliked this sort of thing but it had to be faced, they were finished. Something had run out, the chemistry was wrong – however you chose to describe it, no amount of talk was going to put it right. He perhaps needed a wife whereas Brown wished to live with a man as a comrade. The subordinate role drove her mad, and so the sooner they ended it the better. 'I understand more than you think,' he said, 'but there's not very much I can do.'

'You mean we should split?'

'I think so.'

'Oh, Steve.' She rolled across the bed and rested her head on his chest, feeling the rise and fall of his lungs. She had a fear of growing old alone. 'But what will I do?'

'Get a job. You should have a job, you know.'

'A job. Oh shit.'

'It's just that you get bored, I'm just the same.'

She turned away and curled herself into a ball, her regular sobbing position. She was a noisy laugher, a noisy lover come to that, but the quietest of sobbers. Roscoe heard only the catches in her breath and felt a slight tremor in the mattress. He left her alone for a while, then leaned across and touched her on the shoulder. 'Come on, cheer up.'

She rolled back towards him. 'Oh Steve, Steve. What will become of us?'

'God knows.'

'We had something, didn't we?'

'We did.'

'Still fancy me?'

'Stop fishing. You know I do.'

When he kissed her she tasted of pot, but he was used to that, and wanting to end things well he made love to her with concentration. It turned out no better than average, though Brown cried aloud, as she always did. In the effort to lose herself she would let loose amazing obscenities, urging him to hurt, kill, obliterate her. Roscoe was used to that too, but of what was it a symptom in Brown? For her, it seemed, obliteration was more the point than pleasure, as if in one black, ultimate climax she could shake off her womanhood for ever – or prove it beyond any doubt perhaps? Roscoe did not know. He found her mysterious.

7. The Faint Whiff of Espionage

Meanwhile Marsden drove back across the Midlands to Oxford, still feeling miffed by the size of Roscoe's fee. It was cynical, he thought, it was insolent; but at least it showed nerve, and that Stephen had to a fault, like his father Dick, a man who kept flying back, using up his luck until his plane hit the sea.

Memories of the war evoked an odd response in Marsden. He felt a pang of pure envy for those men who had vanished with such style, escaping the ordinariness of life. Richard Roscoe, for instance, survived in the minds of his friends in a sort of amber glow, forever young, handsome, rich, drinking dry martinis and dancing till dawn at the Savoy, while he, James Marsden, lived on in a small flat in Kensington, a bit of a pansy, getting on now, with a bee in his bonnet about Palestine. That, Marsden knew, was what his friends said, and as he drove through the orange-lit suburbs of Nottingham he thought with sudden vehemence how much he disliked his country – a cramped and tawdry place, overrun by a boorish and self-indulgent people. He wondered why he had ever come back to it. He hated London. Depressed to be at his flat or club, he had recently taken to going to the cinema alone, until rescued from inaction by his friend Saladin.

He reached Oxford in the early hours – it was now Friday, September 8th – and parked outside the house where St Anthony's had lodged him. Bassam had the room next to his and below was Michel Yaacov, the affable young Israeli major. Marsden distrusted Yaacov, believing he was only at the conference to spy out the opposition's mood.

It was therefore a shock to find him in Bassam's room, sitting with a book while Bassam lay snoring on the bed in his clothes.

Marsden stood gaping in the door. Yaacov switched out the light and led him back into the corridor. 'Bassam said you'd come,' he whispered, and seated in Marsden's room he explained what had happened. The story of Gessner's assault filled Marsden with horror, amazement and finally deep foreboding, which was not the least soothed by Yaacov's fluent apology. 'That's the trouble, you see, we have our Black Septembers. And at times like this it's hard to control them.'

Trying to conceal his unease, Marsden wished Yaacov good night, closed the door and went to bed. Though exhausted, he could not sleep. Since middle age he had suffered from insomnia, brought on by the least disturbance to his mental equilibrium or digestive system, and when he knocked on the door of Bassam's room next morning he was ready to show a little temper. Getting no reply, he walked in.

Bassam was still asleep in his clothes. He rose slowly, responding with difficulty to Marsden's questions. He had been the victim, he said, of a stray Jewish crank who was looking for an Arab to thump.

'But why here? Why you?'

Bassam shrugged dozily and put on his glasses, which Yaacov had strapped into shape with Elastoplast. 'I suppose St Anthony's is a rather good hunting ground at the moment.'

'So where's this chap Zeiti?'

'I'm afraid he had to go – flight to Damascus this morning.'

'Does he know about this?'

'Oh yes, came round after.'

'And you don't think he's anything to do with it? This attack I mean, it couldn't have been meant for him?'

Bassam mumbled in a negative fashion as he peered at his bruise in a mirror.

Marsden dropped irritably into a chair. 'All right then, tell me about him.'

Zeiti, said Bassam, was a friend of his, a student from Berlin who had once done good work for Al Fatah but had lately become disillusioned with the leadership. For the last two years he had played no part in the Resistance, but that was not from choice. All he needed was a suitable banner to follow. 'So I told him a bit about our plans. And he was keen, very keen. I think he may join us.'

'What's he doing here?'

'He's got a girl, in London. We meet when we can.'

Marsden was unhappy. He asked whether Saladin had been informed.

'Not yet, no.'

'We must stick to people we can trust. There's no point in numbers.'

'Oh yes, I agree. But Zeiti's really one of the best. I've known him for years.'

Marsden rolled his eyes upwards, ostentatiously exasperated. 'You've known him for years. Well that's all right then.'

'What about your man? Did you . . .?'

'Yes, I think so. Now if you don't mind I'll go and get some breakfast.'

Marsden jumped up and strode from the room in a mood not improved by the thought of the greasy fry which awaited him.

One floor down Michel Yaacov was also awake. He was sitting with a small tape-recorder activated by a very much smaller microphone-transmitter, no bigger than a thimble, which he had attached by its magnetic base to the desk in Bassam's room. When the reels of the recorder stopped turning he played back the conversation to himself with a satisfied smile. Such behaviour was quite against the spirit of St Anthony's. But worth the risk; because here, it seemed, was the nucleus of a brand new resistance organization, a group which took its orders from a man called Saladin and included in its ranks such ill-assorted types as Bassam Owdeh, Ahmad Zeiti and Colonel James Marsden. . . .

Yaacov replayed the tape, then telephoned the London branch of Mossad, the Israeli intelligence service. They easily identified Samuel Gessner and rang back later in the morning to say that Ahmad Zeiti was an Al Fatah 'active', believed to be a member of Black September and involved in the Munich raid.

The realization that one of the Olympic killers had slipped through his hands left a hard knot of anger in Yaacov's stomach which was with him for many weeks after. But he controlled himself, suggesting to Mossad that Zeiti and Bassam should be followed; that Zeiti should not be molested and that the Men of Zion should be stopped immediately. He would see Gessner himself; meanwhile an effort should be made to identify Marsden's new recruit.

Yaacov's suggestions had the force of orders. The hunt for Saladin had begun, but quietly at first, and well below the surface of public events, which continued to provide more blood and thrills.

In Munich the three surviving Arabs had been shut in separate prisons to prevent any rescue attempt. The Olympic stadium itself was now swarming with police and massive precautions were taken for the arrival of the Duke of Edinburgh and President Pompidou of France. 'Nothing is beyond the imagination of these people,' the police said.

That Friday the athletes were buried in Israel and Abba Ebban, the Foreign Minister, admitted to the press that Munich had ended all hope of peace. 'Peace is not the question on my mind today,' he said. 'The question is how to eliminate this scourge.'

The Israeli cabinet was contemplating several different answers to that question, but the first was traditional.

Late that same Friday afternoon, as the sun was going down and the crowds were packing up along the Mediterranean beaches, the fighter-bombers of the Israeli air force took off from their bases and struck deep into Lebanon and Syria. The planes flew so low over Galilee that people could see the rockets attached to their undersides and seconds later heard the thump of explosions beyond the Golan Heights. Altogether ten targets were hit in the biggest simultaneous air strike ever mounted by Israel.

A military spokesman in Tel Aviv said that every effort had been made to avoid civilian casualties. But as he and his audience knew, precision in such matters is not easy. Most of the targets were close to refugee camps and that weekend as bodies were dug out of the rubble the estimates of dead rose steadily. By Monday the number had reached three hundred, settling back later in the week towards two hundred.

That figure could well have been wrong. The Arabs were known to treat statistics as a tool of propaganda. But allowing for all exaggeration, it could still be said with confidence that many more people had been killed than at Munich, mostly civilians, some guerillas too, but probably no members of Black September.

8. The Girl from Jerusalem

In the Lebanon that day was an English girl called Claudia Lees, a young Cambridge graduate who worked for the Anglican Mission in Jerusalem. Claudia had come to the Lebanon from Israel two days before, flying via Cyprus with a second passport, and that Friday, September 8th, she was touring Palestinian refugee camps with a senior official of the United Nations Works and Relief Agency.

UNWRA, pronounced 'Unrah', was the body which provided the refugees with shelter and medical care. It had done so since 1948 and now the organization and all its works had an air of settled, almost prosperous permanence. Its offices and vehicles belonged to the Middle East as did sand or minarets or camels.

Claudia's escort that day was a Frenchman called Roland Giscard. She had brought him a letter from the priest who was her chief in Jerusalem and on the strength of this Giscard agreed to take her with him on a tour of his establishments in the north. They started early at Shatila, a camp in the suburbs of Beirut, then worked up country to Nahr al-Bared. .

The scene was familiar to Claudia. She had worked among the refugees in Gaza, and one camp was much like another: the classrooms of chanting children, the clattering canteens, housewives defeated by dust and crowds of sullen men without a living. The men in particular made her uncomfortable. Crouched in their tiny prefabricated shacks they dreamed of revenge against Israel, yet were patently, laughably far from making it a fact. For these men of the camps that grand final slaughter was all in the mind; the reality was impotence and shame. Claudia felt the force of their frustration almost as a sexual threat, and she shrank from it. The women she pitied, and more so the children.

Following the tireless Frenchman from camp to camp, through the heat and all-pervading dust, she was struck by the sheer intractable size of the problem. This was home for over half a million people. Their number had multiplied since the exodus from Palestine and was multiplying still by natural increase. In the camps which dated back to 1948 the original shelters had almost disappeared under home-built extensions of adobe and breeze blocks, their symmetrical pattern dissolved into the close brown-walled chaos of a normal Arab town. Along the pitted dirt streets commerce had sprung up, cobblers and greengrocers, tailors and cafés and barbers – and that, Claudia knew, was the trouble. The temporary soon became permanent; camps became towns, refugees from one land the citizens of another. People adapted, people forgot. To be forgotten was the nightmare of Black September.

At one point Giscard gave voice to her thoughts. 'The world is full of refugees,' he said. 'The Armenians, for example – who remembers them? We call them refugees only so long as they want to go home. That is what is so extraordinary about the Jews, for two thousand years they dreamed of going back. And now it is these people, kicked out by the Jews.'

Giscard was a typical UNWRA official, unemotional and weary. His job required him to be neutral but privately he was on the side of the Arabs.

'For me the problem is simple,' he said later. 'I work for the United Nations and Israel has no respect for that organization. Many times the UN has requested fair treatment for these people, but always the Israelis do nothing. When Israel obeys the UN the problem will be solved.'

Claudia knew it was not quite as simple as that but did not feel equipped to argue. Instinctively she sided with the Arabs, but that was a bias she dared not admit. The issue was impossibly complicated, and the more she went into it the more confused she got. Trying to keep an open mind, she ended up impressionable as wax, bearing the stamp of the last person she had spoken to. Such flabbiness was irritating to an educated girl, the more so to Claudia since by nature she preferred to be committed.

But that day she felt carefree. One could only take so much of other people's misery, and simply to be out of Israel was a relief – that cramped, obsessive nation behind its walls of wire. The Lebanon had quite a different air to it, more natural, more relaxed, all the intricate strands of its history woven into a harmonious pattern of people and land. At first glance it might have been Greece or Yugoslavia, until one passed the glossy green dome of a mosque or a bus packed with men in white kefias, the universal headshroud of the Arabs. The towns were of flaking brown stucco, the balconies of their old French villas festooned with pink geraniums. The sun was shining with that exceptional hard bright clarity it seemed to have in the East and over to the left the sea was brilliant blue, frothing against the white pebble beaches. All along the coast fishermen were standing with rods on the rocks, heads up into the breeze.

Giscard was chatting about the villa in Tangier he had bought for his retirement.

He had a colonial look to him; an old-fashioned Frenchman of the kind who had governed Algeria, short and solid, with hair cut *en brosse* and the complexion of a lizard. He wore shoes with extraordinarily thick crêpe soles, as if to add to his height, and as he talked he smoked continually, pulling out the crumpled packet from the pocket of his shirt and flicking up one cigarette at a time like a conjuror.

They drove through Tripoli and continued on north until they came to the last of the camps; it spread along the seashore, bisected by the road. Giscard stopped the car just short of it and got out. To the left was an orange grove and ahead of them an almost dry stream meandered through reeds and patches of green towards the beach.

'Nahr al-Bared,' said the Frenchman, pointing forwards. 'It means Cold River.'

Claudia joined him, smoothing out her jeans and feeling her blouse damp with sweat. 'How many here?'

'Registered refugees, about eleven thousand. The total population is higher, of course.'

Giscard looked at his watch. Soon it would be dark. From the roofs of the camp wraiths of smoke drifted into the sky, which was empty except for a distant formation of planes to the north, glinting silver as they banked above the sea. Beside the car an old man was standing at the door of his shop. Two people were crossing a bridge which led across the stream to the camp. Some children were playing in the orange grove.

Claudia had turned back towards the car when Giscard heaved her to the ground. Her protests were drowned by the roar of a plane flying low overhead, already climbing as its load exploded in the orange trees. Another plane followed, and another. The noise was unbelievable. It seemed to come mostly from the jets. The explosions were more like blows to the head, stunning metallic blasts of energy and heat followed by showers of stones and twigs and earth. In the short lull between each attack all that could be heard was this steady rain of debris, then another plane dived in. Each time they thought it had finished, it had not. They kept lifting their heads then ducking down again. The explosions came closer. The old man ran screaming from his shop. Giscard's car rocked, its windows broke, the orange trees were splitting into fragments. Claudia pressed herself into the bottom of the ditch, eyes shut, hands shielding her head. The ground was twitching like an animal in pain and Giscard was shouting, it sounded like swearing, he had one arm pressed tight across her shoulders, and then both of them were lifted off the ground and blown sideways, rolling over until they landed up against a tree – and that was the end of it.

The planes boomed away across the sea. Debris continued to fall, clanging on the body of the car, then diminishing to a patter of smaller fragments. They picked themselves up and stood lurching in the vacuum-like stillness. Claudia promptly sat down again, feeling giddy, and Giscard vomited discreetly into the bushes. He was bleeding from a cut on his neck.

Rescuers started to arrive, followed by a crowd of distraught Palestinian women from the camp, their cries competing with the wail of ambulance sirens. Claudia sat by the ditch, mechanically rubbing the mud from her jeans while people rushed past her. The crowd swelled, blocking the road, and then the Palestinian commandos appeared, in red berets and green denim, officiously clearing a way for the traffic. They had used the orange grove as a training ground. Now it had ceased to exist. Gazing at the craters and blasted tree stumps, Claudia could hardly believe she had survived. The air smelt strongly of explosive; terrified children were stumbling down the road.

People were jabbering hysterically all round her, some crying, others laughing for no reason she could see. She wanted to help but could not stand up. She went on cleaning her jeans

Then the press turned up, arriving in cars from Tripoli soon after nightfall. They wanted facts, details and figures. How many planes, they wanted to know. But witnesses differed. Some said two, attacking in rotation, others a dozen. What type? Skyhawks, the experts said, though others said Phantoms, with overhead cover from Mirages. How many hurt, the press insisted, how many dead?

That took some time to find out. It was known that there were children in the orange grove and some of them might still be alive, injured or buried by eruptions of earth. But finding them was made more difficult by delayed-action bombs, which exploded at irregular intervals throughout the night, scattering the rescuers

'What a technology!' Giscard said. It was his only comment.

The appearance of the first dead child caused something like a riot. First the mother keened alone, flinging herself on the stretcher, then the corpse was lifted, displayed, and other women joined her, screeching in unison while the men shouted more in anger than grief, theatrically waving their fists at the sky. More bodies were dug out. Ambulances came and went. Giscard, as senior representative of the United Nations, felt obliged to stay until the toll was known, but Claudia, who had soon seen as much as she could bear, was driven away to Tripoli by the press.

In the main hotel reporters were dictating their stories by telephone. One of them was telling in French how the rescuers' shovels had uncovered two children who had been playing cards, their bodies wrapped together with the cards strewn around them. Moved suddenly to tears, not by the pathos but the mawkishness of this report, Claudia took a room and went to bed.

While she slept a hurried press conference was called in Beirut by Yasser Arafat, the fleshy and unshaven commander of Al Fatah. Arafat controlled the largest of the Fedayeen groups and had risen to dominate the PLO. In default of other contenders he was the spokesman of Palestine. 'Let all the world know,' he said, 'that this people will continue on its path no

matter what the sacrifices are. Dear comrades, be ready and
alert to face all possibilities.'

By the morning the picture at Nahr al-Bared was clear. The
shopkeeper was dead, also the couple on the bridge. The rest of
the casualties were children: eight dead, and twenty-two
injured.

Giscard left the scene at dawn and came to the hotel in
Tripoli, where he made an immediate phone call to Beirut.
He spoke in a low voice and kept his message brief. 'Giscard
here. You should come straightaway. I'll meet you at the
monastery.'

When Claudia came down she found the Frenchman drinking
coffee on the terrace, lifting the cup from a saucer full of yellow
cigarette stubs. In the harsh morning light he looked like the
survivor of a brawl, swollen-eyed, his clothes streaked with
reddish earth. He told her what the casualties were, and added
that two children were missing. 'At least we think they are.'

'They might be somewhere else, you mean.'

'Ah no, they were there in the *orangerie*. I mean we may have
found them.' Giscard glanced up at her sombrely. 'It's hard to
tell, you understand?'

Claudia nodded, remembering the furious grief of a mother
who had clung to the scraps of her son, pressing them vainly
together with blood-soaked hands.

9. The Man at the Monastery

After breakfast Giscard took her back to Beirut in his Peugeot, driving slowly since the windows of the car had been smashed. The glass had been cleared off the seats but a thick crust of glistening fragments covered the floor. Claudia was glad of the air, as if it might blow away memories of the night, and Giscard was forced to stop smoking. Instead he chewed his teeth, working the muscle at the back of his jaw

They returned by the same coastal road, and the day was as lovely as the one before – the same bright sun and cool breeze, flowers everywhere, leisurely crowds in the streets – a scene so delightful, so different from that of the night that Claudia could not react to them both. Now released from shock, her emotions veered wildly, then the joy of survival proved stronger than sorrow for the children of Nahr al-Bared; in fact she felt a barely controllable urge to laugh, and being a conscientious girl, was ashamed of it. Talking loudly to Giscard above the slipstream, she struggled to restore some balance to her mind. She was still slightly deaf from the bombs.

'If only those pilots could see what they do!'

The Frenchman nodded wearily. 'They would be distressed, of course. That is the advantage of technology, it permits brutality by civilized men.'

'You seem very detached.'

'Detached?' Giscard shook his head and smiled. 'I am not detached.'

'Well you seem so.'

'Ah yes. That is something I have practised.'

'Don't you ever feel a need to *act*?'

Giscard looked at her, champing his teeth, but said nothing.

Claudia was provoked by his composure. She wanted to take the matter further. 'I'm just so *sick* of all this charity. It's the same in the Occupied Territories, you know. If the Arabs put a foot out of line the Israelis blow up their houses, boom, just like that, without waiting for the verdict of the courts. Then along we come, the poor old, pious old Anglican Mission, tut-tutting and clearing up the mess. We hand out our tea and our sympathy and perhaps a few pounds' worth of bricks, then away we dash to the next case. It makes us feel virtuous but I wonder if we do much good. Really we're like people who follow a child around, patching up everything he breaks. We smooth the path of violence.' She stopped to consider this idea, and felt unsure of it. 'Don't you agree?'

'Yes, I agree, and so would Black September. Revolutionaries hate charity – it takes away their hate.'

Giscard liked to talk in abstracts, and as he bawled out these aphorisms in correct but heavily accented English, Claudia warmed to him again. Noticing the muscle in his cheek she decided that, outwardly dour, he was in fact prey to fierce emotions, not the cynic he seemed.

The road passed a patchwork of salt pans, the wheels of their wind pumps spinning in the breeze, but Claudia had talked herself back to the night and now she saw women crazed with fear as they scrambled to identify a shape on a stretcher. 'Oh, I wish I could do more.'

Giscard glanced at her sharply, then lifted his foot from the accelerator. 'Do you mean that?'

'Yes of course.'

'You would do something practical to help these people?'

'If I could. But what?'

Giscard seemed about to answer the question; he had slowed the car almost to a stop. His eyes were on her, and now Claudia saw that the urge suppressed in this terse little chain-smoking Frenchman was neither compassion nor despair, but violence. She sensed he was about to say something extraordinary, but he thought better of it and drove on. Claudia felt a twitch of annoyance; she was ready for anything. Deliberately she repeated her answer to the Frenchman's first question. 'Yes, of course I mean it.'

Giscard did not respond. A few minutes later he turned off to the right, towards a small Christian church set against the blue of the Mediterranean, its ancient ochre stones as solid as

the rocks on which it was built. He said it was called Our Lady
of the Sea and had once been a monastery. Pulling up in the
shade of a tree outside the gate, where another car was parked,
he muttered an apology and disappeared inside.

Claudia got out to stretch her legs. Left alone, she thought
suddenly of cold winter mornings in Cambridge – gas fires,
nice people, good books – her life there seemed as distant as
childhood and the don she had almost married, who still wrote
her long and affectionate letters, lost as a childhood friend. She
would not come back until she was ready, she had told him, and
she did not know when that would be.

The other car under the tree was a big white Mercedes with
black tinted windows and a Lebanese number plate. Putting her
face close against the glass, Claudia peered inside and saw it was
empty. Then she sensed a movement behind her and turned
round quickly in fright.

Beneath the tree now was an Arab of classically villainous
appearance, who pulled out a knife and stabbed the air, exposing congealed yellow teeth in a grin as he mimed the fate of
unwary marauders and conveyed without language that he was
the guardian of this important place. His patched khaki caftan
was strapped to his chest by crossed bandoliers, his wizened
brown face wrapped under and over in a red-check kefia.
Claudia later discovered he was called Etienne, a name acquired
in the French Foreign Legion. He was a Gipsy, not an Arab,
and Saladin used him as a bodyguard.

Spreading his fingers to indicate the price, he offered to show
her round the monastery. She paid up and was taken through
the heavy wooden gate into a small paved courtyard. There,
through an open door, she saw some nuns eating lunch round a
table. They had a radio playing loud brassy music, unsuitable
for nuns, and were shrieking with laughter as they passed round
a bottle. Claudia smiled, but when they saw her the party
stopped abruptly. They stared at her in silence. Following the
Gipsy, she climbed a flight of steps to a parapet and saw that
the monastery was built like a fort, with the sea all around it,
lapping the walls.

Standing in that place, Claudia had something of the
Crusader's lady; decorous, even in jeans; waiting on events. A
girl of average height, she was neither plump nor thin but nicely

rounded, with the tender look of one who has been well cared
for all her life. Her appearance, like her manner, was modest,
but mingled with this modesty was pride, shown clearly in the
angle of her chin. Her hair, which was fair and worn shoulder-
length to conceal a birthmark on her neck, was blown back from
her face by the breeze, and her face was the sort which incurs
men's respect – intelligent, serious, pale, with eyes slightly
narrowed by short sight as she watched the sea surge and
recede on the white rocks below.

The music on the radio, she now realized, was the Colonel
Bogey march. Then the sound was cut off as a door slammed.
Unfriendly nuns. Since the bombing raid nothing had seemed
quite real; the impairment of her hearing had put the world at
one remove, as though events were taking place behind a sheet
of glass.

She turned and followed the Gipsy back down the steps and
into a chapel. The interior was festooned with tawdry chandeliers, neglected, except for the Madonna, whose cheap plaster
statue smiled down on a bank of dripping candles. Claudia was
very nearly certain that she believed in God, but did not find
him here. This ubiquitous Gipsy seemed more in the spirit of
the place, pursuing her from ikon to ikon with lecherous little
black eyes. She turned her back on him and hurried out into
the courtyard, where Giscard had now reappeared with another
man.

This second man made a deep and immediate impression on
Claudia. Afterwards she could not say how it was done; she
knew only that she had been totally mastered without feeling
the slightest resentment. Was it simply the strength of his purpose allied to the gentlest of manners? No, more than that.
There was between them, it seemed, an instant mutual understanding and sympathy. She understood what he wanted and
he understood her hesitations, down to the last nuance. Since
he knew her so well it followed that he would not ask her to do
what she could not, and from that it seemed to follow that
whatever he asked her to do she could and would do – must do
indeed, because he assumed that she would. Thus, by some
subtle chemistry, to go against this man's wishes became a
breach of faith

He was also impressive to look at; an elegant figure in a suit, perhaps fifty, with sleek black hair and the delicate features of a high-born Arab. He carried about him an air of great wealth and the almost lethargic authority of a man who had grown up with power. Then Claudia noticed that he was in fact carefully rationing his energy and that the cause of this was some sort of illness: his skin had a jaundiced tinge and his clothes hung loosely on a tall, thin body. When he spoke his voice was musical and soft, with a slight American accent.

'Well, Miss Lees, I hear you want to fight for Palestine.'

'I did say that, yes.'

He watched her carefully, with eyes which were penetrating but not unkind. 'Did you mean it?'

'I'm not sure – it depends what you want. I'm sorry, that must sound rather vague.'

'On the contrary, if you'd said more I wouldn't have believed you. Beirut is full of young Arabs who want to slaughter Jews. They get no further than the bars along the Hamra.'

The man smiled. Claudia smiled back. She wondered who he was. Both the Gipsy and Giscard were treating him respectfully, hanging back as he led her through the gate and out towards a circular bench built around the bowl of the tree where the two cars were parked

'The point is,' he said, talking in the same gentle manner, 'you are willing to help. What we now have to do is find out the limit of that help, because I think it's important that we do not expect too much of each other. Shall we sit down?'

They sat in the shade of the tree and talked for perhaps twenty minutes. At the end the man said that she was to know him as Saladin. Finally it was arranged with Giscard that the Anglican Mission should be asked to extend her stay in the Lebanon.

'Plead shell shock, Roland, anything you like,' said Saladin, then turned back to Claudia to explain. 'You see, there is an Englishman coming to help us, and I want you to meet him.'

10. General Post, and One More Recruit

Saladin's team was taking shape. After talking to Claudia Lees he spent that Saturday, September 9th, among the refugees at Nahr al-Bared, looking for men he could trust, men who would follow Stephen Roscoe.

Claudia and Giscard returned to Beirut, and that day Bassam Owdeh arrived back in the Lebanon. He was met at the airport by Leila Riad, a fellow teacher at the university. Leila, who had taken care of Bassam for years, was no fool; she noticed that they were being followed, so Bassam was cautious in approaching Saladin. He made light of his experience in Oxford, but Leila was worried. She knew the importance to Bassam of routine and security, all the little defences she had carefully erected in their life together. She was frightened that this new undertaking would destroy him. Already he was losing weight, always a bad sign in Bassam.

Saladin was more worried about the followers, and about Zeiti, into whom he initiated certain enquiries of his own.

Zeiti was now at his home in Damascus, where the family reunion was marred by quarrels. Also there was his sister, with the wealthy Libyan she planned to marry. This Libyan, Raoul Shafiq, was loyal to the former King Idris and therefore an enemy of Colonel Gadaffi. Zeiti despised him and the feeling was mutual. Indeed so vindictive was Shafiq, so determined to settle with this troublesome brother that he had already passed the word about Zeiti's association with Black September to a Jewish acquaintance in Paris who was known to pay well for such information. In Damascus the two men almost came to blows. Zeiti insulted his sister and left in a rage for Beirut, but despite these upheavals a date was fixed for the wedding. Shafiq kept the MZ in touch.

That weekend, September 9th and 10th, the press was full of the Israeli bombing and on Saturday General David Elazar, the Israeli Chief of Staff, appeared on television. 'Air raids are not the only means of hitting back,' he said. 'There are other ways, and we will use them.'

That was the sort of remark which usually prefaced an overland raid into Arab territory, but it could also mean that the Israeli government had decided to reply to Black September by less conventional methods.

What those methods were cannot be proved, but in the months following Munich the press began to speak of a secret new military unit in Tel Aviv called 'God's Wrath', which was said to be liquidating Palestinian terrorists abroad. Certainly a number of Arabs died mysteriously in Europe, and in April 1973 the Israelis mounted a spectacular commando raid on Beirut itself. Three senior officials of Al Fatah were shot at close range in their flats and Yasser Arafat himself escaped by pure chance.

But with or without the aid of God's Wrath, the Israelis were very well able to handle Black September on their own; the last thing they wanted, now or ever, was help from such as Sammy Gessner.

Mossad had by this time traced Gessner to a hotel in London, and on Sunday Yaacov arranged to take a walk with him in Kensington Gardens. Neither man mentioned their confrontation at St Anthony's and Gessner, who understood the shyness of officials, did not ask Yaacov his name or question his authority. He confined himself to tactical advice. What Israel ought to be working on now, he said, was the total reconquest of Solomon's Kingdom. 'We could take Syria tomorrow. I tell you, man, we could beat the hell out of the Syrians.'

Yaacov smiled his superior smile. 'Yes, but do we need to? Do we want to?'

'Yeah, I want to, I want to very much. For me Damascus is a Jewish city.' Gessner prodded the air with a finger as he talked. 'God gave us that land, we should take it back.'

'We might have to wait a while.'

'Yeah, we can wait. He's in no hurry.'

Gessner walked on, chewing gum, while Yaacov politely suggested that the best thing the Men of Zion could do for

Israel was disband. 'And keep away from Zeiti. We have plans
for him.'

'Come on, let me waste him. Do you a favour.'

'Not those sort of plans.'

'Where is he?'

'Damascus.'

'That's a Jewish city, man.'

'So's New York,' Yaacov said dismissively, glancing at his
watch. 'I must go.'

'Have a nice trip.'

'Good-bye now.'

'Shalom.'

They parted by the Albert Memorial. Yaacov went straight
to the airport and flew back to Israel. Gessner walked on to
Berkeley Square, where he joined a crowd of Zionist demon-
strators outside the Arab League building on Hay Hill.

This was the office of Said Hammami, the Arab whom
Roscoe was due to meet on Monday. As local representative of
the PLO, Hammami was held responsible for Munich. Since
the day of the massacre a group of Jews had demonstrated outside his office on Hay Hill, shouting 'Hammami out! Hammami
out!' and on Sunday, when Gessner joined the crowd, it had
swelled with sympathetic onlookers.

With Yaacov now out of the way Gessner meant to have some
fun. He introduced himself to the ardent young Zionists in the
street as an Israeli officer on leave and when the demonstration
dispersed he took a group of them, three youths and a girl, to a
restaurant in Soho. He had served, he said, in one of the armoured units which had stormed the Golan Heights in '67. In his
view the Syrians were the lowest form of life. 'And this guy
Hammami's no better. The PLO supports terrorism, that makes
him an enemy of Israel. I'd like to kill the bastard.'

His companions were impressed, and afterwards one of them,
a boy called David Heinz, took Gessner to his home in Golders
Green.

David Heinz, who was due to play a small but significant part
in the drama of Saladin, was at an unsatisfactory stage of his
life. Having failed to master the guitar, he was working as a
part-time assistant in Hampstead Public Library. His parents
were assimilated Jews, refugees from Austria who had gratefully

adopted the British way of life. His father, an official in the
Ministry of Defence, had wanted at one time to change their
name to Hines, and his mother had a job with the Labour Party.
David's bid for identity was Zionism. Gessner had promised to
speak up in his support, but when they reached the house it was
empty, so they sat in the kitchen drinking coffee.

'What are you going to do with your life, David?'

'I told you, I'd like to go to Israel.'

'Israel? That's a tough place.'

David insisted he had enough of England. 'Like everything
here is too easy, you know?' He waited for the usual interruption,
but now Gessner was silent. 'I mean, I feel guilty when it's so
easy here and our people are in trouble. You know, as you said.'

'I know.' Gessner nodded sympathetically. 'But what you did
there today, that was good.'

'Not much really.'

'No, I tell you, that's good, that's important.'

'Anyone can join in a demo.'

Gessner stood up and paced about the kitchen, chewing
gum. The room seemed too small to contain him. David was
slouched in a chair, a pale flaccid youth with protuberant eyes
and a mop of brown curls, whose clothes made a stab at
current fashion. After a minute Gessner stopped pacing and
stared at him, ostentatiously making up his mind. 'You want
to do more?'

David sat upright, startled.

Gessner barked at him: 'You want to do something for
Israel, right?'

'Er . . . yes.'

'All right, David, here's what you do. You working tomorrow?'

'No.'

'Okay, you meet me at Golders Green subway at nine. I'll be
driving a white Ford station-wagon. And I want you to bring
me a box, about so big, the kind they put groceries in at the
store. Can you do that?'

'Yes, I should think so.'

'Good boy.' Gessner jammed his hat on the back of his head.
'Now I should go before your folks arrive.'

'Don't you want to meet them?'

'Some other time.'

They went outside, and standing beside his mother's roses, watching the man in the black leather jacket walk away, David Heinz felt a thrill of excitement which only later turned to panic.

11. The Promised Land

That Sunday Stephen Roscoe was clearing up his affairs, laying in a store of dog biscuit and leaving instructions for the sale of the grain. He planned to leave home early next morning.

Since deciding to part he and Brown had found a happy mood, which was only disturbed by a small tiff on Sunday afternoon. Roscoe had refused to say what he was doing for Marsden, and this sort of masculine clubbiness was more annoying to Brown than anything under the sun.

Roscoe went off to church without her and afterwards lingered in the pub. By the time he got back she had gone up to bed, so he shut away the dogs and sat drinking alone in the drawing room. That, he decided, was the way he liked it best.

He was easily bored but not fond of change. Harvest evensong had gone as it always had, and that gave him pleasure. The same lessons, the same hymns; marrows laid out exactly as last year round the pulpit. As usual he had sat in the second pew, Mrs Parsons alone behind him and the villagers with their families a little further back. Religion, in the sense of a riddle beyond the stars, had nothing much to do with it. Church was just one of the rituals of Granby and now a pretty rare one, since they only got services at Easter and harvest. For Christmas they went to the cathedral at Lincoln, an outing suggested by the vicar, whose flock spread for miles along the coast.

That night the man had a cold. He kept blowing his nose between the prayers. *Lighten our darkness, we beseech thee, O Lord, and by thy great mercy defend us from all perils and dangers of this night* – comforting words, which made Roscoe feel a boy again, kneeling in this pew with his grandfather. Outside the east wind was buffeting the church and the North Sea fretted at its long concrete barrier, but the magic had been said. Children would sleep safe tonight, pilots would come home.

What had changed was the lesson, or rather his reaction to it, conditioned by recruitment to Saladin. Now the Old Testament read like a Zionist pamphlet, odd fare to serve in an English country church. The text was Deuteronomy, Moses' statement of God's promises on Sinai, read by the vicar in a strong northern accent. *He will bless the fruit of your body and the fruit of your land, your corn and new wine and oil, the offspring of your herds and of your lambing flocks, in the land which he swore to your forefathers to give you . . .*

Roscoe's mind drifted off. The notion that God had drawn the map, he thought, was what inclined good Christian folk to back Israel, that and a feeling that the Jews were more our sort of people than the Arabs, who were pretty much out of the same stable as the Moabites, the Edomites and all that other gang. Such was almost certainly the view of the vicar, who was reading Moses' speech with unabashed relish. *The Lord will take away all sickness from you. He will not bring upon you any of the foul diseases of Egypt* – poor old Gypos, riddled with pox. *You may say to yourselves these nations outnumber us* – ah yes, Israel was outnumbered still, but the Arabs were scattered from Iraq to Morocco. . . .

The vicar's voice rose as he reached the final passage, filling the church to its rafters. *For the Lord your God is bringing you to a rich land, a land of streams, springs and underground waters gushing out in hill and valley* – he had hold of the big brass eagle by its wings and kept lifting his head from the book – *a land whose stones are iron ore and from whose hills you shall dig copper. You will have plenty to eat and will bless the Lord your God for the rich land that he has given you. . . .*

Now, as he sat at home drinking, Roscoe remembered the words. What a stupendous commercial, he thought, what a dream to dazzle for ever the Jews of frozen Russia. No wonder they wanted to go back.

He refilled his glass and then on an impulse, as if in defence against divine wrath, fetched his gun.

This sidearm of Roscoe's is a formidable thing – a Belgian-made Browning Hi-Power, fitted with special wooden grips to accommodate his very large paw. Because, like the Colt, it has few parts and a simple firing action, the pistol has been standard issue for the British fighting forces since 1956. Its principal virtue is its large magazine, which holds thirteen rounds stacked in a diagonal pattern. The ammunition is the same as that used in the Sterling submachine-gun – another convenience – and the whole thing when loaded weighs almost three pounds. It is in fact one of the biggest pistols made, which makes it hard to conceal. But in Ulster Roscoe had carried his in a shoulder-holster with a spring-clip to permit sideways draw and his jackets were so large that its presence against his ribs was not obvious.

He keeps several guns in his house yet never shoots for sport, either animals or men. He just enjoys guns, the look and the feel, the precision of them. He is good with machines and if they are lethal the importance and pleasure of control are increased.

Taking the Browning out of its box he wiped and dry-fired it, then found a box of cartridges and went out to the garage, where he set up a row of empty beer cans and jammed plugs of chewed paper into his ears. He used the classic army firing position, feet apart, knees bent, arms straight out, both hands cupped around the butt. Each time he fired the pistol jumped and flashed, ejecting a cartridge case several feet to the right. He hit four cans out of seven. Not good enough, he thought, and set them up again. With the second magazine he hit three. Worse. Never lick the Great God of Israel like that. . . . He set the cans up again, reloaded, heard a voice behind.

'Hold your fire, baby. Wait till they see the pink of your eyes.'

It was Brown, down from bed in a woolly North African caftan. He kissed her. She nuzzled against him, then became brisk, the frontierswoman. 'Okay, action man, shoot. Let's see what you can do.'

Roscoe plugged her ears, then opened fire again. Responding to the challenge, he hit five cans out of seven. They littered the floor now, punctured and twisted. 'This is no good,' he said, 'target stuff. Set up the bonemeal.'

In an effort to bring life to his garden Roscoe constantly feeds it with fertilizer. The garage was stacked with plastic bags of bonemeal, much more the size of target one should expect to hit, he now explained, in a rapid-fire situation. One aimed for the centre of the body – the important thing was to hit, where

did not matter. 'Now I'll go outside, you set up the bags. Four
will do. Scatter them around, then stand by the door. See how
we go.'

Brown complied, setting up the bags in random positions
round the garage. 'Okay,' she shouted, 'ready!'

Roscoe came through the door exactly as Gessner had done
at St Anthony's. Crouching low, he mimed a draw from the
shoulder and drilled the four bags in slightly less seconds.
'How's that?' he said, straightening up.

Brown inspected the bags, which were leaking white powder
on the floor. 'Pretty damn good,' she said. 'Now, my turn.'

They went on until the box of cartridges was empty. Mrs
Parsons slammed her window but did not interfere. Roscoe
cleaned the Browning, which was hot to the touch, then joined
Brown in bed. 'What fun,' she said. 'Steve?'

'Yes?'

'Can't I come with you? I'll pay my own fare.'

Roscoe was tempted, but said no. 'We ought to give it rest.
Some other time perhaps.'

'Some other time. Okay. Well mind you shoot straight.'

12. Thunder in the Air

During the night a fog rolled in off the sea. Roscoe got up at six and packed his things in the white milky light while seagulls circled and screeched through the murk and Brown sat hunched in an eiderdown. Then they dressed. Mrs Parsons cooked breakfast. No one said much. When they drove away the house was just a grey shape in the mist, and turning his back on it Roscoe felt disloyal, more disloyal to his home than his girl. Travel was like an affair, he thought, a touch of glamour to stimulate the senses, not reaching deep. Like a husband he would come back wondering what had made him leave.

On the platform at Peterborough he said good-bye to Brown, who blinked bravely. It seemed a poor place to end in.

When he reached London Roscoe went straight to see Said Hammami at the PLO office on Hay Hill, where a small crowd of Jews were still demonstrating. Coming out of the lift he was searched by a policeman then hustled past a queue of waiting clients in the corridor. In the event he did not see Hammami but a junior assistant, a polite young Arab, snappily dressed who provided a list of names in Beirut while the Zionists shouted outside. Then Roscoe was led to another office, where he telephoned Marsden.

'Hello . . . Jimmy?'

'Ah, Stephen.'

'I'm on my way over.'

Across the room another young Arab was sitting with a pile of letters and parcels. He picked up each item with the tips of his fingers, examined it carefully, held it up to a light then ran some sort of gadget over the surface of the envelope. Some envelopes he opened, others he placed to one side behind a heavy metal screen. Roscoe realized he was searching for mail bombs.

Marsden was suggesting the best bus to catch when someone interrupted at the other end.

'Just a minute, Stephen . . .'

Roscoe heard voices shouting, then the line went dead.

He left the PLO and caught a bus down to the Embankment. The Atlantic Arab Institute was near the Tate Gallery, but when Roscoe arrived there the street was blocked off by police and a crowd had collected. Further down he could see several fire engines and an ambulance parked across the road; smoke was coming out of a second-floor window, hoses had been run into the building and firemen were running backwards and forwards as a stretcher was brought out.

Roscoe tried to go through, but police barred the way.

Someone pushed through the crowd behind him and started asking questions in a loud American voice. 'What is this please? What's going on here?

Roscoe looked round and saw a short hairy man in a black pork-pie hat, chewing gum. 'It looks like an explosion,' he said.

'Hey, maybe it's the Irish.'

'More likely the Jews,' Roscoe said, then realized the gaffe and started to apologize.

But the man roared with laughter and clapped him on the back. 'That's all right, my friend, all right, no offence. Hey someone *is* hurt.'

Marsden was being assisted into the ambulance with a bulky white dressing round his head. Looking up the street, he signalled to the police, and Roscoe was allowed to go through.

'What happened?'

'Parcel bomb.'

'You all right?'

'Yes. Near thing, though.' Marsden's eyes followed Roscoe's to the stretcher. 'My secretary. She's all right too, just dazed. We'd better get going.'

They arranged to meet that evening at Roscoe's club and there Marsden, neatly stitched, explained what had happened. A youth had delivered a parcel of books for the AAI library, saying that they came from Hammami. No one gave him a glance; the PLO continually generated literature. On the way out he had gabbled a warning at the doorman, who had telephoned up on the internal line. The bomb had exploded as they ran out of the door.

'Changed his mind when he saw your pretty face perhaps,' Roscoe said.

Marsden smiled wanly. The bar of the club was loud with male talk, a dark panelled room with shiny leather chairs. Roscoe had never much liked the place but tonight was in good humour. Then, as he ordered a second round of drinks, Charles Heinz came up.

All Roscoe knew of Heinz was that he was an Austrian Jew, now more British than the British, who worked for the Security and Intelligence Service under cover of a job in the Ministry of Defence. They had met on a course in electronic surveillance and Roscoe had collected the necessary signatures to get him in the club. He remembered an awkward evening at a house in Golders Green, a socialist wife and a mute teenage son. Since then Heinz had evidently prospered; he shone with success and the pleasure it gave him, a small dapper man with a head smooth and white as an egg. Arriving at the bar with his guest he reached up and clapped a hand on Roscoe's shoulder. 'Why hello, old chap, long time no see. Are you staying in town?'

Roscoe sensed a slight stiffening in Marsden but could see no harm in answering the question. He said he was going to Beirut.

'Very nice. Business or pleasure?'

'I'm doing a bit of journalism actually.'

'Really? Well remembering the sort of balls you talk, I expect you'll do well.'

Everybody laughed, not least Heinz himself, who was never quite sure of his jokes although he swore with the best. 'Well,' he said, turning away, 'I mustn't keep Sir Geoffrey from his dinner. Give me a buzz when you get back.'

That was another thing Roscoe remembered: no one could drop names like Charlie Heinz.

'Don't tell me – a friend,' muttered Marsden, employing the Whitehall jargon for spies.

Roscoe pulled a mock-prim face and put a finger to his lips.

At dinner Marsden gave him a press card, wrote out a cheque for £2000, then told him about Bassam Owdeh. 'He's a good chap really, but apt to get over-excited. You'll have to steady him up.'

After brandy and cigars they walked down Brook Street and Roscoe said: 'You know, I think I will take that pistol after all. I'll have someone bring it up to you.'

'Fine. It'll reach you in a day or two.' Marsden hailed a taxi. 'Well, that's it then. Good luck, and when you see Saladin please give him my regards.'

Roscoe said good-bye and thanked him.

'For what?'

'For getting me off that bloody tractor.'

After they had parted Roscoe returned to the club, and settling in the smoke room with a second cigar, rehearsed his knowledge of explosives and the techniques required. Inspecting the damage at the AAI he had thought of the sappers he knew and the quiet men of the Bomb Disposal Squad in Ulster. It was not a field for flashy heroics, not at all the sort of thing for which shooting bags of bonemeal was a relevant exercise. Demolition required only speed and absolute precision, a cool head whatever the conditions, a complete understanding of the power and sensitivity of the materials involved. Well, he knew about that. He was trained. He could do it. Given that always necessary measure of luck, he would bring the money back to buy new gutters for his house.

Yes, Roscoe was confident that night in his club and did even wonder briefly whether this bang he was going to arrange for a man called Saladin might echo round the world like thunder. One did not have to be on one's fourth brandy to see that it could happen. The issues at stake were tremendous, but for that very reason he cleared them from his head. The way to approach this, he told himself, was to treat it as a technical problem, because to measure the results of his actions would only spoil his nerve. Mountaineers avoid looking down, priests cannot question God. Soldiers, too, should keep their minds on the job.

PART TWO

Friends and Enemies

September 12th–September 15th, 1972

1. Disconnection

Next day the Olympic Games ended. The Germans gave three million deutschmarks to the dead athletes' families. The dead terrorists were buried with full honours in Libya and everywhere the Arab-Israeli war reached a new pitch of violence. Said Hammami survived, but later his PLO colleague in Paris was killed by a device which exploded when he picked up the telephone. Both sides mounted a campaign of murder by mail and the first Jew to die was Dr Ami Schachori, Agricultural Attaché at the Israeli Embassy in London. His stomach was blown out by a letter bomb posted in Holland.

On the morning that Roscoe left London the Israeli cabinet held a meeting described as emotional and later that day Mrs Golda Meir made a speech to the Knesset, Israel's parliament. This was her first public statement since Munich and to hear it an eager crowd flocked past the guards and into the flat-roofed building like a Japanese temple which straddles a hill in central Jerusalem. Soon every seat was taken in the plush semicircular debating hall and the gallery above, where the public waited expectantly, watching proceedings through a sheet of bullet-proof glass.

Born in Russia in 1898, Mrs Meir was now seventy-four. Her appointment as Prime Minister was a compromise made necessary by the rivalry of Israel's two most powerful generals, Moshe Dayan and Yigal Allon, but in times of crisis hers was the presence which could hush the unruly voices of the Knesset. At such moments her ancient grizzled head, survivor of the pogroms of Kiev and three wars against the Arabs, seemed the very face of Israel. Often she spoke her mind bluntly, but on this occasion measured her words with care, confining herself to a bitter condemnation of the Arab regimes who had failed to curb the terrorists.

'We have no choice but to strike at them.'

In London the attack on Marsden's office caused a short-lived sensation. David Heinz escaped detection and was quickly removed from the country by his father. Shocked by his son's prompt confession, Heinz let the boy go to Israel, a decision in which he was helped by the fact that Harold Wilson, who lived down the street, had sent his son Giles to a kibbutz.

Marsden patched up his office and continued his lonely defence of the Arabs. That Tuesday he went to King's Cross to meet Nina Brown, who delivered Roscoe's pistol. Brown, still curious, tried to find out what was up. She had no success. Later that day she travelled back to Granby, where the atmosphere was hollow but friendly. Mrs Parsons, it seemed, was prepared to call a truce. In Roscoe's absence the two women got on surprisingly well, and drinking ginger wine in the kitchen Mrs Parsons came up with what seemed to Brown solid wisdom.

'It's hard for a girl on her own. But men want too much. We're betwixt and between, like.'

'Betwixt and between. Yup, that's me.'

'Miss him, do you?'

'Not much.'

'No, well I dare say you're better on your own.'

While they discussed him, Roscoe was above the Mediterranean in an airliner starting its descent to the Lebanon. He had used the time to read a paperback history of Palestine, but the book lay unfinished on his knees as he peered through the window and wondered what was to come. Outside it was dark. The plane was so high that it seemed to be motionless, but night had rolled quickly to meet it. The Alps, Yugoslavia and Greece had been left behind and now Cyprus was passing below, scattered lights and shadowy mountains rising from a moonlit sea. The flight went on to Australia. Roscoe felt strangely disconnected from his life. Granby was a memory, Beirut a name on the map; between them the only reality was this airborne hotel, floating through limbo with a payload of garrulous Chinese and Aussies drinking beer.

His neighbour was also bound for Beirut, a young television reporter called Dominic Morley, under orders to bring back an interview with Black September.

'I thought they never gave interviews,' Roscoe said.

'So far, mate, so far.' Morley pulled a book of travellers' cheques from his pocket and riffled them like a pack of cards. 'It talks, you know.'

He had been in Vietnam the week before and was due in the States to cover the approaching presidential election. Though not yet thirty, he had wild strands of grey in his hair and the ulcerous look of a man on the run. He was only still when sleeping. Once awake he would start to fidget, smoke, chatter, call the stewardess.

Roscoe assumed he had been briefed by Hammami.

'Hell no, Hammami knows nothing.' Morley leaned down and tapped the briefcase between his feet. 'I've got names in here the Israelis would give a lot to see. I tell you, mate, if I can set this up we'll sell it all over the world.'

Roscoe nodded, convinced, and picked up his book. 'Mind if I read?'

'Carry on, carry on. Don't have time myself.'

2. The Bloody and the Wet

Roscoe did not know much about the history of Palestine but since Marsden's visit he had worked at it, seizing odd moments to read, and now the basic steps to deadlock were clear in his mind.

First, for reasons of their own, the British had given a home to the Jews; since then the behaviour of the Nazis had provided an overwhelming moral case for this Jewish resettlement, but only in the mind of the West; the Arabs, understandably, said it had nothing to do with them; they just wanted their land back, even if some of it had been sold to the Zionists at quite a good price; but the Jews had waited two thousand years for this patch and now they meant to stay . . .

'One side is bloody and the other is wet,' so Roscoe had been told by a friend in the Foreign Office. He suspected the verdict was just. Coming up to the present, he had studied the facts more closely.

In 1948 the British had gone home, leaving the two sides to battle it out. Six thousand Israelis had been killed. King Abdullah of Transjordan had sent his army to the help of the Palestinian Arabs, but they could do no more than hold a line down the middle of the country, a line which had then become the frontier of Israel. What remained of Arab Palestine was incorporated into the neighbouring states; Gaza in the south went to Egypt, and the main western rump to Transjordan, which was renamed Jordan.

This absorption by Jordan was resented by the Palestinians. They lost no time in murdering Abdullah and since then had taken several shots at his grandson Hussein. The area disputed, known as the West Bank, was what Saladin envisaged as the nucleus of a new independent state. His plan was still secret but was sure to cause a storm, Roscoe knew; no Palestinian leader had dared to talk of less than total reconquest.

Nor had any Arab country dared to recognize Israel, as Saladin proposed to. Since 1948 there had been a continuous succession of frontier incidents, which twice had exploded into war. In 1956 the Israelis had advanced as far as the Suez Canal; only very strong American pressure had forced them to withdraw. Then in 1967 they attacked again, provided with all the excuse they required by the Arabs' incautious belligerence.

The fighting was over in six days and had ended in overwhelming victory for the Israelis, who drove the Egyptians out of Gaza and Sinai, taking everything as far as the Suez Canal. This time they kept it. They cleared the Syrians off the Golan Heights and seized the West Bank from Hussein. Most important of all they had taken Jerusalem, David's city, which since 1948 had been divided by the armistice line.

Now, in 1972, the situation was static. The Jews controlled the whole of what had once been Palestine; Jerusalem had been annexed and declared the capital of Israel. The other conquered lands, called the Occupied Territories, were run by the Israeli army under what was supposed to be a temporary arrangement. But lately Jewish settlement had started, and General Dayan had said the occupation might last fifteen years.

Talks had sometimes seemed about to begin, but never had. In effect the Arabs had agreed to make peace if Israel withdrew to the 1948 line, but the Jews were demanding a more secure frontier, and nothing would persuade them to give up Jerusalem. They wanted talks before withdrawal – or did they? Did they want any talks at all? Roscoe, for one, suspected not: a view strongly influenced by Marsden. The way he saw it the Israelis liked the map as it was and the gamble of Mrs Meir's regime was that nerve and superior force could keep it that way.

As such gambles go, it looked a safe one. Since 1967 the Arab states had failed to hit back. To carry on the fight the Palestinians had formed their own commandos – the Fedayeen – but this guerilla army had fragmented into many different groups and was no threat to Israel. Despite the PLO, the Resistance was divided from top to bottom. The wretched Palestinians did not even have an undisputed leader, and to Roscoe this seemed the fundamental weakness of their cause.

All they need now, he thought, is a couple of half-canned Englishmen. He put away the book as the big plane tilted in the dark and homed on the lights of Beirut. Morley had collapsed into an exhausted sleep, but when the stewardess woke him he strained at his seat belt, ready for the off.

They stepped out together into the warm eastern night.

Morley was greeted by two Lebanese and driven away at speed. Bassam Owdeh was also at the airport but had noticed he was still being watched. He made no move as Roscoe passed through and took a taxi to his hotel.

3. The Student from Baghdad

Beirut was well up to Roscoe's worst forebodings, a big commercial city, flash, noisy and hot, piled on a cluster of hills beside the sea. His hotel was surrounded by bars with names like the Roxy and Go-Go, gaudy neon and bored girls in red-lit doorways. Nothing much Arabian about the nights here.

But next morning it looked better. He opened the shutters of his room to find a view of the harbour, a wide sweep of brilliant blue water between clifftop suburbs. At the far end he could see the cranes and funnels of a port, but on this side motorboats were weaving frothy patterns on the bay and further out white yachts leaned in a breeze. Luxury hotels crowded the shore. Down the road he could see the Saint George, the grandest of them all, girls in bikinis stretched out beside its pool. The sun was dazzling, already hot. The Lebanese rose early, he discovered, and aimed to finish work by the middle of the day. The afternoon cooled quickly and night came abruptly at six.

He had woken up sticky with sweat. Seeing others do it he went for a swim, Beirut being one of those cities, like Rio, where you can dive off the street into the sea. The water was clean, though not as cold as he liked it. Back in his room he took a shower and ordered breakfast.

As he sat drinking coffee a girl in a nightdress came out onto the balcony next to his own, shielding her eyes against the sun. Something told Roscoe she was English, her pale skin or her hair, or perhaps something else – a sort of reserve in her bearing. She was scanning the harbour, unaware of his presence.

'Hello,' he said.

Claudia was startled.

'Oh, hello,' she said, blushed and retreated.

Back inside her room, brushing her hair, she wondered

whether this was the man whom Saladin wanted her to meet –
Stephen Roscoe. She decided to ask him his name, but when
she looked out he had gone. Leaning over the balcony, she saw
him drive away in a taxi.

Not expecting Saladin to get in touch that day, Roscoe had
decided to substantiate his cover by calling on the rest of the
Resistance. With a letter from the London office of the PLO in
his pocket he went to see Al Fatah, whom he found in one of
many identical concrete apartment blocks scattered on a dusty
red plateau above the sea. The showpiece of the suburb was the
Kuwaiti Embassy, a monument to oil, its coloured tiles and
cupolas gleaming in the sun like Hollywood Arabia.

His taxi driver insisted on parking at a distance, leaving
Roscoe to approach the Fatah building on foot.

It seemed deserted, then he saw that someone was watching
him from an upper balcony. He went in and up to the second
floor. Immediately a door opened, held on a chain, and a dark
face challenged him in Arabic. Roscoe passed the PLO letter
through the gap and after a pause was let in. Three young
Arabs were waiting inside, one of them holding a Russian
Kalashnikov assault rifle. They searched him in silence then
passed the letter round among themselves. Roscoe mentioned
a name which the man at the PLO had given him.

'I've come to see Abu Omar.'

They looked at him suspiciously, then led him through an
empty flat to an office at the back, where a dark slender youth,
improbably handsome in a crisp white shirt, was sitting at a
grey steel desk. His eyes scanned the letter through half-closed
lids then he rose and shook Roscoe limply by the hand, exhibit-
ing perfectly even white teeth in an automatic smile. His name
was Walid Iskandar. Abu Omar, he said, was just a password.

'You see, Mr Roscoe, we have to be careful.'

Showing Roscoe to a chair, he switched on a fan. It blew a
cloud of dust across the room and ruffled his papers, which
were held down by cartridge clips.

'Will you take some coffee?'

Roscoe said he would and pulled out a notebook. He could
not think of anything to ask.

The boy with the rifle had resumed his patrol of the balcony,
though nothing was moving on the bleak surrounding waste-

land. Roscoe could see his taxi parked at the top of the cliffs and beyond it the sea, now grey in the heat.

'Yes, we must be careful,' Walid said. 'There are many Israelis in Beirut.' He pronounced it 'Issrah-aylies' in the Arab manner, adding both music and menace to the word.

'Would they attack you here?'

'Oh yes.' Walid smiled again and spread his hands, like a man regretting the weather. 'They will shoot us or bomb us. They are strong and we are weak. We must be patient.'

The bloody and the wet, Roscoe thought, and allowed Walid to tell him the story of Al Fatah.

This, he knew, was the oldest and largest of the several resistance movements. Yasser Arafat, its chief, had been accused by the Israelis of controlling Black September; but this connection, if it existed, had not been proved.

Walid did not discuss it, pointing out instead that Al Fatah meant 'The Conquest' in Arabic.

That, Roscoe knew, was a misnomer. Since the Six Day War of 1967 the Israelis had crushed all resistance within the Occupied Territories and ringed them with ever more elaborate defences, until the Fedayeen were losing eight men in ten on raids across the border.

Walid did not deny it. He told the story with a sad, resigned smile. 'This man was there,' he said.

One of the youths on the door had come in with two cups of coffee and glasses of water. He laid them on the desk, then lifted his trouser to reveal a plastic leg.

'A mine,' Walid explained with tragic eyes.

On the wall behind his head was a photograph of King Hussein of Jordan. Roscoe noticed that someone had touched up the royal smile with biro, inking in vampire teeth and dribbles of blood.

'The man is a traitor,' Walid said. 'We shall kill him in the end, as we killed Abdullah. The only good Hashemite is under the ground.'

The threat was uttered softly, with a smile.

The Dwarf King they called him in Al Fatah, the Butcher of Amman, but Roscoe remembered a shy man at Sandhurst with a passion for sportscars. In 1970 the Palestinians, led by Arafat, had tried to tip him off his throne; the King had delayed his counter-attack until the last possible moment, but once the order was given his Bedouin army had set about the task with enthusiasm, shelling refugee camps in Amman and driving the Fedayeen across the hills with tanks. Now Al Fatah was exiled to Syria and Lebanon; men playing soldiers in the hills, school-boys drilling in the camps. This pretty young spokesman, stranded in a suburb of Beirut.

Roscoe drank his coffee, which was strong and very sweet. It turned to black slime in the bottom of the cup. 'You speak good English,' he said.

Walid was staring through the window, as if at a life that might have been. He said he had broken off his studies at Baghdad University to join the Armed Struggle. 'Will you stay in the Lebanon for long, Mr Roscoe?'

'A few weeks perhaps.'

'Then I think you will see something.' Again the film-star smile. 'The Lebanese are like Hussein, they do not want war. But they do not have a choice.'

Roscoe recognized an exit line. He got up to go. At the door Walid asked if he knew a man called Morley.

'Yes, he works for Canadian television.'

'Why is he here?'

'He wants to talk to Black September.'

'Then he will not succeed.'

Walid shook hands, not smiling any more. Roscoe saw that something had upset him, and later realized it could have been his own insufficient reaction to the plastic leg, or perhaps a hint of sympathy for Dracula Hussein – or was it that one usually compliments a man on his English if it is, in fact, slightly less than perfect? Walid's beautiful smile could have been erased by any one of these things or by something else too subtle for an Englishman even to guess at, for what mattered to the Arabs was not the words spoken but the subtle vibrations of feeling beneath.

In this they were like women, and Roscoe was ill-equipped to deal with them. He took people as they came; he preferred plain speech. With Walid he was vaguely aware that he had fluffed his lines, but where exactly he had given offence he could not begin to say. He walked away wondering what would become of the student from Baghdad and decided he would probably end up as a receptionist in one of those expensive hotels on the waterfront. Had he been told that morning what Walid Iskandar would do for Saladin, he would have found it hard to believe.

4. Confrontation

Roscoe's taxi was waiting on the clifftop.

As he approached it another car drove past and took the road towards the Fatah building, which it circled slowly once, bouncing and lurching through the copper-coloured dust. Then it came back without stopping, turned towards Beirut and drove away fast. Roscoe stared at this car in surprise. Then he woke his driver and asked him to follow it. He had recognized the man in the back as the loud-voiced American in the crowd outside Marsden's office.

Roscoe's reaction was swift, because this chance encounter confirmed a suspicion already in his mind. He was now almost certain that this was the man who had blown up the AAI; a man who could not have been in Beirut for more than a day, but was already reconnoitring Palestinian offices. Therefore pursue, enquire. Day one, mission one. Yes, it was better than farming.

'Come on, Yussef, buck up. Follow him.'

'Okay, okay, keep your pants on.'

'Not too close now. That'll do nicely.'

Roscoe's driver was not the right man for a car chase. His name was Yussef Trabulsi, a fat Lebanese with gold about his person; gold watch, gold pen, gold ring and gold teeth. He was a motorized currency exchange, who carried dollars, pounds, deutschmarks and francs in his wallet and knew the going rates in his head. He drove a big blue Chevrolet with one hand on the horn, treating all other vehicles as a challenge to his manhood, but he would not risk a scratch, or trouble of any sort. Al Fatah was trouble, and cars which reconnoitred Fatah offices were deadly trouble. As Roscoe urged him on he disentangled his hand from a chain of beads and began to protest more loudly. 'Fedayeen lousy buggers, I take you swim, fish, casino, cedars, everything hokay. You want nice woman?'

'No thanks.'

'How many wives you got?'

'No wives.'

'Whassa matter, you gay boy?'

'No, Yussef, I'm a secret agent. If you follow that car I'll pay double, how's that?'

'Pounds sterling?'

'If you like.'

'Pound sterling sick.' Yussef made a wobbly motion with his hand. 'You got dollars?'

They cruised along the wide coastal road which led back to central Beirut. A sudden strong wind was blowing off the hills above the city, a hot white blast which seemed to come straight from the unseen desert beyond, driving litter across the red waste ground and down to the beach below. Even the Chevrolet rocked; Yussef gripped the wheel to hold it on course. Standing level with the cliffs were tall eroded rocks which soared from the waves like gigantic Henry Moores. Gessner's car was eighty yards ahead.

'Close up a bit,' Roscoe said.

'You like to see bazaar, holy mosque? I take you cheap.'

'Just go where they go.'

Buildings closed in, the same random deployment of concrete apartment blocks, but denser now and taller. Yussef turned off the seafront and plunged into the stream of service taxis, a lesser form of transport than his own, battered old diesel Mercedes which drove on fixed routes around the city, like a permanent stock-car race.

'Corniche Mazraa,' he announced. 'Very nice, very expensive. Like Regent's Park.'

They passed the Russian Embassy and the PLO headquarters, then the car ahead turned left and stopped. Gessner got out and disappeared down a sidestreet.

'Pull in here,' Roscoe said. 'Tell me where they go. I'll see you back at the hotel.'

Yussef reached for his beads and drove away.

Roscoe tailed Gessner into a poor district, where the buildings were older. They were being demolished and replaced by taller ones, gimcrack constructions propped in flimsy wooden scaffolding. Pneumatic drills hammered the air above the ceaseless blaring of car horns.

He saw Gessner turn into a bar and found him there drinking
a milkshake. He had crumpled the straw in one fist and was
drinking straight out of the glass. As Roscoe sat down at his
table he raised his head in surprise, pink ice-cream round his
mouth. Roscoe assisted his memory. 'London, day before
yesterday. We saw that explosion.'

Gessner snapped his fingers. 'Hey that's right, I remember.
Well how about that.'

'Small world.'

'Sure is, buddy. Say, how's your friend?'

'He's all right,' Roscoe said. 'Just a cut.'

'Lucky, eh?'

'Yes.'

'What happened?'

'Parcel bomb. But they were warned – I expect you saw it in
the papers.'

Gessner returned Roscoe's stare. 'Well, that's nice,' he said.
'So maybe the Jews aren't such bad guys after all.' Then he
smiled broadly and held out his hand. 'Sammy Gessner.'

'Stephen Roscoe.'

'Pleased to meet you, Stephen.'

The bar was empty except for the two of them. Gessner drank
back his milkshake and shouted for a napkin. He had shed both
his hat and his black leather jacket but was running with sweat
nonetheless, a heavy man of overbearing physical presence with
thick dark hair on his forearms and chest but not much left on
his head. Coming up behind him Roscoe had noticed the butt
of a revolver in his trouser pocket.

They began a wary conversation. Roscoe said he was in Beirut
to do a story on Black September.

'What's your opinion of those people, Stephen? What do you
write about people like that?'

Roscoe repeated the verdict of Hussein. 'They're animals.'

'Animals. I'm glad to hear you say that.'

'What about you? What brings you here?'

Gessner paused, then a slow conniving smile spread across
his face. 'Beirut's a nice place. They do a good milkshake.'

Roscoe smiled back to show he understood perfectly.

A waiter brought napkins. Gessner wiped his mouth and
nodded at a building across the street. 'Know what that is?'

Roscoe saw yet another apartment block, tiers of pitted concrete balconies mostly occupied by washing lines. On the second floor a group of young Arabs, all in black shirts or sweaters, stood smoking and talking. 'No', he said, 'what's that?'

'The PFLP.'

'Ah, the Marxists.'

'This is where they print their magazine.'

'I was going to call on them. Perhaps I will now.'

'Then you could do me a favour.' Gessner pulled a photograph out of his wallet. 'Take a look at that.'

Roscoe saw a strip of contact prints, front and side views of the same head; it looked as if it came from the police. 'Who's he?'

Gessner unwrapped a stick of gum and put it in his mouth. 'Someone I'm hoping to meet.'

'Name?'

'Zeiti, with a zee. He's a student, from Berlin.'

'And you think he's in there?'

'Could be.'

'Where can I find you?'

'I'll wait here.'

'I mean later – if I see him.'

Gessner chewed rapidly, shifting the gum from side to side of his mouth. The movement acted like a valve, releasing pressure; the rest of him was still. 'I'll be around,' he said.

Roscoe stood up, pretended to hesitate, then handed back the photograph. 'We scribblers aren't supposed to get involved, you know.'

'Yeah, that's right. I forgot.'

'Anyway, I'll go and take a look.'

'You do that.' Gessner raised one hand palm outwards, opened and shut it in sarcastic farewell. 'Take care now, scribbler.'

Roscoe crossed the street towards the PFLP, unhurried but with a slight prickle of the spine, such as a matador might feel as he turns his back on the bull.

5. Marching to Paradise

PFLP – the initials meant Popular Front for the Liberation of Palestine. A left-wing splinter group of the Resistance, it aimed to unite the Arab world in a Marxist revolution, but had itself been splintered by quarrels. Now its main claim to fame was historical. The Front had been the first to practise terrorism abroad when in 1970 its guerillas had hijacked three aircraft to an airstrip in Jordan, providing Hussein with the excuse to retaliate.

But Roscoe found more life here than at the Fatah office. People were arguing, typing, telephoning, and a printing press was working at the back. Plastered all over the walls was a poster bordered in black of a neat-looking man with a moustache. This was Ghassan Kanafani, he learned, a leading intellectual of the PFLP killed in July when his car had been shattered by explosive packed in the exhaust. Kanafani's comrades did not want to forget him; to keep the pain fresh they kept glancing at his face. Most of them had grown moustaches like his and Roscoe noticed they were all wearing black. Black and red were the colours of revolution, he thought; death and anger, blood and hate – or was it the limits of revolutionary presses?

Waiting for an interview he sat and watched a boy stamping envelopes, content in the task, and not for the first time thought how pleasant it would be to belong to a cause, all questions answered, marching to paradise with your friends. But what was an Englishman supposed to get worked up about? England was football and TV, people washing cars in the suburbs. Commitment was blood on a pavement in Ulster and wondering if you had hit the right man.

Time passed. The busy men in black came and went, like an order of monks.

'Mr Roscoe?'

'Yes.'

'Come this way please.'

Roscoe followed the envelope-stamping boy and after showing his press card was taken to see a man called Adnan Khadduri; a small man in steel-rimmed spectacles sitting behind a big desk. A meeting was just breaking up, and as his comrades filed out of the room Adnan raised his fist in a revolutionary salute. The self-conscious gesture looked ridiculous – an intellectual playing man of action.

Beside him was Zeiti, a very different type; dark, good-looking, tall, very thin, with his limbs sprawled casually over a chair. He had a head of unruly black hair in the Che Guevara style, much longer than in Gessner's photograph.

As Roscoe introduced himself Adnan inclined his head formally, consenting to an interview. No coffee at the Popular Front.

The room was lined with posters. One of them showed a boy commando leaping barbed wire and another said LA JEUNESSE ACCUSE L'IMPERIALISME. Above the door was a photograph of airliners exploding in the desert – the moment of glory – and propped in one corner, the plaque of an American embassy, which someone had been using for target practice.

Adnan's English was good, but slow. He spoke with intense concentration, like a man who has suffered a stroke. 'We are more united than we appear,' he said, referring to factions within the Resistance. 'We just follow different methods, that is all.' When asked to define the aims of the Front he answered in the voice of a man repeating a prayer. 'One united Palestine – a secular, democratic, socialist state, where Arab and Jew will live as equals.'

That was what Al Fatah said, omitting the socialism, and to Roscoe it sounded too good to be honest. 'But that state will be controlled by Arabs, because there are more of you. So in fact what you're saying is Israel must go.'

'Not exactly, Mr Roscoe. What must go is the Zionist state. The Jews will be welcome to stay.'

'Even the ones who came from Europe?'

'They will be free to leave, or cooperate.'

'Perhaps they'll be dead.'

'Of course, there will have to be a war. But this time a people's war, and afterwards we shall hear no more of this racialist nonsense.'

'What about the land they've taken over?'

'Land will belong to the state,' Adnan said, sounding a little like Moses on the mountain as he talked of this political Eldorado. 'You speak of this always as a *racial* question, Mr Roscoe, but we do not see it like that. Israel is an imperialist aggression against our territory, begun by the British and continued by the United States.'

Zeiti lit a long filter-tipped cigarette and leaned back with a smile – the smile of a cynic who listens to an idealistic friend. His clothes were not black, merely sober in hue, close-fitting and much too expensive for a Marxist.

Adnan went on, staring down at his desk, emphasizing each slow point with a downward stroke of his fist. 'American capitalism, that is what we have to defeat. It may take many years but in the end we shall succeed, because justice cannot be defeated.'

'How many years, would you say?'

'Twenty, perhaps even fifty.' Adnan looked up defensively; a timid sort of man, bolstered only by dogma. 'Is that so long a time within the perspective of history? Remember, Mr Roscoe, the Crusaders were in Palestine for almost a century – the Jews have only held it for twenty-five years.'

Zeiti interrupted. 'Five,' he said.

They looked at him in surprise. Five years. Yes, that was true. The Israelis had not held all Palestine till 1967.

'Excuse me,' Roscoe said, 'is your name Zeiti?'

For a moment Zeiti was immobile, then he took a long pull at his cigarette and slowly exhaled through his nostrils. 'I don't give my name to English journalists.'

'I only ask because there's a chap across the street who wants to kill you.'

The printing press clacked in the silence. Somewhere a phone was ringing. Zeiti repeated the routine with his cigarette then carefully stubbed it out. Was this an English joke?

Adnan looked at Roscoe, then at the surface of his desk. No, it was not a joke.

Roscoe took them both to a window at the front of the building. 'He's sitting in that bar. His name is Gessner. He's carrying your photograph and he's armed. He thinks I'm on his side.'

'Well, perhaps you are,' Zeiti said.

Roscoe obediently held his arms wide for a search, amused by the irony. Warning Zeiti had been his first partisan act. 'I understand you have to be careful, so what I suggest is you stay here and watch. I'll go down and talk to him, then get out of the way.'

Zeiti ran his hand through his hair, which was stylishly cut, black and glossy as crow's feathers. His eyes were black too, bright and alert. 'You'll tell him where I am,' he said.

'I might, you can't be sure. But what can he do? He can't come and get you and he can't wait for ever. You, on the other hand, can disguise yourself or find another way out the building. True?'

'True.'

'Or if you feel like a scrap, you can go down and take him.'

Zeiti looked hard at Roscoe then seemed to decide they were two of a kind. His face cleared suddenly into a piratical smile. 'I see you've done this before.'

'Oh no, I'm a beginner.'

'Thanks anyway.'

Roscoe shook hands and said good-bye, then went across to the bar. But it was empty, so he stepped back in the street and made a 'nobody here' signal up towards the PFLP, spreading his hands. Zeiti and Adnan were on the balcony; they waved to him and turned back inside.

Roscoe stood in the street for a moment, looking up and down it. The day was still getting hotter. The men on the building sites had rags round their faces, but the wind had slackened.

Feeling thirsty he returned to the bar and walked up to the counter, and only then realized his mistake. That signal to the PFLP had been stupid, because Gessner was still in the bar. The eyes of the barman were the clue – wide with fright and flicking to the left, towards a doorway screened by hanging strips of plastic.

'A beer please.'

The barman poured a glass of beer. The strips of plastic were motionless. Roscoe was braced now, light on his feet, tensing his muscles; yet none of this showed. He appeared the tired Englishman, propping up a bar.

Without a glance at the curtain he drank down his beer, knowing that Gessner would not shoot. His brain was functioning better now, adrenalin pumping. The trick was to be ready without appearing to be ready.

Still Gessner did not move.

Perhaps he was waiting for Zeiti to come down; perhaps he hadn't seen the signal at all. Then as Gessner came through the plastic, sallow round the lips, fists bunched, Roscoe knew that he had.

'Hello there. Thought you'd gone.'

Gessner said nothing, too angry, too confident to fake goodwill. He walked forward.

Roscoe, still casual, took his elbows off the bar and turned to face him. He had thought it might be the knee but it was clearly going to be the fist.

Gessner came on without pausing. He meant to hit Roscoe in the crutch, for a start, but something went wrong. The target turned to air, his fist crashed into the bar. He could not have been more surprised. The last thing he saw with any clarity was the barman ducking in terror and then his faculties were stopped by a blow to the side of the head, where it joined the neck, just below the ear. After that he was conscious but inoperative. His feet were kicked from under him, the tiled floor hit him in the face. The Englishman was taking his pistol. He tried to roll over, get up, but his limbs would not behave. Then the pistol came down on his head.

Roscoe put the Smith and Wesson in his pocket. Two small children were watching from the street, no one else. The barman peered cautiously over the counter. 'Stay there,' Roscoe said to him. 'Pour me another of those beers.'

The barman stared at Gessner.

Roscoe tried his most reassuring smile. 'A beer – one for you, one for me, okay?'

The barman nodded, then fumbled nervously for glasses.

Roscoe dragged Gessner through the plastic curtain and quickly searched his pockets, discovering a packet of condoms, a carton of King Edward cigars and a street map of Beirut. He put the map in his pocket. Gessner's passport confirmed his name; his job was described as 'private enquiry agent'. Inside it was a three-week tourist visa for the Lebanon, issued at Beirut airport on Tuesday morning. Inside his wallet was the photograph of Zeiti, also a snap of two small boys grinning happily as they stood on a lawn in the full-dress uniform of American footballers. Other contents of the wallet: a wad of money, a credit card, a US driver's licence and several calling cards of a company based in Paris. Roscoe took only the licence and one calling card. He could not find what he wanted most: an address in Beirut, or any other clue to Gessner's business and contacts in the city. But now it was time to go.

The barman had not strayed, the beers were ready. Roscoe drank his down quickly, then paid and left the scene.

6. Something between a Bang and a Thud

The working day was over; office workers were spilling out into the streets. Feeling hungry now, Roscoe took a taxi to his hotel, where Yussef was waiting for his money. He said he had lost the other car in the traffic.

'Never mind,' said Roscoe. 'Thanks for trying anyway.'

'What is this? You say double.'

'But you lost them.'

'I follow, like you say, maybe Jew buggers kill me. I take you Fedayeen, you pay double.'

'There you are then. Two more.'

'You want taxi tonight? Casino, nice girl?'

'We'll see.'

Roscoe went into his hotel and found a message from a man called Giscard, inviting him to lunch at the Saint George. He walked round there straightaway.

The land wind had dropped; sky and sea were blue again. Speedboats of every description were moored to small wooden jetties alongside the road. Choosing a deserted one, Roscoe strolled down it and dropped Gessner's pistol into the water.

The Saint George had gone for old-world elegance. Its lobby was panelled, decked out with gleaming brass lamps and buttoned leather, air-conditioned to the temperature of a London club in winter. Uniformed pages stood about in the deep dull silence of luxury and one of them led Roscoe through to a terrace overlooking the bay, where wealthy Lebanese and French merchants, diplomats, foreign correspondents, American oilmen and a minor British pop star were eating lunch under an awning. As always the prettiest girls were escorted by revoltingly tanned old men. There too was Dominic Morley, in conference over a champagne bucket.

Roscoe felt vaguely annoyed by the sight – he has an odd

puritan streak, the product no doubt of his Yorkshire ancestry – and as he followed the page through the pink cloths and clattering cutlery he thought of Adnan Khadduri, batting away at the brotherhood of man. Adnan's word for Saladin would be 'adventurist'.

Claudia was sitting at a table in a corner with Giscard. As Roscoe approached across the terrace she wondered if she would like him. She did not expect to; army officers were not her style and this one looked, she thought, typically archaic, ridiculously British, a very tall man with short neatly parted yellow hair. His face on the other hand was not quite what she had expected; it seemed to be marked by some private sadness, and that she found intriguing. His clothes were really awful, exactly the sort of thing a soldier would wear when out of uniform – baggy check shirt, khaki cord trousers and desert boots. Like her father he probably refused to throw anything away. His skin was still adjusting to the climate.

'Here he is,' she said.

Giscard jumped to his feet. 'Ah, Mr Roscoe. My name is Giscard – and this is Miss Lees. It seems you two have met already.'

'Yes, so we have.'

'Please, take a seat. Now what will you have?'

'Oh, any kind of fish. And a green salad please.'

'Lobster?'

'No, something with fins. Whatever they catch.'

Giscard selected a fish. The waiter asked Roscoe if he was staying in the hotel.

'No I am not,' said Roscoe curtly.

Claudia was disappointed. Oh dear, she thought, he's rude. Roscoe caught the look on her face and quickly made amends. So, he thought, here is a girl who doesn't like bad manners. Quite pretty too, in a nunnish sort of way . . .

This mutual appraisal continued during lunch. Subjected now to the full beam of Roscoe's gentlemanly charm, Claudia decided he was not too bad – not stupid either; he had evidently done some homework on the Middle East. And Roscoe liked what he saw of Claudia, clean and cool in a crisp cotton dress, more like a nurse than nun. He noticed that she screwed up her eyes, as if she needed glasses, and thought before she spoke. Her remarks were intelligent, carefully weighed – not a bit like poor old Brown. She probably had a degree.

Already knowing Claudia better than Giscard could, he was amazed that she had joined Saladin – if she had. Not being sure, he kept off the subject and told them about his talk with Adnan.

'Ah yes,' said Giscard, without scorn or enthusiasm, 'the Arab Awakening. They all talk of that, even Fatah.'

Roscoe instinctively took to this short bristly Frenchman, leather-skinned, weary-eyed. 'And you don't believe it will happen?' he said.

Giscard picked his teeth. 'The Palestinians are never prepared to do the right thing until it is too late. Always one step behind, you see. Now that victory is impossible they want to fight a war, but that chance was lost in 1967.'

'Adnan is talking revolution.'

'Ah yes, it has to be a holy war. Marx is the prophet.'

Giscard then pointed out something which Roscoe had forgotten. It was the Popular Front who had sent three Japanese to Lod airport in May, a suicide squad who had gunned down twenty-seven people in the passenger reception lounge before they were stopped.

'Not so pretty, eh?'

Roscoe shook his head, feeling foolish.

Giscard threw away the toothpick and lit a yellow cigarette. 'We have things to discuss, but I will put to you one question, Mr Roscoe. How long can these people last without a land, I mean survive, as a people?'

'I haven't a clue.'

'Not much longer, I think. The Jews, you see, have learned to exist on an idea – that is what has kept them together, an idea of themselves, nothing more. But the people of Palestine are not so strong, not so crazy if you like.' Giscard leaned forward, talking with the cigarette drooping from his lips. 'Now the organization to which we belong' – the sweep of his hand included Claudia – 'has the courage to face this reality. We have a practical programme to win back a part of the land, and if we are successful they will then have a place on the map, you see – a government, a capital, a seat at the UN . . .'

Giscard was interrupted by an indistinct noise, something between a bang and a thud, which shook the whole city and seemed to gather strength as it reverberated back from the hills around the bay. It came from quite close. Claudia thought it was a supersonic plane; Roscoe knew an explosion when he heard one.

The waiter brought coffee and the bill. Giscard paid it and sat back, about to continue his pep-talk. Roscoe was held by his eyes, which were empty of hope but had a stubborn glint – the eyes of a man who proclaims the world is flat, sticking to his point although the audience is drifting away. He had seen that look in Marsden, and would see it again in Saladin, men who continued to fight for a country that had ceased to exist.

Claudia poured out the coffee. The wine had brought a flush to her cheeks. Somewhere in the city a siren was blaring: the urgent hee-haw of an ambulance or police car.

Giscard lit another cigarette and glanced round the terrace, which was now almost empty. 'Well, Mr Roscoe, are you with us?'

'So far.'

Claudia glanced at Roscoe's face but the challenge had produced no change of expression. He had rather impressive eyes, she thought, very pale blue, which stared at you unblinking when he talked.

'There is an operation tomorrow night,' Giscard said, leaning inwards now and lowering his voice. 'We would like you to assist.'

'An operation?'

'We are putting a man into Israel. The objective is to get him across the frontier then return to Beirut.'

Roscoe was silent for a moment, then said he would like to know more before he went further.

'But naturally. What would you like to know?'

'Everything I need to. What you plan to do, when, how – I made that condition quite clear.'

'Very well, please ask me what you like.'

'With respect, I'd rather hear it from Saladin.'

'Ah.' The Frenchman was pulled up short. 'That is a new condition.'

'It is.'

'You insist on a meeting?'

'I do.'

Giscard nodded. 'I will see,' he said, then sat back, smoking thoughtfully.

Roscoe glanced sideways. All through this he had been bothered by the presence of a man at the neighbouring table, a sleek Levantine in a beige suit who was lunching alone, reading the Beirut *Daily Star*. The man's meal had lasted as long as their own and his paper was propped against a carafe of water, folded as it had been for the last half hour. A slow reader therefore; a slow eater too, who left the restaurant minutes after Giscard.

Alone together, Roscoe and Claudia transferred themselves to a pier which jutted out into the bay below the terrace. Claudia sat in the shade of a parasol while Roscoe borrowed some trunks from the hotel and dived in. He struck out into the bay in a vigorous crawl which soon became a dignified breast-stroke, then returned by easy stages, floating on his back until the cold reached his bones. As he hauled himself out Claudia passed him a towel.

'Tell me, what did you think of him?'

'Giscard? I rather like him.' Roscoe dried himself vigorously, methodically, starting at the top and working on down to his toes. 'Have you met Saladin?'

Claudia seemed embarrassed by the question. 'Oh – yes, he's very impressive.' She changed the subject, asking Roscoe what he thought of the plan.

'Politically, it sounds very sensible.'

'Yes, but is it possible? There's so much hate – you've no idea. It'll be like stitching a septic wound.'

'Well it must be worth a try. We've got a better chance than Adnan, surely?'

'Oh yes. Poor Adnan.'

Roscoe rolled the wet towel into a headrest, placed it on a mattress then stretched out at her feet. 'There's really no need to feel sorry for the likes of Adnan. They've got this music going in their heads, you see – as long as they can hear it they're happy.'

'What about you? No music?'

'Sorry, not a toot.'

Claudia smiled, leaning back in her deckchair drowsily. 'Really, when you think about it, idealism is a male thing, isn't it?'

'Is it?'

'I think so, yes. Women aren't so good at ignoring the facts.'

'What rotten luck they do have,' Roscoe said.

Claudia extended one bare foot and kicked him in the ribs. 'What I mean is they might pursue an ideal, but they'd have a much clearer idea why it suited them to do it.'

Roscoe gave an ambiguous grunt. The motivation of women was not his best subject.

Claudia examined the body spread below her, long and bony, not very attractive, though the muscles had not yet melted into fat. Face and hands were brown from work in the fields, the rest white. She felt strangely excited, not so much physically as by the startling intimacy of the situation: two total strangers flung together in this hare-brained enterprise. She was glad he had turned out polite.

Roscoe, too, was reassured by Claudia. Saladin's psychology was sound.

It was soon four o'clock. A cloud of brown smoke had risen from the centre of the city, drifted out across the bay and dispersed. Giscard had not reappeared. After twenty minutes on the pier Roscoe jumped to his feet and started to put on his clothes. 'I'm off,' he said. 'Going to look around.'

'Aren't we supposed to wait here?'

'I shan't wander far.'

Claudia gathered up her things. 'In that case I'm going back to the hotel. That wine has finished me off.'

On their way out through the lobby they came across Dominic Morley, pink with heat and wild-eyed with frustration. The hunt for Black September was not going well, it seemed. Roscoe asked what the trouble was.

'Bloody Arabs, that's what. If this was Saigon I'd have set it up by now.'

Claudia gazed at him in wonder. To charm the refugees he was wearing an off-white safari suit with a pink chiffon scarf round his neck. Waving his arms about, he took them through his day. Doors had been closed in his face, it seemed, messages ignored, appointments broken. He asked if they had heard the explosion and said it had killed a university professor called Owdeh, a man he was hoping to interview for the moderates. 'Just my bloody luck.'

Roscoe had stiffened at the name. 'Bassam Owdeh?'

'Yes, do you know him?'

'I was hoping to meet him.'

'Well forget it. His car exploded over there this afternoon. Blew the poor bastard to bits.'

7. Post Mortem

Claudia was not much perturbed; she clearly knew nothing of Bassam. But the news had an odd effect on Roscoe, making everything brighter, sharper, faster, louder, as if his senses had been tuned up a pitch. He recognized the feeling and enjoyed it – in fact he could not live without it, and seeing this now with sudden clarity he knew he would join Saladin, because the urge to risk his neck was irresistible.

He wondered how the plan would be affected. Marsden had said Bassam was the most important man.

Leaving Claudia at the hotel he went off alone to investigate and found the site of the explosion in the Rue Omar Ben Abed el Aziz, near the gates of the University. Fire engines, an ambulance, police – the scene was like that outside Marsden's office but the crowd much bigger, more excited, its Arabic gabble suggesting to Roscoe the panic of animals disturbed by a predator or oncoming forest fire. At the centre of the hubbub was a group of European journalists and from them he picked up the facts.

Bassam Owdeh had lived in a block of university flats set back from the street behind a small garden of palms. Underneath was a basement garage, reserved for the use of AUB staff. Bassam himself had not owned a car – he preferred to let his girlfriend Leila drive him – but he often collected her Morris from the basement, bringing it up to her at the garden gate. That day, at 3.20 p.m., the car had blown up as he sat behind the wheel. The flats were now evacuated, charred and drenched but not badly damaged. The body had been taken away and the press were waiting for Leila Riad.

Roscoe's main informant was a man called Nick Cassavetes, a Greek-American agency correspondent who seemed to be taking a particular interest in the matter. When Leila came out

Cassavetes pursued her with questions, but she would say nothing, simply shaking her head and cringing behind an escort of police.

After she had gone the story of Bassam Owdeh's death was passed round, repeated, expanded, improved, and those who had been there longest became absorbed by questions of technical detail. How, for instance, had the charge been triggered? By electrical connections to the ignition or a timing device? The police were reported to have found a clock in the wreckage. Cassavetes was keen to get the right answer but Roscoe had now seen enough. He turned to go, and only then noticed the man he had first seen at lunch, the slow paper-reader, the nibbler of food, now standing on the edge of the crowd. Ducking back, he tugged Cassavetes round by the sleeve. 'Now tell me, who's that?'

'Where?'

'Tall chap, over there.'

'Guy in a suit?'

'That's the one.'

Cassavetes shook his head. 'Dunno, I never saw him before. Hey, you heard about this clock?'

'Yes. Interesting.'

'Sure is.'

'I'm going now.'

'Okay, man. See you around.'

Roscoe left Cassavetes to it, detached himself from the crowd and walked back towards the Saint George. The other man followed, making no attempt at concealment, quickening his pace to catch up. Roscoe waited until he was close behind and then swivelled to face him, poised to kick, hit or dive between two parked cars. But the man smiled and held out his hand.

'Good afternoon, Mr Roscoe.'

'Hello. Who are you?'

'My name is Anis Kubayin. So far you have known me as Saladin.'

8. The Meeting

Roscoe was not sure what he had expected; an older man perhaps, white-haired and statesmanlike, certainly not this dandy
in a beige mohair suit. Could this be the leader of whom Marsden
spoke with such awe?

In fact Saladin – Roscoe never thought of him by any other
name – was the wrong side of fifty, but had no grey in his hair,
which was pure black and oiled so it stuck to his skull in the
style of Valentino. On closer inspection it was clear that he was
old, and not in good health. His face was cadaverous, the
yellowish skin collapsing inwards round his cheekbones and
neck. But this only made him look more dubious, like an ageing
gigolo who had dieted too hard. Having introduced himself,
he took a Turkish cigarette from a flat gold case and fixed it in
a holder with delicate fingers. Claudia, who noticed men's
hands, said afterwards that Saladin's were beautiful; but Roscoe
was staring at his big silk tie, which flapped in the breeze
revealing the label of Saks in New York.

And Saladin was doing his share of appraisal, looking Roscoe
over with a smile which was friendly but reserved. 'Welcome to
Beirut,' he said, then immediately apologized for the odd procedure at lunch. 'It's just that I do have to be very careful.'

'Naturally,' said Roscoe, not yet much impressed. Then he
passed on Marsden's salaams, which Saladin took with a small
ceremonial nod, as if they were his due.

'How is Jimmy?'

'Three stitches in the head, otherwise well.'

'Yes, I heard about that. Nasty business.'

That led to discussion of Gessner. Roscoe reported his adventures of the morning and Saladin showed a keen interest,
looking through the documents from Gessner's wallet. 'And he
was looking for Zeiti?'

'Yes.'

'Zeiti's one of ours, you know.'

'No, I didn't know.'

Saladin looked thoughtful, but said no more on the subject.

They had now come back to the Saint George, where parked
in the forecourt was Saladin's car, the same white Mercedes
with darkened windows which Claudia had seen at the monastery. Inside were three men. One was Giscard, and of the second
Saladin said merely: 'This is Bernard Refo, our very good
American friend.' Oil or CIA, Roscoe wondered, but did not
ask, reaching back for a handshake.

The third man was a Semite, smiling benignly behind thick-
lensed spectacles. 'And this is Arnold Cohen, who will shortly
be going to Israel on our behalf,' said Saladin, now also smiling.
Everyone was smiling. 'Considering he's just had such a nasty
accident I think he looks very well, don't you?'

But Roscoe was quick on the uptake, and he too was smiling
as he shook the hand of this third man. 'Mr Owdeh, I presume?'

The smiles broke into guffaws; the car was full of childish
male glee as Saladin drove fast through the city and up towards
the overlooking suburbs, handing over for Roscoe's inspection
an expertly faked British passport. Inside it was Bassam's
photograph but the name Arnold Cohen, residence London,
occupation travel agent. Pinned to one of the visa pages Roscoe
found a completed Israeli immigration form dated Thursday,
September 14th. That was tomorrow.

It was of course the best way to vanish, the only way with no
questions asked, as Saladin now explained. An anonymous body
equipped with the right clothes and papers, blown apart,
identified by friends; exit Bassam Owdeh, lecturer in Oriental
Studies, murdered by the Zionists in Beirut. Two days later
enter Arnold Cohen, a British Jew visiting Israel from London.
No questions asked.

Roscoe was impressed by the subterfuge. A controlled explosion, one charred corpse and no other casualties – that
implied expertise, which he guessed had come from the
American. This in turn made him wonder why he himself had
been hired; one professional was surely enough. The answer
he arrived at but never confirmed was that Refo's connections
were too sensitive to permit him to operate in Israel.

The rest of that brief car journey was devoted to discussion of the planned border crossing. Giscard took out a map and explained how it would be done, then Bassam produced another map, a hand-drawn diagram of the section of fence he intended to jump. Roscoe was struck by their professional approach.

By late afternoon the five men were sitting on the terrace of a villa in the hills above Beirut, a small but luxurious residence rented by Saladin since his arrival from the States. Patrolling the garden with an old .303 rifle was the Gipsy whom Claudia had met at the monastery. Below them spread the bay and the city, its noise now muted to distant fanfares of motor horns. Lights were coming on as the sky grew darker.

Saladin said the Gipsy would be going to the border – 'a useful little chap' – and then added, conveying to Roscoe with the merest glance that he did not want Bassam to know what they both knew: 'There'll also be a fellow called Zeiti. He's on trial, so if you go along keep an eye on him.'

Roscoe nodded.

'Now, gentlemen, enough of the border. Mr Roscoe has asked to be taken completely into our confidence and I think we must honour that request.'

Giscard, Bassam and Refo murmured their assent.

'When he has heard what we propose he is at liberty to decline our offer and return to England – in which case I am prepared to rely on his continued discretion.'

The others raised no objection.

'Now, Stephen, how much do you know?'

Roscoe briefly repeated what Marsden and Giscard had told him of the political objectives.

Saladin lit a cigarette as he listened; its tip glowed faintly in the gathering dusk. 'Yes,' he said, 'that about covers it. We intend to redraw the map, making allowance for a Zionist state, which I take to be a regrettable but now irreversible fact.'

Roscoe was struck by the bald effrontery of this statement but did not feel tempted to laugh or even question it, being already under Saladin's extraordinary spell. The man had a quiet authority belied by his clothes. Still talking of his political plans he then explained the importance of Bassam's mission, which was to rally support in Israel and the Occupied Territories – a campaign which would come to a climax in early November. 'The slower we are to organize the more likely to fail, through betrayal or Zionist counter-tactics. So we must be quick, and we must be dramatic – this is something that you, Stephen, may find hard to appreciate. It was your compatriot Lawrence who said that the Arabs can be swung on an idea. Well that's true, but take it from me, to swing them you need style. I therefore have no chance at all unless I can achieve some heroics, and that's what I want from you.'

'Heroics?' repeated Roscoe flatly, unable to see in the dark whether Saladin had tempered this with a smile.

'Heroics,' came the equally flat reply. 'Shall we go inside?'

9. 'It must fall flat'

The meeting transferred from the terrace to the house.

Refo, who knew his way around, took orders for drinks and mixed them from a well-stocked cabinet. He was fortyish, monosyllabic, Ivy League, a buttoned-up man in a button-down shirt. Roscoe, still pondering his origins, inclined towards CIA and was not much comforted. Refo, he thought, would be helpful as long as the going was good but would vanish at the first hint of trouble, reappearing years later as US Vice-Consul in Manila or Monrovia – anywhere a long way from here.

Bassam was an enigma; a nice man, but shy, who kept bumping into the furniture. Sometimes he followed the proceedings with eager little nods and at other times his mind seemed to wander, abandoning his body in uncomfortable positions.

Saladin was now unrolling two maps on a table, the first a map of Israel and the surrounding states, the second a street plan of Jerusalem. Then he called the meeting to order.

'Now gentlemen, the heroics. First let me define the problem.' Once again he opened the flat gold case and carefully screwed a cigarette into the short amber holder, pausing until this operation was complete. 'What we need is some show of muscle by the forces of compromise, enough to get Golda Meir off her ass. Whatever it is it must put us in the headlines and keep us there, and this requires in my view some sort of action in Israel. But any such action must be gauged very carefully for its political effect. It must be sufficient to get me an audience in any refugee camp but not so drastic the Jews refuse to deal with us. So what do you suggest, Stephen?'

The question took Roscoe by surprise. 'I imagine they'll be pretty upset whatever we do.'

Saladin held up a slim correcting finger. 'Not necessarily. If we can pull off something bold and at the same time not vicious many of them would, I think, quietly applaud. Ah, they'd say, here is an Arab we can talk to, a man who speaks for his people and does not murder children.'

'Or athletes.'

'Or indeed athletes.'

'I gather you want me to blow something up.'

'Go on.'

'A military installation?'

'Too well protected.'

'A public building then.'

'Let's see what's available.' Saladin leaned over the street map. His hair shone black in the overhead light and coming off his person was the smell of some luxurious lotion. 'Jerusalem,' he said, 'central area. This western part has been in Jewish hands since 1948. Here's the Knesset, and beside it Mrs Meir's office. Next door the Ministry of the Interior. Foreign Affairs here, Ministry of Pensions and National Insurance right behind it, and over here the Mayor's office.' He paused, as if choosing which one to hit, then shifted his hand to the eastern side. 'This part used to belong to Jordan, but since '67 they've been bumping up the Jewish population – creating facts, as they call it. They've built housing estates here, here, and here' – the amber holder darted round the map, cigarette still unlit – 'also here, all on Arab land.'

'I thought we didn't want casualties,' Roscoe said.

Saladin twisted to look at him quizzically. 'Suppose the building was empty? A government office, built on Arab land and not yet occupied – how would that be?'

'Better.'

'Then what about this, my cautious English friend?' Saladin took out a ballpoint – gold again – and drew a small circle round an area hatched to indicate rock. 'It's not shown on any map yet, but on that site there's a new Israeli building, eight floors high, the ugliest damn thing you ever saw in your life. Show him the pictures, Bernard.'

Refo took a folder from his briefcase and passed over a series of photographs. Taken from various angles, they showed a rectangular concrete building with small square window-holes, unglazed.

The room was silent as Roscoe looked through the dozen

prints, already making rough calculations in his head. 'It looks like a prison,' he said, and was surprised when everyone laughed.

Saladin explained that this monstrous piece of architecture had been dubbed 'Alcatraz' by the press and the name had caught on. 'There have been a few protests, even in Israel.'

'What's it for?'

The Israelis were cagey on the point, replied Saladin. At first they had described this Alcatraz as a university biulding, passing the expenditure through the Knesset on the educational budget; but in construction it had emerged as offices, and now it had been re-allocated for purposes unknown. 'Unknown to the public, that is.'

Roscoe smiled. 'But you know better.'

'Indeed we do. Have you heard of Shin Beth?'

'It's their Security Service.'

'Correct – the equivalent of your own MI5.' Saladin tapped the circle on the street plan. 'Well this is their new headquarters. It will be announced as a post and telecommunications centre, but our information is that the top five floors are reserved for Shin Beth and Special Branch, plus various units of the army.'

Roscoe picked up the photographs again. 'So this is the target?'

'That's the target. I don't just want it damaged, mind. It must fall flat.'

Saladin's eyes burned bright, and this fighting talk drew a hiss of amusement from Giscard, who slapped his hand on the table muttering the single French word *'plat'*.

Roscoe turned back to the circle on the map, checking the surrounding pattern of buildings and streets. 'It'll be a big bang.'

'Bigger the better,' said Saladin. 'As you see it's in an isolated site, so you won't do much harm. We have the plans here, architect's drawings etcetera. If you agree to take on the job, I'd like you to look at them and make out a list of what you'd need.'

'May I look at them now?'

'By all means.'

Refo spread the plans on the table and at a nod from Saladin explained various features of this unusual building. The Israelis' intention, he said, was to use the three lower floors for a genuine branch of the postal department; the rest would be gradually occupied by the security services. There would be two lifts, one for the postal staff, serving their floors only, the other reserved for the use of the security men. This second lift would pass by the postal floors and run directly from the basement to the upper part of the building. Leading into the basement was a ramp, down which vehicles could drive into an underground garage. At one end of the roof was a helicopter landing pad and at the other a small but sophisticated interrogation centre, sealed completely from the outside world.

Roscoe absorbed this information, then turned to Saladin. 'I suppose there's a work gang?'

'There is, and they're Arabs.'

'So I'd have to do it at night.'

'Yes, you would.'

'Is the place guarded?'

Refo rested a finger on the plans. 'Two sentries. One here, at the entrance, and another in the basement.'

'How often are they relieved?'

'Every four hours.'

Roscoe was silent for a moment, and then he looked at Saladin with the merest embryo of a smile. 'In that case we'll have to relieve them rather earlier than they expect.'

Saladin beamed with delight.

'I don't get you,' said Refo.

Roscoe turned to him. 'Could you tell an Arab from a Jew in the dark?'

'I guess not.'

'And suppose this Arab was wearing Israeli uniform. Suppose he said hello to you nicely in Hebrew . . .'

Refo got the point.

Saladin glanced round at the others, noting their approval. Then he pulled out a pad and became brisk. 'How many men would you need?'

'Four or five,' Roscoe said, 'that ought to be enough.'

'Must they have military experience?'

'No, I'll train them. You'd have to allow me some time for that.'

'Must they speak English?'

'One must.'

Saladin made a list on a pad. 'This training – you'd need a quiet place for it.'

'Yes I would. Well away from everything.'

'Some equipment too.'

'Yes.'

Saladin turned to Refo. 'That means two supply lines, to Beirut and Aqaba.'

'No problem,' said Refo.

Roscoe asked why to Aqaba.

Saladin moved to the second map. Yes, he said, it had to be Aqaba, because the best way to get a load of heavy equipment over the border was to ship it by night across the narrow strip of water separating Jordan from the Israeli coast south of Eilat. The frontier there was lightly guarded. From the landing point the sabotage party would proceed to a hideout, then on by road to Jerusalem the following night, then back across the border to Jordan. The whole operation should last no more than two days. There were many points of detail to discuss, but that was the essence of the plan. What did Roscoe think?

Roscoe said he would like another drink.

Saladin sat down, looking spent, and at last lit his cigarette. 'If we can bring this off,' he said, 'it will be the biggest operation ever carried out by a Palestinian commando force. But what is more important, Stephen' – and here he took Roscoe by the arm, fixing him with eyes like the ancient mariner's – 'it will have the support of the world. Remember, this Israeli annexation of Jerusalem has been unanimously condemned by the United Nations . . .'

Roscoe nodded, a trifle impatiently. He did not need convincing on this score, and when Refo brought his drink he turned the talk back to practical details. He kept them at it for an hour, going through every stage of the plan, altering it at several points to his own satisfaction. Then he took the job.

10. An Unexpected Complication

After the meeting Giscard drove him back into town, leaving the others at the villa. Roscoe had promised to take Claudia out to dinner but was more than an hour overdue. He was not much troubled by that, remembering her part in the subterfuge at lunch. Now he in his turn had agreed to a deception; Saladin's instructions were that she should be informed about the border crossing but not about the raid on Alcatraz.

Roscoe arranged to eat with Giscard but when they reached the hotel they found her waiting in the bar with a book. Roscoe apologized; Claudia said she did not mind. He saw that she meant it, and was touched. Brown would have been in a rage.

Over drinks Giscard explained the resurrection of Bassam Owdeh as Arnold Cohen and outlined to Claudia the plan for the frontier. He said she could ride with the party as far as Tyre, then took himself off diplomatically.

The night was fine, warm and close, with a full white moon above the glare and blare of the city. After Roscoe had cleaned up and changed, he and Claudia walked round the bay.

She asked him what he thought of Saladin.

'As you said, impressive.'

'I'm sorry about lunch. I thought that was all rather silly.'

'Well, they have to be careful.'

'Yes, I suppose so.'

Roscoe asked how she had spent the afternoon.

'Oh, just sleeping. So you think this thing is worth taking seriously?'

'Yes, of course. Why not?'

'I don't know. It just seems, well, so outlandish. Blowing up corpses, false passports – I wonder if we haven't got into something absurd, and rather futile.'

'Futile? I wouldn't say that. A long shot, perhaps.'

'Very long I'd say.'

'Maybe so. The Palestinians are in a bad way. But consider the alternatives.'

'I just wonder how one man can do much about it.'

'I expect people said that to Lenin.'

'Lenin! I hadn't quite put him in that class.'

Time would tell, Roscoe said, not entirely happy with this comparison himself.

'So you honestly think he can succeed?'

'I think he's got a chance. I intend to help him anyway.'

Claudia absorbed this, walking in silence for a while, then her face cleared. 'All right then, if you will, I will. But I must admit it scares me. You don't know what a relief it is to discuss it with someone I can understand.'

Roscoe smiled at her. 'Most people seem to find me rather perplexing.'

Claudia responded with a smile of her own. 'Do they now. Well, at least you're English.'

The restaurant was an old Arab house by the port, thick white walls and ornately carved doors, a courtyard open to the sky, cushions and very low tables set out in arbours of plants. The food came all at once in small dishes, houmous and similar paste, shish kebab, olives, balls of goat cheese, mint salad, other salads finely chopped, vegetable rissoles and flat discs of un-leavened bread. Claudia knew what was what. As she picked among the dishes Roscoe asked what had made her join Saladin, and she told him about Nahr al-Bared. 'That's one reason. But I sometimes think I'm only doing it because I'm fed up with myself.'

'Fed up?'

'Yes, I'm so dull.'

'What rubbish.'

'No, I mean it. All my life I've felt on the edge of things. I keep expecting something to happen, but it doesn't. Sometimes I try to make it happen, but I either lose my nerve or make a bosh of it. When I went to Cambridge I had dreams of running a *salon*, all the most brilliant people in the university sitting around in my room being brilliant while I dished out my best China tea – and you know what happened?'

'What happened?'

'A lot of boring men in duffle coats turned up and wouldn't go away.'

Roscoe laughed, and then Claudia asked him in turn why he had joined Saladin.

'They're paying me.'

'Oh.'

A waiter brought wine. When he had gone Claudia asked Roscoe what he was being paid for, a question which he answered vaguely, saying that in view of the dangers Saladin wanted a military man. That led to discussion of his past career, which he described in a self-dismissing way, sensing that this girl would not approve of soldiers. But Claudia, not wanting to offend him and genuinely curious besides, made a point of being impressed.

'What an exciting life you've had.'

'No, pretty quiet on the whole. Patches of excitement.'

Claudia held out her glass for more wine. Soon the bottle was empty. Roscoe called for another and they talked of other things, swapping items of their past, laughing a lot, progressing rapidly towards a friendship which surprised them both. Indeed that was already too mild a way of putting it, for whether from pressure of external circumstances or internal needs Stephen Roscoe and Claudia Lees grew fond of each other so quickly it embarrassed them. Each, being nervous of this unexpected complication, tried to slow the process down. But besides their own caution there was nothing to stop them. As soon as they had glimpsed a little of each other they knew they would like the rest. They had the feeling of having met before, perhaps because each corresponded to an image already existing in the mind of the other, a subconscious ideal now suddenly precise and made flesh. Claudia liked Roscoe's laugh – it changed his face completely – and he was delighted to find that she had a zany streak, revealed when he asked her if she would like to see a belly dance.

'A belly dance?'

'A belly dance.'

'I should like to see a belly dance very much indeed.'

Yussef had mentioned a place, and they walked there after dinner. It was a rickety bar overlooking the sea, painted turquoise and red. Down by the stage a bunch of young Arabs were getting drunk on whisky. The prostitutes sat together in a huddle wearing synthetic wigs and fishnet stockings. Fans redistributed the smoke and a bent old woman wandered through the crowd with garlands of magnolia. Claudia chose one and draped it round her neck, obliging Roscoe to buy it. Then they found a table at the back and drank beer.

On stage was a singer, President Sadat to the life – the same trim moustache, the same bank-manager suit – but he had more success with his public, who clapped and shouted for more as he clung to the microphone and poured out his soul in a lilting Arab melody, strangely hypnotic as it crept up the scale then dropped back, never straying far from the dominant note, while behind him a five-piece band, also in suits, slogged away at the accompaniment – two violins, tambourine, zither and bongo drum. Conversation was impossible.

After half an hour she appeared, a big girl, soft and white, stroking the air and grinding her pelvis in a half-hearted fashion. The audience cheered like a football crowd, urging her on, and after many pauses to rest she did reach some sort of climax, mouth open, eyes closed, fat breasts squirming in the tight tasselled costume, white hips a-quiver. Roscoe and Claudia exchanged British smiles.

The show stopped abruptly when one of the drunks in front flung a bottle on stage and was removed by the tambourine man, who doubled as bouncer.

Roscoe and Claudia walked out into the night, now cool by comparison. 'The fabulous East,' he said.

'Land of Venus,' echoed Claudia. 'This is her birthplace, you know.'

'It's certainly venereal.'

'Almost makes me miss Israel.'

'No belly dancing there, I suppose.'

'No indeed.'

Claudia threaded her arm into his as they walked up a narrow street plastered with portraits of Nasser, which flapped in the slipstream of a sportscar, reminding her of other things missing in Israel. 'No sportscars, no jet set, no nice clothes in the shops. Even the food's pretty plain – and they don't drink, you know.'

'Will they let me in?'

'Are you coming?'

'Perhaps. Depends what he wants.'

'Well you won't like it much, I can tell you. It's a very dull place, and rather frightening – no, I shouldn't say that. There's lots to admire. Perhaps it's just me.'

They could not sustain their cheerful mood. Having bolstered Claudia's resolve, Roscoe himself was now struck by doubt. 'I'm not used to being anti-Jewish.'

'We're not, we're anti-Zionist. There's a difference.'

'I hope so.'

'In fact I'm not even anti-Israel,' said Claudia. 'It's just that they will push their luck.'

'And no one dares protest, because we feel guilty. It's our fault they're there after all.'

'Is it? Is it *our* fault – yours and mine? I strongly distrust that collective-guilt approach, especially when it's spread across several generations. The past explains the present but shouldn't excuse it, surely. Not for us.'

'No, I suppose not, but it's difficult, isn't it? Goes against the grain. Many of my best friends etcetera.'

'Yes, it is difficult.'

When they reached the hotel they collected their keys from a sleepy receptionist and Roscoe found a brown-paper package waiting in his pigeon-hole. No stamp, his name scrawled in capitals. . . . Testing the weight of it, he stepped after Claudia into the lift. 'I'll see you at eight,' he said. 'Giscard's bringing the car round then.'

'What a strange man he is. Don't you feel there's some kind of force in him, trying to get out?'

'Maybe. But that's true of most of us, isn't it?'

The scent of magnolia pursued them down the corridor, sickly-sweet. Claudia was wilting as fast as the flowers round her neck. At her door she paused. 'Well good night, Stephen, and thanks so much. I'm sorry, I seem to have got rather gloomy.' She smiled and shook his hand. 'But I'm really very glad you've turned up.'

Roscoe said good night and went into his room. He switched off the air-conditioning and opened the windows, then sat on his bed and listened to her moving about, thinking of her pale clean skin and quiet voice, that wry self-deprecating smile. When he heard her put out the light he opened the package.

As he had guessed, it was his Browning. Marsden must have a friend on an airline.

Roscoe checked the working parts of the pistol, then tucked it under his mattress. He was well content with his day, looking forward to the next. He spent his last waking moments reviewing the plan to get Bassam into Israel. He could see nothing radically wrong with it, but a number of questions still hovered in his mind, questions which he now thought he should have had answered. All of them centred on Zeiti.

11. Suspicions in Gaza

Saladin was working on the answers to those questions, but at this stage the principal threat to his plans did not come from Black September. It came from the subtle and energetic mind of Major Michel Yaacov, who as Roscoe and Claudia left Beirut next morning was studying the story of Bassam Owdeh's murder in the Israeli papers.

Yaacov was sitting at the time in his office at Gaza Command. The room was grey-washed and bare; a desk, two armchairs, maps on the walls. Outside as inside the building was austere, a bureaucratic fortress on the outskirts of the town. It was known as a Teggart Building, one of many such constructed by the British during the last troubled years of the Mandate, well-defended compounds of concrete which the Israeli army had used since the Six Day War to administer the Occupied Territories.

Yaacov's post in this administration was unusually high for a man of his age and rank, and he owed it mainly to his understanding of the Arabs. Born in Marseilles but raised in colonial Algeria, he had returned to France with his parents in 1947 then come to Israel at the age of seventeen. Thus most of his life had been spent among Arabs; he had studied their customs, religion and history; he spoke their language and knew how their minds worked. Though his loyalty to Israel was total, he believed in a single cooperative destiny for the two Semitic races. That was a long way off; first there was a war to be fought, and won; but when the reconciliation came, Yaacov hoped to have a hand in it. His ambition was boundless.

He was a handsome man, with thick dark hair; brown-eyed, soft-spoken, donnishly scruffy. His olive-green uniform was unpressed and worn carelessly, but he carried the natural authority of intellect and sex appeal.

With him in Gaza he had an assistant, a pretty young sergeant-majorette called Ayah Sharon, and that morning when she brought in coffee she found him poring over the Hebrew papers, all of which had given a double-column spread to Bassam Owdeh's death.

'Shalom,' he said, without looking up.

She dropped some documents in his tray and walked out again, bare tanned legs under a short khaki skirt, gold bangles clanking on her wrist. The Israeli army was not like any other.

Yaacov drank his coffee and read on.

He was sorry about Bassam, remembering their walk together in the park at Oxford, the arguments always leading nowhere. Bassam was a loss; Bassam, if he could have calmed down, had been the sort of Arab with whom the new Middle East might be built. Who, then, had killed him? It looked too thorough for an Arab vendetta, and if it was Mossad then something had gone seriously wrong. They were supposed to be watching him, not blowing him up.

Yaacov made a phone call to Tel Aviv, but Mossad denied all knowledge. He turned back to the papers.

The photograph, he noticed, was an old one. Bassam was much fatter these days, and he wore different glasses. In fact the picture in their own files was more recent than this. . . .

Yaacov's pride was his brain. Like a chess champion he was always pleased to find someone he could play with, but to date had never come across an Arab whom he could not outwit. The Arabs, were easy to beat because they made a great noise about their objective and then lost sight of it in their excitement, whereas a Jew always knew what he wanted but was careful about stating it openly, a habit acquired perhaps from living in hostile societies. Paradoxically it was the Arabs who had a reputation for cunning; but what made them difficult to trust was what made them easy to beat – their perversity. Cunning they were not, in Yaacov's opinion.

For instance, this photograph; a typical piece of hamfistedness. It was so misleading it made one ask why, bearing in mind that Bassam was involved in a new resistance effort. And then one remembered that he spoke fluent Hebrew. . . .

As suspicion hardened into near-certainty Yaacov rose from his desk and stood by the window, his habitual thinking position.

For a man who believed in an all-Semitic future the view which met his eyes was bleak. In Gaza the military occupation was a painfully observable fact. The ramshackle, sprawling Arab town was overlooked by Israeli sentries at several high points and through it drove Israeli jeep-patrols on roads cleared like fire-lanes by Israeli bulldozers. In Gaza you could feel the hate, and it had always been so. Here had lived that old foe of Israel, the Philistines. In Gaza Samson had dragged down the enemy's temple on his head.

But today Yaacov's mind was not on the future or the past. He reviewed what he knew of Saladin. A report had come in that this exotic codename applied to a wealthy Palestinian Arab called Anis Kubayin, but apart from this he knew no more than he had at St Anthony's. Whoever this Saladin was, Bassam and Marsden were working for him; Zeiti had joined them then flown to Damascus, where Mossad's agents had lost him; and someone else had been recruited in England by Marsden, identity still unknown. The situation was complicated by those lunatics MZ and their roving thug Gessner, who was clearly undeterred by the talk in Kensington Gardens. Gessner had almost killed Marsden and was now said to be in Beirut, still gunning for Zeiti. He must be stopped. With Bassam now out of the picture, Zeiti was the best lead to Saladin.

Returning to his desk Yaacov called in Ayah Sharon and dictated a list of instructions. Later that morning she telephoned Lod, who were sent a better picture of Bassam; Ashdod and Haifa were also warned. Yaacov even considered where Bassam might hide if he got through the net – a population centre probably. . . .

But that was jumping too far ahead, he thought, and returned to his ordinary business. In an odd way he almost hoped Bassam would succeed, but knew he would not.

12. Calculations in Tyre

Yaacov's pride was his brain, but his weakness was too much faith in it; he was apt to judge his enemies by the standards of his own logic. Thus it did not occur to him that Bassam would come in across the northern frontier, because for one thing the Israeli army was preparing to cross it in the other direction, and for another the whole of southern Lebanon was in a state of near-warfare between the Fedayeen and the Lebanese army, who were trying to keep the Palestinians under control.

Since Munich each side had taken up positions for another round of this three-cornered battle. The storm was expected to break any moment, and to Claudia it seemed that a hush had come over the country. Having now escaped the racket of Beirut, she and Roscoe were driving southwards in a rented Volkswagen Beetle. With them was the Gipsy, and his wizened head leering from the back had put her on edge.

The countryside was pretty and calm, a softer landscape than the north. Along the coastal plain neat rows of orange trees stretched from sea to mountains, the fruit almost ripe but not yet yellow, still concealed in the dark glossy foliage. The road was lined with avenues of tall eucalyptus and beside it ran the derelict railway which had once connected Cairo to Istanbul. They had just passed through Sidon, a quiet town set around a squat Crusader fort, when Claudia opened the glove compartment.

'What's this?'

Roscoe was annoyed that she had found it. 'As you see, a pistol.'

'Yours?'

'Yes.'

She turned the Browning over in her hands, a heavy thing of blue-black metal, cold to the touch. 'Have you ever used it?'

'No, it's never been christened.'

'Surely you can think of a better word than that.' She put the pistol back and snapped the glove compartment shut. 'Blooded, maybe.'

A few moments later they drove into Sarafand, where Bassam and Zeiti were waiting.

Claudia expected a town, but it was just a fishing village; primitive houses scattered round a bay, brightly painted boats on the flat reflecting water. All round it were banana plantations, dense walls of green behind which some Fedayeen units were said to be hiding. According to Giscard the Israelis came by here every day, cruising up and down in patrol boats, and once they had picnicked on the beach. Claudia believed him. The picnic was typical, she thought, the sort of story Israelis often told about themselves. They liked to paralyse their enemy with acts of bravado.

Roscoe parked the car on the road and led the way down to one of the fishermen's houses. The exterior was just a cube of clay, but inside they found a home, clean and neat; two rooms with bedding stacked against the walls, a wardrobe, plastic flowers, a portrait of Nasser. The old man who lived there invited them to sit on a mat where Bassam and Zeiti were already installed, drinking coffee.

Claudia noticed that Zeiti greeted Roscoe with surprise and then as a friend. Bassam's disguise was quite comic; he was wearing dark glasses and a plain white kefia attached to his head by a double black cord, like an oil sheikh. Clutching a travel bag, he sat crosslegged on the mat with the look of a man awaiting execution.

The Gipsy squatted outside on his heels.

The day was bright and hot. The beach was fringed by palms, date-clusters bursting like fireworks below the drooping leaves. Through the open doorway Claudia could see them perfectly reflected in the water, until the Gipsy spoiled the picture with a pebble. Inside the hut the old man was talking on happily, rolling cigarettes for Roscoe and Zeiti. He had nothing good to say about the Fedayeen, brushing his palms together as if to dismiss them as dust.

Claudia listened sadly. Underneath the headlines this was the constant reality: refugees and peasants squabbled for their

miserable portion, too often duped to expect any change. Most
of the world lived like this old fellow, and always the saint on
the wall. Here it was Nasser, elsewhere Kennedy, Lenin, Pope
John – cheap tinted faces beyond reach of disillusion.

Later in the morning she and Roscoe drove on with Zeiti to
Tyre, where Saladin's military contact was waiting to brief
them.

'Poor old Bassam,' Zeiti said, 'he's scared to hell.'

'Well, wouldn't you be?' Claudia instinctively sided with the
chubby professor. She got the impression that for Zeiti fighting
Jews was a hobby; he could as well have been a racing driver.

Further down the coast the traffic thinned out; the countryside was less well tended, the houses dilapidated, and in Tyre
the hush was complete. Outside its Palestinian slums the town
had a dead, deserted air. Ribby dogs scavenged undisturbed in
the streets and the harbour was empty, two grey naval vessels
anchored at its mouth.

Saladin's contact was a Lebanese officer called Hourani,
related to the Kubayin family by marriage. He gave them
lunch in a government restaurant by the beach, spreading a map
on the table in what was supposed to look like a journalist's
briefing for Roscoe. Claudia saw that at another table Morley
was getting the genuine thing. She waved, but he ignored her.
He was still in his safari suit. She could hear enough to tell
that the army were refusing him permission to film on the
frontier.

Roscoe and Zeiti made marks on the map as Hourani spoke
rapidly in French, giving them up-to-date details of roadblocks,
Lebanese positions, Fedayeen activity, Israeli frontier patrols.
The indiscretion was making him sweat, Claudia noticed – or
was it the heat in the restaurant? The walls were plate-glass,
overlooking a long sweep of sand which stretched to the
frontier.

After lunch Roscoe and Zeiti returned to Sarafand, leaving
her in Tyre to inspect the excavations, which was what she had
come for, because this little port had once been the centre of
the world. City had been built on top of city, Phoenician,
Greek, Roman, increasingly splendid; from Tyre the famous
cedars had been shipped to build Solomon's temple and Dido
had sailed to found Carthage . . .

History was Claudia's hobby, and as she strolled through the ruins she felt as happy as she ever did, running her knowledge-able eye over the arches and cisterns and sarcophagi, the elabor-ate Roman brickwork and lovely slim green-veined pillars. She rebuilt the city in her head, restored the colonnades and filled the streets with people. And once or twice she thought about Roscoe. She knew that he liked her and that made her feel comfortable, as if she had money in the bank. But she did not see any particu-lar reason to draw it.

13. Night March

Putting Bassam into Israel was harder than Roscoe expected.

The first problem was to get within walking distance of the frontier. To avoid the roadblocks south of Tyre they returned to Sidon then drove inland, looping back south on a minor road which would bring them close to the border. But this detour looked simpler on the map than it turned out to be. By the time they were travelling south it was night and the minor road had turned out to be no more than a track, which dipped, rose and twisted through the thickly wooded hills of central Lebanon. Roscoe drove as fast as he could since each hour of darkness was precious, but to save the Volkswagen's springs he was frequently forced to slow down, skirting minor landslides, deep ruts and potholes. The moon was full and amazingly bright, drenching the landscape in a colourless glare, and as they mounted a final ridge they looked south into Israel – distant waves of hills, like a frozen sea beneath the moon. Then the road dropped sharply and emerged in Nabatiya.

Nabatiya was a Fatah command centre flanked by a big refugee camp, a frequent target of the Israeli air force. But that night it was quiet. People lay asleep on the pavement like heaps of old clothing. Roscoe and his friends passed through un-challenged and kept going until they came to a point where the road twisted down to the River Litani. On the edge of the drop was a derelict farmhouse, just as Giscard had described it. Ahead of them now was a Lebanese defensive position and further down a checkpoint on the river. From here they could go no further by car.

Roscoe turned off the road and parked in a lean-to at the back of the house while Zeiti and the Gipsy followed on foot, scuffing over the tyre-tracks. In the next five minutes they made ready as quickly as they could, changing into dark warm clothing and checking their weapons. Zeiti unveiled a Mauser automatic, to

which he fixed a shoulder stock. Watching him, Roscoe noticed
his confident handling of this unusual weapon. Bassam was un-
armed; he had only his travel bag. As to other equipment, they
had a small extending ladder to carry, also a signal torch, a map,
a nylon rope, a compass with good fluorescent markings and a
pair of binoculars – items provided by Giscard. Roscoe had
made up a paste to darken his skin and as he applied it the
Gipsy said something in Arabic which made Zeiti laugh. No one
had thought to bring food, but the Gipsy had a bottle of water.

In theory Bassam was in charge but now that the problems
were physical it was Roscoe and Zeiti who took joint command,
collaborating easily and ready to defer to the instinctive field-
craft of the Gipsy.

They locked up the car and set off in file with the Gipsy in
front, then Bassam, then Zeiti and Roscoe carrying the ladder
between them. Zeiti had hitched the Mauser over his shoulder
with an improvised sling. It was now ten o'clock. They aimed
to reach the border about 2 a.m. They had six miles to go, not
an impossible distance in the moonlight, and at that stage
Roscoe felt confident.

The walking was easy at first, hard-baked earth still faintly
scarred by plough-marks. But the man who farmed this land
had fled from the fighting and now his only crop was thistle,
tall weeds which grew to waist-level and rattled when disturbed.
Ahead of them the ground sloped steeply down to the river,
and across the valley, about two miles away, it rose to a level
rather higher than where they now were. On the opposite skyline was a light which Roscoe made out through the binoculars
to be an illuminated petrol sign. They took a bearing on it, but
the Gipsy soon put the compass in his pocket and followed his
nose, tacking down the hillside as it turned to rock and scrub.
The moon was a help but it made them uncomfortably visible.
Hourani had warned them that this was an area disputed between
the Lebanese and the Fedayeen, either of whom would shoot on
sight.

Descending, they could see the valley floor below them,
orange groves and cypresses stretching to the dark hills opposite.
Then they heard the river, a sound like a far-away football
crowd. Then the road reappeared, doubling back across their
front towards a Bailey bridge on the right. On the bridge was a

Lebanese military checkpoint now illuminated by the head-lights of a passing truck. Roscoe inspected it through the binoculars: the usual striped boom and sentry box, soldiers in greatcoats down to their ankles and behind them a sandbagged emplacement. Above the sandbags he could just see the barrel of a heavy machine-gun, American he thought, with searchlight attachment.

The Gipsy then led them in a dash across the road and on down towards the river. For a moment they were totally exposed, crossing bare ground between the road and the first line of orange trees. They ran close together, crouched low in line abreast. The noise of the water was growing all the time – and then the dogs began to bark.

There must have been three or four of them tethered round the checkpoint, more effective than any human sentry. They had taken no notice of the truck but now the one closest to the river gave the alarm. He set off the others, and suddenly the night was alive with the shrill continuous barking of watchdogs. The orange grove was only a short way ahead; Roscoe would have run for it, but the Gipsy knew better. Instantly he dropped to the ground and a few seconds later the searchlight came on, a shattering white blaze, eclipsing the moon.

They were caught in its beam, huddled close, faces pressed flat into the ground.

Roscoe watched Zeiti's finger fumbling for the trigger of his Mauser. Too late for that, he thought. 'Keep still,' he hissed, his senses recording each detail of the moment, the taste of the earth in his mouth, Bassam's legs shaking beside him, the deadly white incandescence above and all around. The dogs were still barking. A soldier shouted – and then it was dark again. The beam moved away from them, raking the floor of the valley. Then it went out.

They sprinted on forward into the orange grove and through the long grass between the rows of trees, bumping their heads against the low-hanging fruit, then over a water-conduit and into a younger plantation, which offered scanty cover but ended in a line of tall cypresses, black spears against the pale sky. The dogs started up again but this time the Gipsy kept going, over a wall and into a ditch, a trench of deep shadow which led to the river.

The Litani at this point was fast but not deep. After pausing to rest they walked upstream, away from the army post, until they came to a stretch where the water was foaming over rocks. The Gipsy crossed first, tying the rope to a tree on either side and stretching it taut as a handhold for Bassam and Zeiti, who followed with the weapons and equipment. Roscoe came last with the rope lashed round his waist.

It took them an hour to climb out of the valley, which was brutally steep, an escarpment of knife-sharp rocks and thorn bushes rising almost sheer from the river. At the top they collapsed exhausted in the shadow of the petrol station. Bassam was walking like a drunk, almost at the end of his strength. It was half past midnight.

But the rest was downhill, and now they could see where they were going. From this high point it seemed that the whole Middle Eastern battleground was spread below them, a vast hushed moonlit arena. The lights of distant villages flickered like the camp-fires of armies, ragged and yellow on the Arab side, in Israel a bright greenish blue. In front was Metullah, the northernmost Israeli settlement. They could see it quite clearly, an orderly pattern of bungalows surrounded by watch-towers and a high wire fence. At the edge of town arc lamps were beamed into Lebanese territory, supplemented by a searchlight which blazed to life at unpredictable intervals. Distances were shrunk by the silence. In Israel a car was changing gear; in a village to the left a door slammed. Miles away a dog barked, answered by another.

Zeiti lit a cigarette and the Gipsy passed round his bottle, but the water was not much comfort. It passed straight into their systems, leaving their mouths dry and still full of mucus. Bassam was lying on his back.

'Better keep going,' Roscoe said.

Zeiti glanced at his watch. 'Yes, we don't have long.'

They examined the map, then picked themselves up and started down the hill to Israel

14. The Fence

They had gone a few yards when the Gipsy raised his hand, then signalled them urgently back into the lee of the petrol station.

Zeiti cupped his hands to Roscoe's ear. 'Fedayeen,' he breathed, and two minutes later they appeared, eight men climbing towards them in file, unmistakably identified by the curved magazines of their Soviet rifles. One of them carried a rocket-launcher. They passed within twenty yards of the petrol station then disappeared to the left, padding through the night with the weary boredom of men on manoeuvres.

Automatically Roscoe had drawn his gun and flicked off the safety catch. A futile gesture, but comforting. Steel in the hand.

Haste was impossible. A thin screen of cloud had drifted over the moon, reducing its light. Bassam was so tired his legs had turned to rubber; going downhill he could hardly control them, and several times went sprawling. He was not just exhausted but terrified, especially of dogs. Each time one barked he twitched, and sometimes he stopped dead, trembling, until gently urged on. Roscoe was now less confident. Bassam was cracking and it was past 3 a.m. The deadline was dawn, which would come about four.

They made it with only twenty minutes to spare, approaching the border across a jumbled rocky wasteland providing sparse cover. On the Israeli side they could see apple orchards, and then a plantation of pine. Just where the pine trees began, almost hidden in their shadow, a watchtower overlooked the fence. Bassam, who seemed calmer now, had been counting the watchtowers. He whispered something in Arabic, then turned to Roscoe.

'This is the one.'

Roscoe nodded and peered at the fence, which was less than a hundred yards away. His mouth was utterly dry.

The Israeli frontier is an elaborate, multiple death trap. The basic obstacle is an eight-foot mesh fence which expands at the top into three horizontal strands of barbed wire. Planted at intervals along it are steel-plated watchtowers manned by the army or Border Police, and running inside it, from the Mediterranean to the Gulf of Aqaba, is a track for patrols. This track is surfaced with a deep layer of sand which gets inspected for footprints and swept clean each morning by a vehicle trailing brushwood. Either side of the track are minefields and trip-flares and scattered all over the border area, on the Arab side as well as the Israeli, are small electronic devices which will pick up the least disturbance or sound. The fence itself is electrically sensitive and at some points connected to unmanned machine-guns which will fire automatically on the point where a breach has occurred.

Hundreds of Fedayeen have been killed on this obstacle course, but Roscoe and his friends had one great advantage denied to the ordinary raiding party. The sentry in this watch-tower was an agent of Saladin, a young Sephardic Jew in the Border Police who had provided full details on this stretch of frontier and was waiting to help them across. He was due to be relieved at 4 a.m., so they had only fifteen minutes left; but now they had to move more cautiously than ever, dragging their bellies over smooth rock and patches of wiry vegetation – a writhing, sweating human snake in the dark. Roscoe's senses were blunted by exhaustion. At each pause he had an urge to lay his face in the stones and go to sleep.

Twice they had signalled and got no response. Now they dared go no closer. If they had picked the wrong tower the answer would be a blinding light and bullets.

'Try again,' Bassam whispered.

Roscoe laid his gun on a rock, pulled out the signal torch and shone it straight ahead. Three short flashes.

No answer.

Roscoe signalled again. They waited, staring forward at the outline of the pines. Then at last there it was: a short green wink in the blackness. Immediately they got to their feet and walked straight up to the fence, keeping their eyes on the circular cabin of the watchtower.

A red light.

They stopped, close to the wire. Roscoe saw something move in the pines beyond the fence, perhaps an animal. Bassam saw it too.

The sentry adjusted his torch for long beam and flashed it on a segment of fence to their right. They moved along to that point and waited again. They were now out of sight of the neighbouring watchtowers, hidden by the lie of the land and the trees.

Another green wink from the tower. The signal to go.

Bassam embraced Zeiti, then grabbed Roscoe's hand. 'Goodbye – and thanks.'

He was shaking all over.

Zeiti propped the ladder against the fence, resting it against the nearest strand of wire at the top, then he and the Gipsy held it steady as Bassam climbed clumsily, nervously, an overweight professor with no strength left in his legs on a ladder which would not keep still because the wire was not taut enough to hold it. At the top he paused and reached down for his bag. Roscoe passed it up. Bassam threw it over and straightened up for his leap. Then he lost his nerve and crouched again, clutching the top of the ladder.

Zeiti urged him on.

'Jump!' cried Roscoe.

But as Bassam dithered the wire had sagged beneath his weight, tangling with other strands, and that must have triggered the alarm. They did not immediately realize what had happened. There were no bells or sirens, only a gabble of Hebrew on the radio in the watchtower and then the noise of an engine starting up, followed by two hollow bangs. Roscoe recognized the note of those reports, but now it was too late. Bassam had already jumped, or rather fallen, just as the flares burst above them, providing a perfect view of the disaster. He had caught his foot in the wire and gone over in a somersault, falling flat on his back in the sand of the patrol-track, where he now lay stunned.

The engine, they now realized, belonged to a vehicle of the Border Police approaching down the track.

There was only one thing to do.

Since Zeiti and the Gipsy were holding the ladder, Roscoe scrambled up it and jumped.

As he did so a man ran out of the trees on the Israeli side, charging at him with a branch of pine. Roscoe prepared to defend himself; but the man ran straight past him, picked up Bassam's bag and started to smooth out the sand with the branch – all this in the noonday blaze of the flares. Roscoe grabbed Bassam round the chest and hauled him off the track. The other man came behind sweeping, then threw away the branch and took hold of Bassam by the feet, swivelling him round to take the lead. 'This way,' he said, 'quickly', and plunged through the barbed-wire defences at the edge of the wood, grunting with the effort. A short man in shirt-sleeves, strongly built; not young, but cool in the head.

Zeiti was no fool either. As he fled from the fence he shouted 'Back tomorrow', then his voice was lost in a burst of fire from the watchtower. At the edge of the trees Roscoe glanced back to see him sprinting over the rocks with the ladder, the Gipsy close behind, while the sentry fired tracer to the left in an effort to mislead the patrol.

Quick thinking. Bravo Saladin and his brave Jewish friends....

Bassam was now semi-conscious, staggering between Roscoe and the helpful stranger as they slithered downhill through the pines. The vehicle was almost upon them and the spasmodic rattle of the sentry's weapon had been joined by the heavier beat of a machine-gun, more flares, rifle fire, a crescendo of noise – then silence. As the firing stopped Roscoe let go of Bassam, drew his gun and dropped flat on his stomach, twisting to face up the hill. They had come perhaps forty yards into the wood. Police were running up and down the fence. He could see their half-track parked beside the tower, an ungainly thing in pale desert paint, and then the flares fell to earth and the night closed in again, blacker than before.

So this is Israel, he thought. Well, at least I've got my passport.

PART THREE

Alarms and Excursions

September 15th — October 25th, 1972

1. Schoolchums

The patrol were questioning the sentry in the watchtower. They had a swivel-mounted searchlight on the half-track and as its beam probed the trees Roscoe pressed his face into the aromatic pine needles, embracing the soft earth of Israel, like a homecoming exile. But the danger was past. A few minutes later the patrol drove off, leaving a new man in the tower.

Bassam had almost recovered now, but walking through the pines he kept a hand on Roscoe's shoulder. The other man carried the bag and led them downhill to a small van concealed in the trees beside a road. As soon as they were safely away, Bassam introduced him.

His name was Eytan Horowitz, an Israeli whom Roscoe came to admire; a big generous man, of great warmth and childish enthusiasms. Irrigation was his subject and he held a teaching post at the Hebrew University in Jerusalem. But his home was a kibbutz in the north, and that was where he took them now, puffing at a gnarled briar pipe as he drove.

Horowitz and Bassam had known each other since childhood, Roscoe learned. Their families had been neighbours in Haifa, where both boys had attended a local British school. But this life had ended in 1948. Just before the British evacuation Horowitz's father was murdered by an Arab revenge squad and two days later both Owdeh parents were killed in the Jewish bombardment of Haifa. Bassam, a wandering orphan in the wreckage of the city, was rescued by a Catholic priest and taken to live with relatives in the Lebanon. Horowitz's mother remarried and went back to Europe, leaving her son on a kibbutz.

Roscoe asked how the two men had come to meet again, and found another British connection. They had spent a year together at St Anthony's, where Horowitz had written a thesis proposing a Middle Eastern Water Authority.

'Sixty-three, wasn't it?' Bassam said.

'Sixty-three,' agreed Horowitz, and added for Roscoe: 'Of course we've met a few times since then. Conferences, you know, that sort of thing.'

'But this is the first time in Palestine,' said Bassam, 'since schooldays anyway. Quite an occasion.'

Horowitz unclamped his pipe. 'An occasion bloody nearly ruined by your inability to climb a wire fence.'

They both laughed loudly, exchanging soft friendly punches. Bassam admitted that he never was much good at sports and Horowitz said he would open a bottle to celebrate as soon as they got in. 'Zionist plonk, just the thing for a Muslim.'

Roscoe was moved. Good old England, he thought. Sports days, a bottle of plonk; but not quite as silly as it sounded. A sense of fairness, that was English too, a product not often found in these parts.

A few minutes later they arrived at Kibbutz Kfar Allon – an orderly lay-out of spruce modern buildings and trees with their bowls painted white, as in a barracks. Then a bungalow; a girl at the door looking scared. 'My God, what a night,' she said. 'I've been waiting . . .'

Horowitz patted her on the head. 'Come on, let's go in.' He led the way through the door, closed it, then did the introductions. 'This is Arnold Cohen.'

'Hi,' she said. No smile.

'And Stephen Roscoe.'

'Hi, pleased to meet you. You want to wash?'

Her name was Rachel; an east-coast American, jumpy and thin. She showed them into a small square sitting room, sparsely furnished in Scandinavian style, and then Roscoe saw that the bungalow was in fact divided into three tiny flats, without kitchens or more than one bedroom, for this was a kibbutz, where meals were eaten collectively and children consigned to the communal nursery. Rachel Horowitz had a daughter aged three, of whom there was no trace.

Horowitz opened a bottle as promised, but they were too tired to finish it. Roscoe fell asleep on a rug while Bassam snored beside him on the sofa. The little room reeked of their sweat.

2. The Man from Chicago

Later that morning, standing at the flat's picture-window, Roscoe found it easy to imagine he had not yet woken. Kibbutz Kfar Allon had the quality of a dream.

For one thing it was utterly quiet, perched high in the hills above the northern town of Kiryat Shemona. Outside the window grew a big clump of cannas, scarlet in the sun – and then there were these girls, striding along the gravel paths in shorts. Two of them came by with a milk churn, laughing in the sun-dappled shade as the milk slopped out and spattered their legs. Others were working in the orchards, and far below the orchards Roscoe could see a green plain, fields of what looked like alfalfa, the rectangular ponds of a fish farm and long lines of sprinklers spraying the crops. In the mauve-blue distance was Mount Hermon, wrinkled and bare, hazy in the heat.

Girls' legs and artificial rain: yes, this was Israel, the answer to the ghetto and the death camp. Not to be lightly destroyed.

Bassam joined him at the window, stretching. 'Beautiful, isn't it?'

Roscoe agreed that it was. 'Like a dream,' he said.

'The fact matches the memory. I wasn't sure it would.'

'They've certainly got the place organized.'

Bassam's reaction was defensive, automatic. 'Palestine was never a desert,' he said, pointing to the orchards. 'This was all Arab land – they took it in 1948.' Then he pointed northwards to the barren brown hills of the Lebanon, surprisingly close. 'The people over there used to live here. Imagine that. Bad enough to lose your land, but to watch someone else pick your crops . . .' The sentence trailed unfinished, as Bassam's often did. 'No,' he said, 'you cannot imagine. The British don't know what it means to be a refugee.'

Roscoe found a note from Rachel Horowitz propped between two glasses of orange juice. 'It must feel strange,' he said, 'being back, I mean.'

Bassam was still at the window. 'Yes, it is strange,' he said, then turned round abruptly and fumbled for a handkerchief, smiling at his tears. 'Oh dear me, Mr Cohen will have to do better than this.'

Roscoe felt an increase of respect for this slightly absurd intellectual, giving up life in the quad to win the peasants back their fruit trees. To know, as he did, that those trees had been planted by Jews made no difference.

Bassam blew his nose and took the juice. 'By the way, I must thank you for what you did last night. I really am an ass when it comes to that sort of thing.'

Roscoe shrugged. 'If I'd been holding the ladder it would have been Zeiti.'

'Still, it was good of you. Not in the contract.'

'Talking of the contract,' Roscoe said, 'I'd like you to take a good look at this building.'

'Alcatraz?'

'Yes. Could you do that?'

'I don't see why not.'

'I want to know everything, any small detail. The work force, how many, when they come and go, how far they've got. Scaffolding, how much and where.'

Bassam listened carefully, noting each point with a nod.

'Any sign of occupation. Is the place locked at night? Do the lights work? And there's one thing I do need to know rather badly.'

'What's that?'

'Are there any lifts?'

'Two, I thought.'

'Yes, but have they been installed? If not, you'll probably see them outside. A couple of big square crates.'

'And this is important?'

'It is. Let me show you.' Looking round the flat Roscoe found paper and a pencil, then drew a quick sketch. 'Now, it's got to fall flat, right? Well, it's a steel-frame building – these vertical supports hold it up. But what holds it steady against any side-shock is this, the lift shaft. See that cross-bracing?

If we blow out that and put some smaller charges here, on the side, the whole thing should keel over.'

'Down the hill?'

'Down the hill.'

Bassam grinned excitedly. 'I'm looking forward to this.'

'Yes, it should be rather fun.' Roscoe scrumpled up the drawing and flushed it down the lavatory. When he came back he said: 'Tell me some more about Saladin. What's he been doing all his life?'

'He's a businessman actually, from America.'

'Really?'

'Not in origin, of course. The family come from Jerusalem – they've lived there for centuries.'

'Pretty grand people then.'

'Quite grand. Businessmen really. After 1948 their property was on the wrong side of the city, so they moved abroad, to Beirut, the States – except Saladin himself, that is. He stayed in Jericho, working in a camp.'

'Was that unusual?'

'Oh yes,' Bassam said, 'the people in the camps are the poor. The middle class fared rather better, and it's they who run the Resistance. Saladin feels strongly that if the people in the camps had a chance to speak up, they might settle for less.'

'We'll soon find out.'

'Indeed. Anyway, in 1967 the Israelis took Jericho too – and that was a turning point for most of us, you know. It was clear then that Nasser couldn't help us, so we either joined Al Fatah or gave up. Saladin gave up. He went to Chicago and made a pile of money importing steel cable from Germany. In fact that's where I met him – I was lecturing at Northwestern.'

'What made him come back?'

'He's dying.'

'Dying?' Roscoe said, startled.

'Yes, I'm afraid so.'

'What of?'

'I'm not sure exactly – he doesn't discuss it. Some kind of cancer.'

'How long's he got?'

'About two years I gather. Maybe more, maybe less.'

'Not long then.'

'No. We're in a hurry.'

As they talked they each took a shower, shaved and dressed.
Rachel Horowitz had laid out a clean shirt for Roscoe. Bassam's
bag was full of clothes bought in London, including a skullcap,
which he patted on the back of his head. 'Now,' he said, 'how
do I look?'

'Jewish to the core.'

'Swine.'

They laughed and sat down, waiting for Horowitz, who had
said he would take them on a tour of the kibbutz. It would be
a good test for Bassam, whose cover was scout for a London-
based travel firm, in Israel to work out tours of the Holy Land.
The agreed story was that the three of them had driven up from
Tel Aviv, Horowitz, his old friend Cohen and Roscoe the
journalist.

3. A Surprise in the Cowshed

It was hot in the room and to Roscoe the silence seemed loaded, as before a storm. He thought of Claudia, years away in Tyre, and wondered what she would do. His instinct was to protect her, but he knew she would resist it.

Bassam smoked one of Rachel's cigarettes and tried out a few words of Hebrew, then Horowitz arrived and Roscoe got a better look at this unusual Israeli. He was a broad, squat, powerful man with a genial face, double-chinned and sun-burned under a tight cap of curly black hair; a man of constant talk and infectious energy. He regarded the tour of the kibbutz as an irresistible practical joke and after briefly rehearsing the story they set off, walking along the sun-dappled paths and calling first at the office of the Kibbutz Secretary, who greeted them as if he had better things to do.

Horowitz had lived in this kibbutz since boyhood but was not on good terms with its dominant clique, who valued his knowledge of modern farming methods but disliked his radical views.

Next came the laundry and clothing store, where liberated women sat stitching. The clean clothes were stacked on slatted shelves, each shelf labelled with the name of a member. It re-minded Roscoe of prep school.

Then the underground shelters, built against Arab attack; then a fine gymnasium and the fruit-packing station, where a weary youth stood below a mountain of apples and complained that the volunteers were smoking pot. The volunteers, Roscoe learned, were the temporary help, youngsters who came out from Europe and America to do their bit for Israel. According to Horowitz the members of the kibbutz resented them, partly because they were needed for their labour – membership was falling – but mainly because, having come, having seen, they went home.

'Rachel was a volunteer. I'm afraid she sometimes regrets it.'

They found her at the school, where she taught the youngest class. She looked happier there.

It was a bright modern school and the children were like any others, doing constructive things in the sun. One of them, a little girl with ribbons in her hair, ran forward and stretched out her arms to Horowitz, who hugged her like a bear and made her squeal with the bristles on his chin. Roscoe asked her name.

'Lois,' said Horowitz, the proud father.

Rachel lit a cigarette. 'Oh boy, that's good,' she said, lifting her face and closing her eyes as she pulled the smoke down. 'Good, good, good. Well, Mr Cohen, would you like to join a kibbutz?'

Bassam took a moment to react. He looked at her blankly, then at his feet, as if to make sure they were there. 'Oh yes, I would,' he said. 'But I'm not sure I'd get through the medical.'

Rachel gave him a wry look, which made Roscoe wonder if she knew, but Horowitz thought it a marvellous joke. He laughed so much he had to put his daughter down. Then a bell rang, and Lois ran to join her classmates. As she disappeared into the school Roscoe glanced at both parents for a sign of frustrated possession, but saw none.

After the school they visited the dairy, where an English volunteer was hosing out cow dung. His face was still pale, untouched by the sun, and Roscoe thought he had seen it before. Then he recognized the timid boy he had once met in Golders Green. It was young David Heinz.

Feeling ready for lunch, Roscoe did not say hello; nor did David, out of shyness, though he watched them all the way through the cowshed.

'Let's eat,' said Horowitz.

'Good idea,' replied Roscoe, and as he followed his host towards the smell of food wondered what had possessed Charles Heinz, the most English of Jews, to send his son to a kibbutz. The puzzle remained, but did not worry him. He thought he had not been recognized and reckoned that even if he had it did not much matter, since his presence in Israel would not be seriously at odds with what he had told Charles Heinz at the club. He therefore said nothing about it to the others, and as they sat down to mutton stew and cabbage in the crowded refectory of Kibbutz Kfar Allon all three turned their minds to this first test of Bassam Owdeh's cover.

4. The Planners

And it went without a hitch. Bassam gave a faultless perform-
ance as a passing British Jew; a family man, sober and business-
minded, living in St John's Wood but looking for a cheaper
place south of the river; a regular attender at synagogue, shaky
on colloquial Hebrew, in deep awe of Israel and its hard young
citizens. He had thought out the role and he carried it off to
perfection. Afterwards Roscoe and Horowitz slapped him on the
back. Bassam beamed proudly, and they returned to the flat in
a mood of self-congratulation; there was business to discuss,
but first they relaxed while Horowitz made coffee and spoke in
defence of the kibbutz.

'Kids get screwed up by their parents – it hurts to admit, but
it's true just as often as not. The family is not such a perfect
institution in my view. Here our women are free, and nobody
grows old alone. We Jews have always been good at ideas, you
know, and this one, the kibbutz, it's a damn good idea. Speaking
for myself I believe it is the model for future society, and that's
why I get so depressed to see us going back to the territorial
imperative and racial integrity, all that primitive nonsense of
which we've been the victims. It's so stupid.' He was kneeling
on the floor, wrestling with an electric percolator. 'You saw how
it was there at lunch,' he added, 'Cowboys and Indians, Us and
Them. They're good kids really, but all their lives they've been
taught to hate the Arabs.'

Bassam was sympathetic. 'Funnily enough I felt no animosity
at all,' he said. 'Just pity, like you. One gets the same feeling at a
Fatah parade.'

Roscoe said he didn't think Israel could really be blamed on
the Jews, at which Horowitz let his hands drop to his side and
blew out his cheeks, exhausted by the folly of the world, or the
difficulty of percolating coffee. 'Ah yes, blame isn't easy. I mean,

I can understand Golda Meir and Dayan – they think we can't survive without a state, and history persuades them that anything is justified to make that state bigger and stronger. I understand that, I sympathize. Most of my relatives were killed by the Nazis. But I don't agree with it – in fact I believe it could well be the death of us.'

'Try the plug,' Roscoe said.

'The plug? Yes, the plug. Good idea.' Horowitz bent to the task, but could not keep his mind on the technical problem. 'One day the Arabs are going to get organized and then bam, back to Germany we go.'

'We're working on it,' Bassam said lightly.

Horowitz let the quip pass, standing up with a sigh as the percolator started to bubble. He pulled out his pipe and patted his pockets for tobacco, then forgot the tobacco and stared through the window, at the orchards and the flowers and the bungalows, still bright as a colour transparency. He stood like that, as if he had caught sight of something unusual, and then said, speaking slowly now: 'However well it started, our settlement in Palestine has become an imperial venture out of its time. I feel in my bones it can't last.'

Bassam and Roscoe sat silent. For a full minute none of them spoke and outside was no sound, not even a dog. Then Horowitz turned and waggled his pipe at them.

'If this war goes on, the world will be involved. The Jews will be blamed for it, and that could bring a new persecution, worse than before.'

Bassam nodded, now solemn again.

Roscoe inspected the percolator. 'I think perhaps this coffee's ready.'

'Go ahead, go ahead, help yourself. So you see, my friends, that's why I support Saladin – for the sake of the Jews. I love these people and I love this land, but I know that to stay here we must share it. What we need now is a whole new initiative, a gesture of trust from those who see the danger, and ideas, ideas. We should build a new kibbutz of Arabs and Jews and take away the kids from their mothers. . . .'

Bassam tittered. 'Now *that* I might join.'

Horowitz found tobacco in a drawer and sat down, smiling broadly. 'Not such a bad idea, eh?'

Later they got down to business, discussing their campaign for Saladin, and watching them Roscoe was again moved, as one is by the friendship of a Negro and a white man. He was also encouraged by their competence and felt he could now say to Claudia, in answer to her question, that this operation was worth taking seriously. The planning of Horowitz and Bassam was meticulous, inspired. Both men appeared to regard this as the most important task of their lives; each of them had an excellent brain and now put it to work. They had long lists of people to contact, with addresses and telephone numbers and a system of symbols under which each potential supporter of Saladin was graded by importance, accessibility and political colouring. They had a list of journalists similarly graded and calendars, one each, on which were plotted week by week the steps in an escalating publicity drive. In a house in Tiberias were facilities for printing leaflets. Bassam produced blocks and finished artwork for display advertisements, prepared to the page sizes of the Hebrew and Arabic press. Space for some of these ads had been paid for already by a company newly registered in Tel Aviv. The company's account was full of real money, but the directors and their specimen signatures were false; Bassam and Horowitz both held cheque books. Bassam was also carrying a very large quantity of cash, enough to see him through to the end.

They had given some thought to security too. For all written messages they had established a book code, to which the key changed daily. For telephone calls they had a password, which also changed daily, and an instant signal to say if the line was insecure. If out of contact they had a system for getting in touch through classified announcements in the *Jerusalem Post*. They had dead letter boxes scattered through the country and a series of safe houses, one of which was Claudia's flat. Bassam, like Yasser Arafat, planned to keep on the move all the time. As well as the passport of Arnold Cohen he had the plastic computerized identity card of an Arab resident in Israel. Horowitz too had a set of false papers. Each had a gadget which at the touch of a button would incinerate the contents of their briefcases. They were as well prepared as any pair of amateurs could be – in fact there was surely a professional touch here, Roscoe thought. Again he wondered about Refo.

The two men worked all afternoon, stopping when Rachel returned from the school, resuming when she went to play basketball with the volunteers. Later she came back and cooked up a vegetable broth on the single electric ring in the flat. Roscoe had assumed she was not in the know; now it came out that she was, but did not want to have any part in the business. She served up the soup with a plate of olives and chunks of bread. They finished the wine, wished each other luck and drank to the glory of Saladin. Then Horowitz took Roscoe back to the frontier. ·

So as not to repeat the risk to the sentry, he chose a different crossing point, a deserted spot between the watchtowers. Climbing the fence Roscoe once again triggered the alarm, but this time evasion was easy; all he had to do was run. Guided by the petrol sign he used the same route as before, reached the derelict farmhouse soon after midnight and fell asleep in the back of the Volkswagen, waiting for Zeiti and the Gipsy. He assumed they would return to that point, but they did not. He slept on, until woken at dawn by a shattering explosion.

5. At the Eye of the Storm

This was the attack on Al Fatah, expected since Munich. At first light that morning, September 16th, three Israeli armoured columns stormed into the Lebanon and Roscoe was caught in the path of the eastern assault group, which had thrust across the border at Metullah and was aimed at the Fatah command post in Nabatiya.

Most of the Fedayeen had withdrawn into caves around Mount Hermon, but the Lebanese put up a spirited defence, laying down heavy artillery fire in the path of the advancing Israelis. One of their batteries was ranged on the road leading up from the Litani bridge, just below the point where Roscoe and his party had turned off to the farmhouse. The first shell was quickly followed by another, and then they were falling in clusters, straddling the road. . . .

It took Roscoe a moment to realize the situation he was in, and then he was out of the Volkswagen, sprinting head down between one salvo and the next towards a rocky gully further down the hill. He flung himself into a thicket of camel thorn and felt the spikes rip along his back as he squeezed between the rocks. For a while he kept his head down, then raised it cautiously to watch the battle.

The Israelis were in British-made Centurions, advancing in file. One tank had been hit and was slewed across the road, but they quickly cleared a path and pushed on, showing the coolness under fire of kibbutz-born man.

The tanks did not pause, but a small squad of infantry, coming up behind, stopped to search the house. They found the car, discussed it for a while, then left it where it was. The shellfire stopped; more Israeli infantry rolled by, and then the scene was quiet, the road deserted. The damaged Centurion was well down the hill.

Roscoe returned to the car and took out his map. The fighting had moved to the north of him, blocking the route to Nabatiya, but he saw there was another way to Tyre, more direct, along a road which Hourani had advised him to avoid. He decided to risk it and drove down to the river, ignoring the shouts of Israeli engineers now working on the abandoned tank. At the checkpoint on the bridge, now manned by Israeli military police, he used the same tactics: straight through, foot down, blind to all signals. Pulling up the opposite slope he heard a blast on a whistle and a shot clanged into the Volkswagen, but nobody bothered to chase him and so he continued, trusting to luck and the confusion of battle, along a rough road which led west to Tyre through the arid hills south of the Litani.

The Israelis were everywhere. The sky was crowded with their aircraft, dive-bombing targets to the north. Troops were combing each small mountain village, searching, interrogating, lining up suspects, instantly demolishing with explosive or bull-dozers a building in which they had evidence of Fedayeen activity. Their weapons were NATO self-loading rifles and Uzi submachine-guns, which they wielded with total assurance. Though obviously efficient they were the most ragged-looking army that Roscoe had ever set eyes on, long-haired, unshaven, dressed in faded green denim with buttons undone and straps hanging loose, big American helmets tipped back on their heads. They had a piratical air, like their black-patched com-mander Dayan, and before them the Arabs were cowed, watch-ing speechless as their houses were destroyed.

Approaching Juwaiya, Roscoe was stopped by an Israeli officer and told he could go no further. The Fedayeen had set up an ambush in the town and firing continued sporadically through the afternoon and night. The Israeli casualties were flown out by helicopter, two dead and six wounded. Again Roscoe slept in the car.

Next morning he moved on, passing through bullet-pocked houses some of which had crumbled like rockfalls into the street. He came across the same Israeli officer herding prisoners into a truck, and then saw a face he knew. Conspicuous among the abject crowd of captives was Walid, the spokesman of Al Fatah in Beirut, still in his white city clothes.

The sensible thing to do was drive on; but Roscoe, a trained fighting man, was slightly ashamed by his non-participation in this unequal battle, so he stopped the car and stepped out, protesting in a tone of decent British outrage that this man was his interpreter, from whom he had been separated in the fighting. The Israeli lieutenant eyed him dully; a young man, close to the limit of exhaustion. Roscoe pressed his attack, drawing from his wallet the card which Marsden had given him. 'You can't treat the press like this, you know.'

'He was carrying a weapon.'

'Naturally. We have to protect ourselves.' Roscoe revealed the Browning in his pocket.

The lieutenant took his press card, inspected it suspiciously, handed it back. Then he called Walid forward and examined a label round his neck. 'This man belongs to Al Fatah.'

'Absolute nonsense, he works for me. I insist that you release him at once.'

Walid watched this confrontation with tragic black eyes, resigned to his fate but pleased no doubt to have it recorded. Then the officer took the label off his neck and told him curtly to get in Roscoe's car. The Israelis were now in a hurry to go; because of the overnight hold-up this unit was last to reach the border.

Roscoe drove on.

Walid was ungrateful. As they passed through Juwaiya he spoke only once, when Roscoe asked what he was doing there.

'Fighting for my country.'

On the edge of town they came across a car squashed flat by an Israeli tank, human limbs projecting from the crumpled metal. Seven people had been inside it.

Walid was provoked to a muttered exclamation of rage and Roscoe experienced his first bad moment of doubt. Despite Ulster he retained a tenuous belief in the rules of war. He wondered if he should have stayed at home.

On the outskirts of Tyre Roscoe was arrested at a Lebanese roadblock. Again he played the press card, but to less good effect. The Lebanese soldiery were furious; they seemed about to beat him up, until Walid protested, breaking silence to deliver a long harangue in Arabic. The Lebanese wavered, then relented. Roscoe thanked Walid as he drove on through, and then spotted a second familiar face. Leaning on a taxi beyond the barrier was Dominic Morley, now wispily bearded.

'These buggers won't let me through. What's going on?'

'Tell you later,' called Roscoe. 'Sorry, can't stop.'

'All over, eh?'

'Yes, I'm afraid so.'

Tyre was crowded with people who had fled the Israeli attack. Having dropped Walid in the central square Roscoe found Claudia sitting in the bar of a hotel by the harbour. With her was Saladin. They jumped up delightedly when he appeared and after a moment's hesitation Claudia, to Roscoe's surprise, embraced him.

'We thought you were dead,' she said.

'Yes. Well, here I am.' Roscoe felt her cheek against his stubble and at the touch of it realized that since leaving Israel he had thought of little else except this nice English girl, waiting to meet him. 'Good to see you,' he said.

Claudia replied with a squeeze, then detached herself.

Saladin stepped in, extending one hand for a shake and laying the other on his shoulder, a gesture of affection which for one fleeting moment, never repeated with quite the same force of near-hallucination, made Roscoe see this man as his father. He saw too, now that Bassam had told him the truth, that Saladin's eyes burned with more than political zeal. They had the bright, urgent look of the dying.

He sat down and told his story, which Saladin interrupted only once, to ask what he made of Eytan Horowitz.

'A good man.'

'But?'

Roscoe smiled, as if he had been caught out at cards. There was no hesitation so slight than an Arab could not spot it. 'Well,' he said, 'it's not for me to say, but I wonder how much you could ask of him. I doubt if he'd agree to any violence.'

Saladin nodded. 'That confirms my own impression.'

Claudia was listening carefully to this, but the subject was dropped.

Saladin ordered drinks then sat in silence until he had all the facts, from Sarafand to Kibbutz Kfar Allon and back again to Tyre. 'Well done,' he said, 'a very good effort. So where's my little Gipsy?'

'Out there somewhere, keeping his head down.'
'While you dash back to protect the young lady.'
'That's it.'
'Let's hope he survives.'
'Oh, he'll survive. His kind always do.'

A waiter brought bottles of beer and three glasses, laying out dishes of carrot and pistachio nuts in the Lebanese manner. Claudia nibbled a carrot as Roscoe filled his glass and drank thirstily. Saladin asked another question.

'Zeiti now. A good man?'
'Useful. Bassam thinks a lot of him.'
'But you think he's a spy.'

Roscoe put down his glass with the blank blue stare which Claudia had seen at the Saint George. 'Why should I think that?'
'Let's say you have doubts.'
'Doubts. Yes, perhaps. But it's no good asking me, I've only just got off the plane. Can't tell one Arab from another.'

Claudia thought this an insolent remark, but Roscoe as usual meant what he said and Saladin had been around Englishmen most of his life. He chuckled, then took a little sip of his beer and wiped his lips with a forefinger.

'My friend, you are right to have doubts. He is a spy.'

Claudia suppressed her surprise, deferring to the mood of manly silence. The bar was deserted, as was the hotel above; too close to trouble for the tourists, too expensive for the new refugees. She had sat here each night with Morley, talking of life and the media.

Saladin had paused for a reaction from Roscoe, but getting none, he went on. 'Zeiti belongs to Black September. He's reporting back every move we make.'

Roscoe asked him what he would do.

'Nothing for the moment. As long as he's with us they won't bother with another infiltrator.'

'I suppose they want to know who you are.'

'I expect they do already, so tomorrow I shall call my press conference. Then I'm going to disappear.'

'A bit rash, wasn't it,' Roscoe said, 'to send Zeiti with us to the frontier? Knowing what you do, I mean.'

'Alas, I didn't know, not till yesterday. He didn't see the passport, did he?'

'No, I don't think so.'

'Good. You'll have to stay close to him. Just keep me alive if you can.'

Roscoe continued to revise his opinion of Saladin upwards, seeing now even in the dandified clothes evidence of will to survive, a brave show of style to cloak the rotting tissues beneath. Now there is an irony, he thought. This man is dying and wants only to live, while I, alive and well, flirt with death.

Saladin stared across the harbour at a fishing boat, cutting towards them through the flat water. 'Bassam is a very brave man,' he said. 'I just hope to hell the Israelis don't catch him.'

Roscoe's eyes shifted to the boat and as it passed close in front of them he tensed, working out what he would do if a gunman were hiding in the bottom. A superfluous precaution; the boat passed on. Still, you never knew. . . .

Saladin stood up. 'Would you excuse us, Miss Lees? I'd like to take a look at this fellow Walid.'

'Of course.'

Claudia watched them walk away, the dusky matinée idol and the tall English gent. A couple of museum pieces, she thought, but noticed for the first time that Roscoe's presence affected her. When he was with her she felt indefinably better than when he was not. More at ease in a dangerous situation, she told herself, resisting the notion that he made her feel happier or, God forbid, more complete.

6. Truth and Dare

Saladin drove back into Tyre in the big white Mercedes. Wherever the Israelis struck was a good hunting ground for recruits, for men so angry that they might risk all to retaliate.

On the way he detailed some facts he had gleaned about Gessner. The company in Paris, he said, was cover for a Jewish vigilante organization called the Men of Zion. The MZ were chasing Zeiti because he had been involved in Munich, and were not to be fooled with. They had killed about fourteen people already.

But Roscoe's mind was not on Gessner; he was wondering if Horowitz knew about Alcatraz, and now asked.

Saladin replied that he did not. 'But I think he'll soon have to. Bassam will tell him when he thinks the time is right.'

'That'll be a risk.'

'Yes it will. Does it worry you?'

'No, but if he's going to be told I think it should be fairly soon. I'd like to know how he reacts before we cross the border.'

Saladin took the point. He had various methods of communicating with Bassam, through intermediaries in Rome and London, where Marsden had set up a bogus travel agency to act as Arnold Cohen's employer. Equipment had also been provided for a radio link between Horowitz in Israel and Giscard in the Lebanon. Each party would listen in daily at prearranged times; transmissions would be coded, and restricted to emergencies.

Roscoe then asked what was next on the programme and was told he had a few days off. Within a week the task force would be ready and the training ground arranged; until then he could take it easy and think about his plans in more detail.

This delay was welcome to Roscoe. Since his arrival in Beirut the pace had been demanding.

Saladin parked the car and they walked together through the crowd which had gathered for the market in tales of Israeli atrocity. Walid was sitting apart, refusing to boast to the rabble, which made Roscoe wonder if he might have misjudged him.

'Leave this to me,' Saladin said. 'I'll be in touch. For the moment I suggest you devote yourself to Miss Lees.' He raised an arch eyebrow, as between ladies' men. 'Got some money?'

'Yes, Jimmy gave me some.'

'Good-bye then, and thanks.'

Roscoe walked back to Claudia's hotel and took a shower while she changed into a white cotton dress with embroidery round the neckline and hem. When he came back into the room she gave him a mock-coquettish look, spinning on the balls of her feet, like a dancer, to make the skirt billow out. She said she had bought it in a Palestinian gift shop as an act of solidarity.

But her taste was good, and so were her legs. Roscoe approved. Brown had always worn trousers.

Then they set off for Beirut in the Volks, through the groves of bananas and oranges and lemons and medlars, past Sarafand and on through Sidon, where oil tankers stood out to sea and sucked the West's black blood from a pipe which traversed Arabia.

'Stephen, there's something I want to ask you.'

'Yes?'

'You're going to do something which I don't know about, aren't you?'

Roscoe had lied to her twice; now he could not. 'I think you should keep out of that.'

'So it's true.'

Roscoe continued carefully. 'Tomorrow Saladin is going to make his proposals public. If he gets no response from the Israelis . . .'

'Which he won't.'

'. . . we may have to twist their arm.' He went on before she could speak. 'Now don't ask me how – you've seen what he's like, he's not a vicious man. Just take it from me, it'll be all right. But I want you to keep right out of it.'

'Don't worry, I intend to.'

'Do you want to drop out altogether?'

S.—F

Claudia thought before replying. 'No, I've given him my
word. I'd like to do something to help.'

Roscoe then asked what the Israelis would do if they caught
her in undesirable political activity.

'I expect they'd deport me.'

'That's all?'

'I don't think they'd bother to do more.'

'Well be careful.'

'You too.'

That was as far as they discussed it at the time, though each
wished later they had been more explicit. They drove on in
silence for a while, and then Claudia, pursuing some thought-
association of her own, asked Roscoe what had made him leave
the army.

'It's not much fun these days.'

'You enjoy risk, don't you?'

'Yes, perhaps I do.'

'Why?'

'Makes life more interesting, I suppose.'

She asked him if he had killed a man, and he told her about
Malaya and Cyprus. Ulster was covered by the Secrets Act, but
in fact there was not a great deal to confess, in terms of quantity
at least. Warfare, he told her, was mostly just waiting, weeks of
boredom then seconds of danger, not enough time to be
frightened. Death came by surprise. One moment you were
bored, the next you were asking what had happened and someone was bleeding on the ground. When you got a close look at
it, death was always casual.

'Are you scared of it?'

'No, I don't think so, not much.'

'Do you want it?'

Roscoe turned to look at her, startled by the question. 'Good
heavens, no. I like to cheat it.'

'Isn't that a rather twisted kind of pride?'

Roscoe said it was normal but knew it was not. Death was
casual; but so, for him, was existence – except that now, here
and now in this car with this girl something seemed to be
stirring, a first intimation that dodging bullets was a poor way
to make the sun shine brighter.

Claudia looked at the sea, then came back to the subject.

'You know,' she said, 'when those bombs were falling at Nahr al-Bared I wasn't really scared. But I do remember thinking what a waste, to get myself blown up on holiday. One's death should have a purpose, don't you think?'

'Ah yes, a purpose. Not easy to find.'

Roscoe stopped to examine the map, then turned off the coast and followed a winding road into the hills. Claudia asked where they were going. 'Wait and see,' he said, guessing from her face what was next.

'Do you believe in God?'

'No.'

'Not even Jesus?'

'Jesus more than God. What about you?'

'Both,' she said, 'I think.'

Roscoe drove through Beiteddin and found them at a place called Maaser es Shuf, erupting from the hillside like fantastic geological formations.

'Oh', she cried, 'the cedars,' and kissed him on the cheek.

They lay side by side on the grass and watched the trees stir above their heads as the sun dropped quickly into the sea. It seemed the place to talk about old loves. Claudia said she had given up a don to see the world and Roscoe reported his affair with Brown.

'She hates to live alone, you see, but can't play the wife. Wants to be one of the boys.'

'She sounds very nice. I'd like to meet her.'

'The mistake was to bring her to Granby. Put too much strain on it.'

The cedars whispered, a thousand years old, their trunks gnarled and pitted like rock. Once they had covered the mountains, but some had gone for roofbeams, others into ships, others into sleepers for the Turkish railway. Now of all the great forest only a few small copses were left, here and further north, collapsing in the weight of winter snow.

Claudia turned on her side, propping her head on one elbow. 'Tell me about Granby.'

'Flat, windy, cold. Big brick house, a few fields. Not a tree for miles.'

'Now there's a thing you'd die for.'

'Granby? Yes I would.'

'Ha! I hear Al Fatah talking.'

Roscoe grinned up at her. She had gone through all the attics, letting in the air. He felt ransacked. 'I don't think I've ever answered so many questions in my life.'

'Do you mind?'

'Not at all.'

She smiled down at him, her pale face framed by the spread of black branches above, her breasts pulled back tight by the bodice of the white Palestinian dress, and to Roscoe it seemed that in this superior position, in her smile too there was the hint of a challenge. Again he was reminded of a nurse. He himself was the patient, diagnosed and tucked up by this superior figure in white, who knew very well that he wanted to kiss her. She knew it and was waiting to see if he would dare.

But he did not dare. In this respect at least he was a cautious man, and later that night in the Beirut hotel he wondered if he might have been bolder, what with the cedars whispering and the rumble of war rolling off to the south, leaving the two of them in peace for a moment which might not recur.

7. Manhunt

By sundown the last Israeli troops had withdrawn from the Lebanon, loading their tanks onto wheeled transporters to protect the roads of Galilee. At the border they were greeted by enthusiastic crowds, including a group from Kibbutz Kfar Allon who handed round baskets of apples. The soldiers waved happily as they handed in their flak jackets and dispersed in a fleet of waiting buses.

A military spokesman in Tel Aviv said that sixty guerillas had been killed and 150 buildings demolished. In Beirut the Lebanese put their casualties at sixty-one dead, wounded or missing.

No figures were announced by the Fedayeen, who were blocked from their original positions on the border by the Lebanese army. Yasser Arafat protested in vain and the editor of the Cairo paper *Al Ahram* compared their fate to that of the Apache.

Three Israelis died in the action, and that evening Golda Meir broadcast a message to their families. 'The sacrifice of our dear ones sharpens our awareness of the dangers that have still not passed,' she said, ending with a prayer that the next year should be one of peace, for this Sunday, September 17th, was the eve of Yom Kippur, the solemn day of fasting and penitence which ushers in the Jewish New Year. As the Israeli troops returned from the Lebanon a special bus took the religious ones straight to a synagogue in Safad.

On Monday Saladin called his first press conference in a Beirut hotel, but its local effects were disappointing. The reaction of the Israeli papers was predictably derisive, and even in the Arab press comment was slight and in the main disparaging. In the organs of Al Fatah and the PFLP he was denounced as a traitor and threatened with 'the wrath of the Palestinian people'.

Elsewhere he did rather better. His initiative was reported by two big American dailies; short pieces appeared in many European papers, and even *Pravda* had a cautious word to say. Outside the Middle East reaction to his proposals was in general favourable, and the French got particularly excited. Led back to a pro-Arab policy by De Gaulle, they were now titillated by a three-page photographic story in *Paris Match* under the headline SALADIN: EST-CE L'HOMME QUI VA GAGNER LA LUTTE DE PALESTINE?

Immediately after this burst of publicity Saladin disappeared. The villa in the hills above Beirut was left empty, the white Mercedes abandoned in its garage. Journalists who tried to seek him out were forced to draw on the gossip in Beirut, sometimes supplemented by an unexpected phone call from the man himself. Only the correspondents of the *Washington Post, Le Monde* and the *Guardian* were conceded an interview, all three being led by a tortuous procedure to the same late-night rendezvous.

This sudden fame did not impress the Israeli government, but they did think it worth some retaliatory action. Before he gained credence Saladin must be stopped, one way or another; the task did not call for a new special unit but it did need a central coordinating man, and in view of his knowledge of the people involved, Yaacov was given the job.

To begin with he handled it alone, since in his normal capacity in Gaza he could call on the services of other departments. Later his staff grew considerably, and a senior man was brought in, but to Roscoe it always seemed that Yaacov was in charge. Above him the chain of command was obscure, and remained so.

His first task was to find Bassam Owdeh, but this proved unexpectedly difficult. The police and Shin Beth had drawn blank, Lod and Haifa had failed to pick him up; yet Bassam was in Israel, of that Yaacov was soon left in no doubt by many small pieces of evidence. Bassam was in Israel, and within days he had tapped the most promising source of support for Saladin, the rich old Arabs of the West Bank who did not want Arafat's war but did not like Hussein either. Wisely he kept clear of Gaza, where Al Fatah and the PFLP retained active cells, but he or someone else was at work among the parties of the extreme Israeli Left who supported a Palestinian state.

Then advertisements were placed in the Arabic press; leaflets and posters appeared in Nablus and Hebron. For correspondence and handouts Bassam was using an IBM typewriter and a French photocopier, but the police failed to match them with those used in any Arab office. He also had the telephone number of every major journalist in Israel. . . .

This was the sort of intellectual challenge which Yaacov enjoyed, and he did have one temporary advantage. He had seen through the 'death' in Beirut, and Bassam himself did not know that. He was therefore now travelling in Israel and the Occupied Territories unaware that his description had been circulated among the security services, and the fact that Yaacov did not catch him in this early stage must be counted bad luck – or good, if your sympathies lie with Bassam.

But the situation altered when Bassam was put on his guard by a series of mistaken arrests. He then promptly went to ground, and did so professionally. After that he never appeared in the same place twice, never lingered or gave advance notice of his movements, making first contact through trusted intermediaries and refusing to attend any meeting except in conditions of absolute security. He also had papers enabling him to pass as a Jew, Yaacov realized, and this exposed a basic weakness in Israeli security procedures, which were not geared to manhunts among the Jewish population. The routine at roadblocks was to concentrate on Arab cars and buses, waving all other vehicles through with the minimum delay.

Normally the wanted man's identity would now have been broadcast, but with Bassam that tactic was ruled out, since a public hue and cry would instantly make him a hero. So while the press were beginning to write him up, the Israeli government continued to deny his existence.

Yaacov now needed a break, and he got it in London.

In attempting to identify Marsden's recruit Mossad's first step had been to contact their colleagues of the British Secret Service, with whom they enjoyed good relations. But in this case the British were shy, Marsden having once been one of their own. Anti-Zionist he was, they admitted, prejudiced even, but otherwise an absolutely straight-down-the-wicket sort of chap. Mossad thought otherwise. They searched Marsden's office and flat, but found nothing of interest.

Then they were rescued by a phone call from Charles Heinz.

8. Yaacov Agonistes

On receipt of his son's first letter from Kibbutz Kfar Allon Heinz had become curious about Roscoe's surprising rate of travel. Remembering the encounter at the club, he looked up the file which he knew existed on Marsden and there found a record of the earlier enquiry from Mossad. This coincidence did not amount to much, but was just enough to act on. Heinz owed the Israelis a favour in any case; the embassy had whisked David away with such convenient speed he suspected they knew the reason. So he phoned them from a call box in his lunch hour – a piece of excellent good fortune for Yaacov, but for Saladin a serious new complication, as yet unsuspected.

From London a telegram was sent to Mossad headquarters in Tel Aviv. An automatic cross-check then produced Roscoe's name from the computer-memory of Aman, the military intelligence department, who had debriefed the Israeli Lieutenant in Juwaiya. This information was collated and passed on to Yaacov, who had closed his office in Gaza by this time and established a base above the Army Press Office in Beit Agron, Jerusalem. On reception of the message his chess mind went to work and made the connections in less time than it takes to recount them.

Comparing the reports of David Heinz and the lieutenant, he concluded that Roscoe could only have reached Juwaiya from the kibbutz in so short a time by jumping the border. And if he had jumped out, he had probably jumped in. Therefore he had come in with Bassam. Therefore the place to be looking was Kibbutz Kfar Allon.

But Yaacov did not go there immediately. First he called on the Border Police in Metullah, who confirmed that two un-explained frontier incidents had occurred on September 15th: an attempted inward crossing in the early hours, and an outward one that night. Yaacov showed more interest in the first and interviewed the sentry concerned, a young Sephardic Jew called Tzachi, who claimed that no crossing had occurred within his field of vision. Yaacov instructed Shin Beth to put him under surveillance, but before that could be done Tzachi jumped the fence himself and was shot by a Lebanese patrol half a mile from the frontier, thus becoming the first man to die for Saladin.

Yaacov was more cautious in probing the kibbutz. Next morning he borrowed a civilian shirt and trousers and posing as an official of Ulpan, the body which arranged Hebrew courses, he had David Heinz brought down to the language school in Kiryat Shemona.

David was dozy with fatigue, smelling of cow dung. Yaacov asked how it was going.

'Hard work.'

'Think you'll stay?'

'I don't know. I might.'

'It's your country.' Yaacov smiled with friendly contempt, sorting through some papers in his briefcase. 'By the way, we sent an English reporter up here the other day – Stephen Roscoe. Did you meet him?'

'Yes – he's a friend of my father's actually.'

'Asked the right questions, did he?'

'He looked a bit bored.'

'Did he go around alone?'

'No, he was with Dr Horowitz.'

'Anyone else?'

'Yes, there was another man.'

Yaacov held forward a photograph. 'This man?'

'Yes. He was wearing different glasses.'

'Did they talk to you?'

'No, just walked through.'

'Did you see them again?'

'At lunch, yes. They sat together.'

'But not after that.'

'No – except Dr Horowitz, he comes up at weekends.'

'Yes, I see. Now, about this course. . .'

David found himself agreeing to learn Hebrew. Yaacov was quietly terrifying.

After this interview Yaacov stood at the window of the school,

thinking of Tzachi's defection and death. It depressed him, the
more so because of the beauty of the view – all those sprinklers
making rainbows in the sun across the flat green fields to Mount
Hermon. Yaacov loved his country, right or wrong, but he knew
why this unhappy sentry had run from it.

A summary report had already arrived from Shin Beth which
revealed that Tzachi had come from Baghdad, an involuntary
immigrant, as were many Eastern Jews. In Iraq his father had
been a prosperous merchant but now the old man drove a taxi
in Nazareth. Unable to get into university, young Tzachi had
joined the police and had then taken up with the Israeli Com-
munists, which must have brought him into the orbit of
Horowitz.

Such stories were common, Yaacov knew, though they usually
ended short of treason. The Eastern Jews – the Sephardim –
were the proletariat of Israel. Power was in the hands of the
Europeans – the Ashkenazim – who controlled the Knesset and
the army. The Ashkenazim saw Israel as a refuge for international Jewry, to be built with the help of their cousins in the
West; the Sephardim drove the taxis and took a less missionary
view. Cousins to the Arab, they were tired of paying taxes to the
dream, tired of watching all the best flats go to immigrants from
Russia. Saladin would find many friends among the Sephardim.

Yaacov saw the danger clearly. There was an underlying split
in the house of Israel, and Bassam was already gnawing at it, a
termite in the timbers. He must be smoked out quick . . .

And now it seemed he would be. The advantage was with
Yaacov as he closed on the kibbutz, armed with new information
and spurred on by anger – not at Bassam or Saladin or anything
Arab, but at Dr Eytan Horowitz, the irrigation expert who instead of digging ditches was undermining the patriotic zeal of
his students with Marxist abstractions. Yaacov could now arrest
Horowitz and have him interrogated, but he decided to wait
and catch Bassam as well, along with any others who might be
involved in this business.

Next day – it was now late September – Kibbutz Kfar Allon
was offered three helpers by a military settlement on the border.
They volunteered to work in the orchards but had in fact come
to look for rotten apples. Two of them were agents of Shin
Beth, the third a girl from Special Branch. Other police came

in as electricians, searched the Horowitz flat and left a listening device in the telephone. Horowitz's rooms in Jerusalem were also searched and bugged. He was shadowed wherever he went, but Rachel was temporarily out of reach, having gone with Lois to see her mother in New York. Preparations were made to watch her on return.

Yaacov was confident that one or the other would lead him to Bassam, but once again was thwarted, this time by the whim of a woman. Rachel, it seemed, had had enough of kibbutz life, enough of Eytan Horowitz too. She refused to come back. Israeli agents found her living in Brooklyn with an ex-volunteer, but she said she knew nothing. Then Horowitz himself, either shocked by this event or alerted to the danger he was in, disappeared without trace.

Dismayed by this lost opportunity, Yaacov asked for extra staff at Beit Agron and was given them. His best hope of success now lay with Mossad in the Lebanon, to whom he had supplied two further names: Stephen Roscoe and Walid Iskandar. The latter, whom Roscoe had rescued in Juwaiya for reasons unknown, was revealed by Aman's computer to be a spokesman of Al Fatah.

But Mossad were foxed; they could trace neither man. Roscoe had left his hotel in Beirut, Walid had vanished from his office in the suburbs. Nor had Zeiti been seen or heard of since his departure from Damascus.

So by mid-October the Israeli operation against Saladin had come to a stop on all fronts. About the movement's leader, Anis Kubayin, a great many facts had now been assembled but not the one that mattered, his whereabouts. He had dared to visit three refugee camps, Beqqa in Jordan and two others in Syria, where his speeches had drawn large crowds. In every camp the passage of his agents was marked by a scattering of leaflets, a paper trail leading to no one, nowhere. His base was assumed to be somewhere in the Lebanon, but no more was known. The Kubayin family were ignorant of his plans; many of them thought he was mad. All his friends and associates had been screened without positive result, and this deepening mystery had added spice and interest to his cause. Beirut was now teeming with investigative reporters and several television companies were seeking an interview.

But Saladin refused to be lured into premature exposure, and Yaacov noticed this restraint. He saw that the whole campaign was phased, building slowly, and he wondered about it. Then through various small clues, he got wind of the fact that some sort of climax was due in early November. He wondered too about that. He stepped up the search, but had no better luck as the weeks of October slipped by.

Yaacov's only consolation was to be rid of Gessner, on whom he had intended to exert some pressure through the CIA. That turned out to be unnecessary. For whatever reason Gessner had already left Beirut by air on September 19th. What Yaacov did not know is that he was due to return there by sea, acting on new information received by the MZ, and the likelihood is that Gessner himself did not know it when he went to the Casino on a final spree.

9. 'Faites vos jeux'

The Casino du Liban, up the coast from Beirut, is like a piece of Las Vegas. It has a spectacular floor show, bars, loud music, pretty girls, rows of fruit machines, backgammon, roulette or chemmy, whatever you want, all provided in a sprawling white palace on the seashore. Gessner went there on Monday, September 18th, the evening before his return to Paris. He had a Filipino girl on his arm and when he took her upstairs to the roulette he came across the man he had been hoping to meet since the previous Wednesday.

Roscoe and Claudia were there for a lark. It was her last night in the Lebanon too. They were standing at one of the less expensive tables, leaning together, arms linked behind their backs as they watched the play. Claudia had lost a little, then stopped. But Roscoe was deep into the game, a cigar clamped between his teeth as he put down fistfuls of plastic chips on the green baize. He gambled as he lived, inclined by nature to bets which were neither flashy nor disorganized, merely perverse. He liked to test his luck. That night he was putting his money exclusively on red. Each time he won he left his stake down, each time he lost he doubled it. He had started with a chip worth approximately one English pound and had lost three times in a row – £1, £2, then £4. Borrowing from Claudia, he put down £8.

'You're mad,' she said.

'Nonsense. Perfectly logical.'

She stood on her toes and whispered in his ear: 'Mad.'

The croupier's face was expressionless as his rake hovered over the chips. *'Rouge, monsieur?'*

'Yes, red.' Roscoe refused to be bullied into French.

More chips rained onto the green, clattering softly as the croupier scooped them into place. He was wearing dark glasses, as were most of the players. The big chandeliers were excruciatingly bright.

The ball bounced and rattled round the wheel, then settled. '*Trente-six. Rouge, pair et passe.*'

Claudia hopped up and down. 'Red! Stephen, you won, you *won*! It's red!'

'Try to keep calm.'

Roscoe reached forward and took his chips off the table, throwing some back for a tip. Then he turned to go, but Claudia stopped him. 'Just a minute. When's your birthday?'

'May 13th.'

'Okay. Put it on thirteen.'

'What, all of it?' Roscoe stared at her, then at the chips in his hand. 'This is over the maximum.'

Claudia insisted. She pooled all their chips, divided them into three equal stakes and lost the whole lot in consecutive turns of the wheel, watching with a satisfied smile as their last bet fell into the coffers of the croupier. 'Now that's what I call gambling.'

Roscoe too was smiling as he led her away from the table. He stubbed his cigar in an ashtray, then standing in the centre of the room, under the bright chandeliers, he pulled her towards him and kissed her on the lips. Claudia did not resist; nor did she respond. She allowed it to happen, and when he released her she was blushing, but the smile was still there, a glimmer of challenge in the eyes. So he kissed her again, longer, harder, and this time she opened her mouth and kissed him back, putting her arms round his neck and pressing herself against him in a rather surprising manner for a girl from the Anglican Mission.

Someone was bound to object.

'Hey, feller.'

Roscoe felt a tap on his shoulder. 'Oh hello,' he said, 'it's you.'

Gessner wagged a finger at him. 'Not here, feller, please. This is a respectable place.'

'She seduced me. Good night, Mr Gessner.'

'She looks a nice English lady.'

'Yes, well you never can tell.'

'Maybe she should know something.'

'What's that?'

'Maybe you should tell her you screw around with Arabs. I mean, she could pick something up.'

Gessner had detached himself from the Filipino girl and was

standing with his hands loose, feet set apart. He came up to Roscoe's chest but seemed to Claudia the stronger party, a bull confronting a giraffe.

She expected a fight, but Roscoe turned away. 'Come on, let's go,' he said, and walked from the room. He seemed to have dismissed the matter from his mind, but as soon as they were outside he grabbed her by the arm and ran to the darkest corner of the garden, pulling her down beside him as he crouched behind a thick screen of bushes.

Seconds later Gessner came out, without the girl. He ran in the other direction, towards the car park, then came back a few minutes later and prowled the garden with a drawn revolver, passing close by where they were, panting and swearing as he stumbled about in the dark. He circled the garden twice, then gave up and went back inside. Claudia was seized by a late fit of trembling, of indignation too, at being drawn into this murderous game. She started to protest, but Roscoe put a finger to her lips, then patted her consolingly as he led her away, keeping all the time to the shadows at the edge of the garden.

That was the last of Claudia's adventures in the Lebanon. Next day she flew back to Israel.

10. The Mysterious Greek

Left alone in Beirut, Roscoe completed his plans. He had two further meetings with Saladin at Giscard's home and was sent the latest details of Alcatraz by Bassam. For the rest of his time he swam, sunbathed and shopped. He wrote a letter to Mrs Parsons enclosing a list of instructions for the upkeep of Granby and sent Georgie a fine Arab dagger for his birthday, brass-sheathed and lethally sharp, quite unsuitable for a boy of four. For Brown he bought an embroidered caftan and wrapped it round the dagger in an airmail parcel. The postage cost more than the gifts.

Within a week, as promised, Saladin's preparations for training were complete, and on Monday, 25th September, just before the agents of Yaacov came looking for him, Roscoe left Beirut. With him went Zeiti and the Gipsy, back from the border unscathed, and Walid, who had now been enrolled. They were driven by Giscard to a house in the remote northern mountains of the Lebanon, where a comprehensive store of equipment was waiting. The Frenchman took a week off to stay with them and next day drove down to Nahr al-Bared, where he picked up two more recruits, Fuad and Ibrahim. That made six. Roscoe put them to work, and they were at it for a month without a break.

Thus for most of October Yaacov was baffled; he could not find any of the men on his list. But the unresolved question is, who did the searching in Beirut?

Mossad undoubtedly had several men in the city, all of whom may have been engaged against Saladin. Nevertheless it seems almost certain in view of what followed that Yaacov's main agent there was Nick Cassavetes, the correspondent whom Roscoe had met outside Bassam's flat.

He worked for a small American news agency which had made its name reporting the truth from Vietnam. Following this radical tradition it tended to give a good press to the Arabs, and since their arrival in Beirut Cassavetes and his wife, both still in their twenties, had become minor stars in political society. They knew the top people in the PLO and Al Fatah and were considered to be good friends of Palestine. They said they were naturalized Americans, born in Athens, and they certainly spoke Greek. In fact, their former friends are now convinced, they were Israelis – either Jews born in Greece who had moved to Israel or children born in Israel of Greek-speaking immigrants. Before coming to the Lebanon they had lived in Washington, where both went to college and Cassavetes had worked for two years as a reporter.

People remember him as a man of utterly deadpan manner, neat and sober in appearance; his wife too was rather forbidding, an athletic girl with short-cut dark hair. They drank fruit juice. Neither smoked. A serious and undramatic couple, they were no doubt dedicated to their profession.

The proof that they were Israeli agents is that six months later they completely disappeared. Journalists do not simply vanish, especially with their wives; but spies whose cover is broken have no choice. The timing was also significant. The Cassavetes were last seen in Beirut on April 10th, 1973, driving out of the city with the men of God's Wrath after the seaborne attack on Al Fatah. That could just possibly have been a journalistic assignment, but the couple did not reappear to explain. The assumption must be that they had helped prepare the raid and were somehow compromised.

The previous October, 1972, Cassavetes was certainly asking after Roscoe. He questioned every pressman in the city. He also showed a quite disproportionate interest in Bassam Owdeh's death, constantly harping on the subject as he strolled with his contacts in the shade of the banyan trees where the AUB students hold their rallies. Once he called on Leila Riad, saying he was doing a feature on the late professor, but she showed him the door. The press officers of the PLO and Al Fatah remember him enquiring after Ahmad Zeiti and Walid Iskandar. They could not help.

If Cassavetes was working for Yaacov he had a bad month, and by the fourth week of it he must have started to wonder if Saladin or any of his men existed. But this despair was premature; his persistence was about to be rewarded.

11. A Narrow Escape

Yaacov, conducting a much bigger search in Israel, found it near-incredible that the nation which had traced Adolf Eichmann could not catch Bassam Owdeh, a notoriously vague academic at large within their own borders.

But Bassam stayed loose, and all through October continued to prepare the ground for Saladin. The two Arabic papers of the Occupied Territories began to discuss the prospects for an independent Palestine. The Israelis censored what they could, but could not censor the air; several Arab radio stations were now giving time to tape-recorded statements issued by Saladin. On October 19th a group of Jewish students joined hands with their Arab contemporaries and marched through the streets of Jerusalem in favour of the project. The march was quickly broken up by the police but succeeded in seriously disturbing the Israeli government. Pressure was now brought on Yaacov for results, his resources further increased.

But Saladin stayed quiet in the wings, awaiting his moment to step on the stage. He was not yet ready to join the Israeli-Arab drama, which continued to play to packed houses, the plot developing as follows.

In Libya Colonel Gadaffi closed the last Christian church and banned the consumption of alcohol by diplomats. He was planning to merge his country with Egypt, but the scheme later ran into the sands. 'Everyone in the Arab world is lost,' he said, 'and does not know where the solution to the burning problem lies.'

Immigrants to Israel reached a new high that autumn, swelled by refugees from the Soviet Union. The Arabs watched this figure as Israelis watched the number of Soviet technicians in Egypt. Sadat had dismissed the Russians from his territory in July, but now they increased their presence in Syria.

In America the election was approaching. President Nixon received five million dollars in Jewish contributions.

Mrs Meir told the Knesset that Israel's war against the terrorists could not be limited to defensive means, but turned shy when questioned on the point by a group of trusted journalists. 'Suppose some acts have been done,' she said, 'only you, the press, don't know about it. Would you expect me to tell this intimate forum right now what, if anything, has been done against terrorism?'

On October 15th the Israelis bombed Fedayeen bases at Sidon and Sarafand and President Sadat found his oratorical form. 'The cry which should fill our ears now is the cry of sweat and blood and hope,' he said, 'there is no place in our struggle for tears.' But in General Dayan's view the chances of a military victory by the Arabs had been much reduced. He called for further Jewish settlement in the Occupied Territories and said that Israel should now make the borders it wanted, 'because we now hold in our hands the design for our future'.

All through these weeks the postal war continued. Israeli embassies were deluged with booby-trapped mail and on October 25th a number of parcel bombs posted from Belgrade reached officials of the Palestinian Resistance. The PLO representative in Libya was blinded, but in Beirut the parcels exploded prematurely. A postman and a secretary were treated for serious facial injuries.

Wednesday, October 25th – that was the day on which Saladin too had a nasty shock.

Early that morning the task force had come down from the hills and dispersed for a day's home leave, their training complete. Having put them on buses to various destinations, Roscoe and Giscard reported to the monastery for a final briefing, but when they got there it was deserted, so they waited in a small dark apartment overlooking the courtyard.

This was Saladin's hideout and it smelled of his disease – a dank whiff of urine and decay. There were maps on the wall, a telephone, two small steel filing cabinets and a combination safe. Otherwise the furniture was monkish; a bed in one corner, wooden chairs on a flagged floor.

They waited there, drinking sweet minty tea as Giscard reported the progress of Bassam and Horowitz in Israel. Both men, he said, were now being hunted and so were more or less immobilized. But their task had been splendidly achieved, since the whole of Israel and the Occupied Territories was in a state of acute expectation.

Roscoe asked if Horowitz knew about the raid on Alcatraz.

'Yes, he's been told.'

'What's he say?'

'He'll help.'

'Really? That's excellent. We're on our way then.'

But Giscard looked anxious. He glanced at his watch, then made a phone call: no answer. He was smoking ceaselessly, his usual strong-smelling brand. Roscoe strolled about the monastery. Like Claudia he was touched by the spell of the place, but standing in the chapel he had a quite different experience from hers – a sudden feeling of proximity to that strange young Jew in the ikons. This was the land that man had walked, or near to it, and some of the mystery seemed to linger in this ancient shrine. It was rather disturbing. . . .

Then a car pulled up outside and Saladin came through the gate. He was walking unsteadily, his suit stained with blood.

Roscoe hurried forward to help, but Saladin waved him back. 'It's all right – I can manage. Let's go inside.'

A few minutes later, changed into fresh clothes, he told them what had happened.

Since losing the Gipsy to the task force he had been looked after by Hourani, the Lebanese officer in Tyre, who had taken leave from the army to act as chauffeur and bodyguard. That morning they had gone to meet Refo at the airport and were on their way back to Beirut when the car had been overtaken by another and riddled with bullets. Hourani, who was at the wheel, had been killed – his was the blood. Refo, though only slightly injured, had been detained in hospital. Saladin himself was unhurt and had come on as soon as he could. 'A very near miss,' he said.

Giscard was brewing more tea. 'Was it Fatah?'

'Oh yes. No question.'

'How do you know?' Roscoe said.

'They were Arabs – I saw them.'

'What were they using?'

'Kalashnikovs. Hell, can those things shoot. . . .' Some
of the terror of the occasion was briefly reflected in Saladin's
face.

'Yes, it's a pretty good weapon,' Roscoe said. 'Very rapid
fire. You were lucky.'

Saladin drank his tea, fitting a cigarette into the short amber
holder, carefully as always but now with an unmistakable
tremor of the hand. His face was drawn and hollow, his eyes
glowed hotter than before. 'We shall have to do something
about Hourani's wife,' he said to Giscard, and as arrangements
were made for the widow's welfare Roscoe heard a sum mentioned which would make her rich for the rest of her life.

They then turned to business, going through the whole plan
from the beginning: what to do in Syria if anything went wrong,
procedure for Jordan, collection of equipment in Aqaba, the
crossing of the Gulf, the hideout in Israel, the final approach to
Jerusalem. Roscoe explained again how Alcatraz would tumble,
and Saladin was satisfied.

'Now,' he said, 'I should tell you how I plan to announce
it . . .'

The meeting lasted two hours, and as Saladin talked on
Roscoe noted that like Marsden's, like Giscard's, his eyes were
always quite close to despair. He seemed now in this dark cell
to be willing himself to believe that it would happen, that in a
matter of weeks he would be the spokesman of his people,
jetting round the world from conference to speech to deferential
television interview. It was so courageous that Roscoe did not
have the heart to express any doubts and found himself saying
what was wanted, as perhaps did Giscard, until the three of
them were deep into the fantasy.

Yet by Middle Eastern standards was it so fantastical?
Nothing, after all, could be more improbable than Israel itself
– two thousand years of nostalgia suddenly translated to the
map – and even the great universal god had been invented here,
as if on this blank drawing-board of sand it was easier to sketch
a grand design. In Granby it would have sounded bunk; back
in Granby you would laugh and change the subject, but here
you could believe, absorbing the tradition of the desert, where
there never had been a great deal to do except get yourself
killed for an idea.

So at least Roscoe reflected as he travelled back to Beirut with Giscard.

That evening he went drinking in various bars of the city and word must have spread that he was back, because next morning Cassavetes came round to his hotel, asking questions.

PART FOUR

Fantasy and Death

October 26th, 1972

1. The Road to Damascus

But Cassavetes was a few hours too late. Roscoe had already started on the long eastward-looping overland journey which was to bring him back to Israel. Early that morning, Thursday 26th October, he left the Lebanon for Syria, travelling in a big blue Chevrolet saloon. Also in the car were Walid, the Gipsy and the two refugees from Nahr al-Bared, Fuad and Ibrahim. Zeiti had travelled ahead to Damascus for his sister's wedding.

At the wheel was Yussef, Roscoe's original driver, who had picked them up early from the Place des Canons and was now driving fast through the clouds which cloaked the hills behind the city. Roscoe was paying him in fresh dollar bills but Yussef was unhappy, working it off on the horn. He did not like making this trip, he did not like the look of the passengers. The only thing he liked was the fare.

'Who are these men?' he said.

'Friends of mine.'

'Fedayeen?'

'Just friends.'

'Fedayeen no bloody good, make trouble for Lebanese people. Why you go to Syria?'

'I am a tourist,' Roscoe said deliberately. 'This man Walid is my guide, these others are visiting their families. I want you to remember that.' He took out his wallet and revealed more dollar bills.

'Syrians bad people. Zero class. They cut your throat.'

'We'll take care of them. Just get us there alive.'

The Chevrolet swerved to avoid an oncoming bus then dropped through the clouds into sunlight, swooping round bends with a hiss and a squeal of tyres towards a vast green plain which faded to the burnt brown shades of the desert. They were now at the crest of the pass which leads east from Beirut. It snowed here in winter, but this was October and black long-haired goats were still grazing on the grass between the ski-lifts.

Roscoe opened a window as the air grew warmer with their descent. Now that things were on the move he felt cheerful. This was the job for which he had left Granby, and since that night long ago in his club his attitude had altered. He was no longer the neutral technician but committed now, to Palestine, and also to Claudia, for whose sake he hoped to kill no one. Those commitments were not ranked; they sat side by side in his mind and he had not examined them for any contradiction. He was in that most happy condition for a fighting man, his skills at the service of a cause in which he could see no fault.

In the previous month he had used all those skills to prepare the operation now beginning, but it was Claudia he was thinking of that fine October morning as the car swooped down towards the plain of eastern Lebanon. He tried to resurrect her all of a piece but could only see independent bits of her, first one and then another – the way she squinted at those dishes in the restaurant, the birthmark on her neck, her legs below the Palestinian dress, the look in her eyes when he kissed her at the Casino . . .

After the incident with Gessner they had found a beach and walked along it in the moonlight. But the mood between them was disturbed.

'What a horrible man,' she had said.

'Gessner? He's a joke. A bit pathetic really.'

'He would have killed you.'

'I dare say.'

'So you'd have shot him first?'

'If I had to.'

'That's what soldiers always say, isn't it?'

Inexplicably irritated, she had kicked off her shoes and waded into the sea while he sat glum on the beach. He was easily persuaded that she was too good for him. It hurt, nonetheless.

After a while she had come back and sat down beside him. He had got up to go, but she had put a hand on his arm. 'Stephen, promise me you won't do something you're ashamed of.'

'I have certain standards. But you know how it is – soldiers always say that.'

'Please, don't be cross. Sit down, talk to me. You dislike yourself, don't you?'

'Not really.'

'It looks like that to me.'

'Perhaps I do, now.'

'Not before?'

'Before I could live with it.'

'So what's different now?'

She knew, but since she asked he would tell her. 'You,' he said.

'Me?'

'I mind what you think.'

She had taken her hand off his arm then, as if to relieve him of her presence. He could not see her face in the dark but knew when she spoke that she was smiling. 'You want to know what I think, Stephen dear?'

'Yes. What do you think?'

'I think I like you very much.'

She had said it in the sort of voice which bright English girls reserve for such confessions – surprised, amused, objective – as if she had spotted something curious under a microscope. And he, still guarded, had mumbled that his feelings were similar.

'Say it then.'

'I like you very much. I shall miss you. How's that?'

'That's all right.'

Cautious statements; but the words were a deed, a fact had been created. For a moment they had sat on the sand in awkward silence then Claudia had taken the initiative, running her lips across his cheek towards his ear. 'Kiss me again,' she had said, breathing right into him with that startling skill of hers, 'come on, kiss me.' And so he had kissed her, and then the last door banged open and he had let the warm essence of her fill that empty place where he lived, so orderly and safe but really very dull, and now seen at last for what it was, the result of timidity or perhaps just of laziness, since in matters of the heart he always played safe, preferring a life of routine to the troublesome business of human relations. But that had all ended one month ago; that whole safe, manageable, solitary life had ended on a beach in the Lebanon as he kissed her and pushed her back down on the sand. . . .

Or had it? Had anything significant happened at all? She had occupied his thoughts, even more so in absence, but now he could not remember her, and with the memory had faded the warmth, as hard to recall as a summer day in winter.

That vexed Roscoe, it worried him. It made him think something must be wrong with him, and so another reason why he was glad to be on the move was that this road led to the bridge across the Jordan where she would be waiting. The others would cross from Aqaba but he was to go into Israel on his passport, over the Allenby Bridge, where Claudia would meet him. Yes, there was much to look forward to in Israel. There things would be decided, and he would take them in order. First he wanted to get to the Jordan, to see her again; then on to Jerusalem and do the job cleanly, in a way she could respect, or tolerate at least. Because his contract must be honoured, he had got her agreement to that on the beach, without however specifying what was to be done. She had not asked him and he had not told her. She had offered to meet him, that was all. The rest had been left in the air. . . .

The car was on the flat now, racing through apple orchards, neat fields of cabbage and onions, vineyards and trailers piled with sugar beet. Further east the fertility diminished, it was back to figs and goats again, looking at a distance like swarms of black flies on the plain. Close up ahead were the hills which marked the border with Syria.

Roscoe put Claudia from his mind and reviewed the progress of the previous month.

Nothing for a long time had been so enjoyable as the weeks spent training in the hills above the monastery. There he had taught his team to shoot, more for reasons of morale than any specifically murderous intention. He had taught them to handle explosives, how to set a detonator and where to place the charges to blow a building flat. Echoes had bounced around the rock as bursts of nine-millimetre ripped into targets concealed between the olive trees and derelict farmhouses vanished into dust and flying stone. He had shown them how to operate a radio, use natural cover, read a map, march at night, protect themselves from air attack; and the Arabs had taught him how to live in the heat, how to ration his energies and do without water and where to find food when there seemed to be none.

Each week he had watched their discipline improve. Four desperate men, a Gipsy and an English professional – it was not a bad team, he thought.

The Gipsy's two talents were murder and survival. He would of course desert them in a corner, because gipsies do not die for politics. Walid on the other hand was fanatical; he would march until his feet bled, as if doing penance for the wasted years in Al Fatah. Fuad and Ibrahim, the two new recruits, wanted only revenge, dour family men in their forties who had lost friends and relatives to the Phantoms of Israel. At first they had seemed unsuitable material, but the stint in the hills had put pride in their eyes and vigour in their limbs; they had even been seen to smile once or twice. Now they sat in the back, either side of the Gipsy, perhaps wondering whether they would see their families again and probably not caring much. If they died in Jerusalem their sons would remember them with pride.

The plain was behind them now as Yussef took the car into the second range of hills and on towards the Syrian border through crags of white rock etched sharp against the sky. Cultivation had ceased; the light was so fierce it scorched the eyes. Here again Roscoe felt that sudden sharp focus of the senses, and knew it had to do with the presence of death – because that was another thing about the Middle East: there was death in the air here, distinct as a smell, which gave to the act of existence this hard, bright edge.

Down the road now was the frontier, surrounded by long-distance trucks, Mercedes and Berliets, colossal wheeled caravans of the desert with intricate floral designs on their bodywork and number plates showing that they came from as far as Iraq and Kuwait.

Yussef drove past them and parked at the head of the queue. 'Syrians no good,' he said, 'zero class,' and walked off to the customs post.

Roscoe got out to stretch his legs.

The heat was like a blow to the head. The truck drivers sat in the shade of their vehicles, in no hurry to move. An old woman scavenged in the garbage which lay about the valley, her feet stumbling over the rocks in old laceless army boots. Other women sat beside the road, shielding their faces with veils against the dust.

A land of death, a land of dreams . . .

Watching the old one, Roscoe made the connection. Back in
little old England, so tidy and green, a man could live for himself, sufficient to himself; a land without extremes had bred a
prosaic people. But here, out in these dusty wastes, the life of
an individual man was so meagre and fragile that he would seek
to transcend it. Yes, this desert man required fantasy as others
need bread, and rather than wake from his dream he would
gallop to death – might even long for it, preferring the green
grass of paradise to the knowledge he'd been fooled. Yes, that
was it, that was what reeked in the air here, not death but *death-
wish*, the special brand of madness of the Semites. And this
being so, it was surely no accident that the only man suggesting
a settlement was dying of natural causes; a man in effect already
dead, and so without delusions. . . .

A few minutes later Yussef returned from the customs post.
'Everything hokay,' he said, and drove on to immigration
control. They disembarked again, each holding his papers for
clearance, and pushed into a hall full of peasantry shouting
through the grills at Syrian officials – and there too was Dominic
Morley, shouting the loudest, pink-faced in his off-white safari
suit. 'Television,' he was screeching, press card in hand, 'see
this? Te-le-vision . . .'

Roscoe watched the drama unobserved, and when his own
passport was safely stamped *Tourist* stepped forward to console
the defeated.

Morley looked up in surprise. 'Oh hello,' he said, 'you still
around? The bastards won't let me through.'

'So I saw.'

'Bloody Arabs.'

'Still chasing Black September?'

Morley glanced round in alarm, then led Roscoe outside.
'Careful, man, we could get lynched.'

'Surely not. Had any luck?'

Morley shook his head dejectedly. He had managed by this
time to interview Arafat, but his masters had sent him back for
more. 'They want film on this guy Saladin, but shit, man, where
is he? I tell you, I've had enough. I could grow old here.'

Roscoe asked if he was going to Israel.

Morley replied that he was; he would be there in a week.

'Where will you stay?'

'Jerusalem.'

'What hotel?'

'The American Colony. Why, are you going there?'

'I'll be there,' Roscoe said, 'on the sixth. Can you wait?'

'I don't know . . .'

'I could have something for you.'

Morley's eyes sharpened. 'Hey, what is this? You're in on something.'

Roscoe smiled enigmatically. 'If you get your name in lights you can buy me a drink.'

'Come on, man, open up.'

'See you on the sixth then. The American Colony.'

Saladin's men were back in the Chevrolet. Yussef rapped the horn. Roscoe said good-bye and as he passed on into Syria looked back to see Morley's car manoeuvre through the trucks and head towards Beirut. He wondered what Saladin would think of the idea.

2. All the Beauty is Within

Syria was soldiers and dust. Half the male population was in uniform, clapping and singing as they rode along in trucks, thumbing lifts outside camp gates, drilling at the trot on dusty parade grounds, and the dust covered everything, boots uniforms and vehicles, bleaching the sparse vegetation and the black crinkly hair of the soldiers to the universal khaki of the desert. No rain had fallen that year. The staple industry of Syria was war against Israel, subsidized by the Russians, and here for the second time – the first was in Juwaiya – Roscoe felt a twinge of unease at what he had got himself into, an instinct that something quite nasty could happen and a sudden desire to be out, if not back to Lebanon then quickly on to Jordan, where the madness might be less he thought, tempered by the noble traditions of Sandhurst and the Bedouin.

His Browning was in a shoulder holster under his jacket. Walid too was armed. The Gipsy carried only a knife.

Shortly after 10 a.m. they reached Damascus, a city which bore the grandiose imprint of the French – parks and squares and boulevards succumbing to neglect. The buildings were crumbling, the roads cracked as if by an earthquake. Rising to the north was a range of white rock, its lower slopes littered with the shacks of refugees.

Yussef pulled up at the New Ommayad Hotel, where disconsolate Russians sat drinking orange juice under the fans and a party of French milled about in the lobby, on a side-trip from a cruise ship berthed in Beirut. Fuad and Ibrahim waited there while Roscoe and Walid went off to find Zeiti. The Gipsy walked behind to check they were not followed.

Roscoe had mixed feelings about Zeiti, who throughout the period of training had seemed as committed as the rest – energetic, resourceful, a guerilla natural-born, who enjoyed the

whole business as he himself did. To refuse him home leave
would have made him suspicious, nor could he yet be abandoned, since the only safe policy was to keep him with the party
until the objective had to be revealed. But he would without
doubt have used this interval to report to his masters, and so
the rendezvous agreed was the tomb of Sultan Saladin, a senti-
mental gesture but also a prudent one, since ambush would be
difficult in a public place. Roscoe was nervous about it all the
same and glad to have Walid along, of whom he now had a
high opinion.

They walked a few yards apart, past a cavernous barracks.
The parks too were crowded with soldiers, lying in groups on
the grass, strolling about hand in hand. In the centre a dense
throng of people surged through the streets, parting only for the
buses, battered old charabancs with vertical exhausts. Spivs
were hawking Kent cigarettes and a boy was making money
with an air rifle, offering the chance to fire a suction dart between the tits of a famous Western cover girl.

In character if not in distance Damascus was a long way from
Beirut. This was Arabia, and one of its least accessible cities at
that. Here the people were harder, poorer, swarthier, proud to
the point of permanent anger and charged – or so it seemed to
Roscoe – with a quivering potential for hysteria. Walking on
through them he was as conspicuous as an infidel in Mecca, and
yet he felt invisible. No one looked at him or tried to sell him
anything. Only beggar children touched him, little fingers
creeping into his until slapped away by angry adults. If the
Syrians had to let an Englishman into their capital they preferred to ignore him.

Walid smiled back across the heads of the throng as they
pushed their way through the Souk al Hamadiya, a tall dark
arcade with curved iron roof, like a London railway terminus.
The Gipsy caught them up. No one was behind, he said.

At the end of the souk they came to the Ommayad Mosque.
Walid took Roscoe inside and proudly showed him the interior,
the glass chandeliers and tall Roman columns. Fathers and sons
sat cross-legged on the acres of carpet, the women white-
sheeted in a separate enclosure. Birds swooped and circled
below the painted roof, a soft flap of wings above the murmur
of talk. People walked around in their socks or just rested, as

s.—G

they used to in cathedrals, and at the far end an old man stood
kissing the tomb of John the Baptist.

'For us he was a very great prophet,' Walid said.

As the mosque filled for prayer they strolled out into a wide
adjoining courtyard, where they sat for a while in the shade of a
flanking colonnade and looked across the freshly hosed paving
towards the minaret where Muslims said Jesus would touch
down on Doomsday. It was a beautiful place, clean and cool
and quiet, shutting out completely the dust and uproar of the
city.

'That is the Arab way,' Walid said. 'All the beauty is within,
you see.'

Roscoe looked at his watch as the sheikh's voice began to
recite the Koran. It was almost eleven.

'We'd better go,' he said.

Walid stood up reluctantly, brushing down his freshly
laundered clothes. 'It is not far from here.'

They recovered their shoes and worked round the walls of the
mosque to the right, through a quarter where the houses seemed
to grow from the sediment of history, their walls stuffed with
chunks of Roman pillar and Byzantine masonry. Walid said
Damascus was the oldest city in the world and now Roscoe saw
what an Arab town should look like: a human hive sculpted
from the earth, proof against desert winds and sun. The streets
were like tunnels and full of strange sights – cripples on trolleys,
men smoking water-pipes, a barber's shop converted to shoe-
shine – and through a beaded doorway he caught a glimpse of
a steam bath, morose-looking men wrapped in towels sweating
in silence round a pool. They passed through the gold market,
a dull glint of loot in the dark – and then Roscoe heard a word
he knew.

'*Salah-deen!*'

He turned in surprise to see a gang of small boys, grinning and
barefoot.

'*Salah-deen!*' they shrilled, tugging at his sleeve as Walid led
the way down an alley which ended in a small deserted square
below the northern wall of the mosque. In the centre stood a
squat stone building with a dome ribbed like a melon, at which
the boys pointed, dancing in the dust.

'*Salah-deen! Salah-deen!*'

Roscoe distributed coins and they scampered off in search of more suckers as the Gipsy appeared from the shadows, his wizened face grinning like a monkey's. There was no sign of Zeiti.

'You two go that way,' Roscoe said.

They divided, worked round the sides of the square, then met behind a clump of tired trees in front of the mausoleum's entrance. Roscoe scanned the black bars of shadow, dry in the mouth.

'Stay here. I'll go in.'

Walid looked puzzled. He did not know – none of them did – that Zeiti belonged to Black September. He asked what was wrong.

'Nothing probably. Just keep your eyes open and cover me – the way we practised it.'

Walid nodded, looking hurt. He knew now there was something Roscoe had not told him, and anything less than perfect trust was disappointing.

Roscoe signalled to the Gipsy to come with him.

3. Blood on the Carpet

Inside the mausoleum it was dark, musty like an unused church. The floor was strewn with carpets, the walls set with porcelain tiles and strips of black basalt.

When they saw it was empty the Gipsy retreated back into the sun and squatted on the doorstep to smoke a cigarette, his hand cupped around it. For these travels he was wearing a suit – only the jacket did not match the trousers and both looked as old as himself, the sort of clothes which turn up in auctions of dead men's effects. His head was still wrapped in a red-check kefia.

While they waited Roscoe strolled around inside, stooping to catch the garbled English of an elderly caretaker.

So this was the tomb of the great man himself, scourge of the Crusaders, saviour of Jerusalem. It had a Germanic look, like the vaults of the Hapsburgs in Vienna, and sure enough the caretaker said it had been built by Kaiser Wilhelm II. The sepulchre was raised on a platform and above it hung a lamp engraved with the monogram of Wilhelm and his Ottoman ally, Abdul the Damned.

Outside the boys had found another client. Again they were chanting the name Saladin, and now for the first time Roscoe was struck by the power in that word. Its tame English spelling, even in the more correct version of Salah-ed-Din, gave no hint of its forceful sound in Arabic – that short double bark, then a catch in the throat and the long third syllable expelled through the teeth.

'*Salah-deen!*'

More than a name, it was a battlecry. With that cry the cowed ranks of Palestine would rise to claim their rights. . . . So thinking, exultant with the giddy romance of this whole brave adventure, Roscoe turned towards the door and saw that

Zeiti was standing there, framed in the brilliant shaft of sun. He was wearing a white shirt and tight-fitting jeans, carrying a shoulder bag of Syrian Arab Airways.

Roscoe was concealed by the tomb. Zeiti stepped into the dark, peering round as he approached across the carpets. Then a second person came through the door. It took Roscoe a moment to recognize Gessner, and another to gather his wits. But Gessner did not pause; he had come a long way for this, followed his man, chosen his moment. He pulled a pistol from his belt, planted his feet and aimed at Zeiti's back. Roscoe shouted, Zeiti dived, and the first bullet hit the platform of the tomb. Zeiti scrambled sideways, yelping in pain as Gessner fired again. Gessner's two shots were muted by a silencer but were followed by two more, the stunning reports produced by a Browning, like iron doors slamming in the resonant building. As Roscoe fired twice into his middle Gessner bellowed then lurched forward, doubled up, clutching his stomach, trying to get his gun up, until the Gipsy yanked back his head and slit his throat. He then collapsed on the floor with the sound of a man being violently sick as Roscoe ran past him and out through the door. The boys were sprinting away in every direction. The caretaker stood open-mouthed, then sank to his knees. Walid was running from the trees. 'Hang on to him,' Roscoe shouted, pointing at the caretaker, then ducked back inside.

Gessner was flapping on the carpet, spouting blood. The Gipsy stood watching with a grin until Roscoe leaned down and fired again, point-blank to the skull.

Then Zeiti stumbled forward, clutching his arm, eyes rolling upwards. Roscoe caught him. 'Can you walk?'

Zeiti's answer was inaudible. They had both been deafened by the shots, so Roscoe had to shout and gesticulate.

'Take it easy, you're okay. Walid, hold him. Now let's get out of here, quick.'

Released by Walid, the caretaker fell to his knees again. Roscoe hauled him to his feet, shouting 'Keys! Tell him to give us the keys.'

That was done, and they locked the door behind them, leaving Gessner where he was. Roscoe dragged the caretaker with him by the collar. 'Don't run,' he shouted, 'walk,' and then they

were back in the tunnels of the city, zig-zagging blindly away
from the mosque. Only Zeiti knew Damascus well enough to
get them out of the maze. 'How are you doing?' Roscoe bawled
at him. 'Keep moving, keep moving. Straight on . . . then left?
Come on then, let's go.'

Brown adobe tunnels, a blue strip of sky between the eaves.
More people now, children following. . . .

'Don't run! Zeiti, listen, we've got to get out of this. I want a
road. Can we get a taxi? Left again here? Well done, you're
okay, keep your arm up, keep it up – there, hold it like that.'

An old man with mules; a scooter, swerving back to look. But
no police, no soldiers. Traffic. A road up ahead. . . .

'Well done! Walid, are you listening? Here's what I want you
to do. The rest of us will go on to Jordan, you stay behind here
with Zeiti.'

'No,' said Zeiti, 'no!'

'Shut up. Walid, keep him with you, understand?'

Walid was steady now, concentrating.

'Keep the taxi and take Zeiti on to an address which I'll give
you. When you get there ask to speak to Rashid Fawzi, repeat
Fawzi. Don't speak to anyone else. Tell Fawzi you've come
from Saladin, tell him the dead man is a Zionist agent, we've
got the only witness and we're going straight on to the frontier.
Then leave Zeiti there and come on yourself as soon as you can.
We'll wait for you in Jordan. Hold him, hold him up – that's it,
one arm each. Now quick, a taxi . . .'

'There's one over there,' Walid said, and after that for a little
while longer it was all talk and action, as they drove through the
city then scrambled back into the Chevrolet, though even while
this was going on Roscoe could hear the doors slamming in his
mind, shutting out the helpless Jew on the carpet. Well, it was
done, and within minutes his gun was out again, levelled at
Yussef below the dashboard.

'Take us to Jordan. That's what I paid you for.'

Yussef was truculent. He had got a look at Zeiti.

'Finish! No more,' he shouted, 'I go to Beirut,' then he said
something in Arabic sufficiently offensive for Fuad to punch
him in the back of the neck. The caretaker was crying, the Gipsy
had his knife out, the car was a tin box of male sweat and panic,
death skipping about inside it like a roulette ball as Roscoe

rammed the Browning into Yussef's side, sank it right up to the trigger guard in the soft rolls of flesh and yelled 'Drive!'

Yussef's eyes bulged. 'Hokay, we go,' he said, managing to sound simultaneously outraged and pliant, 'no trouble please.' He patted back the gun then accelerated forward with his hand on the horn, through the shambles of Damascus and out through the suburbs, scattering children, chickens, goats, past the shells of old cars and buildings half-finished or half-ruined. Soldiers leapt out of the shadows thumbing lifts, jumped back as the car gathered speed, and then they were away on the road south to Jordan, a narrow strip of tarmac which led across a rolling brown plain to the hazy horizon.

Roscoe kept his eyes on the receding city, but nothing came after them. The road was empty behind and in front, perfectly straight and flanked by an endless line of telegraph poles. Where it met the horizon it seemed to melt to water, but something was coming towards them now, it seemed to be suspended above the liquid shimmer then materialized into a bus. Pebbles and rocks slammed into the belly of the Chevrolet as Yussef drove past it at speed, two wheels clinging to the tarmac. It would take him three hours to get to the frontier.

Roscoe relaxed and lit a cigarette, suppressing a tremor in his hands. His pulse slowed to normal. Images of Gessner's last moments hovered like bats at the edge of his mind.

The caretaker pulled himself together. The others began to laugh and chatter, but to Roscoe they seemed far away. He heard them from a distance and thought they were like silly children, but no sillier than he, with his dreams of a good clean fight and a girl at the end. No fight was clean, he of all people should have known that, because however it started, it ended with blood on the floor and this feeling of nothing, this numbness. Like sex, the more often you did it the easier it got, the more casual.

When he thought of Gessner he felt only sorry for himself, but was not the least tempted to renege on Saladin. On the contrary now he felt compelled to go on, like a drunk or a gambler reverting to type, and was almost relieved to have lapsed, because this functional numbness was the right mood for battle, temporarily lost to a girl in the Lebanon, now recovered.

Suddenly exhausted, he lit a second cigarette to keep himself awake. The road stretched ahead. Yussef had the needle up to eighty. Far to the right were the blue hills of Golan and over in the east the desert which stretched to Iraq; but here, either side of the road, the same never-ending, rolling brown plain – arable land, Roscoe thought, from the scratches on its surface, though he could not imagine what grew here. The villages were barely discernible, of the same stuff and colour as the earth, a scatter of brown cubic shapes in the emptiness.

So they raced on, and Syria reeled past like a film, a scratchy old sepia flick with odd bits of action – a boy holding out a brace of quail, another boy galloping nowhere on a donkey; women with preposterous loads on their heads; a group of them, gathered round a water pipe. The water was splashing down into a conduit, a beautiful arc of it, precious as diamonds.

The sight provoked thirst. The Gipsy passed forward his bottle.

Roscoe took it from him with a smile. You murderous little monkey-faced monster, he thought. We are two of a kind, you and I.

Fuad and Ibrahim were dozing now and between them the old Syrian caretaker sat with pleading eyes. Roscoe informed him he was not going to die then thought for a while about the Jordanian frontier. They would have to part with Yussef when they got there; no through traffic was allowed. Half the Arab world was trying to kill Hussein, so in Jordan there was going to be a search. But Saladin had said he would have a man there. Saladin had a man everywhere.

They passed through Deraa, where the Turks had done something nasty to Lawrence, and soon after that reached the Syrian border post. Half-expecting arrest, they walked through without incident as Yussef turned back to Damascus with the caretaker. Walid had done his work well.

In Jordan a long queue of vehicles was waiting to be searched. The police wore starched shorts and spiked sola topis and next to the customs shed was a building more splendid than anything in Syria with a sign up in English and Arabic saying TOILETS.

Roscoe was worried about the search, but then out through the gates of a military compound strode a smart army officer, and with him another man, silver-haired and nimble of step.

'Jimmy!'

'Hello, Stephen.'

'What the devil are you doing here?'

'Inspecting the troops,' Marsden said breezily.

4. Sour Dreams

Saladin's allies in Jordan were three Palestinian army officers, two of whom had lost their nerve the previous day – hence Marsden's unexpected presence. The third was the man with him now, a young major of infantry called Muammar Nazreddin, who was on the King's staff; a slim man, dashing, moustached, about forty but younger in appearance, who had lost his right hand to an Israeli mortar bomb. Sandhurst had left its mark too. 'Good to have you with us,' he said to Roscoe, holding out his left hand reversed for a shake. The other was a rigid leather glove.

Roscoe was very pleased to see him. All power in Jordan stemmed from the palace, and with Nazreddin on their side they would have no problems. Without him they would have been finished. Nazreddin had assembled the equipment required for the assault; he was also providing a base in Aqaba and would prepare their return across the border into Jordan. Now he volunteered to wait for Walid.

Marsden took Roscoe and the others on down to Amman, talking of Gessner as he drove.

'What typical bloody Jewish foolishness, to go blasting off in Damascus.'

'Foolish or brave,' Roscoe said, 'depending on your prejudice.'

'How the hell did he get there?'

'God knows.'

Later the details emerged. Gessner had boarded the French ship in Istanbul, using a West German passport and timing his arrival in Damascus to coincide with Zeiti's return there. The murder was splashed all over the press. In the end Al Fatah took the credit, though for two days Marsden was worried that Roscoe had been compromised.

Driving down through Jordan he fretted all the way, his early good humour turned to petulance, as if the killing was a piece of regrettable indiscipline. When they reached Amman it was dark. Marsden dropped the others at a modest suburban hotel and took Roscoe on to the Intercontinental, preserving the concept of an officers' mess.

The Intercontinental outdid Kubla Khan; it was a palace on a hill, marble-floored, air-conditioned, with fountains in the lobby, two swimming pools and décor from the Arabian Nights. Roscoe followed a porter up to his room and ordered a bottle of whisky. He drank some, took a shower, drank some more, topped up his glass and put on a clean shirt. He felt extremely hungry.

Marsden was waiting in the penthouse restaurant, where they ate overlooking the lights of the city while a girl at a piano sang Beatles oldies. At the bar was a man Roscoe thought he knew from Beirut, and sitting at a table in the corner a noisy Scandinavian airline crew. The eye of the stewardess was roving.

Marsden continued to fret. 'Putting it away a bit, aren't you?'

'Killing Jews is thirsty work. What's yours?'

'No more for me.'

What very poor taste, Roscoe told himself, to let the man think I am drinking to forget. I'm not drinking to forget. I'm just drinking.

Marsden then asked about Claudia. 'What's she like?'

'Full of charity.'

'Any good to us?'

'I don't think she's been much involved.'

Marsden picked at his steak. 'That chum of yours, Nina Brown . . .'

'Brown? What about her?'

'After you'd gone she kept on at me. Wanted to know where you were, ringing up all hours. She was keen to come out here, but I said it wouldn't do.'

'Quite right.'

'She's living in your house, you know.'

'She's still at Granby?'

'Said she was a farmer.'

'Well I never. Good old Brown.' Roscoe pushed away his plate and helped himself to one of Marsden's thin cheroots. 'Tell me, who's this Refo?'

'Do you need to know?'

'Don't be silly, man, I'm into this deeper than you.'

Marsden was persuaded to divulge. He lowered his voice. 'He works for an oil company – one of the big boys. That's a natural alliance if you think about it.' He paused, then said something more prophetic than he knew. 'If war breaks out again the Arabs could turn off the tap.'

'So this company is backing a settlement with the Palestinians.'

'Hitherto prevented by lack of a suitable negotiator.'

'How much are they doing?'

'Money, logistical support. I'd better not tell you who they are.'

'No, don't bother. Mystery solved.'

Roscoe cast a bleary eye at the airline crew. The pilots had gone off to bed; she was stuck with the steward.

Marsden signed the bill. 'Don't get drunk, there's a good chap. I'll say good night now.'

'Good night.'

Left to himself, Roscoe moved to the bar and settled on a stool beside the man from Beirut, who swivelled and held out a hand, as if he had been waiting to talk. It was Nick Cassavetes.

Roscoe asked what he was drinking.

'Just orange.'

'Nothing in it?'

'No thanks.'

Cassavetes had flown in from Beirut that day. He said the agency wanted a piece on Hussein's divorce from Muna, the English girl from Ipswich who had borne him two sons. 'A real sob story.'

Roscoe agreed, Muna had been wronged.

Cassavetes retailed the latest royal gossip, dipping into his orange juice with a small snuffling laugh. Afterwards Roscoe could not remember much about him, and there was in fact little to remember. Cassavetes had no distinctive traits, no character almost. The man was as dull as his clothes, which were utilitarian, without any style new or old. A most unusual journalist – except in his curiosity about other journalists. He asked Roscoe what he was doing in Jordan.

'Oh just swanning about, you know.'

'Come through Syria?'

'Yes, got in tonight. Not bad, is she?'

'Excuse me?'

'Over there, in the uniform.'

'Yeah, cute. How long are you here?'

'A few days.'

'In Amman?'

'Thought I'd look at the country.'

'Then where?'

The questions came slightly too fast. Even Roscoe, in his present fuddled state, was alerted. He excused himself as the air hostess got up to leave, still escorted by the steward.

She hesitated, smiled, agreed to dance. Her name was Anna, from Denmark; a big girl, bulging up against him. They danced until the steward left, drank, then danced some more. Cassavetes left. The pianist left, putting on a tape. They danced until the tape ran out. Roscoe made a suggestion. 'All right,' she said, and when they got to his room undid her uniform, opening her arms with a friendly Danish smile as her big breasts swung loose. Roscoe pushed her down on the bed. 'Yes,' she said, 'yes, go on, do it,' and he did it, what he had not done to Claudia, plumbed between her strong Danish legs, pinning back her arms as she heaved about beneath him, plumbed and ground his teeth and thought out with it, this is it, this is what it comes to, blood and sperm and bullets, nothing else to do but shoot and fuck and shoot . . .

Afterwards he lay with his eyes shut and listened to her breathing beside him. He could smell her, the most intimate smell of a girl he did not know. Already he was wondering what had possessed him.

'You English are so rough,' she said.

'I'm sorry.'

'No, I like it.' She stroked his spine. 'You're so strong. Oh, Stephen . . .'

Roscoe turned over and gently pressed her back, revolted by the use of his name. 'You should get some sleep now.'

'I will sleep with you, and in the morning . . .'

He smiled and shook his head. 'It's a nice idea, Anna, but you'd better go.'

She looked at him with wide, hurt eyes. 'Will I see you again?'
'No, I don't think so.'
'All right, I will go. Good-bye, Stephen.'
'Good-bye, Anna.'

That was the last event of the day and he forgot it with the rest. After she had gone he span away into sleep.

Later he woke feeling ill. He had dreamed he was walking down a line of kneeling men, who pitched forward into a trench as he shot them one by one through the back of the skull. They were dressed in the clothes of the dead, unmatching suits and old overcoats, but when they fell into the trench they were naked, a tangle of limbs, flapping feebly. He moved along the line, then came to a woman who had coarse grizzled hair tied back in a bun – even from behind he recognized Golda Meir. But when she tumbled into the trench, he saw he had shot Mrs Parsons.

Having woken, he was sick. And then he was laughing – at the dream, at himself, and at the Intercontinental tumblers by the basin, which were wrapped in paper bags marked STERIL-IZED FOR YOUR PROTECTION. He unpacked one and rinsed out his mouth, then came back to the window of the bedroom.

Outside it was just getting light. Beyond the plate-glass Amman was a spread of white boxes pierced by tall minarets, pencil shapes aimed at the grey sky like missiles, and from each of them now came the amplified groan of a muezzin, dragging the city from sleep into prayer.

Roscoe listened to the sound, watched the light grow. A new day, another city; sleeping near by a stray fellow-animal injected with his seed, and over there another one, dead from his bullets. Well, what the hell. It all came to nothing in the end, so the best you could do was laugh at the joke. Laugh, do your job, take the money. Kill if you had to, survive as long as you could. Enjoy what you could, because at the end there was nothing. . . .

Still clutching a sterilized glass he watched the sky turn pale above Amman, and again he chuckled wryly, struck by the notion that if this was the dawn of his death he was in the right condition to greet it – empty in heart, mind, stomach and scrotum. Then he sat on the bed and took out his gun, field-stripped it and laid out the parts on a handkerchief. He pulled strips of rag through the barrel until they were coming out perfectly clean, and then held it up to his eyes, angling it to catch the first rays of the sun.

Oh yes, he thought, I'm ready.

PART FIVE

Move and Counter Move

October 27th – November 5th, 1972

1. The Midnight Caller

It was Friday, October 27th – dawn in Amman but in Granby just after midnight, and as Roscoe cleaned his pistol Nina Brown was lying on the floor of his drawing room, her head propped against the belly of a mastiff, her feet on the polished brass rail of the fender. The room was lit only by the fire. Outside an east wind was hurling the sea against the wall, such a fury of water and air that she could hear the surf even with the gramophone on. But here it was warm, it was comfortable.

The stubble had been burnt and ploughed in, the grain sold in Lincoln. She had ordered more fuel for the boiler and made a quilt out of Indian cottons for the bed. Georgie was going to nursery school, a daily detachment which had greatly improved their relations.

Life had been further enhanced by the arrival that day of a small flat parcel, posted from Fort Worth, Texas. Inside was a paperback novel and the message *Sweet dreams, Nina girl, love Jim*. The pages had been hollowed out with a knife and packed with a polythene bag of brown powder. Now she had got one rolled and was smoking it.

She remembers the moment because of what followed. Watching the flames, listening to the music and the surf, she was wondering how many men she had had in her life.

Georgie's father had taken her to a motel called The Firebird. She had cancelled the abortion on an impulse, but when the idea became flesh she could never quite believe what she had done. Georgie was cute, but she saw him as an independent wonder of nature rather than a creature of her own. She did not feel at all the way a mother ought to feel. That visceral change, self-fulfilling, self-annihilating, which had claimed all her friends one by one, had passed her by. A biological fault in herself, she sometimes thought – or perhaps something lacking in the act of conception. Events at The Firebird had been a disappointment. There had been others better, many others. Too many. She stopped counting.

She thought about Jim out in Texas, then about Roscoe, God knew where. Sometimes she missed him. She kept certain snapshots in the memory – out on the sand with his dogs, screwing up his face as he cut a cigar, the way he rubbed tonic on his hair – the *smell* of that stuff! It lingered in the bedroom, permeated deeper than her own scents of musk and patchouli. The wardrobes were clogged with his heavy shoes and shaggy patched jackets, preserved by Mrs Parsons with mothballs.

Roscoe haunted his house like a man recently dead and like a new widow Brown expected him to walk through the door any moment. But as soon as it happened they would quarrel, she knew. The next day or the next she would get a pain in her neck, a pressure in the head like a migraine. She would be foul again and he would kick her out. To avoid that she ought to remove herself now, but the prospect of London was daunting. She was too old to be a vagabond; the jobs she might enjoy sh e could not get, the jobs she could get she did not want. She could not think what to do and so had stayed at Granby, prolonging a life that was over, like a widow.

She finished the joint and made another. The flames had risen higher, enveloping the log. The house creaked and rattled in the wind. The gramophone had switched itself off but she lay where she was and smoked on, half asleep, until the phone rang.

'Hello?'

A man asked to speak to Stephen Roscoe.

'He's not here,' she said.

'Is he abroad?'

'I don't know where he is. Who is this please?'

'A friend of his. Surely you know where he is.'

'No, I'm sorry, I don't.'

'It's important,' the man said. 'I have to get in touch with him.'

'I'm sorry, I can't help you.'

He had a quiet voice, polite yet insistent, with a slight indefinable accent. He repeated his question, then asked when Roscoe would be back.

'I don't know that either.'

'But you're living in his house, Miss Brown. You and your child.'

'You know my name?'

'Yes I do.'

'Who *are* you?'

'Please tell me everything you know about what Stephen Roscoe is doing . . .'

'The heck I will.'

'. . . and you will come to no harm.'

'Harm? Did you say harm?'

'That's right.'

'What is this, some kind of threat or what?'

'Call it a warning.'

'Well whoever you are you're wasting your time. I don't know a thing.'

'Who sent him to Beirut? Was it Marsden?'

'Look, man, I don't know who you are, I don't know what any of this is about, right? So do me a favour and get off the line.'

'Miss Brown . . .'

'Sorry, brother, some other time.'

'Don't hang up, Miss Brown. Please, that would be stupid. We are not far away. We shall kill your child first, and then you.'

The sea sounded ready to come over; the room seemed suddenly cold, the house as frail as cardboard.

'Miss Brown? Are you there?'

'Yes. Yes, I'm here.'

'I think you know we mean it.'

'Okay, I believe you. Just go ahead and tell me what you want. But please, will you leave my son out of it?'

'Answer my question. Where is Stephen Roscoe?'

'Jesus, I'm telling you the truth, I don't *know*. He went to Beirut on a job. That's all he told me, a job in Beirut, nothing else. He's been gone six weeks and he didn't say when he'd be back.'

'What about Marsden?'

'He came here, a few days before. They went on the beach. I don't know what they said.'

'And that's all you know?'

'Yes.'

'No letters, no postcards?'

'One from Beirut, about three weeks ago.'

'What did it say?'

'Nothing. No news, I mean.'

'Okay, I believe you.' The man's voice shifted to a friendlier tone. 'Your friend Stephen Roscoe is a very stupid man, Miss Brown. If you want him back alive you must cooperate. Otherwise I cannot guarantee it, do you understand?'

'I understand,' said Brown.

The man then instructed her to find out from Marsden, on the pretext of some domestic emergency, where Roscoe was at that moment. He said he would call back at noon and rang off.

Brown immediately woke Mrs Parsons. They held an urgent conference in the kitchen, then Mrs Parsons cabled her sister in Withernsea, a seaside resort east of Hull. Brown packed a suitcase, then loaded a shotgun from the rack and collected her car from the garage. Mrs Parsons woke Georgie, wrapped him in blankets and laid him on the back seat.

'You'll like Withernsea. It's a lot more lively than what Granby is.'

Brown hugged her. 'Thanks, Katie. Sure you won't come?'

'No, it wouldn't be right, not with him away and all. Anyroad they'll not bother me, not with them dogs about.'

'You'd better call the police.'

'Don't you fret, love. I'll be all right.'

Brown said she would telephone Marsden in the morning – Roscoe had left the AAI number – then drove off, keeping the shotgun beside her on the passenger seat.

The wind was so strong it almost blew the car off the road, but she held the wheel hard, driving as fast as she dared between the dykes. She was frightened but not altogether unhappy, because at last she was into the action and also for a moment there, glancing behind her at the little black head in the blankets, she had felt as a mother should feel.

2. Preparations in Jordan

Three hours later Brown was on the ferry to Hull, watching its screws churn across the muddy Humber while Roscoe enjoyed calmer waters, swimming in the pool of the Jordan Intercontinental. Deeply tanned girls lay round him on mattresses, their curiosity concealed by dark glasses. The Scandinavians had gone. A barman was distributing iced drinks and Marsden sat reading an Arabic paper, which was full of Gessner's murder, a quarter of its front page devoted to a ghoulish picture of the corpse.

Watching both Englishmen from an upper balcony was Nick Cassavetes. He had come to Amman on a hunch, having learned from the hotel receptionist in Beirut that Roscoe had a visa for Jordan, and now that his quarry was in sight he meant to stay close.

After curing the night's excesses with some strenuous lengths, Roscoe climbed out of the pool. Marsden glanced up at Cassavetes.

'Who's he?'

'An American. Agency correspondent. Too nosy by half.'

Roscoe told what he knew of Cassavetes and Marsden said he would check on him. They sat where they were for half an hour, then Roscoe got dressed.

At noon an official car called to take them to the Basman Palace. They were through the lobby and into it before Cassavetes could get off his balcony. From the hotel they were driven through the diplomatic quarter of Amman, past the city's Palestinian ghettoes, then through a heavily guarded iron gate and up a tarred drive to a solid-looking mansion on a hill. That day the King was not in residence.

They were met by a palace official and escorted up a broad flight of steps, across a tiled hall, through a series of heavy

double doors manned by veteran soldiers of the Desert Patrol,
then in yet further, down corridors more hushed, past sentries
from the faithful Circassian Guard in fur hats and black
cossack uniform, and finally into an anteroom, plainly furnished. Waiting there Roscoe glanced through a narrow barred
window and caught sight of an anti-aircraft gun in the garden,
its barrel projecting at the empty blue sky through a camouflage
net.

'Getting the red carpet, aren't we?'

'It's just Nazreddin's way of showing us how grand he is.'

'So the King doesn't know?'

'Certainly not.'

'I thought he was in favour of a settlement.'

'Not if it means a Palestinian state.'

'So Nazreddin's taking quite a chance?'

'Well, he won't get beheaded,' Marsden said, and then the
official came back and they were taken on through to an office,
air-conditioned, screened by blinds, without a trace of paper-
work. Nazreddin appeared to have nothing to do but await
their arrival. As they came through the door he jumped up
from his desk with a smile, clicked his heels and showed them
to a sofa. Coffee was brought in, and after the customary
pleasantries Marsden asked whether the villa in Aqaba was
ready.

'Not quite. Usual bloody cock-ups. You'll have to hang
about for a day or so.'

Roscoe then asked about the truck.

'That's ready, and the other stuff. We'll go and take a look
if you like.'

Nazreddin locked his office, put on reflector glasses and took
them outside to his car. First they went to pick up the others,
now rejoined by Walid, then Nazreddin drove to an army
camp south of Amman where he unlocked a room behind the
quartermaster's store and showed them the equipment he had
assembled.

It consisted of two semi-rigid inflatable fourteen-foot
dinghies, with Evinrude outboards and paddles for the final
approach. On the floor was a pile of webbing haversacks for
carrying the explosive. Laid out on a table were two signal
torches, a VHF transmitter-receiver, three walkie-talkies,

compasses, two Very pistols and assorted cartridges, flares, a crate of 9 mm ammunition and four Uzi submachine-guns. There were also seven Israeli army uniforms, made up by Nazreddin's tailor to measurements provided by Roscoe from Beirut. Refo was bringing the boots; also two outboards of a type which made less noise, the explosive and all ancillary detonating equipment.

That was the more important delivery, but this stuff mattered too, and so Roscoe took his time, inspecting and testing each item carefully. His intention was that the task force would masquerade as an Israeli army unit. Thus he hoped to travel through Israel unnoticed and to take the sentries at Alcatraz by surprise, getting up close enough to disarm them. That might need a few words of Hebrew but would not work at all unless the uniforms looked right. He turned to Nazreddin and thanked him.

'Excellent, excellent,' Marsden said.

Nazreddin asked whether they wanted a rocket-launcher.

'Certainly not,' said Roscoe with a smile.

'Just let me know. Whatever you want.'

'This will do fine.'

After that they walked over to the MT park and inspected a Dodge one-ton truck of the type used by the Israelis for transport of infantry. Bassam had obtained a similar vehicle in Israel, which Roscoe and his men would use for the assault and also for the getaway into Jordan, crashing through the border fence at a pre-selected point.

'Who's the driver?' asked Nazreddin.

'Ibrahim. He used to drive a bus.'

Ibrahim stepped forward.

'Good show,' said Nazreddin, and sent to tell the camp commandant that a section of his fence was about to be flattened, courtesy of the King. Then he climbed up into the cabin, followed by Roscoe. Ibrahim got behind the wheel, and after a few false starts drove them out of the camp.

From there they headed into the desert, hurtling past camels and black nomad tents pegged like a bats' wings to the earth. Following Nazreddin's directions Ibrahim turned up a dirt track which led to a derelict fort on the horizon. He was soon in command of the vehicle, wrenching the gears up and down

and kicking at the heavy steel clutch until the engine was
whining in top. Maximum speed was just short of fifty.
Nazreddin grinned at Roscoe behind his mirror glasses. 'All
right?' he shouted.

'All right!'

Ibrahim pulled up beside the fort and they sat for a while in
the shade of its walls. To the east was a flat expanse of nothing,
a quiver of heat where the land met the sky. Nazreddin blew
smoke rings into the motionless air. 'This is a hell of a thing
you're going to do,' he said. 'Could change the whole picture.'

'Let's hope so.'

'I hear you knew Hussein at Sandhurst.'

'Only slightly.'

'He's a romantic, but also a realist. When we get this thing
going he'll help.'

'It's amazing he's hung on so long.'

'Stephen, this whole bloody kingdom is amazing. Abdullah
just got off a train from Medina and claimed it. The British
were too surprised to stop him, and then they rather liked the
idea. A home for the Hashemites, a home for the Jews – we're
living on a map drawn by British adventurers.'

Roscoe nodded, abashed.

'Well, it's not your fault. You're going to change it, right?'

They returned to the camp by a different route. Two
hundred yards from its fence Nazreddin made Ibrahim stop
and explained the basic rules of border-hopping, in Arabic and
English. If you have enough speed, he said, go for a post,
which will snap or bend flat under impact and pull the wire
under the wheels. If your momentum is slight, however, aim
between the posts; the wire will then give for some distance
but may stall the truck, in which case be ready to jump on the
bonnet and over.

Ibrahim nodded as he listened, a sturdy little man of few
words. Beyond the fence a small audience waited: Marsden
and the others, a few Jordanians in uniform. Ibrahim started
up, accelerated, went for a post. Roscoe held tight. Nazreddin
shouted 'Tallyho!' as they hit, but the post misbehaved,
sheering off at the base but staying vertical, pinned against the
front of the truck. Then more posts came away, to left and
right, until a wide section of fence was being swept across the

open ground of the camp, causing the audience to scatter and run. Ibrahim kept going. Roscoe saw that Marsden was about to be caught by the wire. He shouted. Ibrahim kept going, and then the fence gave way, some wires twanging apart, others screeching as they dragged across the metal of the truck. Ibrahim drove on a short distance then stopped. Roscoe patted his shoulder. Nazreddin laughed and said the Jews built better fences. Marsden clapped derisively.

In the late afternoon they left the camp and drove west, to a high observation point above the Jordan valley, from which they could discuss the merits of various exit points from Israel.

This was in fact Mount Nebo, where Moses had glimpsed the Promised Land before dying. The site was marked by a Dominican church and all round it Jordanian sentries were posted on the summit with binoculars. Only the soft clank of goats' bells disturbed the high breezy silence. Behind the church a huge iron cross thrust into the sky.

'They built it for the Pope,' explained Nazreddin, 'when he came to Israel, you know.'

Roscoe was surprised the Pope could see it.

'Oh yes, you can see Jerusalem from here.' Nazreddin pointed to a ridge in the distance, shielding his eyes against the setting sun. 'There, you see? That's the Mount of Olives.'

Roscoe peered westwards, and thinking of Claudia, just beyond that blue ridge, felt a little like a refugee looking at the home he had lost.

Between the two high points was a vast hazy chasm, very deep and miles across, running north and south across their front. At its bottom the Dead Sea shone like molten gold and north of that was Jericho, a distant smudge of green, and north again the Jordan, a faint scar along the darkening valley.

Marsden, too, seemed affected by the view. 'The cockpit of the earth,' he said, and then Nazreddin brought them back to practicalities.

'Where will you hole up?'

'Aqabat Jabr.' Roscoe pointed downwards. 'It's an empty refugee camp near Jericho.'

'I know, I grew up there.' Nazreddin dispelled his embarrassment with an unaffected smile. 'We keep a permanent watch here, so when you're ready to come out I suggest you fire a Very light.'

'Wouldn't radio contact be better?'

'We'll work that out too – frequencies, codes, we can keep it very simple. But you might not have time, so we'd better have a back-up procedure.'

Nazreddin then said that in his view the best place to attempt the drive out was the flatlands immediately north and south of the Dead Sea.' He took out a classified military map and pointed out the relevant Israeli positions, access roads and minefields. To help Ibrahim see where to breach the fence, marker flags would be planted on the Jordanian side.

'I've chosen four alternative crossing points. We'll take a look at them tomorrow . . .'

3. 'He is Coming'

Forward two days now – to the morning of Sunday 29th October, when Claudia, travelling in her little white Fiat, crossed the landscape below Mount Nebo. The road which she took strikes east from Jerusalem through the Judean wilderness, then drops sharply to Jericho and continues on north up the Jordan to Galilee.

This was the West Bank, the territory where Saladin hoped to reconstitute Palestine. Claudia knew every part of it well, but rarely came this way since the Mission found most of its work in the population centres of Nablus, Ramallah and Hebron. In those towns Saladin's name was now on everyone's lips, and on many walls too – slogans daubed in paint, scrubbed away by the authorities, repainted the next night; posters ripped down but always reappearing, leaflets thick on the ground in café and mosque and bazaar. It was astonishing what Bassam and Horowitz had done in so short a space of time, and she was pleased to have helped.

But here, along the lonely eastern road she had taken this Sunday, there was not much population to win. The Jordan valley itself was desolate and sere, the river hardly more than a ditch between sterile deposits of silt. The Israelis' occupation was discreet: a few slabs of concrete in the hillsides, coils of wire, an occasional jeep. The tanks were out of sight.

Further north the picture changed dramatically. Passing into Israel proper, she drove through industrial kibbutzim, neatly cultivated fields and grids of irrigation pipes. The land turned from brown to green, and then through the trees appeared the water which Jesus had fished, vivid blue and ruffled by a breeze. Claudia turned left and followed the lake's western bank to Tiberias, where she waited in a restaurant for Bassam.

This would be their first meeting for a fortnight, but before that she had seen quite a lot of him. She had driven him about the place and run various errands, even gone ahead of him once to a rendezvous to check the coast was clear. He had used her flat for meetings and had stayed there occasionally, collapsing exhausted on her spare bed. He worked hard for the cause – too hard, she thought. Each time she saw him he was thinner. Sometimes his energy was feverish, and then his talk would grow disjointed, his clumsiness worse; at other times he sat inert and mute for long periods, as if paralysed.

Why he had called her to Tiberias she did not know. She could tell from his voice on the phone it was important, but could not guess the reason.

While she waited she ate an Israeli breakfast, a meal she had come to enjoy – smoked carp, tomato and cucumber, olives, raw onion, a cold hard-boiled egg and cream cheese. Then she poured herself more coffee and sat back, looking across the lake to the Golan Heights, a forbidding natural barrier which rose to the border with Syria.

When she thought of Stephen Roscoe she submitted her feelings to cautious analysis. There was something almost pat about their relationship, which made her wary, but the truth was she missed him, more than expected, and in a particular way. In his company she had felt relaxed, as if a threat had been lifted – relieved, as if spared a task – and what, alas, could that mean except that she was not, after all, a modern girl? Independence appealed to her in theory but in practice was tiring. Her spirit kept failing, more from loss of interest than will. She was not good at living for herself, she had decided, and that was what had drawn her to Saladin.

She remembered the kiss on the beach. She was glad he had stopped where he had. Thinking back to that time in the Lebanon she remembered how it felt to be with him – that easy symbiosis – more precisely than the man, and that surely proved it was more than a superficial attraction. But perhaps it would all turn to nothing when she saw him again. She must be prepared for that. . . .

'Hello there.'

It was Bassam, sidling furtively round the big eucalyptus which overhung the terrace. He was wearing his usual dark

British suit, too heavy for the weather and now hanging loose on his frame. On his head was an embroidered Jewish skull-cap.

Claudia greeted him affectionately and led him to her car. Scrambling in beside her he forgot one leg, on which he closed the door, then he sorted himself out and took a leaflet from his briefcase.

She glanced at it without absorbing the contents, noting only that the text was set out as usual in Hebrew, Arabic and English. But this, Bassam said, was the most complete statement yet of the movement's political aims. Copies would be distributed in Israel and the Occupied Territories throughout the coming week, coinciding with similar publicity in the camps – the final build-up.

'To what?'

Bassam looked excited. Today, he said, two meetings had been organized, one of the leading Arabs approached by him, and another, here in Tiberias, of the main representatives of the Israeli Left.

Claudia was puzzled; a cardinal rule had been to avoid large meetings. Surely this was a risk, she said.

Bassam replied that it was, smiling mysteriously.

'Then why do it?'

Bassam continued to smile. 'He is coming.'

'What do you mean? Who's coming?'

'Our Lord and Saviour.'

Then Claudia caught up with him. '*Saladin?*'

'Revealed from heaven with his mighty angels, in flaming fire taking vengeance on them that read not my leaflets.'

Bassam shook with laughter, but Claudia was appalled. 'He's coming here,' she said, 'to *Israel?* Is that wise?'

'It's essential.'

'But how? I mean how will he get here?'

'By courtesy of UNWRA.'

Bassam explained that only vehicles of UNWRA were still allowed to use the road which ran from Beirut to Haifa, a closely guarded diplomatic privilege which Giscard had found a way to exploit – the ultimate sin for a neutral official. After weeks of careful machinations by the Frenchman Saladin was coming through as a Palestinian doctor employed by the World

Health Organization in Geneva. If things had gone as planned they would be in Tiberias within the hour.

Claudia's instinct was to flee straight back to the Mission, but she collected herself and started the car. Bassam guided her to a house on the outskirts of town, where they picked up Horowitz, and then she drove on to the rendezvous, a hostel on a hill above the northern shore of the lake, which was, as it happened, the site of the Sermon on the Mount.

4. The Return

Horowitz did not have much to say. Claudia had only met him twice but noticed he was now much fatter; he had swollen as Bassam had shrunk, and the pep had gone out of him. Also between these two men there now seemed to be some tension. She gathered they had not met for some time. Having parked at the rendezvous, which was deserted, she left them together and walked off to explore.

Beside the hostel was a Franciscan church. Peering in through a window she saw that the walls beneath the dome formed an octagon lit by eight glass panels which recorded the beatitudes in vivid purple lettering. The sun was shining through the one which said BEATI PACIFICI, but she did not take it as a sign.

The two men were strolling about the hostel's garden as they waited, along gravel paths arranged in a geometric pattern under a dense grove of trees. The lake was below, Capernaum to the left and away to the right the hills where Sultan Saladin had caught the Crusaders. The sun was dazzling, a quivering intensity of light over all the parched uplands, but below the trees it was shady and cool, the air stirred lightly by a breeze. Claudia was nervous. Something was about to go wrong, she felt.

When she rejoined them Bassam and Horowitz were discussing a truck, a Dodge one-tonner they had bought from a fruit merchant and were having resprayed at Beersheba.

'But will it look right?' Bassam asked anxiously. 'Remember it has to look like a military vehicle.'

'My dear friend,' Horowitz said testily, 'all you have to do is get the thing *dirty*. If it's so damn dirty you can't see the colour then it has to belong to the Israeli army, right?'

Claudia thought this quite funny, but neither man laughed.

Bassam asked who would be taking the truck down to Eilat; he thought it would be better left there for collection.

'That's up to you,' replied Horowitz.

'But you know I can't drive.'

'Roscoe can take it down himself.'

'All right, you can pick it up together in Beersheba. But you'll have to drive – he won't have his uniform.'

Horowitz shook his head. 'I'm not going.'

'But I told you, he wants a Hebrew speaker. Why couldn't you go? You could wear your uniform.'

'Because I am trying to keep out of jail.' Horowitz spoke as if to a child.

'But there aren't any roadblocks, we've checked. You'd be all right.'

Horowitz lowered his head and closed his eyes, breathing deeply through his nose as if for Yoga. Claudia saw that he was trembling, but whether from fear or annoyance could not tell. Then, head still lowered, he opened his eyes and said in a measured voice: 'Obviously you don't understand, so let's get this straight. I support your political objectives but I will not commit any violence against my own country. I won't assist it, I'll have nothing to do with it.'

Bassam was dismayed. 'But, Eytan, I told you . . .'

'Yes, you told me – too late.'

'You didn't object.'

Horowitz nodded, still looking at the ground. 'No, I did not. That was my mistake.'

'You said you'd help.'

'Well now I've had time to reflect – haven't I?' Horowitz lifted his head with a sarcastic smile.

Bassam pleaded with him. 'I told you, no one is going to get hurt.'

'Oh no? Bassam, you are a naive man.'

'Stephen knows what he's doing.'

'Stephen Roscoe is an adventurer. He'll kill anyone who gets in his way. He killed the Irish, you think he won't kill Jews? Hey? What do you think about that?'

Bassam turned to Claudia for help, but Horowitz pulled him back roughly by the sleeve. 'Damn it, how the hell am I going to get out of this country? Tell me that. If I stay they'll lock me up, but how can I get *out*?'

So that was it, thought Claudia, seeing now that the situation was hopeless for Horowitz; even Saladin's success would make no difference to his plight. He was doomed to flight or jail, and according to Bassam had lost his family to a hippy in New York.

As he vented his despair his whole body sagged, as if deflated. He let go of Bassam and spoke more calmly. 'I have given my life to this country. I don't want to leave it, but what can I do?' He hung his head again and shook it, dripping tears on the gravel. 'Nothing,' he said, 'there really is nothing I can do.'

Bassam put a hand on his shoulder and the two of them walked off.

Left alone, Claudia sat on a bench provided by the Church of God Prophecy, Cleveland, Tennessee. For a while she looked blankly at the lake, her mind in a turmoil of sorrow for Horowitz, anxiety for herself and frightened curiosity about Roscoe's mission. But that she would not ask about. Better not to know, she thought, and to calm herself took out the leaflet which Bassam had given her. Turning to the English section she read the introductory passage and then came to Saladin's proposals, which were set out in five short paragraphs.

Objectives

1 An independent state of Palestine based on Gaza and the West Bank, neutral, demilitarized, protected by international guarantee. Recognition of Israel as defined in 1948. Frontiers to be agreed by negotiation, mutual renunciation of force.

2 Open borders between Palestine and Israel, patrolled by UN forces. Free passage of persons and goods but no rights of residence or property for either race within the territory of the other (except Arabs residing in Israel since 1948).

3 Immediate resettlement of refugees in Palestine, assisted by a programme of international aid. Refugees not wishing to return become citizens of the Arab states where they reside and receive compensation from Israel.

4 East Jerusalem to be capital of Palestine, West Jerusalem capital
   of Israel. Restoration of 1948 armistice line, but city to retain
   open status as at present. Joint supervisory municipal commission
   under UN chairmanship. Old City to receive international status
   under UN control, religious questions to be referred to an inter-
   denominational body.

5 These measures to be preceded by a plebiscite of the Palestinian
   people, supervised by the UN and leading to a democratic
   assembly temporarily sited in Beirut. Formation of provisional
   Palestinian government representing majority opinion to conduct
   negotiations.

Claudia read these proposals through twice. How reasonable
they were, she thought, how obviously right. But were they
possible? The situation seemed long beyond reason. Some of
these ideas would just make the Israelis' laugh; they would
rather go to war again than give up Jerusalem, and would it
really help to 'twist their arm'? That was how Stephen had put
it. For God's sake what *was* he going to do?

She stared at the lake again, more frightened than before.
Then Bassam came back and sat beside her. 'Well, what do
you think?' he said, pointing at the leaflet.

'I think it's very good. Clear and sensible.'

'The first paragraph was difficult. We wanted to leave some
border options open.'

Claudia glanced at it again. 'Very diplomatic,' she said. 'I
hope you succeed.'

'Ah, we're a long way from that.' Bassam nodded his head
towards the car, in which Horowitz was now sitting. 'We've
lost him, I'm afraid.'

'What will you do?'

'We can get him out, but that will have to wait. The important thing now is to keep him well hidden.'

'Are you worried he'll defect?'

'No, he won't do that. That's why he's so miserable.'

Bassam wiped his glasses, deliberately calm, frowning in
thought, and Claudia noticed the effort in this self-control.
Bassam had often seemed volatile, almost flippant; but now he
was sober, in contrast to Horowitz. He was full of surprises,

she thought, therefore easily misjudged. Faced with this final test, he seemed to be gaining in strength. As his body was leaner so his mind was more incisive; all the fat in his character had been stripped away, at what psychic cost she could only imagine. She had the feeling he would either succeed or snap permanently.

He took off his skull-cap, as if suddenly struck by its absurdity, and put it in his pocket. 'It's today that worries me,' he said.

'These meetings?'

'We've kept them as small as we can. But we can't repeat them, so everyone's got to be there – everyone who counts, and that includes some I'm not sure of. It's a hell of a risk. Yaacov could be on to it.'

'Who's Yaacov?'

'A very clever man.'

Bassam explained about Yaacov, who had now been identified as the man charged with stopping Saladin.

Claudia asked if there was anything she could do, hoping the answer would be no.

'Yes, there is. I'll give you some of these leaflets, and a special enclosure, which I'd like you to post to the press corps tonight. I've got the addresses in the car. Can you do that?'

'Yes of course.'

'And another thing. There's a Canadian television crew arriving tomorrow, a fellow called Morley . . .'

'Little Dom!'

'You know him?'

'Oh yes, we're old friends.'

Claudia had started to tell Bassam about Morley when they heard a powerful car horn and turned to see a big white American station-wagon with UNWRA in bold blue letters on its flanks. As it braked at the hostel they looked towards it, open-mouthed, half-expecting disaster, but then out he stepped, theatrically, as if from a coffin sawn in half – Saladin!

Immediately Claudia was won again. The man was so charming, so brave. He greeted her with a warm handshake and in his eyes she saw gratitude. She too now knew about his cancer, but noticed that the illness had receded in response to the advance of his hopes; he looked stronger than he had in the Lebanon, his step was light. He was dressed in a suit no

doctor could afford, but the ruse at the border had worked –
the Israelis scarcely bothered to check UNWRA vehicles. He
told them about it excitedly as he strode to the edge of the
trees and looked out across Galilee, breathing in the air and
slightly raising his hands, like a man come to claim his kingdom.

Bassam was speechless with relief. He could not stop laughing.

Giscard stood behind, avuncular, lizard-like, smirking as he
lit a yellow cigarette. '*Bonjour*, Miss Lees. You are well?'

'Yes, very well thanks.'

Horowitz came over from the car, slow-footed like a boy in
disgrace, but was promptly acclaimed as the architect of victory.
He smiled through his tears apologetically and in that moment
Claudia saw that he would after all go through with it, because
he had nothing more to lose. All Horowitz had left was here: a
few friends, a political idea and this spellbinding man who
embodied it.

'Now, there's a lot to discuss,' said Saladin briskly, and led
them to a corner of the garden to confer.

The plan was to travel from the Mount of the Beatitudes in
convoy, proceeding immediately from the meeting with the
Jews in Tiberias to the one with the Arabs in Ramallah, then
on to a safe house in Jerusalem. Claudia's car would be used
for the approach to each rendezvous; otherwise the men would
ride with Giscard in the UNWRA vehicle. The important
thing, explained Bassam from experience, was to keep moving
fast and once hidden, to stay put. But he was not entirely happy
with the plan. 'The question is,' he said, 'how much do they
know?'

5. The Trap

The answer to that was that Yaacov knew more than even Bassam suspected. Ayah Sharon had by this time made a chart for the wall of his office which identified all the people working for Saladin except two – Claudia Lees and Roland Giscard. The chart was designed like a genealogical tree, with Anis Kubayin at the top. At the bottom it branched into two lists of names, some Arab and some Jewish – people whom Saladin's agents were known to have contacted in Israel and the Occupied Territories. Each of these lists contained a number of informers and in view of this Yaacov was surprised that Bassam and Horowitz were still on the loose. That they were was to their credit; both men had been cunning and cautious. Yaacov admired such technique, and was almost disappointed when Bassam made the blunder of calling a meeting in Ramallah.

The venue was an old Arab house on the eastern fringe of town, white-walled, flat-roofed, with a crenellated parapet. Rather prettier than anything the Jews had built, Yaacov had to admit. He was watching it from the window of a petrol station opposite, at the junction with the road to Jerusalem. With him was a senior official of Shin Beth and an officer of Special Branch. Two Israeli soldiers dressed as Arabs were sitting on the pavement outside the gates of the house. Another two were watching the back. Linked to Yaacov by radio but well out of sight was a military unit with a van for removal of suspects.

The time was 12.30, approximately three hours after Claudia had met Bassam in Tiberias.

The house belonged to Suleiman Najjar, a former mayor of Ramallah. An old man now, slow and fat, his white hair topped by a fez, Najjar was sitting on the porch in a rocking chair,

cooling his face with a round wicker fan like a ping-pong bat
as he waited for the meeting.

His guests arrived in quick succession, two dignified figures
in chauffeur-driven cars, then a younger man who drove himself, then another on foot, then three others arriving together
in a taxi. Seven altogether.

Yaacov knew them all, and the only one for whom he felt
unrelieved contempt was the young one, who was his informer.
He watched them enter his trap with a mixture of self-satis-
faction and sadness, understanding what attracted them to
Saladin's initiative and knowing too the caution with which
they would approach it. Their first concern would be their own
interests, which they had learned to protect through all manner
of political upheaval. Though the Israeli regime was a great
deal more repugnant than the Turkish or the British, their
urge to do anything about it was blunted by apathy and
intricate internal rivalries. To unite them in the interests of
Palestine would require a real feat of persuasion: Bassam alone
would never achieve it, which led one to wonder what exactly
was the purpose of this incautious gathering. It must have been
called to hear something or someone important. Saladin himself
was alleged to be somewhere in the Lebanon, but Mossad had
completely failed to find him . . .

Yes, thought Yaacov, today could see the end of it.

He kept his eyes on the house.

For a while the seven Arabs stood talking on the porch, then
Najjar took them inside. The windows were shuttered. The
house stood white and blank in the sun while the chauffeurs
squatted together in the garden, smoking in the shade.

Time passed, and while he waited Yaacov reviewed the
latest facts at his disposal about Saladin. He now knew that
Roscoe had turned up in Jordan, having come from the
Lebanon through Syria. Marsden was also in Amman and both
had been seen with Nazreddin, who was on Hussein's staff.
Roscoe had four men with him. Gessner had been killed in
Damascus, probably by Zeiti, who was now no longer with the
party – Mossad were reporting rumours in Damascus of
another casualty. So Gessner and Zeiti were out of the picture;
but Roscoe was in Jordan, a highly trained soldier, recruited
for what?

Yaacov now suspected that the climax to Saladin's campaign might be violent. He was under strong pressure for results and knew he had little time left. Two days before he had been worried, but now his luck had turned. He had Roscoe hooked in Amman and a net round this house in Ramallah, into which Bassam would swim to address his little meeting, perhaps some bigger fish, but certainly Bassam . . .

But Bassam was late, unless he was in there already.

When Yaacov next looked at his watch it was 1.30, and about that time a telephone rang inside the house. Then a man in dark glasses appeared on the porch.

Yaacov recognized Hakim, Najjar's eldest son, who ran the family business. Hakim came down the steps and spoke to the chauffeurs, two of whom went behind the house. Then he walked to the gate and looked up and down the street. Then to Yaacov's consternation he questioned the two Israeli soldiers, one of whom spoke Arabic, but not well enough for this. Hakim told them to move on and they shuffled off obediently, acting out their part. Yaacov and his two companions ducked out of sight as Hakim stared in their direction, then they saw him stride quickly back to the house. Half a minute later Najjar's guests appeared in a body, hurrying down the steps towards their cars.

Bassam's caution had saved Saladin. He had phoned from a few miles north, asking for a search in the vicinity of the house. Already Hakim Najjar was back on the line and minutes later Giscard had the UNWRA vehicle turned round and speeding to Jerusalem by an alternative route. Claudia trailed behind, along with her bootload of leaflets.

Yaacov had been foiled, but he still hoped to do himself some good. He ordered his men to close in. Najjar's guests were herded back into the house and searched one by one. Each was carrying a copy of Saladin's new manifesto. The house was also searched, but yielded only leaflets.

Najjar submitted with a saturnine smile while his son muttered insults and his womenfolk fluttered in fright. When his friends had been released he took Yaacov into his study, a cool book-lined room ornately furnished, and offered him coffee. Yaacov was gracious in defeat. In faultless and circumlocutory Arabic he went over the legal restrictions on political activity and suggested that, in view of the prosperous and tranquil conditions now prevailing in the West Bank, to which the illustrious Najjar himself had so significantly contributed, involvement with adventurers like Saladin was unwise, not to say regrettable foolishness. With goodwill and moderation on both sides a political settlement would be reached in due course, Arab and Jew would live together as they had in the past and time would heal the wounds inflicted by war.

Yaacov did the talking. Najjar merely smiled, gently fanning his face as he made his short reply. 'Time, my friend, is what you have to fear.'

Yaacov did not need reminding of that. As soon as he saw his trap was sprung he had ordered up roadblocks round Ramallah, but knew it was too late. From Najjar's house he returned to his office in Beit Agron, where Ayah Sharon was waiting with further bad news.

Bassam and Horowitz had been seen in Tiberias that morning, she reported, at a gathering of Israeli radicals which had been addressed by Saladin himself.

Yaacov nodded wearily – he had expected it – and flopped into the chair behind his desk, momentarily beaten. His shirt was stained with sweat from the vigil in the petrol station. Ayah lit him a cigarette. She ran his office efficiently but rarely got the chance to offer comfort, and the moment quickly passed. Yaacov returned to the chase.

The meeting in Tiberias, it emerged, had been prepared with more care than the one in Ramallah. Those present had been summoned to the town individually, on various pretexts, then called at short notice to a room in a hotel. None had known what to expect or could now say where Saladin had gone.

Yaacov believed them. Nine Jews had been invited to this gathering of whom two had afterwards volunteered information to the police. In the following hours Yaacov worked through the other seven and narrowed down his interest to a man called Livner, an elderly Israeli citizen of Christian faith and British origin whose file recorded that he had once been a teacher at the school in Haifa where Bassam and Horowitz were pupils. Livner now lived in Tiberias and a search of his house revealed conclusive evidence that Horowitz had hidden there – a bed in the basement, an IBM typewriter, a French photocopier, a radio with range for the Lebanon. Livner was promptly arrested and brought to Beit Agron, but after questioning him into the night Yaacov decided he knew nothing of importance, consigned the old man to summary detention and laid himself down on a bed in his office.

He slept for two hours and woke heavy-hearted, expecting a summons to Mrs Meir's office. By tradition in Israel the penalties for military failure were swift and severe.

But no such summons came. Instead, at 9.30 that morning, Monday 30th October, a black saloon car pulled up at Beit Agron and out of it stepped a man whom Yaacov knew to be one of the hardest in Israel; a tall man, dark-suited, granite-faced, with grey hair shaved close to his skull.

This late arrival in the story of Saladin was Menachem Ariel, and his name was the prettiest thing about him. Ariel had spent his whole life in espionage and underground warfare, having cut his teeth in the Stern Gang. During the sixties he commuted between various Israeli embassies in Europe, where his bleak features could be seen above the chattering diplomatic crowd, moved only by the Coke which he periodically raised to his lips. At this time, October 1972, he was based in Jerusalem, but everything about him was obscure – his functions, his department, his authority, even his home. Although a civilian, he was observed to work closely with the army and police. It was alleged in a German magazine that Ariel was Deputy Director of Shin Beth, and this may well have been correct. A place he was seen at often was Sarafand, not the sleepy fishing village in the Lebanon but the military detention centre of that name in Israel, and of one thing there is no doubt at all: it was Ariel who had supervised the construction of cells and interrogation facilities on the roof of Alcatraz. He visited the building site daily.

From this point onwards he took a close interest in Saladin, and Yaacov, while continuing to run the operation, was obliged to report to him.

Their working session that Monday began with a review of everything that had happened so far, and Yaacov shirked no ignominious detail. But worse humiliation was to come. He had not yet looked in his tray and so had not seen the document which Ariel took from his briefcase and passed forward, saying it had been received through the post that morning by every major journalist in Israel, foreign and local. This was of course Saladin's trilingual leaflet – no surprise in that – but stapled to the front of it was a sheet of typescript which read as follows in its English version.

A MESSAGE FROM SALADIN

GENTLEMEN OF THE PRESS:

ENCLOSED IS A STATEMENT OF MY OBJECTIVES.
PLEASE STUDY IT CAREFULLY. TODAY (29TH OCTOBER)
I CROSSED THE BORDER INTO OCCUPIED TERRITORY.
I AM NOW IN JERUSALEM, WHERE MY FAMILY HAVE
LIVED FOR MANY CENTURIES. I AM WILLING TO
NEGOTIATE PEACEABLY WITH GOLDA MEIR WHENEVER
SHE SO CHOOSES. BUT UNTIL THAT TIME COMES
I AM FORCED TO RESORT TO HARSHER METHODS.
YOU WILL THEREFORE SHORTLY BE INVITED TO
WITNESS A DEMONSTRATION OF FORCE WHICH WILL
PROVE TO THE WORLD THAT THE RIGHTS OF THE
PALESTINIAN PEOPLE CAN NO LONGER BE IGNORED.
PLEASE AWAIT FURTHER COMMUNICATION.

ANIS KUBAYIN
(SALADIN)

6. Final Manoeuvres

Goaded, supported, advised if not actually directed by Ariel, Yaacov now attacked his task with almost frantic energy, working round the clock for three days, catching naps in his office when he could. Shin Beth, the army and police were all jumping to his orders. But as with Bassam, so with his chief: the problem was to trace the man without provoking a public hue and cry, or at least without adding to the general hubbub now existing.

The suppression of publicity was more successful than the search. At first Saladin's threat of violence was widely reported, his message reproduced on many front pages. But when he did not follow it with immediate action, interest tailed away and comment turned derisive, laced with discreditable details about his private life, some true, some invented by the Israeli propaganda machine. The European press continued to give the matter space and ironically the best American coverage came from the agency for which Cassavetes worked. But by way of example the Hebrew papers ignored the story completely, and outside the Occupied Territories the Arab press was still largely hostile. Several television crews came hotfoot to Jerusalem, but when nothing occurred only Morley stayed on, drinking alone in the bar of the American Colony.

This lack of reaction, while welcome to Yaacov, impeded the manhunt, since most of the Israeli population were quite unalerted to the danger. Few people knew what Saladin or either of his two lieutenants looked like. Those who did, however, were used, and among the people brought down from Kibbutz Kfar Allon to assist the authorities was David Heinz, who was posted at an outdoor café on the busiest street in Jerusalem. He sat there each day drinking beer with a plain-clothes policeman, content to be released from picking apples.

Others who could recognize Bassam or Horowitz or Saladin were deployed at similar points in the city, and some in Tel Aviv. Photographs of the three wanted men were posted in every police station but no extra roadblocks were set up, since that would have given an impression of emergency. Yaacov in any case had no faith in such methods, preferring to rely on good intelligence. All Saladin's likely contacts were kept under strict surveillance, in particular journalists who might accept his invitation to a 'demonstration of force'.

These methods also produced no result; Saladin lay low. But Yaacov was unworried, because he held a winning card, and that was Roscoe.

A report had come in that this English 'journalist' had applied for permission to cross the Allenby Bridge. Yaacov had expected that, and now he prepared an elaborate reception. From the moment Roscoe entered Israel he would be followed, and as for his men, they would not even get in, because now they had revealed where they planned to cross the frontier. The Israeli Border Police had seen them inspecting the fence in the area of the Dead Sea. Yaacov sent back a congratulatory message, repeated his alert to all border units between Jericho and Eilat, and went home to sleep.

All he had to do now was wait.

7. A Snag in Aqaba

In the meantime Roscoe had completed his southward journey to Aqaba, having parted with Marsden. On return from Mount Nebo they had found a telegram from the AAI reporting the threat to Nina Brown, so next day Marsden had flown back to London while Roscoe and Nazreddin collected the others and drove down to inspect the exit points on the border.

On arrival in Aqaba Roscoe had examined the layout with interest, since this was where the raid into Israel would start. Aqaba on one side, Eilat on the other – the two towns were split by the frontier, but so close they seemed one, a continuous fringe of docks, hotels and villas at the northern extremity of the Gulf, that narrow arm of water reaching up from the Red Sea. He was pleased to see that it was in fact as narrow as it looked on the map, also calm. The distance between the two coasts did not look impossible for three Arabs and a Gipsy to cross in the dark, if helped by their Jordanian friends. He was encouraged.

Nazreddin had then showed them to their base, an isolated house at the eastern end of the Jordanian beach. Next day the equipment which Roscoe had inspected was delivered, and on Wednesday, November 1st, Refo arrived in a pick-up loaded with explosive.

Roscoe had asked for a type known as RDX, a powerful but stable explosive which could be moulded into any shape required.

In fact Refo could not lay his hands on RDX but supplied a near-exact American equivalent called Plastex. It arrived in the form of slim tubular cartridges, packed in 5-lb cartons. The cartons were in fibreboard cases lined with polythene, ten in each case. Refo delivered sixteen cases, total weight of explosive 800 lb. That was a lot. Detonated all at once it would make a

very big bang, but to flatten Alcatraz as required – not simply
damage it but bring it right down – would require a big bang,
Roscoe knew. In fact he had asked for more explosive than he
needed, to allow for contingencies; he intended to use only
600 lb for the destruction of the building. That was still a lot.
A sapper could have done it with less, but Roscoe had not had
a chance to examine the premises and wanted to be sure of
results.

The first job was to unpack all the explosive and mould it
into 50 lb charges. These charges were then rammed tight into
the haversacks, sixteen in all, four of which were spare. Into
eight of these explosive packs were incorporated heavy industrial magnets, the idea being to attach the haversacks to the
vertical rails in the lift shaft of Alcatraz. Another four packs
were to go along the base of an outer wall. Thus the building's
central support would be destroyed and a simultaneous shock
delivered to one side, causing the whole rectangular structure
to tilt into a rhombus, and then on over and down, until
flat.

Detonation was to be electrical, and timed. For this purpose
Refo had supplied several boxes of detonators, little pencil-
shaped things, copper-sheathed, with negative and positive
leads. When the time came two of these would be stuck into
each of the charges and connected by ordinary electrical wire,
red and black, to control boxes. The control boxes could be set
to produce the detonating electrical impulse at the time
desired. They could also be connected to each other, to make
sure of simultaneous explosions.

There was nothing very difficult about any of this except that
with so many wires in the dark, on enemy ground, one could
get in a muddle. But much could be done by way of preparation:
cutting the wire into appropriate lengths, stripping the ends for
connection and so forth. This Roscoe did in the house in
Aqaba. The actual setting of the detonators would be left until
they reached the hideout in Jericho.

Much could also be done by way of rehearsal, and with this
too Roscoe was busy in Aqaba. He spent six days there, each
of which was occupied fully with practice and briefing. Working
from the architect's plan laid out on the floor he showed where
the charges must be placed and how they would bring down

the building. He went through the drill many times, allotting specific simple tasks to each man. The Uzis were test-fired in the desert and the Israeli uniforms tried on, now complete with high-laced boots brought by Refo in appropriate sizes.

At night they drove down the coast to practise with the dinghies – and at that point a problem arose. Fuad, Ibrahim and the Gipsy were no good on water. Walid was competent, but could not control two craft at once – they were in any case difficult to manoeuvre accurately with paddles. Roscoe consulted with Nazreddin, and they agreed, for the crossing of the Gulf an extra man was needed.

Once again Nazreddin obliged, producing an old Bedouin sergeant called Mukhtar, who had had commando training; a squat, grizzled man with a face like carved wood. Mukhtar made no secret of his contempt for Palestinians but seemed content to serve under an Englishman. He immediately took charge of amphibious operations. The team was strengthened, but suffered a disturbance to morale. Walid felt slighted and the others were suspicious, though they could not deny Mukhtar's value on the water.

Worried that quarrels would break out in his absence, Roscoe took Walid for a walk down the beach on the evening before he left for Israel. The Gulf was calm, a deep trench of flat silent blue, turning almost purple where it stretched away south between the steep rocky coastlines of Sinai and Saudi Arabia.

'I see you don't like Mukhtar, but you must admit we need him.'

Walid conceded the point with bitter reluctance. 'You know what those Bedouin did to us.'

'Yes, I know. But we can't always choose the allies we would like.'

'Hussein is *not* my ally!' Walid pointed down the coast towards the King's retreat. 'He is worse than the Jews.'

'Hussein knows nothing of this. If he did he would try to prevent it.'

'That is not what Mukhtar believes.'

'Let Mukhtar believe what he likes – he'll do a better job for us. I consider you in charge here while I am gone, but I trust you to keep your feelings under control.' Roscoe gestured up the beach towards the last Israeli border post, from which coils of rusted barbed wire spilled down across the sand into the water. 'It's them you have to worry about, not Mukhtar.'

Walid smiled in apology, his black eyes softening into intimate friendship. Laundered at every opportunity, his white shirt and trousers looked almost as good as when he left Beirut. 'You are right,' he said, 'excuse me.'

They kept their distance from the frontier, sitting on the sand among a crowd of bathers. From there Roscoe pointed out the point on the Israeli coast where he and Horowitz would wait to meet the dinghies. 'Shall we run through it again?'

'If you wish.'

Walid displayed his perfect white teeth in genuine amusement at these anxious repetitions of his new English friend. They had already run through it many times.

A few minutes later they walked back, watching the motor-powered dinghies of two Israeli night patrols arc into the Gulf from the far side of Eilat. That would be the danger, thought Roscoe, the patrols and the sonic devices in the water, and the searchlights and God knows what else. If they had Phantoms they had night-eye equipment.

Then Walid said: 'Why are you doing this, Stephen? Why are you risking your life like this for Palestine?'

Roscoe almost replied 'For the money,' then noticed it was not in the script. 'Because I believe in it,' he said, and held out his hand as they came back up to the house. 'Good-bye, Walid. Be careful.'

'Good-bye, my friend. Good luck.'

Roscoe said good-bye to the others then left for Amman with Nazreddin, harrassed by the thought of contingencies he might have overlooked. He felt suddenly exhausted, feverish. The road stretched from nothing to nowhere, a thin band of tarmac through flat rock and scrub. Camels were grazing in the distance around the tents of the Bedouin, and at one point the car pulled up for a train, an ancient steam engine panting black clouds into the dusk as it dragged a load of phosphate to the sea. This, said Nazreddin, was the famous Hejaz Railway which had once linked Medina to Istanbul. These tracks had carried the troop trains ambushed by Lawrence, in fact this very engine had been dug from the sand . . .

Roscoe fell asleep. He did not want to hear about Lawrence.

They reached Amman towards midnight and Nazreddin went home to his wife. He was returning to Aqaba next day.

Waiting up in Roscoe's room at the Intercontinental was Marsden, back from London with a bottle of Scotch. His face was grave. He reported that in his view Brown had been threatened by the Israelis.

Roscoe drank a tumbler of whisky, then poured himself another. 'I'll have to be careful then.'

'You'll go through with it?'

'Yes.'

'You look done in.'

'I think I've got flu. All that messing about in dinghies.'

'That's all we need. Better go to bed then.'

Roscoe refilled his glass. 'This is the cure. Well provided.'

Marsden lit a cigarette. 'That journalist fellow . . .'

'Cassavetes? Is he still here?'

'He seems unusually anxious to keep you company.'

'Perhaps he likes me.'

Marsden did not smile. He puffed at his cigarette, as if it might pollute him. 'Did you know he's going to Israel?'

'Really?'

'Yes, I'm afraid so. He's going in with you, over the bridge.'

PART SIX

Winners and Losers

November 6th — November 9th, 1972

1. The Hardening Mood

The date was Monday, November 6th, the time about 8 a.m. as Roscoe left the Jordan Intercontinental for Israel. The attack at Alcatraz was set for two days ahead. Saladin was ready to step from the wings.

But that November was not a good month for the peace-makers.

In Germany what everyone feared had now occurred: Black September had hijacked a Lufthansa plane and forced the release of the three surviving terrorists imprisoned in Munich. The Israelis were enraged by the Germans' timidity, which Mrs Meir called 'shocking, a disgrace to the spirit of man'. She recalled her ambassador from Bonn. The Israeli air force bombed camps near Damascus. Forty-five people were killed.

The three released terrorists were taken to Libya, where they held a press conference. 'We are not savages,' they said. 'We hoped our operation in Munich would succeed without bloodshed, but after the German betrayal we knew we had to die. This was also obviously the fate of the hostages.'

Afterwards they vanished, running from God's Wrath. They were assumed to be concealed by Gadaffi, who boasted of a secret volunteer army. Gadaffi was begging for trouble, and now King Hussein caught the hardening mood. In a speech to Jordan's parliament he said that he was not, as was widely suspected, prepared to reach a settlement with Israel. 'We will never bargain.'

But this tough talk did not deter his enemies. A frustrated Jordanian pilot dive-bombed the palace in Amman and the King was taken to hospital with shrapnel in his thigh. An officers' plot was exposed, organized by Black September, financed by Gadaffi. Libyan Radio said it would not be the last. 'The Arab masses will continue to struggle.'

Sadat too survived a coup in Cairo, the third attempted that year. In the absence of diplomatic progress his position was becoming intolerable. He could not make peace or war, and so veered between the two. 'He resembles nothing so much as a rat in a trap,' wrote the correspondent of the *Guardian*. 'Each new dash to some illusory exit is a bit more frantic than the last.'

Sadat's dilemma was the fine point of balance of the whole Middle East. In that ordinary brain the future would be settled. Saladin was hoping to push him into peace, but that month the Egyptian president told a meeting of his closest advisers that he meant to 'start a fire' across the Canal.

And in Tel Aviv Mrs Meir expressed a rare doubt. 'The facts may lead us to the conclusion that the Arabs have at present no prospects to win a war,' she said, 'but the next thing we know could be a catastrophe.'

All through that month the postal duel continued. A London diamond broker lost his fingers to a letter bomb, one of twelve addressed to Jewish firms in Britain. The method employed was a strip of plastic explosive enclosed in two pieces of cardboard and triggered by a spring. Commander Matthew Rodger of Special Branch issued advice to anyone receiving such letters from abroad. 'Take the damn thing to the bottom of the garden, well away from the children, and leave it there.' On no account should the letters be immersed in water, he said, or the envelopes would become soggy and weak, thus releasing the spring.

The Post Office feared that the Christmas mail rush might be used to launch a new campaign. 'You can't inspect thirty million letters a day,' said a spokesman. 'That is the size of the problem.'

Israel had its scares, too. Three letter bombs were found in Kiryat Shemona. One was addressed to President Nixon.

2. Face to Face

No, the times were not propitious, but Roscoe had a clear plan of action in his head as he drove to the frontier.

Today he would see Claudia, reconnoitre Alcatraz, meet Saladin. Tomorrow night, Tuesday, he and Horowitz would go down to Eilat, pick up the others and drive back up to the hideout at Jericho. All day Wednesday for final preparations, then into Alcatraz as soon as it was dark. Disarm the sentries, mine the building, set the control boxes; then on to Saladin's press conference. Boom, sensation, flight. Saladin back to Beirut with Giscard, the rest into Jordan and home . . .

That was the plan and it was clear, but he knew that nothing ever went according to plan, nothing in the world and especially not military situations. In battle as in life the trick was to cope with surprises, foresee them as far as you could, have a new plan ready and activate it fast.

Yes, he thought, there were many possibilities, some foreseen, some undoubtedly not, and the odds on coming back up this road in good order were not marvellous. But then they might be lucky. There was always luck, and he believed in his own. He liked to test it, but he would look after it too, because it was a friend.

He relaxed in the car, feeling the aspirin take effect. Marsden was with him. They did not speak as they drove past Beqqa, the biggest of all the refugee camps, a city of asbestos, tin and rags, its prefabricated hutches almost in sight of the land lost to panic and war.

Even from a distance Roscoe sensed the despair of the place, and was glad to feel a boost of moral purpose. He also felt abominably ill – and that was a joke. An officer in the army of the righteous ought not to catch flu. The plan made no provision for flu . . .

West of Beqqa the road came over a crest, then dropped to

the lowest point on earth. The Dead Sea appeared to the left,
a steaming vat of turquoise fringed by white crystal, and ahead
was the Jordan, a line of reeds along the valley floor. The air
became clammy and hot, pervaded by the strange salt smell of
condensation.

Roscoe's ears sang with the desert, he sweated and streamed
in the heat. Just short of the river he said good-bye to Marsden,
then sat beneath the brilliant red blossom of a flame tree as his
luggage was hoisted on a bus. Other passengers crowded into
the shade, mute as cattle, while the driver shouted for suit-
cases, packing them tightly on a roof rack.

Half an hour later nothing had happened. No one was
hurrying to Israel.

Cassavetes was on the bus too. He arrived with a man from
the Jordanian press office and as soon as his papers were
cleared, joined Roscoe under the tree. He wore a nylon shirt
and slacks of artificial fibre secured by a cheap plastic belt. His
hair had been cut. His only luggage was a briefcase and a
Japanese camera slung round his neck.

Surely, said Roscoe, this excursion would queer his pitch in
Beirut?

'That depends what I write.'

'And what will you write?'

'Oh, the usual feature – how the Israelis are blowing up the
Arabs' houses.'

'Are they?'

'Sure they are. It's the penalty for terrorism. Cheaper than
jail, you know.'

'Whose side are you on?'

Cassavetes avoided the question with a laugh; a sniffing
sound, humourless. 'I report the facts,' he said, and looked at
his watch. 'Jesus, what a country. Where have you been? I
missed you at the bar.'

That came ill from an orange-drinker. Roscoe blew his nose.
'Took a look at Petra.'

'How was that?'

'Marvellous. Thought I might do a piece about Lawrence.
Do you realize they're still using the trains he attacked?'

'No kidding.'

Cassavetes lost interest and strolled off. A few minutes later

Roscoe saw him snap an Arab child, rapidly winding on his film and dropping on one knee to alter the angle while the child stood and grinned, framed by a hillside which was littered with military installations. Then the bus driver called all aboard and they bounced down the track towards the Jordan.

Either side of the track were gutted farm buildings and untended fields; the valley was abandoned to soldiery. The bus stopped for a final check of documents, then started forward again, through a thicket of reeds and on to the planks of a bridge. Roscoe took in the scene, his eyes rheumy but noting each detail: the sluggish brown water below, no more than a stream, the Jordanian sentries in the reeds and to the left the old Allenby Bridge, broken-backed girders across which the refugees had filed.

The bus advanced slowly, then braked, as if in fright. The passengers were silent.

A bored Israeli sentry stared at them over the barrel of his gun; a plump face, perspiring, bespectacled, with sideburns. He was walled in by sandbags and shaded by a roof of corrugated iron. To the right was a bigger defensive position, built into a high mound of silt and topped by a flagpost. The flag was white, with two horizontal blue stripes, the Star of David in the centre.

A shout, and the bus started forward again. They were driven up the road and herded into a reception centre, where every bag and parcel was opened, each item of clothing meticulously prodded. It took a long time. Waiting his turn, Roscoe suddenly felt faint and gripped the mesh wall for support. Beyond it Israeli girl soldiers strode about in the sun, wearing short khaki skirts. The Arabs kept their eyes on their luggage.

Not far away was a similar wire-enclosed compound where trucks were being driven two at a time into bays. Saladin had dismissed this method of importing the explosive, and now Roscoe saw why. The Arab drivers stood to one side as their tyres were deflated, their loads of citrus fruit probed with steel rods. Holes had been bored along the sides of the vehicles, the petrol tanks fitted with a special glass panel. Roscoe had never seen a frontier so thoroughly controlled.

He stepped forward as his case was heaved up and opened

the contents spread quickly on a counter. He had nothing to declare.

'Passport.'

He handed it over.

'Sit there please.'

He sat on a low wooden bench with the Arabs and saw his passport handed to a uniformed army major standing behind, who looked him over carefully. Roscoe did not know it, but this was Yaacov.

Next came a personal search in a cubicle and then he was led to an office in a building near by, where Yaacov now sat behind a desk, examining his passport.

'Shalom. Please sit down.'

Roscoe sat on a small wooden chair and immediately started to shake. The room was air-conditioned.

'What is the purpose of your visit to Israel?'

'I'm a journalist.'

'Is that what you said to the Syrians?'

'No.'

Yaacov smiled. Roscoe noticed his extraordinary repose: almost feline.

'How long will you stay here?'

'A few days. Perhaps a week.'

'I see you have given as your address the American Colony Hotel. Can you give us a reference – someone in Israel who will vouch for you?'

'I'm not sure I can. This is my first visit . . .'

'What about the girl in the car park?'

Roscoe felt his face turning pink. Blood was pumping through his head, preventing thought.

'I assume she's waiting to meet you,' Yaacov said pleasantly.

'Oh – will she do?'

'Of course.'

'Her name is Claudia Lees.'

'Address?'

'She works for the Anglican Mission – I'm not sure . . .'

'Yes, I know it.' Yaacov handed back the passport. 'Thank you, Mr Roscoe. That is all.'

'Thank you.'

'Please enjoy your stay.'

3. Cat and Mouse

Roscoe collected his luggage and walked into Israel, pausing at the last wire fence to gather strength. Claudia was standing thirty yards away under a shelter of reeds.

For her this was a turning point, in the sense that catching sight of him now, after six weeks' separation, she accepted the fact that their lives were connected. She had not met a man she liked more, and as long as he existed she would not regard him with indifference. This certainty rode into a place on a wave of girlish emotion, which sent her running gladly towards him.

He was dressed as in Beirut, except that his clothes had deteriorated further. His check shirt was stuck to his thin frame by sweat, his khaki cord trousers deeply creased around the knee. His hair was longer, curling at the edges, bleached and slightly greased so it shone like brass in the sun. At the gate of the border post he had put down his case and leaned against the wire, his body appearing to wilt with the effort of supporting its extraordinary length.

Roscoe saw her come towards him smiling. She was wearing a blue gingham dress and big circular sunglasses, which she took off. Squinting in the glare, her smile breaking into a laugh, she opened her arms and put them round him. He felt her lips against his face. His head was roaring. The sight of her and even more the smell of her, that clean soapy English aroma which he never could hold in his head, had taken his breath away. Once again he was amazed by her openness. She was pleased to see him and not afraid to show it. Trusting, she created trust, just as cynics made the worst come true. He had never met a girl with so little guile.

'Hello.'

'Hello,' she said, hugging him, 'hello, hello, hello.'

'How are you?'

'I'm fine. How are you?'

Roscoe said he was fine.

Claudia had felt his back stiffen, but now it relaxed. 'How brown you are. Oh, I'm so glad to see you.'

'It's mutual.'

She stepped back to look at him, her hands still in his. 'What's the matter? You're shaking.'

'Let's get going.'

He reached for his suitcase, but she stopped him. 'Stephen, you're sick!'

'Touch of flu. Ridiculous bad timing, I'm afraid.'

'You'd better stay with me. I'm an excellent nurse.'

Roscoe said thank you, but no. That would not be necessary, or wise.

She picked up his suitcase, then threaded her arm into his as they walked towards her car exchanging news. Saladin was safe, she said, also Bassam and Horowitz; she had taken food to the flat where they were hiding. And Morley had arrived with a film crew. 'He says if he hasn't heard from you by tonight he'll go home. Poor little Dom, he's scared they'll edit him away.'

Roscoe nodded weakly, and then saw a pressman Saladin could do without.

Cassavetes was waiting by the car.

'Jesus, what a business,' he said, flinging an exasperated hand towards the border post. 'Can you give me a ride to Jerusalem?'

Without waiting for an answer he took the suitcase from Claudia and put it in the boot of the Fiat. He had started to lift in his own when Roscoe laid a hand on his arm.

'No, I'm sorry, we can't. Get a taxi.'

Cassavetes patted his pockets and spread his palms outwards. 'No currency.'

'You'll manage.'

Roscoe signalled Claudia into the car and got in beside her. She looked unhappy. Rudeness upset her; another form of violence. As they drove away she said: 'Who on earth was that?'

'A doubtful customer.'

When Roscoe explained, she was dismayed. 'You mean you're being watched?'

'It's possible.'

'Well it's over then, isn't it? I mean they'll just arrest you.'

'Arrest me? What for?'

Roscoe pointed out that he hadn't yet committed a crime, a remark which Claudia took to mean he shortly would. 'All right then, what are you going to do? You'd better tell me.'

Roscoe hesitated. 'If I do, you'll be an accessory.'

'Yes, I suppose so.'

'I thought we agreed . . .'

'Oh to hell with it. Just tell me.'

So he told her; and she blenched.

'Alcatraz,' she said eventually, '*Alcatraz*? My God. You realize what that place is I suppose?'

'No one seems to know for sure.'

'Well maybe they don't in Beirut, but here they do, everyone knows. Stephen, it's their *new spy headquarters*.'

'Yes, I had heard.'

She looked at him, to see if he was serious, and saw that he was. 'You're mad,' she said, 'you'll never do it. You'll be killed . . .'

'Not if I can help it.'

'. . . and probably others too.'

'Not if I can help it.'

'Oh stop saying that. Don't be so . . . bloody pious.' And then her fright turned to annoyance; she reacted as if she had been tricked. 'I *told* you I wouldn't get involved in anything like this.'

'Well you're not involved, are you? You came down here to meet a friend. You're taking him to his hotel and then you're going back to saving souls.'

'Now you're being nasty.' Claudia's eyes filled instantly with tears, which brimmed, but did not fall. 'That's the first time you've ever been nasty, did you know that?'

'I'm sorry, it's just that you're making me jumpy.'

Roscoe touched her arm, to show that he meant it, and told her not to worry. She shouldn't have asked, he said, and he shouldn't have told her, but now that she knew she must stay clear and try not to worry too much. The whole thing had been worked out; it was better prepared than she realized and if it went as intended no one would be hurt – okay?

'Okay,' she said dully.

He patted her, then noticed that a car had pulled out in the main square of Jericho and was following the Fiat at a distance. He watched it, keeping one eye on the wing mirror. Then he asked Claudia to show him Aqabat Jabr, and a few moments later they passed it.

Roscoe had expected something like Beqqa, but this camp was an old Arab town, a ghost town, acres of brown adobe dwellings crumbling in the heat, a few children playing in the empty pitted streets. He had meant to inspect the place this morning, but did not bother in the circumstances. A first change of plan . . .

Claudia drove on in silence, now repenting her outburst. She had to acknowledge that her presence here was due to her own ambivalent attitude; she could have demanded the truth long ago, but had not. Roscoe was behaving consistently, but in her one ambivalence followed another. She was ready to live with him but would not risk jail for him. Having stumbled on what she thought was love, she was briskly reminded of its limits. Annoyed at herself, muddled and frightened, she had a sudden urge to put her foot down, drive and drive until they reached a place that was safe.

But the road ahead presented only one choice. After Aqabat Jabr they came to a fork – right to Jerusalem or left to the Dead Sea, where several bathing stations lined the shore, tourists lolling like corpses in the treacly water. Claudia turned towards Jerusalem, the car behind turned left. Roscoe saw it go and relaxed, unaware that Yaacov was in a second car further back.

Yaacov had been up since early morning preparing this reception. He even had a helicopter ready in case they took the road to the Negev. But that would not be necessary now. From this point there was nowhere that Claudia could turn off before the outer suburbs of the city, where other cars were waiting to take up the chase.

Roscoe suspected as much. He was going to take no chances. He told Claudia he would hop out somewhere in Jerusalem. She would then please drive on, drop his luggage at the hotel, go home and stay there. From now on she was to have no more to do with Saladin. 'Don't say anything on the phone, don't even talk about it inside your flat. Just carry on with your job, and one day perhaps we'll have a good laugh about it.'

Claudia nodded. 'I'm sorry.'

'Sorry? For what?'

'For being such a coward. I'm just too scared to help you.'

Roscoe smiled at her. 'Your nerves may be bad but your scruples are fine.'

She drove along for a while, and then agreed, in a serious and definite voice. 'Yes, it's not just cowardice – I really do think this is wrong. The point is you can't meet violence with violence. That changes nothing.'

'I disagree,' Roscoe said. 'Violence can change things. It's sometimes unavoidable.'

'It's never unavoidable. Saladin should stick to peaceful methods, like Gandhi. As soon as you blow up that building he's no better than Arafat.'

'You've heard his arguments.'

'Yes, but that's just *politics*. It depends what level you're talking on. Surely the quality of life is more important than any political interest.'

Roscoe thought of Beqqa. 'The quality of whose life?'

'Yours, for a start.'

Claudia's voice wavered; a tear escaped below her sunglasses. 'You're about to degrade yourself, like you did in Ireland, for what? Some superficial notion of honour, which is just an excuse to behave like an animal.' She bit her lip and struck the wheel. 'I'm sorry, that's unfair. I just don't want you to be killed. Oh damn, *damn* this whole thing.'

Roscoe looked away. 'It's too late for this,' he said.

'Stephen, it's *not*.'

'You see, it was me who shot Gessner.'

Claudia half-expected this, and to Roscoe's surprise she took it quite easily; her concern now was more for his physical safety than his soul. As he told her the story she pulled up on the verge and switched off the engine, fishing in her bag for a handkerchief. She did not notice the car which came round a bend below, braked, then overtook them at speed. Roscoe did, but finished his story. 'So you see, might as well go on. In for a penny, in for a pound.'

Claudia took his hand. 'You probably saved Zeiti's life. Anyway, what else could you have done?'

'Violence is sometimes unavoidable.'

She laughed. 'Yes, I've lost that point. I'm just sorry it has to be you.'

'It's a pity we had to meet in this situation.'

'Perhaps in another situation we wouldn't have noticed each other.'

Claudia drove on, and a few miles later they came into east Jerusalem, a haphazard pattern of streets, like Amman. The population of this eastern quarter was Arab but the feel of the place subtly different from any of the cities that Roscoe had travelled through. They were the provinces, this was the metropolis – the metropolis of the world. Christian spires rose among the minarets, a multiplication of temples, and in the face of this abundance of sanctity Roscoe said suddenly: 'I can't guarantee that no one will be killed, you'd better understand that. I'll just try to keep it under control.'

'That's your job, to control it.'

'Yes.'

'Well don't get killed yourself.'

'We're like people with different religions, aren't we? Or rather I have none.'

'You have more than you think,' said Claudia, lifting her hand to the windscreen. 'Welcome to the City of God, Captain Roscoe.'

She slowed down, waving on the traffic behind as they came round the Mount of Olives and reached the point all photographers choose. Spread before them now was a modern town of no particular splendour, built on hills, but rising from a hollow in the centre was what mattered to Claudia Lees and to King Hussein of Jordan and to the late Sammy Gessner: a small brown honeycomb of ancient streets packed tight behind an encircling wall. The wall was made of paler stones and inside it, close in front, was the Mosque of Al Aqsa; on the far side a cluster of churches rose above Calvary and clinging to every bare patch below the battlements were the graves of pious Jews. The basement of Herod's great temple, the only shrine left to them, was somewhere inside out of sight.

Roscoe took it in at a glance, then shifted his eyes towards Mount Scopus. 'There it is,' he said.

Claudia reluctantly followed the line of his finger. 'Yes, that's it.'

Alcatraz was already a landmark; it occupied one of the commanding sites of the city and was taller than anything around it, standing apart on a high patch of rock. Now stripped of scaffolding, it stood revealed as an almost square construction of concrete with no adornment whatsoever. Its name was well chosen.

Claudia chuckled. 'At least you won't be accused of vandalism.'

'I'm going to take a look at it.'

'You ought to be in bed.'

'Now's the time, before they get too organized. What we need to do is get off this road.'

'What about here?'

'Yes, turn here, that's it – now, step on it.'

Claudia turned abruptly right and accelerated up a steep narrow street past the Garden of Gethsemane. At the first sharp bend she was forced to slow almost to a stop and sound her horn. Roscoe had his door slightly open and pitched out suddenly, slamming it behind him. 'Keep going!' he shouted, and then ducked through a gate into the grounds of a church. A monk in white habit was watering flowers. He looked up in surprise. Roscoe smiled at him amiably, then hearing two other cars drive past, ran back down the hill and caught a taxi.

According to the plan he would not see Claudia again until England, but when it occurred to him he had not even said good-bye, he thought he might telephone her later, or even call in at the Mission. There was no extra risk to her in that, he reasoned, since they had been seen together already.

He paid off the taxi at the National Library and walked the rest of the way. Looming closer, Alcatraz looked indestructible, an edifice of such fortress-like solidity that even Roscoe was hard put to imagine it falling. He kept his distance, scrambling over the high surrounding rock and two neighbouring construction sites to obtain different views. The front of the building faced eastwards, towards the ridge on which it was set, and was approached by a newly made access road. On this side was a shallow flight of steps, the main entrance and one sentry. He was standing on the steps, looking bored, his Uzi slung carelessly. On the open ground below the steps several vehicles were parked among the cement mixers and builders' supplies, and there too were the lifts, still packed in their crates.

The back of the building overlooked the city and was perched above a steep downward slope of rock and scrubby vegetation. That was the way Roscoe meant it to topple, so this was the wall to undermine.

On the north side the access road looped round then vanished down a ramp into the basement. From the roof rose a tangle of radio masts and there too was a windowless penthouse – the interrogation centre. The building was almost complete at the top, less so at the bottom, where some of the windows were not yet glazed. But everything tallied with the architect's drawings and Bassam's descriptions. There were no surprises.

Roscoe spent the afternoon on this reconnaissance and in the course of it grew extremely fatigued. Dazed and sweating, he felt his fever rise and found a patch of shade in which to rest. He intended to wait until nightfall. Under cover of dark he would take a closer look; check the routine of the sentries, check the building was empty at night. He hoped it would be empty.

From the point where he was sitting he enjoyed a good view of the city, which did indeed turn the colour of honey in the evening light. He could see the holy places, the strangely phallic tower of the YMCA and off to the right the Japanese outline of the Knesset. On the hilltops were luxury hotels and many blocks of flats, ranged across the skyline like a massive outer wall.

Directly to the west of Alcatraz, across the hollow into which it would fall, was a small new hotel called the Park International. Roscoe could see the plate-glass window of its rooftop reception room.

That was the room where Saladin would meet the press on Wednesday. The time would be evening, just before nine o'clock.

The room had a platform at one end. The press would be expecting someone else, but onto this stage would step Saladin. His speech would be short: an announcement of his identity, a word about the despoliation of Jerusalem, an invitation to look to the left . . . 'and please stand back from the window.' Yes, Roscoe thought, that had better be added – and while this was happening he himself would be somewhere outside the hotel.

If conditions permitted he would fire several flares in the air to illuminate the scene, and at 9 p.m. precisely the two control boxes would deliver their small electric charge to the twenty-four detonators. Morley's camera would record the event.

Some of the press would perhaps turn on Saladin in anger, but by that time he would be gone, slipping quietly with Bassam into the service lift held ready by Horowitz, then out through the kitchens to a car which Giscard would have ready and away in an UNWRA vehicle waiting near by. Bassam and Horowitz into another car, which he himself would have waiting outside the hotel, then back to Jericho and the truck, which Ibrahim drives to safety, smashing through the fence as his headlights pick up the marker flag . . .

Roscoe could see no major fault in the plan but had assembled a small list of queries. Seeing that darkness was still some time away, he walked off to find a call box.

Saladin answered himself.

'Stephen?'

'Yes, it's me.'

'So you've made it.'

'Yes.'

'No problems?'

'Nothing serious.'

'I've been worried. I thought Claudia would call me . . .'

Roscoe explained about Claudia. Saladin understood. They discussed their intervening adventures, then moved on to current business. Saladin said that Bassam and Horowitz had gone out to post the invitations to the press. Roscoe thought a meeting unnecessary; all he needed to know was where to meet Horowitz next day. Saladin told him. They discussed a few other arrangements – the press conference, the escape – then concluded.

Roscoe walked back to Alcatraz and snooped around it in the dark. The Arab workers had gone. Some Israeli technicians came out, and then at six the two sentries were relieved, just as Refo had said. The second one was posted in the basement. The new man in front was lackadaisical; he lit a cigarette and settled down on the steps to read a paperback by torchlight.

Roscoe found a taxi and went to his hotel. Now what he wanted was a drink, a bath, bed. He was sick of hotels but the

American Colony was unusually pleasant, an old Arab house
with a courtyard full of flowers.

There he found Morley, cockahoop at the bar with his crew.
His report had been upgraded to fifty minutes of screen time
and General Dayan had given him an interview. Morley was
riding the crest of the wave, Morley was buying the drinks.
Roscoe took him into the courtyard and told him that the
following day he would receive an invitation to a press conference from a British parliamentary delegation who were
coming to Jerusalem to make a presentation to the Knesset.

Morley was shocked that a man such as Roscoe could have
so little notion of TV priorities. 'Is that all you came here to
tell me?'

'I suggest you attend. Get there early and set up your
camera.'

'Sorry man, we're flying back tomorrow.'

Roscoe went further. 'Cancel the flight,' he said. 'I promised
you a story – this will be the best you'll ever get.'

Morley hovered. 'But what's it got to do with . . .'

'More than you think.'

'You mean . . .'

'You'll see what I mean. Just be there.'

Morley began to get excited. 'I want to hear more about this.
Have another drink.'

But Roscoe refused to say more. He retreated to bed and
passing through the lobby came across Cassavetes, who, predictably, had chosen the same hotel. They exchanged frigid
smiles. Roscoe walked out to the annexe in which he was
lodged. He was crossing the street when he heard a car pull up
behind him and turned to see Claudia's Fiat. She hurried
towards him, and as she stepped into the light he saw the news
was bad.

'They've got Bassam,' she said.

4. The Street of Sorrow

Roscoe was calm. He led her back towards the car. 'How do you know?'

'Horowitz phoned me. He just escaped himself.'

'How did it happen?'

'They were spotted at the Post Office by a boy from the kibbutz. It's my fault really.'

Roscoe thought it might be his, but did not explain. 'Why is it your fault?'

'I was supposed to post those letters. But we were late back from the border and when I didn't ring, Bassam decided to do it himself. Apparently the timing has to be right. They must reach the press on Wednesday.'

Roscoe understood the reason for that. 'So,' he said, 'Horowitz drove him there.'

'Yes.'

'In what?'

Claudia explained that Bassam had given her money to hire a car the previous Friday. Horowitz had abandoned it near the Jaffa Road then immediately telephoned to warn her, suggesting she report the car stolen.

Roscoe thought about that. 'No,' he said, 'keep mum. It's not a bad excuse though, if you get asked.'

Privately he was appalled that she had been so directly involved. This was the car which he would have used to take Bassam and Horowitz to Jericho from the Park International. It should have been hired by Giscard.

'So, new situation. Poor old Bassam.'

'Stephen, he'll talk, I know he will. He's just not strong enough.'

'We can't assume that.'

'You mean you'll carry on?'

'Yes, I think so, I'd better talk to the boss. Let's find a call box.'

Claudia drove away from the American Colony, and just then it started to rain: a rush of wind, followed by an instant downpour. She sat in the car while Roscoe made the call.

Saladin also was calm, though his voice was flat with disappointment. He agreed, it was too late to alter the plan. He had spoken to Giscard, who was willing to proceed. Roscoe said Giscard should hire another car, and then asked about Horowitz. How was he? Still game? There was a pause, then Saladin answered in a manner which made Roscoe realize that Horowitz was listening.

'He's willing to go with you to Eilat.'

Roscoe noted the reserve in that statement. He said he would pick up Walid and the others and proceed to the hideout as arranged. On Wednesday he would telephone from Jericho. Apart from arrests the first sign that Bassam had talked would be Israeli troops around Alcatraz, so someone should do a final reconnaissance, and the man for that was Giscard, who was due to arrive in Jerusalem from Gaza that day.

Saladin agreed with these suggestions, as if they were the best one could do in a hopeless situation. 'We shan't see Bassam again.'

'No, not for a while.'

'Not ever,' said Saladin, sounding suddenly impatient with this British understatement. 'Officially he does not exist here, so they don't have to bother with a trial. They will torture him then kill him.'

'I doubt that.'

'Stephen, you don't know these people.'

'That's true,' Roscoe said. He did not know the Israelis, he did not know the Arabs. He had heard the stories. He thought that Israel might be capable of some pretty rough stuff; he also thought it likely the Arabs exaggerated. Still, however you looked at it, Bassam's arrest was a very bad development.

After the phone call he sat beside Claudia in the car, infected by Saladin's despair. The rain was torrential, gurgling in the gutters, scouring the city of dust.

Claudia too was dejected. 'I knew you'd carry on,' she said. 'Stephen, this really is mad.'

'We'll take it in stages. We can always pull back at the end.'

'And you're not going to change the plan at all?'

'How can we? It's too late for that.'

'It's crazy. He should go back to Beirut and you should get the next flight to London. Try another day.'

'You know it's now or never,' Roscoe said. 'Anyway, what about Bassam? If he holds out, we owe it to him to go on.'

'Oh, the honour of men.' Claudia lowered her head and picked at her dress. 'Poor Bassam, he was such a nice man.'

Roscoe pulled her head to his chest and they sat like that, silent for a while, parked in some street in Jerusalem, listening to the rain, glad to be together.

Roscoe was tired; all his limbs ached, also his head. Claudia too seemed quite spent, and then in one of those startling reversals of mood of which her sex are capable, she kissed him. 'I want to spend the night with you.'

'I don't think you should.'

'Please. I want to.'

'We're being watched.'

'What difference does that make? They'll watch us anyway.'

Roscoe was not in condition to resist. He agreed.

'Hooray,' cried Claudia, 'I've seduced the big soldier. Now I shall cut off his hair.'

Roscoe collected his luggage from the hotel, then she took him to her flat, which was four small rooms above the Anglican Mission, a short distance inside the old city wall. When she unlocked the door he saw cream-painted offices, plain wooden furniture, a crucifix. Upstairs, where she lived, was equally neat: a few dresses and shoes, a few books. She showed him a bed, into which he flopped, first shivering uncontrollably then sweating until the sheets were damp. Claudia played nurse, bringing him a hot drink and aspirin, smiling down as she wiped his face with a flannel. 'I love you, you know that, don't you?'

'I love you too,' he said, closing his eyes as she kissed him and switched out the light.

He fell asleep listening to the rain.

In the morning it had stopped. Claudia woke him early with tea, then lay beside him on the narrow bed. Together they watched the light grow and listened to the city stir about them, the groan of the muezzin, the patter of a mule's feet, a gathering shuffle of slippers on the ancient paving. Roscoe felt better, but strangely light-headed. The sounds in the street were far off, the world beyond this room seemed unreal. Jerusalem and its slowly stirring masses, his own long journey to get here, the prospect of violent action ahead – in all this wild dreaming the only reality was Claudia, breathing now beside him, eyes closed as he stroked her hair and face.

He was like a man who has stumbled on treasure, compelled to make sure of it by touch, but carefully, in case it should come to pieces in his hands; but Claudia, while happy to submit to this, was thinking there wasn't much point in it since he would probably be killed. She asked him what he thought he would be doing a week from today.

'Getting quotes for the gutters. And you?'

'I'll carry on here, I suppose. I may get leave at Christmas.'

'I hope you'll come and see me.'

'Is that an invitation?'

'Of course.'

'Then I will.' She opened her eyes and smiled at him. 'How do you feel?'

'Better. Thanks to you.'

A yellow square of sunlight appeared on the ceiling, and watching it Roscoe had exactly the opposite feeling to the one in Amman. This is the dawn of my life, he thought. All this long time I have been in the dark, but now perhaps . . .

Claudia got off the bed, interrupting the thought, and he watched her pick up the tea cups, moving about in a long white nightdress, her bare feet slapping softly on the tiles. Then she came back from the kitchen and stood by the window, looking down. 'Isn't it extraordinary,' she said, 'to think that Christ died a hundred yards from here?'

Roscoe agreed it was hard to believe. 'Do they know exactly where?'

'Oh yes, there's a horrible church with a hole in the floor. The stations of the cross are an industry – everywhere you go there's a creepy monk holding out a poor-box. It's about as religious as a funfair.'

Roscoe dressed, then joined her at the window. Knowing the Israelis were there, he did not bother to look for them. The

air smelt fresh. Below the window was a steep stone-paved
street descending in steps towards the tunnel of a teeming
bazaar, like a Bible illustration. Christ staggering by with his
cross was as easy to imagine as the hacking Crusaders, or
Israeli paratroops weeping hysterically as they shot their way
back to the Temple. The tourists were like time-travellers,
wandering with their cameras through the Arab kefias, the
starched white wings of Christian nuns and the black saucer-
hats of orthodox Jews.

Roscoe lowered his voice – they had avoided all talk of
Saladin inside the flat. 'What we need now is a place where I
can get out the back. Somewhere near a gate.'

Claudia thought for a moment, then suggested Miss Carter.
'Who's she?'

'A very good friend. She runs a souvenir shop just up the
road – where I park my car. We can go in through the front,
then she'll drive you out in her van.'

'Sounds fine.' Roscoe looked at his watch. He was due to
meet Horowitz at noon. 'Let's have something to eat.'

After breakfast they walked up the Via Dolorosa, where the
shrines were as numerous as shops. Here He was flogged,
here's where He dropped it, this is where His brow was
wiped . . . The tourists' cameras clicked and an enterprising
Arab tried to sell Roscoe a crown of thorns. Claudia was
pensive but Roscoe was almost boisterously cheerful, not at all
in crucifixion mood, his spirits restored with his health. The
world was washed clean, and he was in that happy condition
where even the touch of her arm, linked in his, gave him
pleasure. He could not believe his luck would run out.

Miss Carter was a middle-aged American, bright of eye and
full of indignation against the Israelis. When Roscoe was introduced as a journalist she offered to show him a case in Hebron,
an elderly couple whose house had been destroyed because
their son had helped the Fedayeen. She was due to assess their
need that morning for a private charity. Roscoe said this would
suit him well and ten minutes later was driven away in the back
of her van, explaining that he did not want to be observed,
which Miss Carter agreed was a sensible precaution. Very few
journalists, she said, had the wit or the guts to resist Israeli
guidance.

As soon as they were clear of the city Roscoe joined her in the front of the vehicle. They passed by Bethlehem, then drove on southwards to Hebron, and from there Roscoe took a taxi to Beersheba, where Horowitz was waiting in uniform with the truck, now painted in military drab.

Roscoe was sad to see the change in him: the swelling of the body and shrinkage of spirit. They greeted each other as friends but then could find little to say.

From Beersheba they drove east across an undulating plain where the Bedouin reappeared with their camels, past Dimona, Israel's heavily guarded atomic research centre, then down to the salt plant at Sodom, where they turned south again, following the line of the frontier with Jordan. Nothing went wrong. They ignored appeals for lifts. The road stretched on south free of checkpoints, rising imperceptibly toward sea level and passing King Solomon's Mines, the rich store of copper which Moses had promised his people.

They reached Eilat in the late afternoon, parked the truck and walked along the beach to the border with Aqaba – that tangle of wire spilling down into the sea. And there on the other side was Walid, still dressed for Henley, sitting on the sand as arranged. They gave him the signal then returned to the truck and drove to a restaurant, where Roscoe ate a meal while Horowitz watched him in silence. The water was calm, as before, deserted of shipping. Hippies were camped on the Israeli beach and further along were the tents of an army post. Roscoe saw the usual two dinghies set out for night patrol, then bought himself some whisky and set off with Horowitz about 10 p.m., driving round the shore of the Gulf to the rendezvous, where they parked the truck out of sight and walked down to an inlet concealed from the road. The night was black as could be wished, moonless and tranquil.

They settled down to wait on the rocks at the water's edge. Horowitz did not speak. Roscoe took an occasional swallow of Scotch and thought of Claudia, safe now in bed. Sitting in the dark by the Gulf of Aqaba he pictured their reunion on the platform at Saltfleet-in-the-Marsh, the weed-grown Lincoln-shire station which connected with Boston. He could see it quite clearly. He believed his luck would hold.

5. Like Wolves on the Fold

But Claudia was neither safe nor in bed. As soon as it was clear from Shin Beth's report that Roscoe had evaded surveillance, Yaacov had decided to interrogate her.

Yaacov was by this time more anxious than at any previous point, face to face with not only failure but disgrace. Saladin and Horowitz were still hidden; Bassam had said nothing. Roscoe was again on the loose, and if he managed to get his little team into Israel anything could happen. With Bassam arrested they might change their method of entry and also the target, whatever that might be. Yes, the present situation could be summarized all too succinctly: Saladin was winning hands down.

But Yaacov continued to think coolly. He conferred with Ariel and they decided to do three things.

First, Bassam Owdeh would now be interrogated with the fullest rigour allowed by the classified regulations issued to certain security units and the army. Ariel himself would direct this operation, remaining with it day and night until it was complete. Yaacov would also give it what time he could. Yaacov would play the soft man to Ariel's hard and they would alternate in the usual manner. Owdeh was now at Jerusalem's central police station, where no one had managed to make the slightest sense of what he said. Sarafand was the obvious place to take him, but that was not convenient for Yaacov, so Ariel proposed he be brought to Alcatraz, which was equipped with the relevant facilities. Yaacov agreed and it was done.

Second, military checkpoints. These now seemed a legitimate defensive measure. Yaacov did not expect Roscoe's men to succeed in crossing the border, but if they made an attempt it would certainly be at some point between Eilat and Jericho. They could therefore be cut off by no more than three roadblocks, one between Jericho and Jerusalem, another at Dimona and a third west of Arad. These were set up about 2 p.m., and as each unit phoned in to Yaacov in Beit Agron he marked their positions on a map, secure in the knowledge that if Roscoe was now between Jericho and Eilat, he was trapped.

Yaacov's third decision, taken late that afternoon, was to bring Claudia Lees in for questioning. There was, he reasoned, nothing to be lost by it. Since she clearly knew she was under surveillance she was not going to lead them to Saladin. On the other hand she could be used against Bassam. Suspects were easier to break when there were two; either could be persuaded that resistance was futile, since the other had talked. So Yaacov gave orders that Claudia be brought to the top floor of Alcatraz, where Bassam was now being put through the hoops.

But then he got a second shock. Shin Beth had not only lost Roscoe; they had also lost Claudia, who had vanished inside the old city, along with the agent who was tailing her.

What had happened was this.

After seeing Roscoe off Claudia had returned to the Mission for a normal day's work, which was interrupted in the late afternoon by a man who walked into her office uninvited, a young Arab in European dress and steel-rimmed spectacles who leaned across her desk and said in a soft voice that he had an important message for Saladin. She asked him his name. He replied that he was Adnan Khadduri.

Claudia turned hot then cold. 'What do you want?' she said.

'I must talk to you.'

'Not here.'

'No,' agreed Adnan. 'Please come with me.'

'This place is being watched.'

'We know that, don't worry.' Adnan smiled.

Claudia tried to be calm. There was nowhere she could run, but as long as she stayed in the Mission she was safe. 'We have no wish to be involved with the Popular Front,' she said.

Adnan stiffened in surprise, then sat slowly in a chair, as if wearied by these factional squabbles. 'We are on the same side,' he said after a pause.

'Not exactly.'

'In Beirut, perhaps not. But here there is only one enemy. We must cooperate, Miss Lees. You are in danger.'

'Will I be safer with you?'

'You will be among friends. And if you wish to protect your friend Stephen Roscoe, you will come with me now.'

'Is that a threat?'

'No, no, it is a warning. You see, they are waiting for him.'

'Who?'

'The Israelis have men on the roads. If he tries to come back he will be killed.'

Claudia faltered. 'Are you sure?'

Adnan nodded. 'My information is reliable.'

Claudia appeared to be convinced. 'All right,' she said, 'wait for me outside. I'll be with you in a minute.'

Adnan hesitated, then agreed to leave the room.

Claudia tried to think clearly. She did not dare to use her telephone because of Roscoe's warning. The Mission would shortly be closed, and then she would be alone in her flat. The PFLP were no friends of Saladin; on the other hand Adnan seemed genuine. She could not believe he would harm her. So she cleared up her papers and joined him in the street.

'Stay close to me,' he said, and gave her an encouraging smile.

Claudia did as she was told, but was more encouraged by the knowledge of an Israeli agent behind.

They walked downhill, out of the sunlit streets below the New Gate and into the dark maze of tunnels and alleys of the old Arab quarter. The crowds of hawkers and tourists pressed close around them. Claudia's abduction was so swift she was scarcely aware of it. She followed Adnan through a door and saw a narrow corridor, steps leading down in the dark. Two men were waiting inside, flattened against the wall. One of them took hold of her roughly and pulled her down the steps. The other was Zeiti. He was holding a long-barrelled pistol close to his chest. He did not look at her or speak as she was dragged past him. Adnan muttered something in Arabic and stepped back into the street. Claudia's protests were smothered by a hand clapped across her mouth. She was now at the bottom of the steps, held hard against the wall. Another form obscured the door above, then tumbled down with a cry; Claudia's Israeli shadow landed at her feet. Zeiti almost dived down the steps. The Israeli on the floor was half up, but fell

back with a grunt as Zeiti kicked him in the face. A pistol
clattered to the floor. The man stirred; Zeiti kicked him again,
then dragged him by the collar through a second door, followed
by Claudia and her captor. The door was slammed shut and
Zeiti switched on a light, a single weak bulb suspended from
the ceiling. The room was full of sacks and smelled of spice.
No one spoke. The Israeli was lying face down on the floor,
still stirring feebly. Zeiti heaved him up against a sack and
fired into his chest, then dragged him to a corner of the room
where he quivered and lay still. Adnan came in through the
door and said something to the man holding Claudia, who
released her and went back up the steps. Adnan closed the door.
Zeiti put away his pistol and lit a cigarette. Claudia sank to the
floor, then Adnan pulled out a sack and laid it horizontal to
make her a seat. It was some time before she could speak.
Adnan told her that he and Zeiti had come across the border
from Syria, a combined operation of the Front and Black
September, who now wished to join forces with Saladin. All
she had to do was tell them where he was.

Of the two Claudia thought the soft-talking Adnan more
frightening. She was shocked by his glib deception at the
Mission, almost more so than by Zeiti's casual murder of the
Israeli. She could hardly believe what had happened and for
many hours afterwards half-expected Roscoe to come through
the door, pistol blazing.

6. The Gulf

But Claudia was far from Roscoe's thoughts as he waited for his men beside the Gulf of Aqaba. What bothered him was Horowitz, whose manner was increasingly peculiar. The man seemed to be in some kind of deep, irreversible sulk. Since their meeting in Beersheba he had hardly said a word and as they sat in the dark at the water's edge, waiting intently for the soft slap of paddles, Roscoe could feel the man's hostility and fear.

'Have a slug of this,' he said, holding out the whisky.

No answer.

Roscoe emptied the bottle into the sea. He had had enough himself. But something must be done about Horowitz.

'You're regretting this, aren't you?'

Horowitz did not reply. Roscoe could only just see him, huddled on the rocks a few yards away. A mile to the north the lights of Eilat and Aqaba were spread around the end of the Gulf.

'I said you're regretting this.'

So quietly that Roscoe could hardly hear him above the slop of the waves, Horowitz said yes, he was regretting it.

'I can understand that.'

'Can you?'

'Yes, I think so.'

'I think not,' Horowitz mumbled. 'I think you cannot understand what it means for me to do this.'

'I remember what you said at the kibbutz. It struck me then that Israel must never be destroyed.'

'But that is your job, to destroy. You are a military man.'

'I thought we were creating something. You said yourself you were in it for the sake of your people.'

'That was the theory, all very fine. But in practice it comes down to *this*!' Horowitz flung an angry pebble into the water. 'These people who are coming here, are they any different from the ones who attack us every day? Who murder our women and children?'

'Of course they're different. God knows what passes in their heads, but they're under my command for a start. No one will be hurt if I can help it.'

'*If* you can help it!' Horowitz hissed in disgust. 'Ah, you English are such hypocrites. You like to keep your noses clean, don't you? You pretend to be fair but in the end you are only for yourselves.' He flung another furious pebble. 'How do you know what it means to be a Jew? You cannot know. That is why Israel was created, to protect us from people like this – like you. That is why I ask myself what I am doing here.'

Horowitz ended in Hebrew, perhaps with an oath, and Roscoe saw that it was useless. The mood of the kibbutz was totally lost. When it came to the test, blood was stronger than reason, and Saladin would fail as the poor pious British and all neutral parties had failed, because the forces in play were too strong. Between the fear of the Jews and the pride of the Arabs there was no room for compromise.

This thought had been creeping up on him for weeks and now it struck him with the weight of a hopeless conviction. He felt that he might as well go home.

'Well,' he said, 'we're in this together now, whether we like it or not. So for God's sake let's do it well and talk about it later.'

'Leave God out of it.'

'All right, for the sake of your bloody people then.' Roscoe looked at his watch. 'It's time for the light. Have you got it?'

Horowitz said nothing but passed across a signal torch, pre-set to green and narrow beam. Roscoe took it back to a cave he had found at the foot of the cliffs and switched it on, angling the beam precisely with a compass until it coincided with the bearing on which the two dinghies would approach. Then he clambered back across the rocks and they waited together, not speaking.

The Gulf was like a black hole in space. The line between water and land could not be distinguished; only the stars showed where the sky began. The Israeli patrols had been observed to keep to a pattern, one covering the harbour while the other stayed out in the Gulf. Nazreddin's plan was to distract the outer unit with a Jordanian patrol boat while

Mukhtar passed between, cutting his motors and paddling along a fixed bearing until he saw the signal light. If that had gone wrong there would already have been a commotion on the water. Now Mukhtar's dinghies should be close. The danger was the Israeli sentry in a watchtower perched on the cliffs three hundred yards south. His searchlight had probed the night spasmodically, but now was inactive. The time was 10.55. Five minutes to go. Roscoe strained to catch the slightest sound or movement and then suddenly, miraculously, there they were, coming in one behind the other with a dip and swirl of paddles, right on the hour. He wanted to cheer. Scrambling back into the cave he doused the light, then guided them into a beach below the road. He was knee-deep in water, grasping their hands and slapping their shoulders. Faces were invisible; mutters of Arabic in the dark. Under Mukhtar's direction the dinghies were dragged up, unloaded, deflated, dismantled and hidden with the speed and precision of a military demonstration. Transferring the equipment and explosive to the truck took longer, a laborious relay up a steep twisting path, halted each time a vehicle drove past. Roscoe was handed a bundle by Walid – his Browning and an Israeli uniform. He changed on the beach then followed the last man up to the truck. Ibrahim took the wheel, Horowitz beside him. Roscoe sat behind with the others, placing himself beside the cabin's rear window. They set off. Cigarettes were lit.

The road was unobstructed, empty of traffic, and by the first light of day they were at the Dead Sea, its salt crystals glinting like ice as the sun's early rays struck the walls of Masada to the left. At the northern extremity of the lake Ibrahim slowed down to inspect their escape route, a track leading down to the border fence. Then Jericho came into view and they turned into Aqabat Jabr, the deserted refugee camp, bouncing through its empty rutted streets until they found the building which Bassam had recommended.

It was an old UNWRA garage, built of breeze blocks and roofed with rusting sheets of corrugated iron. Some of these sheets had been pilfered, leaving rectangular gaps through which the sun shone in beams on the rubble-strewn floor. A bleak place, but ideal for their purpose. Fuad and the Gipsy were posted as sentries while the truck was backed into a corner

and unloaded. Horowitz stood to one side. None of the Arabs
had spoken to him. Each party preferred to ignore the existence
of the other and yet they looked a cohesive unit, identically
dressed in green Israeli denim and forage caps, the solitary
Jew indistinguishable from the Arabs.

As Mukhtar and Ibrahim unloaded the equipment Walid
laid it neatly on the floor and Roscoe inspected it item by item.
Nothing was damaged, nothing even wet. Then he gathered
them all in a circle and gave them detailed instructions for the
rest of the day – sentry rosters, weapon-cleaning, preparation
of charges, procedure to follow if disturbed. He was pleased
with the discipline displayed in the night and told them so,
through Walid. After the landing he had noticed they were
silent and nervous, but now they chattered excitedly as they
went about their tasks, obviously delighted with their daring.
They would settle down during the day, he thought. The point
of maximum danger was past. Provided Bassam held out, the
rest should be comparatively straightforward, and the best way
not to think about Bassam was to keep busy.

There was in any case plenty to do. One of the Gipsy's party
tricks was to make a smokeless fire, and so he brewed tea while
the others made ready the detonators, connecting them to
their wires and setting them in the Plastex, carefully coiling the
wires into the haversacks. Roscoe tested the control boxes and
then the walkie-talkies; then the torches, then the radio, which
received an answering bleep from Nazreddin in Jordan. Then
he took out the plans of Alcatraz and went through it again
from the beginning, while Horowitz looked on in silence. In
the afternoon they slept. About 5 p.m. Roscoe drove into Jericho
and telephoned Saladin, who said that Giscard had inspected
Alcatraz and reported all clear. A new car had been hired.
Giscard had gone to the UNESCO Women's Training Centre
at Ramallah but would be back before the press conference.

'All set then,' Roscoe said.

'Yes, all set. Good luck, Stephen.'

'You too.'

'See you soon.'

Roscoe returned to the camp and they loaded the truck,
leaving various items of equipment in the garage. Roscoe
checked everything. Then they set off.

7. The Assault

It was Wednesday, November 8th, time 5.30 in the evening as Saladin's task force left the garage in Aqabat Jabr for the final approach to Alcatraz. On board the Dodge truck in which they were travelling they had 800 lb of Plastex, of which the destructive power can be gauged by the fact that the largest terrorist bombs very seldom exceed 20 lb. The sixteen haversacks into which this explosive was packed were placed behind the cabin of the truck, arranged in a ring around the rest of the equipment and watched over by Fuad, who was armed with a Uzi submachine-gun. The back of the Dodge was covered by a faded tarpaulin which shielded the vehicle's load from view. Under this tarpaulin, just inside the tailgate, sat Walid and the Gipsy, also armed with Uzis. Walid's brief was to watch for pursuers.

They were all wearing Israeli uniform, and their vehicle was of the military type which can be seen every day on the roads of the Occupied Territories.

Ibrahim was at the wheel and Horowitz in the front passenger seat, as the night before. But Roscoe had altered his own position. He was now inside the cabin, sitting on the floor behind the gear lever. By his left hand was Ibrahim's Uzi and on his right side, now carried in a webbing holster on his belt, his Browning pistol. His head was just high enough to see through the windscreen or back towards Walid through the cabin's rear window, from which the glass had been removed.

They followed the same route as Claudia had from the border. The sun was going down, the road busy with end-of-day traffic. Ibrahim took the right fork to Jerusalem and Roscoe settled back, glancing at the fuel gauge as they climbed into the hills. Then they came round a bend – and there was Yaacov's roadblock.

Roscoe jerked upright. Ibrahim braked, but there was nowhere he could turn. He changed down, then moved slowly forward into the queue of waiting vehicles. Roscoe called back a warning to Walid, and immediately Horowitz started to shake.

The procedure which had been worked out was for Horowitz to produce his reservist's papers and say they were on their way back from an exercise – but would he do it? Roscoe could not answer the question with confidence. The likelihood was, he thought, that Horowitz would simply not make any positive effort to talk his way through, passively allowing events to take their course.

This assumption of Roscoe's was probably correct. Horowitz had no intentions of any kind; he was like a man sleep-walking over a cliff, neither consciously seeking disaster nor capable of positive steps to avoid it. The problem of decision was therefore all Roscoe's, and he had a very short time at his disposal. About a dozen vehicles were waiting to go through and the queue was shrinking all the time. Ibrahim continued to drive forward. Horowitz continued to shake.

Roscoe's first move was to take out his pistol. Revealing it to Horowitz without ostentation, he said in what he hoped was a convincing manner: 'If you make a mess of this, I'll use it. Just do exactly what we agreed.'

Horowitz glanced at the pistol in surprise, then his face took on an extraordinary expression, half-smiling, simultaneously terrified and reckless. Roscoe saw straightaway he had made a mistake. The best favour he could do this man was to shoot him, and the threat to do so had merely made Horowitz more likely to defect. For a moment his mind went completely blank, bereft of alternatives. He glanced up the road at the check-point – four vehicles left, one of them a bus – and then on an impulse he did something inspired, a proof of what an artist he is in such situations. He leaned up and yanked the wheel of the Dodge to the left, shouting 'Pull out!' so suddenly that Ibrahim obeyed automatically and before he knew what he was doing had started to overtake the queue. Roscoe punched the horn. 'Go on! Accelerate!' Ibrahim accelerated forwards. The roadblock was temporary; there was no boom or obstacle. The troops inspecting documents turned in surprise, then waved them on through with a nonchalant greeting. Roscoe waved back, keeping his head well away from the window, and then

they were round the next bend and away, speeding unopposed
to Jerusalem.

Roscoe holstered his gun. In seconds the whole upper half
of his uniform had become wet with sweat. He then took out a
map, called Walid forward to the cabin's rear window and
showed him an alternative route for the return to Jericho,
looping northwards via Ramallah. Roscoe told him to sit
beside Ibrahim on the way back and if they came across a
roadblock to follow exactly the same procedure, straight on
through with a toot and a wave. Walid nodded, put the map in
his pocket and returned to his post at the back of the truck.

They drove on, the light fading fast as they climbed towards
Jerusalem. Horowitz was calm now. He said nothing for a mile
or two, then clicked his tongue and smiled. 'You're a pretty
smart guy, Roscoe, aren't you?' He shook his head, the smile
growing wider. 'Pretty smart, pretty smart.' Then he tapped
Roscoe's pistol in its holster, still smiling broadly. 'But you
wouldn't have used it.'

'How the hell do you know?'

'You didn't even cock it.'

'You're not so dumb yourself,' Roscoe said.

They laughed, and recapturing at this eleventh hour a little
of the mood of the kibbutz, both thought of Bassam. Roscoe
wondered aloud what treatment he would get and Horowitz
replied that he hated to think. 'I expect we have some nasty
types in that department.'

'Ever come across them?'

'No, I wasn't much of a soldier. They kept me at a desk.'

Roscoe knew from experience what could be done short of
serious physical damage. The Israelis would certainly allow
themselves as much, probably rather more than the British had
in Ulster, the object being to frighten and bewilder rather than
cause pain. Deprivation of sleep was often enough. The prisoner
was stripped and kept standing until his legs collapsed, jerked
to his feet again, hour after hour: a continuous process of
relentless bullying by two or three men in a small confined
space, sometimes turning to carefully gauged violence, to shov-
ing and jostling, to small sharp blows aimed about the body,
administered either with the hand or a short rubber truncheon
and supplemented by hair-pulling, ear-yanking, tweaking of

the balls, obscene threats. A hood placed over the head to cause disorientation, ceaseless questioning alternately brutal and mild, tape-recorded screams from the neighbouring cell, shots outside the window – there were many refinements and in the last resort drugs, against which the courage of any man was useless. Bassam would break in the end, he thought, but might perhaps last a little longer.

'It depends how seriously they're taking it,' he said. 'My guess is they think we're just a joke.'

Horowitz nodded, unconvinced. 'Let's hope so.'

When they reached Jerusalem it was dark. They drove straight up to Mount Scopus and parked near the Hebrew University, then Roscoe and Horowitz walked forward until they had Alcatraz in view. The work force had gone. While they watched, several cars drove away, some from the fore-court, others coming up the ramp from the basement. One by one the lights in the building were extinguished, until by 6.45 it appeared to be evacuated. Only the stairs and lobby were still lit, and two small windows on the top floor. No movement could be seen inside either. A single light was also burning on the roof and from somewhere up there Roscoe thought he heard the barking of a dog. He did not comment on it. He drew the attention of Horowitz to the sentry in front, just visible in the light still coming from the lobby. 'Now,' he said, 'we're going to do a clean job. No excitement, no mess. But that fellow's life depends on you. The closer we can get to him the better chance he has, and the same goes for the one in the basement.'

Horowitz nodded but did not speak. He had started to shake again.

'Just be ready with the Hebrew,' Roscoe said, 'and leave the rest to me. All right?'

'All right.'

'Let's go then.'

They returned to the truck. Roscoe left Horowitz alone in the cabin while he briefed the others and checked their weapons, cocked now, with safety catches on. He repeated that no one was to fire except on his orders. Walid translated. Then Roscoe wished them luck and returned to his position in the cabin, Ibrahim again at the wheel. The time was 6.55. They started forward, turned right, drove three hundred yards along the ridge then left down the access road. Alcatraz reared close ahead, a massive black square against the night sky, the lights of the city spread behind and below it.

Things happened quickly.

Ibrahim pulled up at the entrance, where one car was still parked. Roscoe and Horowitz stepped out. The sentry came down the steps towards them, his Uzi still slung. He said something to Horowitz, and Horowitz replied. The sentry came on and then was reeling to the ground, felled by Roscoe with the same blow used against Gessner. Roscoe disarmed him and made the Uzi safe while Walid jumped down and applied a chloroform pad to the fallen man's face. When his limbs were slack they heaved him into the truck where Fuad slapped adhesive tape over his mouth and handcuffed him to one of the tarpaulin stays. The Gipsy clipped cuffs on his feet.

Horowitz stood watching, immobile with shock. Roscoe ordered him back into the cabin of the truck. Ibrahim still had the engine running.

Walid took the place of the sentry, installing himself in the shadows with a walkie-talkie. If challenged he had a few words of Hebrew rehearsed.

Roscoe and the Gipsy walked up the steps and through the front entrance. The doors were unlocked, which made Roscoe almost certain that the building was not yet fully evacuated. He did not stop to reflect on it. The floor of the lobby was half tiled, half raw concrete; the lift shaft gaped empty. Roscoe peered into it and saw the expected iron ladder. He sent the Gipsy down it, then returned to the truck.

Ibrahim turned in a circle, round the lift crates and the cement-mixers, then along the north side of the building and down the ramp into the basement, which was lit by fluorescent light-strips in the ceiling. Parked in one corner, at the foot of some stairs, was a car and a military jeep. So someone was still in the building, but if Horowitz had now made this deduction he said nothing of it and Roscoe did not pause for a moment. They drove towards the sentry, who was sitting on the stairs. As they stepped out he jumped up, startled, and unslung his weapon. He challenged them, and this time Horowitz stood speechless, the fright apparent on his face. Roscoe walked forward with a casual 'Shalom', but the sentry cocked his gun and raised the barrel, issuing another sharp challenge. Roscoe stood still. Then the Gipsy came out of the lift shaft, moving like a little brown stoat towards the sentry's back. The sentry turned too late, the Gipsy had hold of him. Roscoe dived forward, knocking back the Gipsy's knife and half-wrenching the Uzi from the sentry's hand in one desperate movement. The Israeli fell over, tugging fiercely at his weapon, then Roscoe had it free and whipped the barrel round on him. The sentry scrambled to his feet, hesitated, looked round and then ran for the ramp – at which point Fuad saved the day. Younger than Ibrahim, a lean wiry man who had shown much agility in the Lebanese mountains, he was out of the back of the truck and across the basement like a sprinter off the starting-block, catching up the sentry, clawing at his uniform and eventually bringing him down on the concrete. Roscoe was hard behind, and then the job was done. He had the man's upper half in a fierce two-armed grip while the Gipsy grabbed his flailing legs and Fuad applied the pad to his face. They put him in the truck with the other, then paused to catch their breath. It was now seven o'clock. Only five minutes had passed since they had left the university precinct.

Horowitz was flapping his hands, almost in tears. Roscoe took hold of him. So far so good, he said, nothing works perfectly but no bones broken, so be thankful for that. Horowitz nodded miserably, collecting himself with an effort. Roscoe was sure that he would not bolt now and so asked him to keep a look-out on the basement stairs. Horowitz agreed, took the sentry's Uzi and a walkie-talkie. Roscoe showed him how to work it, then just as he picked up the third walkie-talkie for himself, it buzzed, and Walid's voice came through to say that a car was approaching the front. Roscoe waited tensely.

Above ground, on the steps, Walid stood back in the shadows as two Israelis, one of them in uniform, one in a suit, hurried past into the building and on up the stairs. The civilian was Ariel, though Walid did not know it. He reported all clear. The time was 7.05.

Roscoe went quickly to work, unloading from the truck one control box and the eight packs of explosive for the lift shaft, distinguished from the others by the keys of the soft-iron magnets which projected through holes cut into the webbing. They were assembled at the bottom of the shaft. Running up the wall of the shaft was the vertical service ladder down which the Gipsy had climbed – in fact there were two ladders, one on each side. Roscoe formed a human chain on each in turn with himself at the top, the Gipsy below him, then Fuad, then Ibrahim at the bottom. The haversacks were passed up the chain, weighing 56 lb apiece with the additional weight of the magnets. Each man had to climb a little with his load before handing it up. As Roscoe passed the ground-floor opening he looked across the lobby for Walid, but could not see him. Having climbed a little further, he began to fix the haversacks into position at the point where the first floor began, jamming each pack against the lift rails then twisting the keys of the magnetic chucks to hold them in position. Then, as the magnets took the weight, he opened the flap of each haversack, looked inside with his torch, took out the wires attached to the detonators and let them fall to the bottom of the shaft. The wires had been coiled with extreme care and small weights attached to their ends to make them fall easily. Before he closed the flap of each haversack Roscoe made sure the detonators were firm in the Plastex, their connections secure. Then he climbed down to meet the Gipsy, coming up with the next pack. It was dangerous, acrobatic work since some of the rails were out of reach of the ladder and to get at them Roscoe had to balance on the cross-bracing – the diagonal pattern of girders which provided the building's main support against horizontal thrust. He worked with complete concentration, his torch clamped between his teeth, his head empty of any thought not prompted by the technical needs of the moment. The building was silent; no danger buzz sounded from the walkie-talkie in his pocket.

By 7.20 it was done. The eight central charges were in position and he was gathering the wires at the bottom of the shaft, black and red, sixteen of each, twisting their pre-stripped ends into two separate leads, negative and positive. He turned to the control box – and then stopped. They could all hear the footsteps, coming down the stairs, still several floors up. Horowitz and Walid yapped simultaneously into their walkie-talkies. Roscoe told them to keep their distance from the exits

and act naturally. He waited, hidden in the shaft with the
others. All torches were off. No one moved. The steps came
closer, then travelled across the ground floor and out the front
entrance. They belonged to Yaacov, who drove away in his car.
Walid was not challenged. Half a minute later he reported all
clear.

Roscoe turned back to the control box, set the timer, twisted
the charging handle, pressed the test button, saw the test fuse
blow then threaded the leads round the two brass connector
studs, which he screwed down tight.

The main task was done. Setting the four extra charges
against the back outer wall took less time. They were placed at
ground-floor level against the building's main vertical supports,
which though now sheathed in concrete could easily be detected
from the shape of the walls. All four packs were connected to
the second control box and this box then linked to the first in
the basement by wires which Roscoe was careful to conceal.

Now the whole job was done. The time was 7.30. Torches,
tools, surplus wire, reserve control box and walkie-talkies were
replaced in the truck with the spare 200 lb of explosive. Ibrahim
took the wheel and they drove up the ramp. Walid climbed
aboard. They went on up the access road to the ridge, turned
left along Mount of Olives Road, drove a short distance, then
stopped.

Roscoe congratulated them all and passed round a hipflask.
Only the Gipsy drank from it. The rest lit cigarettes, except
Walid, who neither smoked nor drank. Horowitz explained how
to find the road to Ramallah, then he and Roscoe stepped down.
They would be in Aqabat Jabr later that night, Roscoe said, but
did not specify a time. He began to wonder how he and Horowitz
were going to get through any roadblocks in a private car. They
might have to try for the frontier somewhere else, he thought,
and so told Walid that if they had not turned up by the following
night he was to take the others on out, warning Nazreddin by
radio first. If they got no answering signal they should go
anyway, firing a red Very light exactly three minutes before
they hit the wire. The sentries should be left in the garage at
Aqabat Jabr, handcuffed to some solid object and given a fresh
dose of chloroform just before departure. They were on no
account to be harmed. Walid absorbed this and then said good-

bye, shaking Roscoe's hand with a proud flashing smile. Ibrahim started the truck and they were gone.

Roscoe and Horowitz walked down from Mount Scopus into Wadi al Joz. From the bottom of the hill Roscoe looked back at Alcatraz and now found it easy to imagine that massive bulk leaping, sagging, tumbling, blown off its perch at 9 p.m. precisely. He was eager to see it. He glanced at his watch. It was 7.50.

Arriving at the Park International he and Horowitz went first to the hotel's car park, where Giscard had left a British Ford saloon for the run back to Jericho. Roscoe looked under a floormat, found the keys, tested the car and reparked it. He took a Very pistol and four flare cartridges from the blouse of his uniform and put them in the boot. Then he and Horowitz crossed the road and went into a block of service flats also owned by the hotel.

One of these flats had been rented by Refo, who used another name for the purpose. Refo travelled constantly during this period between Israel, the Lebanon, Jordan and various destinations in the West, but needless to say he was not in Jerusalem that day. Since October 29th the flat had served as Saladin's hideout in the city, and for that it was ideal, situated as it was in a rich and respectable ghetto much favoured by diplomats and expatriate businessmen, a largely European colony, self-contained, undisturbed, law-abiding, the last place that Yaacov would look. It was also convenient for the press conference, due in an hour's time.

Roscoe had warned Morley to expect an invitation from a British parliamentary delegation, and that delegation was real enough, the first of many such groups to come from all over the world for Israel's twenty-fifth anniversary. They arrived in Jerusalem that evening and next day presented a silver Menora candelabrum to Abba Ebban in the Knesset. The only oddity in their programme was their press conference. The politicians assumed it had been arranged by the embassy in Tel Aviv; the embassy assumed they had arranged it themselves, as politicians will. It had in fact been arranged by Marsden, who had telephoned the Park International from London. The invitations had been printed by Horowitz in Tiberias and posted just in time to reach the press, just too late for awkward questions to gather any weight. The time selected, 9 p.m., was also nicely judged. The MPs' flight from London was due to reach Lod at 8.40, so they could not reach the Park International until Saladin was on his way to the Lebanon.

But these calculations were, as it happened, academic. Because Saladin was dead. He was already dead by eight o'clock that evening when Roscoe and Horowitz, both still in uniform, took the lift up to the fourth floor of the annexe and knocked on the door of his flat.

And instantly Roscoe knew they were trapped. The quietness of the building, the two men in the lobby, the open door further down the corridor – too late the details formed a pattern . . .

8. Flexibility in Battle

The door was held open by someone unseen; beyond it the flat was in darkness.

Roscoe saw that resistance was futile. There was nothing to do but submit.

He stepped forward, felt a gun barrel pressed to his neck and stood absolutely still as his Browning was removed and a hand fluttered over the pockets of his uniform. He heard Horowitz gasp in surprise. Rubber-soled feet were running up the corridor, the flat was full of people moving about in the dark – and then the lights were switched on by the Israeli officer who had quizzed him at the border.

One hand on the switch, the triumphant impresario, Yaacov allowed himself a smile. 'Good evening, Mr Roscoe. I see you've joined the army.'

But Roscoe felt only disappointment.

Saladin was on the sofa. His feet were in monogrammed slippers and one arm was flung outwards, exposing the sleeve of a flamboyant dressing-gown. The amber cigarette-holder was lying on the floor.

Yaacov told his men to leave the room and they were gone with a squeak of rubber soles, closing the door behind them softly. Horowitz sank into a chair, hanging his head over tightly clasped hands.

Roscoe stepped forward and examined the corpse. Its head was twisted sideways, lips drawn back from the teeth, one eye half-open; the skin of the face was taut across the bone, smooth and yellow, the black hair slightly disarranged. One bullet had passed through the chest, another through the side of the neck.

Ah well, it was neater than cancer. But sad, when they had come so far.

Bending down, he picked up the amber holder and put it in

his pocket. Then he turned to Yaacov. 'Did you do this?'

Yaacov denied responsibility.

'Your people then.'

'No.'

'All right, who?'

Yaacov lit a cigarette, pulling out the packet and flicking a flame from a lighter with deft easy movements. 'I think Miss Lees may answer that, when we can find her.'

Roscoe's expression did not alter, but now he was afraid. A chill spread like hemlock through his veins. 'What do you mean?'

Yaacov told him that Claudia had disappeared the previous evening.

Roscoe's fear hardened into angry suspicion. 'But your people were watching her.'

'We lost her.'

'Oh yes?'

'Yes.'

'I don't believe you.' Roscoe pointed to the body. 'If this wasn't your work what are you doing here?'

'It was reported. We found him dead.'

'And then you just hung around in the dark.'

'We were expecting you,' Yaacov said with a nod.

'All right, who killed him?'

'I'd say it was Arabs.'

'Oh yes, you would. And what's Claudia Lees got to do with it?'

'She has been abducted by Black September.'

Roscoe's instincts recoiled. He was not thinking straight, not thinking at all. 'You're a bloody liar,' he shouted. 'Where is she?'

Yaacov was patient. 'Three days ago,' he said, 'Ahmad Zeiti and Adnan Khadduri crossed the border into Golan. We have plenty of evidence for this. You know, and I know, why they took that risk. They wanted to stop you and they had only one way to do it. They knew where to find Miss Lees, correct?'

Roscoe said nothing. Yaacov went on.

'You can admit that or you can deny it, but I can assure you of two facts. Zeiti and Khadduri are in Israel, and Miss Lees was escorted from her office by a man who sounds like Khadduri.

There are witnesses. If you don't believe me, ask the priest she works for.'

Yaacov gestured at the telephone.

Roscoe shook his head and sat down. He saw that it was true.

Yaacov's tone softened. 'We had a man following her, as you observed. We found him dead in a cellar. Where they went after that we don't know – I wish I could tell you.'

'I suppose they'll leave the country,' Roscoe said.

Yaacov shook his head. 'Not Zeiti. He'll want to kill some Jews before he goes.'

'Yes. Very likely.'

Yaacov pulled up a chair and sat down himself. 'Now, I think you'd better tell me what you came here to do.'

Roscoe needed time. 'Could I have one of those?' he said.

'Of course. Help yourself.'

Yaacov passed him a cigarette and lit it. Horowitz was still sitting with his head in his hands. The room had the total, sealed silence of a vacuum. It was furnished like every service flat in the world, comfortable but featureless; a bad place to die.

Yaacov waited.

Roscoe smoked, then looked at his watch. The time was 8.10. New situation; therefore new plan required, and quick. He thought for two minutes before he spoke.

'I'd like to make you a proposition.'

Yaacov raised his eyebrows in amused surprise. 'Are you in a position to?'

'I think so.'

'Very well, I'm listening.'

'Point one,' said Roscoe, 'yesterday I brought five men across the border. They're armed and they've got enough explosive to cause a lot of casualties. Second point, tonight we mined a major public building in Jerusalem. It's due to go up in fifty minutes.'

Roscoe now paused for a reaction, but Yaacov was cool. 'So what's your proposition?'

'Very simple. I will show you which building and persuade my men to desist from further action on condition that you let us go free, and by that I mean all of us – Bassam Owdeh too.'

Yaacov's face was pale with anger as he rose to his feet. 'Even for an Englishman you are unusually insolent.'

He strode to the door and called his men in. Roscoe and
Horowitz were handcuffed and escorted roughly down the
service stairs. Just as they emerged from the building Roscoe
saw Giscard drive into the car park, glance in their direction,
then drive straight out again. He and Horowitz were then
thrust into a van. Yaacov and another man climbed in with
them; the doors were slammed shut, a light came on. The van
started forward, driving fast, siren wailing. Yaacov said something in Hebrew to Horowitz then struck him hard across the
face. Horowitz fell to the floor of the van. The other man
picked him up. Yaacov repeated his question, struck again. He
was taut, white-lipped with anger. But Horowitz would not
speak. Red weals were rising on his cheek. Roscoe watched
passively, gathering his resources, and then the van braked, the
doors were flung open. They were led up a short flight of steps
and through some glass doors into a half-finished building.

Roscoe almost laughed. It was Alcatraz. Yaacov was too
flustered to notice the absence of a sentry, too hurried to see
the wire connecting the control boxes. He took them up the
concrete stairs, dimly lit, past the first floor, the second – half-
finished plasterwork, electric cables snaking from the ceiling –
and on up to the eighth, where work was almost finished. Then
into an office: steel furniture on a tiled floor, fluorescent light,
telephones, two men in shirtsleeves. Yaacov barked at them.
One had raw scratch marks on his face, as if he had been
clawed by an animal. The other went out through a heavy steel
door and came back with a third man, a tall man, granite-faced
crewcut, hard as they come. Roscoe knew the type.

Yaacov and Ariel conferred in Hebrew. Ariel stood for a
moment in thought, then beckoned to Horowitz and punched
him in the groin. Horowitz fell doubled up to the floor, whim-
pering like a dog as Ariel questioned him, kicked him, repeated
the question.

Yaacov turned to Roscoe. 'I think you'd better tell us.'

'I've made my offer,' Roscoe said.

'We could do the same to you.'

'It wouldn't make any difference.'

'Do you want to hurt your friends?'

'You're hurting them. I'm trying to help them.'

Ariel followed this exchange with suspicious little flicks of his head, from one to the other. Roscoe realized he did not speak English.

Yaacov looked at a clock on the wall. It was 8.30. Again he and Ariel conferred, then Horowitz was lifted to his feet and taken out through the steel door. Beyond the door Roscoe could see a flight of steps leading up to the roof. A dog was barking and from somewhere close by came the sounds of a busy communications room – the bleep of Morse and rattle of telegraphic machinery. The noise was cut off with a clang as the steel door shut. Ariel and both his men had gone with Horowitz. Roscoe stood handcuffed in the centre of the room as Yaacov sat down at one of the desks. They were now alone.

'This is stupid,' Yaacov said.

'Why is it stupid?'

'If you destroy a building in this city you will spend many years in one of our prisons.'

'I understand that.'

'You will also ensure the same fate for your friends, including Miss Lees.'

'She has nothing to do with it.'

'Of course she has. The courts will sentence her with you.'

Roscoe said nothing. Yaacov went on.

'You cannot help your friends. You are making things worse for them, and your action has no political significance. It is utterly worthless.'

'I wouldn't say that.'

'So a building is destroyed. The explanation for that will be ours, your case will be dealt with in private. The public will make no connection with Saladin.'

'Now you are being stupid,' Roscoe said. 'You know very well you have no chance whatever of keeping that secret. Come on, accept my terms, what can you lose? Saladin is dead. The best thing you can do is see he goes quietly.'

Yaacov stared balefully at Roscoe then glanced at the clock, which said 8.35. He picked up a telephone and spoke rapidly in Hebrew, put it down, picked up another – an internal line, to judge from the buttons on the receiver – spoke again, put it down, then stood looking at both as if waiting for something to happen. Nothing happened. He lit a cigarette. 8.37.

One of Ariel's men came back into the room, and then

Roscoe was taken through the steel door, accompanied by
Yaacov. They climbed the steps to a corridor lined with six
cells. Bassam was sharing his with an Alsatian chained to the
wall. When he moved the dog bayed and snapped, held inches
out of reach by the chain. Yaacov had the dog taken out.
Bassam slid to the floor, his head dropped forward. He seemed
to have shrunk; his clothes were disarranged, his face unshaven, filmed with sweat. He smelled not only of sweat but of
something more pungent, more putrid. Yaacov addressed him
in Arabic and Roscoe said: 'Don't you believe it, don't say a
thing.' Bassam answered neither. Yaacov reached down and
lifted his head, pointing at Roscoe as he spoke again in Arabic.
But Bassam saw nothing. He was somewhere else.

Yaacov took Roscoe back to the office below. The clock on
the wall said 8.43. A telephone rang. Yaacov seized it, listened,
put it down, picked up the internal line and spoke urgently,
all this in Hebrew. Then he went to the steel door and called
down one of Ariel's men, to whom he gave a quiet instruction.
The man hurried back up the stairs. Yaacov then sat down and
lit a second cigarette. Roscoe stood as before in the middle of
the room. 8.45.

Yaacov was nearly inscrutable, but Roscoe now noticed a
change. In some way the situation had altered, and to Yaacov's
advantage. He was relaxed now, propping his feet on the desk,
tilting back his chair as he smoked. 8.46.

'You amuse me,' he said.

Roscoe failed to see the joke. Yaacov explained.

'You are about to tell me your information, because you have
no choice, and yet you keep up this ridiculous bluff in the hope
of a promise. You expect me to let you go free if I say I will.
That is very English, very arrogant, and in the circumstances,
amusing. You come to my country on a mission of destruction
and then you have the bloody English cheek to appeal to my
sense of honour.'

'Correction,' Roscoe said. 'I'm appealing to your self-
interest.'

'Oh? How is that?'

'No explosion, no casualties, no awkward trials, no publicity
for Saladin – that's a good deal for Israel. But you'd better be
quick about it.'

Yaacov shook his head and smiled. He smoked on in silence. The minutes passed.

8.48, 8.49, 8.50.

That was Roscoe's limit. 'All right,' he said, 'you win. I realize I have only your word, but will you please try to keep Miss Lees out of it?'

'That's your only condition?'

Roscoe said it was.

Yaacov inclined his head graciously. 'I shall endeavour to protect that good Christian lady.'

Roscoe then told him that the building he had mined was this one, Alcatraz.

But Yaacov did not stir; his expression did not alter, his feet stayed propped on the desk.

Roscoe said that if he looked downstairs he would find that the sentries had gone. 'The charges are in the lift shaft and along the back wall. I can disconnect them in a couple of minutes.'

Yaacov's only reaction was a sigh. 'If that is an attempt to escape, it is a weak one.'

'It's the truth, I assure you.'

'And where are your men?'

'I'll tell you later.'

'You will tell me now.'

Roscoe refused.

'Very well,' said Yaacov, 'we shall sit here until you change your mind.'

Roscoe found a chair and sat down, unworried now since he knew how the situation had altered. The clock on the wall said 8.54.

Two minutes later Horowitz was brought in, propped between Ariel's men and followed by Ariel himself. Yaacov questioned him in Hebrew. Roscoe was about to intervene, but then he saw it was unnecessary. Horowitz said nothing. He raised his eyes to the clock and decided to die.

Yaacov too saw that look, and gave up. The room was silent as the hands of the clock approached nine, reached the hour and passed on.

Horowitz was removed. Ariel walked up to Roscoe, seemed about to hit him, then strode from the room. Once again

Yaacov and Roscoe were alone. Yaacov stubbed out his cigarette with a thin smile. 'So you knew.'

Roscoe admitted so, swapping smile for smile. 'What made you look here?'

'A simple matter of deduction. The view from that hotel was limited to Mount Scopus. I didn't think you'd go for the university or the library.'

'Very smart of you.'

'Six hundred pounds of PE – you don't believe in half measures, do you?'

'It's a pretty solid building,' Roscoe said.

'And so it will stay.' Yaacov's smile faded. 'Where are the sentries?'

'They're safe.'

'They'd better be.'

'I'm still willing to negotiate.'

'Mr Roscoe, you have nothing to negotiate with. Your men will take no action without you, and I am sick of your face. Come with me.'

Roscoe's handcuffs were removed. He was taken up the stairs and locked into the cell next to Bassam's. It was a small rectangular room with tiled walls, at one end a mattress with blanket, at the other a hole in the floor with push-button flush. A recessed light glowed dimly in the ceiling and a low hum came from two ventilator grills. The door was sealed hermetically, with a peephole set in the centre. Roscoe explored the place briefly, wondering how long he would be here, then used the lavatory and stretched out on the mattress. He lay still for a while, straining to catch any sound from the neighbouring cells. There was none. He took Saladin's holder from his pocket and examined it sadly; it still smelt of Turkish tobacco. Then he wondered about Claudia and if he could have prayed with any honesty, would have done so for her. Instead he thought how much he would like to kill Zeiti.

When he next looked at his watch it was midnight. He tried to sleep, and did so for a while. He woke to his fate with a shock and then slept again, beginning to accept it – that necessary process of adjustment for prisoners. He would not see Granby for years. His luck had deserted him, but he bore it no grudge. He had pushed an old friend too far.

But Roscoe's resignation was premature; his luck was still at work, guiding Shin Beth to a house on the outskirts of Nablus where a shot had been reported in the early hours. They broke in to find the house empty except for a semi-conscious English girl, quickly identified as Claudia Lees. She was given emergency treatment, revived, taken to an ambulance and her stretcher connected by radio-telephone to Alcatraz. Yaacov told her that Saladin was dead, that her friends had been arrested and the best she could do now was tell him what she knew. Claudia refused. She said she would talk to Stephen Roscoe only, to him and no one else.

At 4.20 Roscoe's cell door was opened. By now deep asleep, he was woken by one of Ariel's men and hustled down the steps to the office below.

Yaacov was waiting with his hand cupped over a telephone receiver. He looked tired now, rumpled and sweat-stained, but his brown eyes were sharp, and again he exploited the advantage of surprise. Without any preliminaries he held out the receiver. 'This is Miss Lees. She wants to talk to you.'

Roscoe blinked, then took the phone. 'Hello . . . Claudia?'

'Stephen? Is that you?'

Her voice was very weak. Roscoe could only just hear it and at the faint sound could barely speak himself for relief. 'Yes, it's me,' he said. 'Are you all right?'

Claudia replied that she was, which considering her condition was a lie of heroic proportions.

'Where are you?'

'Nablus.'

Yaacov was listening on an extension.

Roscoe was thinking as fast as he could, wide awake now. 'They're listening in,' he said, 'so don't say a thing until I tell you to.' Then he asked her to repeat what the Israelis had told her. She did so, pausing for breath, her voice sometimes fading to nothing. Roscoe replied in a deliberate voice that Saladin had indeed been murdered by persons unknown, that he himself and Horowitz were in jail for reasons she knew nothing about, right?

'Oh. Yes, right.'

Then he asked her if she had been kidnapped by Arabs. 'Just answer yes or no.'

'Yes,' she said.

'Were they from Black September or the Popular Front? Just yes or no.'

'Yes, one from each.'

'How long ago did they leave you?'

'About an hour – perhaps more.'

Yaacov interrupted. 'In what kind of car?'

'That's all right,' Roscoe said, 'you can tell him.'

'A grey Mercedes,' she said, 'an old taxi I think.'

Yaacov made to speak again, but Roscoe cut in. 'Now,' he said, 'this is important. Do you know where they've gone?'

'Yes, I . . .'

'Careful now. Wait. Just tell me, is it the place which I asked you to show me on the road?'

'Yes.'

'Okay, that's all I need to know. Now don't say any more, to me or to anyone else. Just go back to England as soon as you can, and if they won't let you, get yourself a lawyer.'

'But Stephen . . .'

'That's all now.'

'Stephen, please, wait. They're going to kill Mrs Meir.'

Both Yaacov and Roscoe were stunned into momentary silence. Roscoe found his voice first. He asked how she knew.

'I heard them talking . . . her name. They kept mentioning . . . I couldn't understand it all.'

'Okay, that'll do,' Roscoe said. 'No more now. Give them back the phone.'

He rang off. Yaacov had already picked up another phone, then a second – a red one which he had not touched before. He was issuing urgent instructions into the first phone, then he put it down and waited for an answer on the red one. He turned to Roscoe. 'All right, now where are they?'

'Do I have a deal?' Roscoe said. 'Come on, make it quick.'

Ariel was now in the room. Yaacov explained to him. Ariel, outraged, looked towards Roscoe then back at Yaacov, raising his voice in angry protest. Yaacov held up a hand to silence him, then spoke into the red phone. Ariel hung back. Yaacov talked rapidly, calmly for perhaps two minutes, nodded as he got the answer he wanted, then passed the receiver to Ariel, whose manner as he took it became deferential. Without waiting for

Ariel to finish, Yaacov turned back to Roscoe. 'All right, you've got your deal.'

'Spell it out,' Roscoe said.

'We must have Zeiti and Khadduri, dead or alive, doesn't matter – and the sentries. If they've been hurt, you stay.'

'Okay, and I want Bassam.'

'Bassam, yes. But not Horowitz. He stays.'

'Horowitz too.'

'I repeat, not Horowitz.'

'Get him here,' Roscoe said.

'You're in no position to argue.'

'Just get him here, quick, or you can bloody well lock me up again.'

So Horowitz was brought down from the cells, blinking sleepily. Roscoe explained the situation to him and Horowitz accepted it without hesitation. 'That's okay,' he said, 'take Bassam and let me stay. I'd prefer it.' He smiled, looking happier than at any time since they had met in Beersheba. Roscoe asked if he was sure. Horowitz said yes, he was sure, and turned back towards the steel door before he could be led. Roscoe could not think of anything to say to him.

Ariel had replaced the red receiver. His malevolence seemed as much directed at Yaacov as at Roscoe. Yaacov ignored him; he was waiting for an answer from Roscoe, who now agreed to the deal. He said his men were in Aqabat Jabr.

'How much explosive have they got?'

'Two hundred pounds.'

Yaacov rolled his eyes to the ceiling. 'And that's where Zeiti and Khadduri have gone?'

Roscoe nodded. 'Have you got any roadblocks?'

'None north of Jericho.' Yaacov thought for a moment, then glanced at his watch. 'They'll be there already. We'd better hurry.'

And so the lines of battle broke, and Roscoe joined forces with his enemy. He found it easy to collaborate with Yaacov, and though he had no guarantee of it, believed the Israelis would stick to their bargain. With Saladin dead the bigger prize was Zeiti and Adnan, each of whom had played a part in recent atrocities. Zeiti had furnished the weapons for Munich and Adnan had helped prepare the Japanese massacre at Lod.

Their capture would be a welcome political sensation, whereas
Saladin was something best swept below the carpet.

Furthermore, as Yaacov had been quick to see, Roscoe
could be useful in the tactical situation now presented. The
problem was not to protect Mrs Meir – already every road out
of Jericho had been sealed and cleared of traffic – but to catch
or kill the two men without casualties. The lethal range of
200 lb of Plastex was considerable. Zeiti and perhaps Adnan
too were trained in its use and would not hesitate to die if they
saw the chance to take a good number of Zionist-imperialist
dogs with them. Once their car was on the road the units at the
barriers were dangerously exposed, and to mount an assault on
the garage was more difficult still. Many might be killed, and
certainly the two captured sentries.

Since this problem was of Saladin's creation it was Yaacov's
intention that Roscoe should solve it, at whatever danger to his
person. He explained the plan he had in mind as they waited
together on the roof of Alcatraz for a helicopter, already now
approaching across the sleeping city from the west. It was 4.35
in the morning, only fifteen minutes since the conversation with
Claudia. The light was dull grey, the air still and warm. All the
spires, towers, cupolas, minarets and domes of Jerusalem projected from a thick haze below them. And standing on that high
point Yaacov and Roscoe were at ease together, two military
men in pre-battle conference. The technicalities were quickly
settled between them.

The helicopter was circling now, descending.

Yaacov asked Roscoe how he had got his men into Israel,
and was told; Roscoe reckoned the dinghies would be found in
any case. But Saladin's route he kept to himself, protecting
Giscard, and also the good name of UNWRA, who went to
great lengths to preserve their neutrality and prevent such
abuse of their diplomatic privileges.

Then Yaacov said: 'I can understand why you joined him.
Partition is the reasonable solution, and one day perhaps it will
come. But not yet.'

Roscoe asked why not, raising his voice against the clatter of
the incoming helicopter.

'Because this is a war,' replied Yaacov, 'and wars are irrational.
They can only be stopped by victory or defeat.'

'Or exhaustion?'

'We're a long way from that. So are they . . .'

Their talk was overwhelmed by the noise of the machine as it skirted the aerial masts and settled on a circular pad at the end of the roof. Bending their heads into the downdraught, Roscoe and Yaacov ran crouched below its blades towards the open door, and were then lifted up, away, up and eastwards over the Tower of Ascension, across the Judean hills and down towards the Dead Sea, now the colour of slop in the early light, as if the blue had boiled out of it. Within minutes they had landed on the open ground outside Aqabat Jabr.

Israeli troops had discreetly surrounded the camp and cleared it of the few remaining inhabitants. Roscoe's pistol was returned and he was given an Israeli jeep. Yaacov waved him on his way. 'Good luck,' he called, but did not look as if he cared. It was simply a suitably English thing to say.

Driving slowly forward, Roscoe braced himself for this final hazard. What he needed now was that cool approach of the technical man, but this time he could not achieve it. Blankness of the mind could no more be willed than sleep. He was frightened, because he wanted to live.

9. Picking up the Pieces

Grey but already too warm – it was the sort of dull day which things seem to end on. The time was approaching 5 a.m. but the sky still opaque, without the usual sunny streaks over Jordan. A thick haze was spread across the valley, blurring shadows, trapping heat, and as in a tent the air was dense, too still to stir the dust which rose in drifts against the crumbling adobe of Aqabat Jabr.

Roscoe was bleary with exhaustion and traces of fever, drops of sweat running off his face as the jeep bounced and lurched over ruts which had set hard as concrete. He drove slowly, then rounded a corner and stopped to collect himself, out of sight of the Israelis but not yet in view of the Arabs.

He stayed there several minutes and found himself thinking at that moment of his father – a mysterious link across the years, through the blood, which was comfort of a kind. Pride of clan lifted his spirit; also there were one or two things he could do.

He rested his eyes on the green of his uniform, wiped his face, breathed deep, flexed his muscles then relaxed, like an athlete preparing to race. Then he took out his gun and felt its heavy blue steel in his hand, the surface of the wooden grip firm against his palm. He was glad to have it back. Subduing his fright with mechanical activity, he removed the magazine from the butt and tested the lie of the ammunition on the spring with his finger, then pulled back the slide and blew into the breech, dry-fired, reloaded, pulled back again to cock, slipped off the safety catch and tucked the barrel down into the holster on his belt, folding back the flap for easy draw. He prepared himself to smile or to shoot, because if Zeiti and Adnan were here almost anything could happen. He did not know how they would react, or how fast, or what the others would do. He had several alternative plans in his mind but was ready to improvise, as ready as he could be. To think more about it would weaken his nerve, so he started the jeep and drove on.

Israeli troops had appeared close behind as they tightened the circle. He could see them in the mirror, taking cover; a stir of green in the empty brown buildings. Then he turned out across a wide space of pale baked earth towards the UNWRA complex at the edge of the camp, and as soon as the garage came in view he saw that things were not as he had left them. Both doors were unguarded. Roscoe chose the right-hand entrance and drove straight in, cut the engine and free-wheeled to the centre of the building, then abruptly turned, braked and rolled from the driver's seat to the ground, coming up with the snout of the vehicle interposed between himself and the group in the corner.

The situation was clear in his head, the best course of action decided as his feet touched the ground.

Zeiti and Adnan were there with their car, an old Mercedes as Claudia had said. Walid was helping them to pack it with explosive. Fuad and Ibrahim sat facing the wall with the two Israeli sentries. Mukhtar was dead by the door, stabbed, to judge from the blood. The Gipsy had gone.

As Roscoe drove in Walid had put down a pack of explosive, begun to crouch then stood still by the car. Zeiti's head was buried in the boot; he had straightened up quickly, then ducked behind the vehicle. Adnan was the only man armed. He was standing by the car with a Uzi submachine-gun and his orders were clearly to shoot. As the jeep rolled towards him he turned and raised the barrel, clutching the magazine convulsively to steady his aim — but then the jeep had veered aside. He had faltered just long enough to lose the advantage, and now Roscoe's pistol was levelled across the bonnet at his chest. Adnan waited for a target but Roscoe's head was barely visible, tucked well behind the Browning as he held it straight out at arm's length with both hands wrapped tight round the butt.

Zeiti was still out of sight behind the Mercedes. Walid was immobile.

Adnan did not know what to do. His eyes were wide with fright behind his steel spectacles. He backed towards the car.

Roscoe thrust his pistol further forward. 'Don't move,' he said. 'Stay exactly where you are.'

Adnan stopped, still ready to shoot.

'Now drop it.'

Adnan lowered the Uzi but kept hold of it.

Roscoe raised the butt of his pistol then slammed it back down on the hot khaki metal of the jeep. 'I said drop it. Go on, drop it.'

Adnan let the Uzi fall and glanced back in distress towards Zeiti, who now cautiously appeared from behind the Mercedes, exposing only the top of his head in the angle of the still-open boot lid. Roscoe swivelled his gun towards the car, aiming for the shock of black hair in the shadows, then stiffened as he saw that Zeiti had a grenade. He was holding it up in his left hand, for Roscoe to see, and now pulled out the pin with his right. Then, his left fist still clutched around the spring-release lever, he held it on top of the packs of explosive already in the boot.

Plastex was difficult to detonate, but a grenade dropped that close might just do it. The car contained enough to blow the garage and everyone in it to pieces. If Zeiti was shot the grenade would be released . . .

Roscoe re-appraised the situation, slightly easing the pressure on his trigger finger. Then he uncupped one hand from his pistol and held it palm outwards in a gesture of truce. 'All right,' he said, 'all right, now let's take this slowly. What the hell is going on here?'

'We're taking over,' Zeiti shouted. His voice echoed through the empty building. 'We're leaving now – don't try to stop us.'

'All right, get going. Walid, stand back.'

But Walid stood his ground. He spoke in the high, clear voice of a martyr. 'I'm going with them.'

'Don't be stupid.'

'You don't understand – I want to go.'

'You're not going anywhere.'

'I'm sorry, Stephen. Zeiti is right . . .'

Roscoe felt rage like an orgasm, contracting his stomach and draining the blood from his face, rushing up through his nerves and out along his arm to the joint of his trigger finger. He held it there, just, at that finely poised extremity as he swung the Browning round at Walid and spoke in a hoarse, stifled voice. 'Do as you're told or I'll blow your fucking head off.'

Walid flinched, then recovered his nerve. He turned to Zeiti, who spoke to him curtly in Arabic. Walid protested, but Zeiti dismissed him then called out to Adnan, who picked up the fourth haversack and put it inside the Mercedes, then got behind the wheel. Zeiti gave another order. Adnan opened the passenger door. Zeiti slammed the boot shut and quickly held the grenade over the pack in the car. Walid retreated a pace.

'Over here,' Roscoe called. 'Fuad, Ibrahim, on your feet, over here – and bring the Israelis.'

Ibrahim got the message, tugging at the two Israeli sentries to follow him. Still hobbled hand and foot, they rolled, crawled, scrambled up and hopped behind the jeep. Fuad and Ibrahim scuttled up behind. Roscoe signalled all four to get below the Dodge, which was parked close beside. Walid started to follow, then stopped.

Without relaxing his firing position Roscoe now called out to Zeiti. 'Okay, off you go. Drive out.'

Zeiti straightened up slowly, still holding the grenade. He now had his Mauser in his right hand. 'Don't try to follow us.'

'We won't.'

Roscoe raised his head slightly and for a second they stared at each other across a distance of perhaps fifteen yards, strangely linked by the equal power to kill, which ran between them like a closed-circuit current. Zeiti's breath was coming fast through dilated nostrils. His left shirtsleeve was bulky from the dressing still strapped round his arm. His face was pale and stiff, his eyes fever-bright and yet distant, as if fixed on some internal purpose. He kept Roscoe in view all the time. He opened his mouth, as if to speak, then ducked down into the car. Adnan started the engine and accelerated forwards, driving out past the body of Mukhtar.

Immediately Roscoe turned to the others. 'Get down,' he said, 'quick,' and pushed them underneath the truck.

Fuad, Ibrahim and the sentries obeyed without question, but Walid hung back until Roscoe hauled him roughly to the ground then dived down beside him as a long burst of automatic fire split the silence, then the whoosh-bang of a bazooka,

followed by a mighty explosion which punched in the garage
like a fist. Roscoe and Walid just managed to scramble underneath the chassis of the truck as the building's front wall
sagged in and then collapsed, bringing down two central
girders of the roof with a clatter of corrugated sheeting.

Heavy fragments continued to fall, clanging on the rusted
sheets of metal. The building stirred and settled, more breeze
blocks tumbled. But the main structure held, and soon there was
silence, the air closing over them like water, hot and still as
before.

Then distant small sounds reached their ears: shouts, and
feet running. Israeli troops swarmed in across the rubble,
lifted the debris off the Dodge and helped them out one by one.
They stood up slowly, stunned and deafened, finding their
feet. Walid must have offered some resistance; an Israeli
soldier clubbed him casually to the ground, then heaved him
up again. Roscoe uncuffed the two sentries, then they all
stumbled outside.

A crowd of silent Arabs had gathered round the open
ground between the UNWRA garage and the camp. The rest
of the Israeli cordon had fanned out to gather in pieces of
wreckage, but there was almost nothing to be found. Only the
chassis of the car was recognizable, a bent grid of steel on the
edge of a shallow smoking crater.

The truck was extracted from the garage, battered but still
working. Roscoe and his three surviving men were herded
aboard and driven under escort to a military camp on the
outskirts of Jericho, where Roscoe was taken to an office.
Yaacov was waiting there, seated at a desk. The mood was cool
but polite. Roscoe was offered a chair and a cigarette. He
wondered what was coming, then relaxed as Yaacov said that
before releasing them he wished to make it clear that further
publicity for Saladin would only make it harder for Horowitz.

'Are you telling me to keep my mouth shut?'

'I'd advise it – for your own sake too. If this morning's
events become known you won't be very popular with the
Arabs.'

Roscoe agreed that was so.

Then Yaacov stood up and they passed through together
into an adjoining office, where Bassam was sitting in a chair

with his hands on his lap, his head hanging forward on his chest. Yaacov spoke to him softly as they came in, but he did not reply. Roscoe could get no answer either. When they touched him he stiffened convulsively, then yielded as they helped him to his feet. As soon as they released him he froze, as if playing statues, so they each took an arm and continued to guide him forward slowly. He walked in small shuffling steps, like a man blind or very old, without volition. Before they put him in the truck Yaacov took hold of his shoulder and pressed it, saying something in Arabic close to his ear. Then he turned to Roscoe. 'Get him to Beirut as quick as you can. Miss Lees will be sent home as soon as she's well.'

Roscoe asked what was wrong with her. Yaacov told him. Roscoe stood for a moment in shocked silence – shocked at the news, shocked that he had not asked earlier – remembering her voice on the telephone. Then he asked Yaacov to take good care of her, to which the predictable reply was that Israel had the best doctors in the world. Roscoe nodded and held out his hand. 'Well, thanks for your help.'

Yaacov was not sure he wanted any thanks. He hesitated, glancing at Roscoe's still extended hand. Then he shook it, and as they parted, smiled. 'Don't try it again.'

'No. I hope, one day . . .'

'Yes, one day. Good-bye now.'

Roscoe climbed aboard the truck. Yaacov issued instructions to two of his men, who came with them as far as the Allenby Bridge, then stepped down and waved them on. Ibrahim took over the wheel. The boom was lifted, and they drove across into Jordan. Roscoe telephoned Marsden from the border post and twenty minutes later they were allowed to proceed. While they waited for clearance Roscoe explained to the others what had happened in Jerusalem, but Walid refused to translate. Roscoe asked what had become of the Gipsy, but got no reply. Bassam sat slumped in the truck. He had fallen asleep.

They travelled in silence, climbing out of the valley. When they reached Beqqa, Walid stopped the truck and got out. Roscoe stepped down to say good-bye, but Walid turned away towards the city of shacks, spat on the ground and walked off.

Marsden and Nazreddin were waiting in Amman. Roscoe reported events, then Nazreddin took Fuad and Ibrahim to

their previous quarters. Roscoe and Bassam were given rooms
at the Intercontinental. Bassam was carried from the truck,
since he could not be woken. A doctor arrived to examine him
but found only bruises.

Marsden booked seats on a flight to Beirut, then returned to
Roscoe's room. 'You did well to get out,' he said. 'It could have
been worse.'

Roscoe lay flat on the bed with his eyes shut. His body was
exhausted but his mind still racing. He was thinking how very,
very near he had come to shooting Walid.

'It was a mess,' he said.

EPILOGUE

Questions
and Answers

1973; Christmas Eve 1972

1. Arab or Jew?

That was the end of Saladin's initiative, and its only result was to reverse the Israeli government's plans for Alcatraz. The building still stands, but is no more than what they say it is – a branch of the postal department.

Saladin himself was soon forgotten. The story of his death blazed and died in two days; by November 12th it was in small print. The press version, inspired by the Israelis and not denied by Al Fatah, was that he had been assassinated by Ahmad Zeiti and Adnan Khadduri, who had crossed the border from Syria for the purpose. That story stuck, and it may just possibly be true. But the more I looked into it, the more I came to doubt it.

Consider first the evidence of Claudia Lees.

She was questioned by Zeiti and Adnan in the cellar for several hours. The attempt to convince her that they wished to collaborate was quickly abandoned. Adnan confessed that they were out to stop Saladin, and in true Marxist fashion tried persuasion through political lecture. He told her that Israel was a relic of colonial times, as doomed as white Rhodesia. Partition, along whatever line, was morally indefensible; Palestine should be restored to its people and the European Jews sent home, as was done for the Algerian French. Persecution of the Jews was a western crime, he said, therefore it was up to the West, not the Arabs, to make reparation. Claudia listened but held firm. Several times the men paused to talk to each other, and this was when she first heard them mention Mrs Meir. She understood a little Arabic, enough to know the talk was of killing. When they turned back to her, their approach was different. Both men told her their personal histories, which were similar to many she had heard. Both came from Jaffa, whence they had been driven as children. Their families had

declined and disintegrated, hounded from place to place by
war. Zeiti told with mounting hysteria how his mother, then
pregnant, had died by the road in the chaos and heat of 1948.
Claudia assured them of her sympathy but still refused to
help. Then Zeiti lost control. He pulled out his pistol and waved
it in her face as he yelled abuse and threats. Claudia became
very frightened. She cannot remember exactly what she said.

But at this point the session was interrupted by the third
man, who returned to the cellar with the news that an Israeli
search was closing in – this was late on Tuesday night. The
cellar was hurriedly abandoned. Claudia was escorted through
the streets at gunpoint, put into a car and driven north to
Nablus. There she was locked in the basement of a suburban
house and guarded by the unidentified man. For the next
twenty-four hours she did not see Zeiti or Adnan, who were
therefore absent throughout the period – from 5 to 8 p.m. on
Wednesday – during which Saladin was shot.

But if it was they who had shot him their action on return to
Nablus was odd. They demanded again to know where Saladin
was hiding, and this time their mood was more desperate.
When Claudia would not answer Zeiti slapped her face – a
turning point. Several times he hit her with the flat of his hand,
shouting alternately in English and Arabic. Claudia stood her
ground; her resolve had stiffened in the long day's wait. The
two men then left her alone in the dark. In the early hours of
Thursday they came back, grim with new purpose but scared,
she thought, of what they intended to do.

Adnan offered no physical violence; the beating was administered by Zeiti, but his blows did not hurt much. They seemed
to hurt him almost more, since any sharp movement made him
wince. This violence was meant to frighten rather than injure
her, Claudia could tell that, and though she was indeed terrified
she did not think Zeiti would do her any serious harm. In his
eyes she saw a look of agonized desperation as her non-coopera-
tion forced him ever further into the role of monster.

This went on for some time, an alternating rough-house and
shouting match, then the two men withdrew for a second time.
When they came back a few minutes later Claudia saw that
Zeiti had his gun out. He loaded and cocked it while Adnan
explained the choice before her. Claudia believed it was a

bluff, but when Adnan held her back against the wall and Zeiti pressed his pistol to her skull, she lost her nerve. She diverted them to Aqabat Jabr, unwilling to die and thinking that Roscoe and his men could cope with this better than she.

But Zeiti and Adnan were encouraged by this to interrogate her further, returning to the matter of Saladin's whereabouts. They kept repeating the question, over and over, until Zeiti suddenly lost patience and shot her through the foot. Then she fainted.

That is Claudia's version of what happened, and it can be argued that her memory is defective; that she gave away Saladin's whereabouts during the session in Jerusalem and Zeiti simply maimed her in Nablus out of spite. But that does not fit her character or his. Claudia is not one to shirk or blur the truth, and Zeiti, while desperate, was by no means irrational – still less so Adnan, whose cruelty was wholly born of reason.

Yet if these two were the murderers of Saladin, their behaviour on arrival at Aqabat Jabr was irrational.

Walid and the others knew only that something had gone wrong, having heard no explosion in Jerusalem at nine o'clock. Then towards dawn they were woken by a scuffle at the door to find Mukhtar dead – no tears for the Bedou – the Gipsy on the run, and here now their old comrade Zeiti, proclaiming Saladin a false god and urging them to rally to the standard of Al Fatah. To this appeal Zeiti would surely have added that Saladin was dead; yet he did not mention it, and for that I have the evidence of Fuad and Ibrahim, who are both sober men with no reason to lie – on this score at least, though they have allowed a somewhat flattering version of their exploits to take root in Nahr al-Bared.

I hoped to check their statements with Walid, but he refused to answer most of my questions. I was told in Beirut that he had joined Black September.

The Gipsy, whom I found fleecing tourists at the monastery, cannot add to the story one way or the other. He bolted when Mukhtar was stabbed and turned up two weeks later in the Lebanon, by some route unknown to any but himself.

That is the case in favour of Zeiti. But if he was not the killer, then who was?

Roscoe himself now accuses the Israelis, arguing that their

motive was as strong as Black September's. Saladin's arrest, he
says, would have made the man a hero, whereas dead he was
quickly forgotten, along with his project for a Palestinian
state, that idea which the Israelis so much feared.

I agree with this verdict, but cannot believe the murder was
sanctioned from above. Saladin's death could also very easily
have made him a hero, and such evidence as we have – the red
telephone – shows a readiness for clemency in high quarters. I
assume the act was done in the heat of the moment, in which
case the only two suspects who can now be identified are
Yaacov and Ariel, and if the choice is narrowed to these two,
there is only one possible answer. Yaacov was found on the
scene of the crime but could not have pulled the trigger himself,
for one simple reason. The official autopsy put the time of
Saladin's death at 7 p.m., and at that time Yaacov, by his own
account supported by the evidence of Walid, was inside
Alcatraz. He did not come out of the building till twenty
minutes later. Ariel on the other hand returned to it shortly
after the murder, and on that the case against him rests, a long
way from proven.   •

In a sense it does not matter who killed Saladin, Arab or
Jew. The forces of compromise merely lost another round to
those of extremism. But assuming it was the Israelis, the
question remains: how did they discover where he was?

One possible answer lies with Dominic Morley. But if
Morley was the link then the main fault, it must be said, was
Roscoe's, whose conversation with him in the courtyard of the
American Colony was careless, to say the least, and can only be
explained by the undue importance he attached to television.
That conversation must have been observed by Nick Cassavetes,
because after it he attached himself to Morley like a leech, and
Morley for his part saw no reason to avoid the friendly Greek-
American from Beirut. He says he quite liked the man.
Cassavetes was free with the drink and Morley quite naturally
told him about the British politicians' press conference, to
which they arranged to go together. This arrangement was
made after lunch on the day of the murder and assuming that
Cassavetes worked for Mossad, it would have been enough to
lead the Israelis to investigate the flats at the Park International.

There is of course another possibility, namely that the secret of Saladin's location was extracted from Bassam, and that was the question I most wanted answered when I took my researches to Israel.

2. The Country of the Blind

I arrived there in December 1973, and the mood which I found differed greatly from that which had confronted Saladin. The Israelis were in a turmoil of self-criticism, shocked by their failures in the Yom Kippur War of the previous October. Some of them were talking in Biblical terms, as if they had been punished for their sins, but for Ayah Sharon, whom I met in Tel Aviv, the sin of Golda Meir's regime was not arrogance but negligence. In her view the only lesson of this latest war was that Israel should go it alone, and the look on her face as she said this remains in my mind – a mixture of fear and pious certitude, of eagerness to live and willingness to die.

When I mentioned Yaacov her eyes filled with tears. 'We were friends,' she said. 'Now he will not see me.'

I asked her why, and then she told me that Yaacov had been wounded in the first few hours of the fighting, when his tank had been hit by an Egyptian missile.

I found him at the flat of his aunt, not far from the hospital in Herzliya which he was still visiting for treatment. He is blind now, bald except for scattered tufts of hair and so badly burned that his features appear to have melted. He sat in the dark and answered my questions in a low slurred voice while his aunt shuffled round him, attending to his needs.

This old woman, Yaacov's only surviving relative, bore the scar of an earlier war. Tattooed on her arm was the number which showed she had been in a German concentration camp, and I found myself watching her for some first-hand evidence of that distant horror which to my generation lives only in a few grainy newsreels. But no shock of reality occurred; in her face I saw only an absolute absence of trust. She had survived. She expected nothing more.

She resented my presence there, but Yaacov insisted on telling me his side of the story, and I formed the impression he was under instructions to do so. Talking of Saladin's political aims he repeated the view of his government that a Palestinian state would be used as a stalking-horse by the Arabs, who, whatever they might say, wanted only the destruction of Israel. The West was easily deceived, he said, but the Israelis and the Arabs understood each other well. The Jews could not survive without a state, the Arabs were determined to destroy that state, and to weigh the justice of various solutions was futile, since justice had nothing to do with it; in a war of survival all that counted was relative power. No peace would last, he said, because the spokesmen of compromise – Saladin, Hussein – would be replaced by others. The Arabs would always be led by a Gadaffi or an Arafat . . .

Yaacov's aunt muttered agreement, hovering protectively about him in the dark. 'They murder our children.'

'Saladin was not a murderer,' I protested. 'He gave strict instructions to the contrary.'

Yaacov was silent for a moment, then lowered his mutilated head. 'He should have made that clearer.'

His mouth seemed to bubble, too full of saliva, and yet he answered all my questions, including the one which mattered to me most.

'No,' he said, 'Bassam told us nothing. He was very courageous.'

'What did you do to him?'

'I myself, nothing.' Yaacov turned his sightless eyes towards me: a conversational habit, useless now. 'How is Bassam?'

When I told him he offered the suggestion that Bassam was a catatonic case. I agreed that was so, but repeated the charge of the doctors in Beirut that electric shocks were the prime cause of damage. Yaacov resisted that, asking if burns had been found on the body. I had to admit they had not. Yaacov nodded, relieved, and sat back in his wheelchair. 'It shows, you know.'

'What about drugs?' I said.

Yaacov did not answer, but turned his ruined face towards the window. 'So Bassam cannot speak and I cannot see,' he said. 'We each pay our price.'

That was the end of our interview. His aunt showed me out, and I walked away feeling that in the two generations of that household I had seen the whole character of Israel – the ruthless reliance on force and the deep psychic trauma which has caused it.

3. The Beginning and the End

That talk with Yaacov was my last piece of business in the Middle East and next day I flew to Tangier to see Giscard, who was last on my list. Of the others I had interviewed all who would talk and will here briefly mention their present situations.

Bassam is in a Lebanese clinic, a pleasant enough place, where we walked together through a garden of palms. He can in fact now talk a little, but only with an agonizing effort of will, like a man with the worst sort of stammer. He closes his eyes and breaks into a sweat, takes a deep breath and opens his mouth; nothing comes out; he tries again, perhaps a third time, until the words tumble out in a rush, so garbled and inconsequential that he seems to take fright, leaves the statement unfinished and clamps his mouth shut. I was strictly forbidden to discuss his experience in Israel.

Horowitz is serving seven years in the political wing of the jail at Ramleh, near Tel Aviv. His trial, in December 1972, was held *in camera* and at Yaacov's suggestion he elected to conduct his own defence without counsel or witnesses. I was not allowed to visit him but he has written to authorize publication of Saladin's story, a formality which Roscoe insisted on.

David Heinz is in the Israeli army, having chosen to stay on at Kibbutz Kfar Allon. I met him on leave there with Hannah, the girl he means to marry, and together they make a good advertisement for Zionism, tanned and well muscled from labour, with that closed look you see in the eyes of true believers. Thus Israel lives on. The assistant librarian from Hampstead takes up the sword dropped by Yaacov.

Bernard Refo, the mysterious American, is now at the Massachusetts Institute of Technology, still hoeing his patch in the misty ground between government and business. He answered my questions by letter, providing me with sheets of typewritten data which on closer inspection turned out to be completely uninformative. Did he work for an oil company or American intelligence? Maybe both. I do not know, but find it quite plausible that Saladin was secretly sponsored in Washington.

Great efforts are now being made from that capital to redraw the map as he suggested, but without Saladin the task is a hard one. No moderate Palestinian leader is in sight; Arafat's star is in the ascendant, Hussein's on the decline. Israel drives a hard bargain, the Arabs have the oil. The ether is crackling with rumours of war and how it will end is hard to foresee.

The skirmishing across the Lebanese border continues. Two Israeli settlements near Kibbutz Kfar Allon have been attacked by Palestinian suicide squads, provoking the usual retaliatory bombing raids and a series of increasingly desperate statements from the AAI in London.

The secretary of that institution is no longer Marsden, whose involvement with Saladin cost him his job. He now teaches Arabic at Sussex University and lives in a small flat in Brighton, surrounded by souvenirs of the East. I asked him what had become of Saladin's money, since Roscoe accepted only £3000. Marsden said that he could only answer for the London account, from which the balance had been donated to a Palestinian orphanage. In general he seemed depressed and unwell and spent a lot of time telling me how much he hates his students.

Giscard on the other hand is thriving. Now retired to his villa near Tangier, he has replaced his wife with a dark-skinned beauty from Senegal. Like Gauguin, he seems to have waited all his life for this break with convention. We sat on cushions wearing caftans and spent a pleasant evening with a water-pipe.

From Tangier I flew back to London, then travelled up to Granby to report on my tour – this was December 1973. Stephen and Claudia Roscoe had been married the previous June and now Claudia was pregnant, supporting her weight on a stick. She will have a slight limp for the rest of her life. Roscoe's wounds are less obvious, and might even be said to improve him. He seems subdued; the bold crusader has become a husband and a farmer, two occupations about which he is equally serious. His care for his wife almost smothers her, but the match is a good one, and watching them together I remembered the previous Christmas Eve, 1972, when things were less tranquil.

That was the day with which I began this account, the day I first heard about Saladin. Roscoe had returned from his adventures a few weeks before and Claudia was just back from hospital in Israel, limping badly, still in pain. Roscoe was reserved with her, determined to be blamed for what had happened. Things were further complicated by the presence of Brown, who had come out of exile in Withernsea, and to add a little edge to the occasion Black September had sent us a Christmas present.

The parcel was small, flat in shape, addressed to Roscoe. The 'e' was missing from his surname and Stephen was mis-spelled 'Steven', which should perhaps have alerted him. Posted in Paris on December 12th, it was wrapped in mauve paper and so successfully made to look like a gift that it ended up under the tree.

I suppose it could have come from the Men of Zion, who are certainly capable of sending a parcel bomb. But the better bet is Black September, who had an equal motive and could have learned of Roscoe's perfidy from Walid Iskandar. More con-clusive is the fact that the British police intercepted several bombs that week, all posted in Belgium or France and addressed to prominent Jews. Each one of these packages was wrapped in coloured paper. A warning had been issued on the radio that morning – in fact it was when I mentioned this that Roscoe, who was starting to tell me about Saladin, stopped talking and was suddenly still. Then he strode into the hall and took Georgie through to Mrs Parsons, came back and went through the parcels under the tree. He picked up the mauve one and carried it out to the garden, instructing me to keep my distance. I watched from about twenty yards away while he crouched on the lawn and ran his hands over its surface. Then he placed it in a yellow plastic bucket and ran a hose out from a tap in the garage. I imagined that this was a safety precaution, but signalling me down with a smile I knew, Roscoe turned on the tap and two minutes later the package exploded, blowing bits of yellow plastic all over the garden.

Roscoe straightened up with a grin, though later he grew
pensive and remarked that if this had happened once, it could
happen again.

It could, but has not. The demolition of that plastic bucket
is the last event in the story of Saladin – though not quite
where I choose to end it, since a better last scene occurred later
that day when we all became involved in the most recent of
the rituals of Granby, instituted by the overworked vicar. A
coach arrived to take the village to carols in Lincoln.

We could see the cathedral from miles away, floodlit on its
hill, and the service inside it was unforgettably splendid.
Candles dripped, organ pipes soared into the dark. The golden-
robed clergy processed down the nave as if on wheels, and a
choirboy sang solo, far away, his voice reaching up like a thread
to the vaults.

I saw Claudia's eyes dampen, and later she admitted to being
much moved. For months she had lived with the cry of the
muezzin, but this was the call to which her own spirit soared,
a boy's voice in a Gothic cathedral, and tonight at least that high
thin sound seemed to carry all the hopes of the West – aspira-
tions she at least understood. She was glad to be home.

Unimpressed by the pomp, Georgie's eyes followed an
independent course, settling on the girl two rows ahead who
had dropped her collection money. While the rest of us sang
he droned along on a note of his choosing, and I saw Brown
press him to her side in relief.

Afterwards we gathered with the rest of the congregation
outside the west front, stamping in the cold as we waited for
the bishop to deliver the blessing. Then his voice boomed
from the sky through loudspeakers, scattering pigeons into the
floodlights. 'GO FORTH INTO THE WORLD IN PEACE.' We
could just see his mitre above the dense throng round the
porch, where he stood at a microphone. 'BE OF GOOD COURAGE.'
He had a real bishop's voice, sonorous and slow – 'HOLD FAST
THAT WHICH IS GOOD' – and after each phrase he paused,
allowing the echoes to die. 'RENDER TO NO MAN EVIL FOR
EVIL.' Down they came one by one, these fine Christian edicts
like the tablets of Moses on the heads of the people of Granby,
on Roscoe and Claudia and Brown and myself and little
Georgie – 'STRENGTHEN THE FAINT-HEARTED' – edicts

which none of us except maybe Claudia thought about much but which coloured our lives nonetheless – 'SUPPORT THE WEAK' – all dreamed up in the desert by a young Palestinian Jew – 'HELP THE AFFLICTED' – and taken together not really a suitable epitaph for Saladin, since he was a Muslim – 'HONOUR ALL MEN' – but apt enough sentiments to round off this long tale of human misadventure. 'LOVE AND SERVE THE LORD . . .'

The bishop's voice rose for the final valediction, then he lifted his hand in the sign of the cross and a low British mumble spread through the crowd, resolving itself into a slightly embarrassed 'Amen'.

I looked to see if Roscoe's lips moved, but they did not. He was standing beside me with Georgie on his shoulders; Claudia and Brown were together in front of him, the villagers behind and around him. For a moment like the rest of us he stood transfixed as all the bells of the cathedral rang out, peal after peal, an overwhelming cascade of metallic sound which set off the pigeons again and tumbled out into the dark beyond the floodlights.

Then he lifted Georgie off his shoulders and turned to his own little flock.

'Now,' he said, 'who wants a drink?'